Books by Saul Bellow

The Dean's December
Him with His Foot in His Mouth
  and Other Stories

Published by POCKET BOOKS/WASHINGTON SQUARE PRESS

SAUL BELLOW

HIM WITH HIS FOOT IN HIS MOUTH

AND OTHER STORIES

PUBLISHED BY POCKET BOOKS NEW YORK

For my dear wife,
Alexandra

POCKET BOOKS, a division of Simon & Schuster, Inc.
1230 Avenue of the Americas, New York, N.Y. 10020

Copyright © 1974, 1978, 1982, 1984 by Saul Bellow
Cover artwork copyright © 1985 Paul Perlow

Published by arrangement with Harper & Row Publishers, Inc.
Library of Congress Catalog Card Number: 84-48322

ISBN: 0-671-55247-3

First Pocket Books printing October, 1985

10 9 8 7 6 5 4 3 2 1

POCKET and colophon are registered trademarks
of Simon & Schuster, Inc.

Printed in the U.S.A.

Contents

Him with His Foot in His Mouth

DEAR MISS ROSE: I ALMOST BEGAN "MY DEAR Child," because in a sense what I did to you thirty-five years ago makes us the children of each other. I have from time to time remembered that I long ago made a bad joke at your expense and have felt uneasy about it, but it was spelled out to me recently that what I said to you was so wicked, so lousy, gross, insulting, unfeeling, and savage that you could never in a thousand years get over it. I wounded you for life, so I am given to understand, and I am the more greatly to blame because this attack was so gratuitous. We had met in passing only, we scarcely knew each other. Now, the person who charges me with this cruelty is not without prejudice toward me, he is out to get me, obviously. Nevertheless, I have been in a tizzy since reading his accusations. I wasn't exactly in great shape when his letter arrived. Like many elderly men, I have to swallow all sorts of pills. I take Inderal and quinidine for hypertension and cardiac disorders, and I am also, for a variety of psychological reasons, deeply distressed and for the moment without ego defenses.

It may give more substance to my motive in writing to you now if I tell you that for some months I have been visiting an old woman who reads Swedenborg and other occult authors. She tells me (and a man in his sixties can't easily close his mind to such suggestions) that there is a life to come—wait and see—and that in the life to come we will feel the pains that we inflicted on others. We will suffer all that we made them suffer, for after death all experience is reversed. We enter into the souls of those whom we knew in life. They enter also into us and feel and judge us from within. On the outside chance that this old Canadian woman has it right, I must try to take up this matter with you. It's not as though I had tried to murder you, but my offense is palpable all the same.

I will say it all and then revise, send Miss Rose only the suitable parts.

. . . In this life between birth and death, while it is still possible to make amends . . .

I wonder whether you remember me at all, other than as the person who wounded you—a tall man and, in those days, dark on the whole, with a mustache (not worn thick), physically a singular individual, a touch of the camel about him, something amusing in his composition. If you can recall the Shawmut of those days, you should see him now. *Edad con Sus Disgracias* is the title Goya gave to the etching of an old man who struggles to rise from the chamber pot, his pants dropped to his ankles. "Together with most weak hams," as Hamlet wickedly says to Polonius, being merciless about old men. To the disorders aforementioned I must add teeth with cracked roots, periodontia requiring antibiotics that gave me the runs and resulted in a hemorrhoid the size of a walnut, plus creeping arthritis of the hands. Winter is gloomy and wet in British Columbia, and when I awoke one morning in this land of exile from which I face extradition, I discovered that something had gone wrong with the middle finger of the right hand. The hinge had stopped working and the finger was curled like a snail—a painful new affliction. Quite a joke on me. And the extradition is real. I have been served with papers.

So at the very least I can try to reduce the torments of the afterlife by one.

It may appear that I come groveling with hard-luck stories after thirty-five years, but as you will see, such is not the case.

I traced you through Miss Da Sousa at Ribier College, where we were all colleagues in the late forties. She has remained there, in Massachusetts, where so much of the nineteenth century still stands, and she wrote to me when my embarrassing and foolish troubles were printed in the papers. She is a kindly, intelligent woman who *like yourself, should I say that?* never married. Answering with gratitude, I asked what had become of you and was told that you were a retired librarian living in Orlando, Florida.

I never thought that I would envy people who had retired, but that was when retirement was still an option. For me it's not in the cards now. The death of my brother leaves me in a deep legal-financial hole. I won't molest you with the facts of the case, garbled in the newspapers. Enough to say that his felonies and my own faults or vices have wiped me out. On bad legal advice I took refuge in Canada, and the courts will be rough because I tried to escape. I may not be sent to prison, but I will have to work for the rest of my natural life, will die in harness, and damn queer harness, hauling my load to a peculiar peak. One of my father's favorite parables was about a feeble horse flogged cruelly by its driver. A bystander tries to intercede: "The load is too heavy, the hill is steep, it's useless to beat your old horse on the face, why do you do it?" "To be a horse was *his* idea," the driver says.

I have a lifelong weakness for this sort of Jewish humor, which may be alien to you not only because you are Scotch-Irish (so Miss Da Sousa says) but also because you as a (pre-computer) librarian were in another sphere—zone of quiet, within the circumference of the Dewey decimal system. It is possible that you may have disliked the life of a nun or shepherdess which the word "librarian" once suggested. You may resent it for keeping you out of the modern "action" —erotic, narcotic, dramatic, dangerous, salty. Maybe you have loathed circulating other people's lawless raptures, handling wicked books (for the most part fake, take it from me, Miss Rose). Allow me to presume that you are old-fashioned enough not to be furious at having led a useful life. If you aren't an old-fashioned person I haven't hurt you so badly after all. No modern woman would brood for forty years over a stupid wisecrack. She would say, "Get lost!"

Who is it that accuses me of having wounded you? Eddie Walish, that's who. He has become the main planner of college humanities surveys in the State of Missouri, I am given to understand. At such work he is wonderful, a man of genius. But although he now lives in Missouri, he seems to think of nothing but Massachusetts in the old days. He can't forget the evil I did. He was there when I did it (whatever *it* really was), and he writes, "I have to remind you of how you hurt Carla Rose. So characteristic of you, when she was trying to be agreeable, not just to miss her gentle intentions but to give her a shattering kick in the face.

I happen to know that you traumatized her for life."
(Notice how the liberal American vocabulary is used
as a torture device: By "characteristic" he means:
"You are not a *good person*, Shawmut.") Now, were
you really traumatized, Miss Rose? How does Walish
"happen to know"? Did you tell him? Or is it, as I
conjecture, nothing but gossip? I wonder if you
remember the occasion at all. It would be a mercy if
you didn't. And I don't want to thrust unwanted
recollections on you, but if I did indeed disfigure you
so cruelly, is there any way to avoid remembering?

So let's go back again to Ribier College. Walish and
I were great friends then, young instructors, he in
literature, I in fine arts—my specialty music history.
As if this were news to you; my book on Pergolesi is in
all libraries. Impossible that you shouldn't have come
across it. Besides, I've done those musicology programs on public television, which were quite popular.

But we are back in the forties. The term began just
after Labor Day. My first teaching position. After
seven or eight weeks I was still wildly excited. Let me
start with the beautiful New England setting. Fresh
from Chicago and from Bloomington, Indiana, where
I took my degree, I had never seen birches, roadside
ferns, deep pinewoods, little white steeples. What
could I be but out of place? It made me scream with
laughter to be called "Dr. Shawmut." I felt absurd
here, a camel on the village green. I am a high-waisted
and long-legged man, who is susceptible to paradoxi-
cal, ludicrous images of himself. I hadn't yet gotten
the real picture of Ribier, either. It wasn't true New
England, it was a bohemian college for rich kids from
New York who were too nervous for the better
schools, unadjusted.

Now then: Eddie Walish and I walking together

past the college library. Sweet autumnal warmth against a background of chill from the surrounding woods—it's all there for me. The library is a Greek Revival building and the light in the porch is mossy and sunny—bright-green moss, leafy sunlight, lichen on the columns. I am turned on, manic, flying. My relations with Walish at this stage are easy to describe: very cheerful, not a kink in sight, not a touch of darkness. I am keen to learn from him, because I have never seen a progressive college, never lived in the East, never come in contact with the Eastern Establishment, of which I have heard so much. What is it all about? A girl to whom I was assigned as adviser has asked for another one because I haven't been psycho-analyzed and can't even begin to relate to her. And this very morning I have spent two hours in a commit-tee meeting to determine whether a course in history should be obligatory for fine-arts majors. Tony Lem-nitzer, professor of painting, said, "Let the kids read about the kings and the queens—what can it hoit them?" Brooklyn Tony, who had run away from home to be a circus roustabout, became a poster artist and eventually an Abstract Expressionist. "Don't ever feel sorry for Tony," Walish advises me. "The woman he married is a millionairess. She's built him a studio fit for Michelangelo. He's embarrassed to paint, he only whittles there. He carved out two wooden balls inside a birdcage." Walish himself, Early Hip with a Harvard background, suspected at first that my ignorance was a put-on. A limping short man, Walish looked at me—looked upward—with real shrewdness and traces of disbelief about the mouth. From Chicago, a Ph.D. out of Bloomington, Indiana, can I be as backward as I seem? But I am good company, and by and by he tells me (is it a secret?) that although he comes from Gloucester,

Mass., he's not a real Yankee. His father, a second-generation American, is a machinist, retired, uneducated. One of the old man's letters reads, "Your poor mother—the doctor says she has a groweth on her virginia which he will have to operate. When she goes to surgery I expect you and your sister to be here to stand by me."

There were two limping men in the community, and their names were similar. The other limper, Edmund Welch, justice of the peace, walked with a cane. Our Ed, who suffered from curvature of the spine, would not carry a stick, much less wear a built-up shoe. He behaved with sporting nonchalance and defied the orthopedists when they warned that his spinal column would collapse like a stack of dominoes. His style was to be free and limber. You had to take him as he came, no concessions offered. I admired him for that.

Now, Miss Rose, you have come out of the library for a breath of air and are leaning, arms crossed, and resting your head against a Greek column. To give himself more height, Walish wears his hair thick. You couldn't cram a hat over it. But I have on a baseball cap. Then, Miss Rose, you say, smiling at me, "Oh, Dr. Shawmut, in that cap you look like an archaeologist." Before I can stop myself, I answer, "And you look like something I just dug up."

Awful!

The pair of us, Walish and I, hurried on. Eddie, whose hips were out of line, made an effort to walk more quickly, and when we were beyond your little library temple I saw that he was grinning at me, his warm face looking up into my face with joy, with accusing admiration. He had witnessed something extraordinary. What this something might be, whether it came under the heading of fun or psychopathology or wickedness, nobody could yet judge, but he was glad. Although he lost no time in clearing himself of guilt, it was exactly his kind of wisecrack. He loved to do the Groucho Marx bit, or give an S. J. Perelman turn to his sentences. As for me, I had become dead sober, as I generally do after making one of my cracks. I am as astonished by them as anybody else. They may be hysterical symptoms, in the clinical sense. I used to consider myself absolutely normal, but I became aware long ago that in certain moods my laughing bordered on hysteria. I myself could hear the abnormal note. Walish knew very well that I was subject to such seizures, and when he sensed that one of my fits was approaching, he egged me on. And after he had had his fun he would say, with a grin like Pan Satyrus, "What a bastard you are, Shawmut. The sadistic stabs you can give!" He took care, you see, not to be incriminated as an accessory.

And my joke wasn't even witty, just vile, no excuse for it, certainly not "inspiration." Why should inspiration be so idiotic? It was simply idiotic and wicked. Walish used to tell me, "You're a Surrealist in spite of yourself." His interpretation was that I had raised myself by painful efforts from immigrant origins to a middle-class level but that I avenged myself for the torments and falsifications of my healthy instincts, deformities imposed on me by this adaptation to respectability, the strain of social climbing. Clever, intricate analysis of this sort was popular in Greenwich Village at that time, and Walish had picked up the habit. His letter of last month was filled with insights of this kind. People seldom give up the mental capital accumulated in their "best" years. At sixty-odd, Eddie is still a youthful Villager and associates with young people, mainly. I have accepted old age.

It isn't easy to write with arthritic fingers. My lawyer, whose fatal advice I followed (he is the youngest brother of my wife, who passed away last year), urged me to go to British Columbia, where, because of the Japanese current, flowers grow in midwinter, and the air is purer. There are indeed primroses out in the snow, but my hands are crippled and I am afraid that I may have to take gold injections if they don't improve. Nevertheless, I build up the fire and sit concentrating in the rocker because I need to make it worth your while to consider these facts with me. If I am to believe Walish, you have trembled from that day onward like a flame on a middle-class altar of undeserved humiliation. One of the insulted and injured.

From my side I have to admit that it was hard for me to acquire decent manners, not because I was naturally rude but because I felt the strain of my position. I came to believe for a time that I couldn't get on in life until I, too, had a false self like everybody else and so I made special efforts to be considerate, deferential, civil. And of course I overdid things and wiped myself twice where people of better breeding only wiped once. But no such program of betterment could hold me for long. I set it up, and then I tore it down, and burned it in a raging bonfire.

Walish, I must tell you, gives me the business in his letter. Why was it, he asks, that when people groped in conversations I supplied the missing phrases and finished their sentences with greedy pedantry? Walish alleges that I was showing off, shuffling out of my vulgar origins, making up to the genteel and qualifying as the kind of Jew acceptable (just barely) to the Christian society of T. S. Eliot's dreams. Walish pictures me as an upwardly mobile pariah seeking bondage as one would seek salvation. In reaction, he says, I had rebellious fits and became wildly insulting.

Walish notes all this well, but he did not come out with it during the years when we were close. He saved it all up. At Ribier College we liked each other. We were friends, somehow. But in the end, somehow, he intended to be a mortal enemy. All the while that he was making the gestures of a close and precious friend he was fattening my soul in a coop till it was ready for killing. My success in musicology may have been too much for him.

Eddie told his wife—he told everyone—what I had said to you. It certainly got around the campus. People laughed, but I was depressed. Remorse: you were a pale woman with thin arms, absorbing the colors of moss, lichen, and limestone into your skin. The heavy library doors were open, and within there were green reading lamps and polished heavy tables, and books massed up to the gallery and above. A few of these books were exalted, some were usefully informative, the majority of them would only congest the mind. My Swedenborgian old lady says that angels do not read books. Why should they? Nor, I imagine, can librarians be great readers. They have too many books, most of them burdensome. The crowded shelves give off an inviting, consoling, seductive odor that is also tinctured faintly with something pernicious, with poison and doom. Human beings can lose their lives in libraries. They ought to be warned. And you, an underpriestess of this temple stepping out to look at the sky, and Mr. Lubeck, your chief, a gentle refugee always stumbling over his big senile dog and apologizing to the animal, "Ach, excuse me!" (heavy on the sibilant).

Personal note: Miss Rose never was pretty, not even what the French call une belle laide, *or ugly beauty, a woman whose command of sexual forces makes ugliness itself contribute to her erotic power. A* belle laide *(it would be a French idea!) has to be a rolling-mill of lusts. Such force was lacking. No organic basis for it. Fifty years earlier Miss Rose would have been taking Lydia Pinkham's Vegetable Compound. Nevertheless, even if she looked green, a man might have loved her—loved her for her timid warmth, or for the courage she had had to muster to compliment me on my cap. Thirty-five years ago I might have bluffed out this embarrassment with compliments, saying, "Only think, Miss Rose, how many objects of rare beauty have been dug up by archaeologists—the Venus de Milo, Assyrian winged bulls with the faces of great kings. And Michelangelo even buried one of his statues to get the antique look and then exhumed it." But it's too late for rhetorical gallantries. I'd be ashamed. Unpretty, unmarried, the nasty little community laughing at my crack, Miss Rose, poor thing, must have been in despair.*

Eddie Walish, as I told you, would not act the cripple despite his spiral back. Even though he slouched and walked with an outslapping left foot, he carried himself with style. He wore good English tweeds and Lloyd & Haig brogans. He himself would say that there were enough masochistic women around to encourage any fellow to preen and cut a figure. Handicapped men did very well with girls of a certain type. You, Miss Rose, would have done better to save your compliment for him. But his wife was then expecting; I was the bachelor.

Almost daily during the first sunny days of the term we went out walking. I found him mysterious then.

I would think: Who is he, anyway, this (suddenly) close friend of mine? What is this strange figure, the big head low beside me, whose hair grows high and thick? With a different slant, like whipcord stripes, it grows thickly also from his ears. One of the campus ladies has suggested that I urge him to shave his ears, but why should I? She wouldn't like him better with shaven ears, she only dreams that she might. He has a sort of woodwind laugh, closer to oboe than to clarinet, and he releases his laugh from the wide end of his nose as well as from his carved pumpkin mouth. He grins like Alfred E. Neuman from the cover of *Mad* magazine, the successor to Peck's Bad Boy. His eyes, however, are warm and induce me to move closer and closer, but they withhold what I want most. I long for his affection, I distrust him and love him, I woo him with wisecracks. For he is a wise guy in an up-to-date postmodern existentialist sly manner. He also seems kindly. He seems all sorts of things. Fond of Brecht and Weill, he sings "Mackie Messer" and trounces out the tune on the upright piano. This, however, is merely period stuff—German cabaret jazz of the twenties, Berlin's answer to trench warfare and exploded humanism. Catch Eddie allowing himself to be dated like that! Up-to-the-minute Eddie has always been in the avant-garde. An early fan of the Beat poets, he was the first to quote me Allen Ginsberg's wonderful line "America I'm putting my queer shoulder to the wheel."

Eddie made me an appreciative reader of Ginsberg, from whom I learned much about wit. You may find it odd, Miss Rose (I myself do), that I should have kept up with Ginsberg from way back. Allow me, however, to offer a specimen statement from one of his recent books, which is memorable and also charming. Ginsberg writes that Walt Whitman slept with Edward Carpenter, the author of *Love's Coming-of-Age;* Carpenter afterward became the lover of the grandson of one of our obscurer Presidents, Chester A. Arthur; Gavin Arthur when he was very old was the lover of a San Francisco homosexual who, when he embraced

Ginsberg, completed the entire cycle and brought the Sage of Camden in touch with his only true successor and heir. It's all a little like Dr. Pangloss's account of how he came to be infected with syphilis.

Please forgive this, Miss Rose. It seems to me that we will need the broadest possible human background for this inquiry, which may so much affect your emotions and mine. You ought to know to whom you were speaking on that day when you got up your nerve, smiling and trembling, to pay me a compliment —to give me, us, your blessing. Which I repaid with a bad witticism drawn, characteristically, from the depths of my nature, that hoard of strange formulations. I had almost forgotten the event when Walish's letter reached me in Canada. That letter—a strange *megillah* of which I myself was the Haman. He must have brooded with *ressentiment* for decades on my character, drawing the profile of my inmost soul over and over and over. He compiled a list of all my faults, my sins, and the particulars are so fine, the inventory so extensive, the summary so condensed, that he must have been collecting, filing, formulating, and polishing furiously throughout the warmest, goldenest days of our friendship. To receive such a document—I ask you to imagine, Miss Rose, how it affected me at a time when I was coping with grief and gross wrongs, mourning my wife (and funnily enough, also my swindling brother), and experiencing *Edad con Sus Disgracias*, discovering that I could no longer straighten my middle finger, reckoning up the labor and sorrow of threescore and ten (rapidly approaching). At our age, my dear, nobody can be indignant or surprised when evil is manifested, but I ask myself again and again, why should Eddie Walish work up my faults for thirty-some years to cast them into my teeth? This is what excites my keenest interest, so keen it makes me scream inwardly. The whole comedy of it comes over me in the night with the intensity of labor pains. I lie in the back bedroom of this little box of a Canadian house, which is scarcely insulated, and bear down hard so as not to holler. All the neighbors need is to hear such noises at three in the morning. And there isn't a soul in British Columbia I can discuss this with. My only acquaintance is Mrs. Gracewell, the old woman (she is very old) who studies occult literature, and I can't bother her with so different a branch of experience. Our conversations are entirely theoretical. . . . One helpful remark she did make, and this was: "The lower self is what the Psalmist referred to when he wrote, 'I am a worm and no man.' The higher self, few people are equipped to observe. This is the reason they speak so unkindly of one another."

More than once Walish's document (denunciation) took off from Ginsberg's poetry and prose, and so I finally sent an order to City Lights in San Francisco and have spent many evenings studying books of his I had missed—he publishes so many tiny ones. Ginsberg takes a stand for true tenderness and full candor. Real candor means excremental and genital literalness. What Ginsberg opts for is the warmth of a freely copulating, manly, womanly, comradely, "open road" humanity which doesn't neglect to pray and to meditate. He speaks with horror of our "plastic culture," which he connects somewhat obsessively with the CIA. And in addition to the CIA there are other spydoms, linked with Exxon, Mobil, Standard Oil of California, sinister Occidental Petroleum with its Kremlin connections (that *is* a weird one to contemplate, undeniably). Supercapitalism and its carcinogenic petrochemical technology are linked through

James Jesus Angleton, a high official of the Intelligence Community, to T. S. Eliot, one of his pals. Angleton, in his youth the editor of a literary magazine, had the declared aim of revitalizing the culture of the West against the "so-to-speak Stalinists." The ghost of T. S. Eliot, interviewed by Ginsberg on the fantail of a ship somewhere in death's waters, admits to having done little spy jobs for Angleton. Against these, the Children of Darkness, Ginsberg ranges the gurus, the bearded meditators, the poets loyal to Blake and Whitman, the "holy creeps," the lyrical, unsophisticated homosexuals whose little groups the secret police track on their computers, amongst whom they plant provocateurs, and whom they try to corrupt with heroin. This psychopathic vision, so touching because there is, realistically, so much to be afraid of, and also because of the hunger for goodness reflected in it, a screwball defense of beauty, I value more than my accuser, Walish, does. I truly understand. To Ginsberg's sexual Fourth of July fireworks I say, Tee-hee. But then I muse sympathetically over his obsessions, combing my mustache downward with my fingernails, my eyes feeling keen as I try to figure him. I am a more disinterested Ginsberg admirer than Eddie is. Eddie, so to speak, comes to the table with a croupier's rake. He works for the house. He skims from poetry.

One of Walish's long-standing problems was that he looked distinctly Jewy. Certain people were distrustful and took against him with gratuitous hostility, suspecting that he was trying to pass for a full American. They'd sometimes say, as if discovering how much force it gave them to be brazen (force is always welcome), "What was your name before it was Walish?"—a question of the type that Jews often hear. His parents were descended from north of

Ireland Protestants, actually, and his mother's family name was Ballard. He signs himself Edward Ballard Walish. He pretended not to mind this. A taste of persecution made him friendly to Jews, or so he said. Uncritically delighted with his friendship, I chose to believe him.

It turns out that after many years of concealed teetering, Walish concluded that I was a fool. It was when the public began to take me seriously that he lost patience with me and his affection turned to rancor. My TV programs on music history were what did it. I can envision this—Walish watching the screen in a soiled woolen dressing gown, cupping one elbow in his hand and sucking a cigarette, assailing me while I go on about Haydn's last days, or Mozart and Salieri, developing themes on the harpsichord: "Superstar! What a horseshit idiot!" "Christ! How phony can you get!" "Huckleberry Fink!"

My own name, Shawmut, had obviously been tampered with. The tampering was done long years before my father landed in America by his brother Pinye, the one who wore a pince-nez and was a music copyist for Sholom Secunda. The family must have been called Shamus or, even more degrading, Untershamus. The *untershamus,* lowest of the low in the Old World synagogue, was a quasi-unemployable incompetent and hanger-on, tangle-bearded and cursed with comic ailments like a large hernia or scrofula, a pauper's pauper. *"Orm,"* as my father would say, *"auf steiffleivent." Steiffleivent* was the stiff linen-and-horsehair fabric that tailors would put into the lining of a jacket to give it shape. There was nothing cheaper. "He was so poor that he dressed in dummy cloth." Cheaper than a shroud. But in America Shawmut turns out to be the name of a chain of banks in Massachusetts. How do you like *them* apples!

You may have heard charming, appealing, sentimental things about Yiddish, but Yiddish is a *hard* language, Miss Rose. Yiddish is severe and bears down without mercy. Yes, it is often delicate, lovely, but it can be explosive as well. "A face like a slop jar," "a face like a bucket of swill." (Pig connotations give special force to Yiddish epithets.) If there is a demiurge who inspires me to speak wildly, he may have been attracted to me by this violent unsparing language.

As I tell you this, I believe that you are willingly following, and I feel the greatest affection for you. I am very much alone in Vancouver, but that is my own fault, too. When I arrived, I was invited to a party by local musicians, and I failed to please. They gave me their Canadian test for U.S. visitors: Was I a Reaganite? I couldn't be that, but the key question was whether El Salvador might not be another Vietnam, and I lost half of the company at once by my reply: "Nothing of the kind. The North Vietnamese are seasoned soldiers with a military tradition of many centuries—*really* tough people. Salvadorans are Indian peasants." Why couldn't I have kept my mouth shut? What do I care about Vietnam? Two or three sympathetic guests remained, and these I drove away as follows: A professor from UBC observed that he agreed with Alexander Pope about the ultimate unreality of evil. Seen from the highest point of metaphysics. To a rational mind, nothing bad ever really happens. He was talking high-minded balls. Twaddle! I thought. I said, "Oh? Do you mean that every gas chamber has a silver lining?"

That did it, and now I take my daily walks alone.

It is very beautiful here, with snow mountains and still harbors. Port facilities are said to be limited and freighters have to wait (at a daily fee of $10,000). To see them at anchor is pleasant. They suggest the "Invitation au Voyage," and also "Anywhere, anywhere, Out of the world!" But what a clean and civilized city this is, with its clear northern waters and, beyond, the sense of an unlimited wilderness beginning where the forests bristle, spreading northward for millions of square miles and ending at ice whorls around the Pole.

Provincial academics took offense at my quirks. Too bad.

But lest it appear that I am always dishing it out, let me tell you, Miss Rose, that I have often been on the receiving end, put down by virtuosi, by artists greater than myself, in this line. The late Kippenberg, prince of musicologists, when we were at a conference in the Villa Serbelloni on Lake Como, invited me to his rooms one night to give him a preview of my paper. Well, he didn't actually invite me. I was eager. The suggestion was mine and he didn't have the heart to refuse. He was a huge man dressed in velvet dinner clothes, a copious costume, kelly green in color, upon which his large, pale, clever head seemed to have been deposited by a boom. Although he walked with two sticks, a sort of *diable boiteux,* there was no one faster with a word. He had published *the* great work on Rossini, and Rossini himself had made immortal wisecracks (like the one about Wagner: *"Il a de beaux moments mais de mauvais quarts d'heure"*). You have to imagine also the suite that Kippenberg occupied at the villa, eighteenth-century rooms, taffeta sofas, brocades, cool statuary, hot silk lamps. The servants had already shuttered the windows for the night, so the parlor was very close. Anyway, I was reading to the worldly-wise and learned Kippenberg, all swelled out in green, his long mouth agreeably composed.

Funny eyes the man had, too, set at the sides of his head as if for bilateral vision, and eyebrows like caterpillars from the Tree of Knowledge. As I was reading he began to nod. I said, "I'm afraid I'm putting you to sleep, Professor." "No, no—on the contrary, you're keeping me awake," he said. That, and at my expense, was genius, and it was a privilege to have provoked it. He had been sitting, massive, with his two sticks, as if he were on a slope, skiing into profound sleep. But even at the brink, when it was being extinguished, the unique treasure of his consciousness could still dazzle. I would have gone around the world for such a put-down.

Let me, however, return to Walish for a moment. The Walishes lived in a small country house belonging to the college. It was down in the woods, which at that season were dusty. You may remember, in Florida, what New England woods are in a dry autumn— pollen, woodsmoke, decayed and mealy leaves, spider webs, perhaps the wing powder of dead moths. Arriving at the Walishes' stone gateposts, if we found bottles left by the milkman we'd grab them by the neck and, yelling, hurl them into the bushes. The milk was ordered for Peg Walish, who was pregnant but hated the stuff and wouldn't drink it anyway. Peg was socially above her husband. Anybody, in those days, could be; Walish had below him only Negroes and Jews, and owing to his Jewy look, was not secure even in this advantage. Bohemianism therefore gave him strength. Mrs. Walish enjoyed her husband's bohemian style, or said she did. My Pergolesi and Haydn made me less objectionable to her than I might otherwise have been. Besides, I was lively company for her husband. Believe me, he needed lively company. He was depressed; his wife was worried. When she looked at me I saw the remedy-light in her eyes.

21

Like Alice after she had emptied the DRINK ME bottle in Wonderland, Peg was very tall; bony but delicate, she resembled a silent-movie star named Colleen Moore, a round-eyed ingenue with bangs. In her fourth month of pregnancy, Peg was still working at Filene's, and Eddie, unwilling to get up in the morning to drive her to the station, spent long days in bed under the faded patchwork quilts. Pink, when it isn't fresh and lively, can be a desperate color. The pink of Walish's quilts sank my heart when I came looking for him. The cottage was paneled in walnut-stained boards, the rooms were sunless, the kitchen especially gloomy. I found him upstairs sleeping, his jaw undershot and his Jewish lip prominent. The impression he made was both brutal and innocent. In sleep he was bereft of the confidence into which he put so much effort. Not many of us are fully wakeful, but Walish took particular pride in being alert. That he was nobody's fool was his main premise. But in sleep he didn't look clever.

I got him up. He was embarrassed. He was not the complete bohemian after all. His muzziness late in the day distressed him, and he grumbled, putting his thin legs out of bed. We went to the kitchen and began to drink.

Peg insisted that he see a psychiatrist in Providence. He kept this from me awhile, finally admitting that he needed a tune-up, minor internal adjustments. Becoming a father rattled him. His wife eventually gave birth to male twins. The facts are trivial and I don't feel that I'm betraying a trust. Besides, I owe him nothing. His letter upset me badly. What a time he chose to send it! Thirty-five years without a cross word. He allows me to count on his affection. Then he lets me have it. When do you shaft a pal, when do you hand him the poison cup? Not while he's still young enough to recover. Walish waited till the very end—*my* end, of course. *He* is still youthful, he writes me. Evidence of this is that he takes a true interest in young lesbians out in Missouri, he alone knows their inmost hearts and they allow him to make love to them—Walish, the sole male exception. Like the explorer McGovern, who went to Lhasa in disguise, the only Westerner to penetrate the sacred precincts. They trust only youth, they trust him, so it's certain that he can't be old.

This document of his pulls me to pieces entirely. And I agree, objectively, that my character is not an outstanding success. I am inattentive, spiritually lazy, I tune out. I have tried to make this indolence of mine look good, he says. For example, I never would check a waiter's arithmetic; I refused to make out my own tax returns; I was too "unworldly" to manage my own investments, and hired experts (read "crooks"). Realistic Walish wasn't too good to fight over nickels; it was the principle that counted, as honor did with Shakespeare's great soldiers. When credit cards began to be used, Walish, after computing interest and service charges to the fourth decimal, cut up Peg's cards and threw them down the chute. Every year he fought it out with tax examiners, both federal and state. Nobody was going to get the better of Eddie Walish. By such hardness he connected himself with the skinflint rich—the founding Rockefeller, who wouldn't tip more than a dime, or Getty the billionaire, in whose mansion weekend guests were forced to use coin telephones. Walish wasn't being petty, he was being hard, strict, tighter than a frog's ass. It wasn't simply basic capitalism. Insofar as Walish was a Brecht fan, it was also Leninist or Stalinist hardness. And if I was, or appeared to be, misty about money, it was conceivably "a semi-unconscious strategy," he said. Did he mean that I was trying to stand out as a Jew who disdained the dirty dollar? Wanting to be taken for one of my betters? In other words, assimilationism? Only I never admitted that anti-Semites of any degree were my betters.

I wasn't trying to be absentmindedly angelic about my finances. In fact, Miss Rose, I was really not with it. My ineptness with money was part of the same hysterical syndrome that caused me to put my foot in my mouth. I suffered from it genuinely, and continue to suffer. The Walish of today has forgotten that when he went to a psychiatrist to be cured of sleeping eighteen hours at a stretch, I told him how well I understood his problem. To console him, I said, "On a good day I can be acute for about half an hour, then I start to fade out and anybody can get the better of me." I was speaking of the dream condition or state of vague turbulence in which, with isolated moments of clarity, most of us exist. And it never occurred to me to adopt a strategy. I told you before that at one time it seemed a practical necessity to have a false self, but that I soon gave up on it. Walish, however, assumes that every clever modern man is his own avant-garde invention. To be avant-garde means to tamper with yourself, to have a personal project requiring a histrionic routine—in short, to put on an act. But what sort of act was it to trust a close relative who turned out to be a felon, or to let my late wife persuade me to hand over my legal problems to her youngest brother? It was the brother-in-law who did me in. Where others were simply unprincipled and crooked, he was in addition bananas. Patience, I am getting around to that.

Walish writes, "I thought it was time you knew what you were really like," and gives me a going-over such as few men ever face. I abused and badmouthed everybody, I couldn't bear that people should express themselves (this particularly irritated him; he mentions it several times) but put words into their mouths, finished their sentences for them, making them forget what they were about to say (supplied the platitudes they were groping for). I was, he says, "a mobile warehouse of middle-class spare parts," meaning that I was stocked with the irrelevant and actually insane information that makes the hateful social machine tick on toward the bottomless pit. And so forth. As for my supernal devotion to music, that was merely a cover. The real Shawmut was a canny promoter whose *Introduction to Music Appreciation* was adopted by a hundred colleges ("which doesn't happen of itself") and netted him a million in royalties. He compares me to Kissinger, a Jew who made himself strong in the Establishment, having no political base or constituency but succeeding through promotional genius, operating as a celebrity. . . . Impossible for Walish to understand the strength of character, even the constitutional, biological force such an achievement would require; to appreciate (his fur-covered ear sunk in his pillow, and his small figure thrice-bent, like a small fire escape, under the wads of pink quilt) what it takes for an educated man to establish a position of strength among semiliterate politicians. No, the comparison is farfetched. Doing eighteenth-century music on PBS is not very much like taking charge of U.S. foreign policy and coping with drunkards and liars in the Congress or the executive branch.

An honest Jew? That would be Ginsberg the Confessor. Concealing no fact, Ginsberg appeals to Jewhaters by exaggerating everything that they ascribe to Jews in their pathological fantasies. He puts them on, I think, with crazy simplemindedness, with his actual dreams of finding someone's anus in his sandwich or with his poems about sticking a dildo into himself. This bottom-line materialistic eroticism is most attractive to Americans, proof of sincerity and authenticity. It's on this level that they tell you they are "leveling" with you, although the deformities and obscenities that come out must of course be assigned to somebody else, some "morphodite" faggot or exotic junkie queer. When they tell you they're "leveling," put your money in your shoe at once, that's my advice.

I see something else in Ginsberg, however. True, he's playing a traditional Jewish role with this comic self-degradation, just as it was played in ancient Rome, and probably earlier. But there's something else, equally traditional. Under all this all-revealing candor (or aggravated self-battery) is purity of heart. As an American Jew he must also affirm and justify democracy. The United States is destined to become one of the great achievements of humanity, a nation made up of many nations (not excluding the queer nation: how can anybody be left out?). The U.S.A. itself is to be the greatest of poems, as Whitman prophesied. And the only authentic living representative of American Transcendentalism is that fat-breasted, bald, bearded homosexual in smeared goggles, innocent in his uncleanness. Purity from foulness, Miss Rose. The man is a Jewish microcosm of this Midas earth whose buried corpses bring forth golden fruits. This is not a Jew who goes to Israel to do battle with Leviticus to justify homosexuality. He is a faithful faggot Buddhist in America, the land of his birth. The petrochemical capitalist enemy (an enemy that needs sexual and religious redemption) is right here at home. Who could help loving such a comedian! Besides, Ginsberg and I were born under the same birth sign, and both of us had crazy mothers and are given to inspired utterances. I, however, refuse to overvalue the erotic life. I do not believe that the path of truth must pass through all the zones of masturbation and buggery. He is consistent; to his credit, he goes all the way, which can't be said of me. Of the two of us, he is the more American. *He* is a member of the American Academy of Arts and Letters—I've never even been proposed as a candidate—and although he has suggested that some of our recent Presidents were acidheads, he has never been asked to return his national prizes and medals. The more he libels them (did LBJ use LSD?), the more medals he is likely to get. Therefore I have to admit that he is closer to the American mainstream than I am. I don't even look like an American. (Nor does Ginsberg, for that matter.) Hammond, Indiana, was my birthplace (just before Prohibition my old man had a saloon there), but I might have come straight from Kiev. I certainly haven't got the build of a Hoosier—I am tall but I slouch, my buttocks are set higher than other people's, I have always had the impression that my legs are disproportionately long: it would take an engineer to work out the dynamics. Apart from Negroes and hillbillies, Hammond is mostly foreign, there are lots of Ukrainians and Finns there. These, however, look completely American, whereas I recognize features like my own in Russian church art—the compact faces, small round eyes, arched brows, and bald heads of the icons. And in highly structured situations in which champion American executive traits like prudence and discretion are required, I always lose control and I am, as Arabs say, a hostage to my tongue.

* * *

The preceding has been fun—by which I mean that I've avoided rigorous examination, Miss Rose. We need to get closer to the subject. I have to apologize to you, but there is also a mystery here (perhaps of karma, as old Mrs. Gracewell suggests) that cries out for investigation. Why does anybody *say* such things as I said to you? Well, it's as if a man were to go out on a beautiful day, a day so beautiful that it pressed him incomprehensibly to *do* something, to perform a commensurate action—or else he will feel like an invalid in a wheelchair by the seashore, a valetudinarian whose nurse says, "Sit here and watch the ripples."

My late wife was a gentle, slender woman, quite small, built on a narrow medieval principle. She had a way of bringing together her palms under her chin when I upset her, as if she were praying for me, and her pink color would deepen to red. She suffered extremely from my fits and assumed the duty of making amends for me, protecting my reputation and persuading people that I meant no harm. She was a brunette and her complexion was fresh. Whether she owed her color to health or excitability was an open question. Her eyes were slightly extruded, but there was no deformity in this; it was one of her beauties as far as I was concerned. She was Austrian by birth (Graz, not Vienna), a refugee. I never was attracted to women of my own build—two tall persons made an incomprehensible jumble together. Also I preferred to have to search for what I wanted. As a schoolboy, I took no sexual interest in teachers. I fell in love with the smallest girl in the class, and I followed my earliest taste in marrying a slender van der Weyden or Lucas Cranach woman. The rose color was not confined to her face. There was something not exactly contemporary about her complexion, and her conception of gracefulness also went back to a former age. She had a dipping way about her: her figure dipped when she walked, her hands dipped from the wrist while she was cooking, she was a dippy eater, she dipped her head attentively when you had anything serious to tell her and opened her mouth a little to appeal to you to make better sense. In matters of principle, however irrational, she was immovably obstinate. Death has taken Gerda out of circulation, and she has been wrapped up and put away for good. No more straight, flushed body and pink breasts, nor blue extruded eyes.

What I said to you in passing the library would have appalled her. She took it to heart that I should upset people. Let me cite an example. This occurred years later, at another university (a real one), one evening when Gerda put on a dinner for a large group of academics—all three leaves were in our cherrywood Scandinavian table. I didn't even know who the guests were. After the main course, a certain Professor Schulteiss was mentioned. Schulteiss was one of those bragging polymath types who gave everybody a pain in the ass. Whether it was Chinese cookery or particle physics or the connections of Bantu with Swahili (if any) or why Lord Nelson was so fond of William Beckford or the future of computer science, you couldn't interrupt him long enough to complain that he didn't let you get a word in edgewise. He was a big, bearded man with an assault-defying belly and fingers that turned back at the tips, so that if I had been a cartoonist I would have sketched him yodeling, with black whiskers and retroussé fingertips. One of the guests said to me that Schulteiss was terribly worried that no one would be learned enough to write a proper obituary when he died. "I don't know if I'm qualified," I said, "but I'd be happy to do the job, if that would be of any comfort to him." Mrs. Schulteiss, hidden from me by Gerda's table flowers, was being helped just then to dessert. Whether she had actually heard me didn't matter, for five or six guests immediately repeated what I had said, and I saw her move aside the flowers to look at me.

In the night I tried to convince Gerda that no real harm had been done. Anna Schulteiss was not easy to wound. She and her husband were on the outs continually—why had she come without him? Besides, it was hard to guess what she was thinking and feeling; some of her particles (a reference to Schulteiss's learning in the field of particle physics) were surely out of place. This sort of comment only made matters worse. Gerda did not tell me that, but only lay stiff on her side of the bed. In the field of troubled breathing in the night she was an accomplished artist, and when she sighed heavily there was no sleeping. I yielded to the same stiffness and suffered with her. Adultery, which seldom tempted me, couldn't have caused more guilt. While I drank my morning coffee Gerda telephoned Anna Schulteiss and made a lunch date with her. Later in the week they went to a symphony concert together. Before the month was out we were baby-sitting for the Schulteisses in their dirty little university house, which they had turned into a Stone Age kitchen midden. When that stage of conciliation had been reached, Gerda felt better. My thought, however, was that a man who allowed himself to make such jokes should be brazen enough to follow through, not succumb to conscience as soon as the words were out. He should carry things off like the princely Kippenberg. Anyway, which was the real Shawmut, the man who made insulting jokes or the other one, who had married a wife who couldn't bear that anyone should be wounded by his insults?

You will ask: With a wife willing to struggle mortally to preserve you from the vindictiveness of the injured parties, weren't you perversely tempted to make trouble, just to set the wheels rolling? The answer is no, and the reason is not only that I loved Gerda (my love terribly confirmed by her death), but also that when I said things I said them for art's sake, i.e., without perversity or malice, nor as if malice had an effect like alcohol and I was made drunk on wickedness. I reject that. Yes, there has to be some provocation. But what happens when I am provoked happens because the earth heaves up underfoot, and then from opposite ends of the heavens I get a simultaneous shock to both ears. I am deafened, and I have to open my mouth. Gerda, in her simplicity, tried to neutralize the ill effects of the words that came out and laid plans to win back the friendship of all kinds of unlikely parties whose essential particles were missing and who had no capacity for friendship, no interest in it. To such people she sent azaleas, begonias, cut flowers, she took the wives to lunch. She came home and told me earnestly how many fascinating facts she had learned about them, how their husbands were underpaid, or that they had sick old parents, or madness in the family, or fifteen-year-old kids who burglarized houses or were into heroin.

I never said anything wicked to Gerda, only to provocative people. Yours is the only case I can remember where there was no provocation, Miss Rose—hence this letter of apology, the first I have ever written. You are the cause of my self-examination. I intend to get back to this later. But I am thinking now about Gerda. For her sake I tried to practice self-control, and eventually I began to learn the value of keeping one's mouth shut, and how it can give a man strength to block his inspired words and to let the wickedness (if wickedness is what it is) be absorbed into the system again. Like the "right speech" of Buddhists, I imagine. "Right speech" is sound physiology. And did it make much sense to utter choice words at a time when words have sunk into grossness and decadence? If a La Rochefoucauld were to show up, people would turn away from him in midsentence, and yawn. Who needs maxims now?

The Schulteisses were colleagues, and Gerda could work on them, she had access to them, but there were occasions when she couldn't protect me. We were, for instance, at a formal university dinner, and I was sitting beside an old woman who gave millions of dollars to opera companies and orchestras. I was something of a star that evening and wore tails, a white tie, because I had just conducted a performance of Pergolesi's *Stabat Mater*, surely one of the most moving works of the eighteenth century. You would have thought that such music had ennobled me, at least until bedtime. But no, I soon began to spoil for trouble. It was no accident that I was on Mrs. Pergamon's right. She was going to be hit for a big contribution. Somebody had dreamed up a schola cantorum, and I was supposed to push it (tactfully). The real pitch would come later. Frankly, I didn't like the fellows behind the plan. They were a bad lot, and a big grant would have given them more power than was good for anyone. Old Pergamon had left his wife a prodigious fortune. So much money was almost a sacred attribute. And also I had conducted sacred music, so it was sacred against sacred. Mrs. Pergamon talked money to me, she didn't mention the *Stabat Mater* or my interpretation of it. It's true that in the U.S., money leads all other topics by about a thousand to one, but this was one occasion when the music should not have been omitted. The old woman explained to me that the big philanthropists had an understanding, and how the fields were divided up among Carnegie, Rockefeller, Mellon, and Ford. Abroad there were the various Rothschild interests and the Volkswagen Foundation. The Pergamons did music, mainly. She mentioned the sums spent on electronic composers, computer music, which I detest, and I was boiling all the while that I bent a look of perfect courtesy from Kiev on her. I had seen her limousine in the street with campus cops on guard, supplementing the city police. The diamonds on her bosom lay like the Finger Lakes among their hills. I am obliged to say that the money conversation had curious effects on me. It reached very deep places. My late brother, whose whole life was devoted to money, had been my mother's favorite. He remains her favorite still, and she is in her nineties. Presently I heard Mrs. Pergamon say that she planned to write her memoirs. Then I asked—and the question is what Nietzsche called a *Fatum*—"Will you use a typewriter or an adding machine?"

Should I have said *that?* Did I actually *say* it? Too late to ask, the tempest had fallen. She looked at me, quite calm. Now, she was a great lady and I was from Bedlam. Because there was no visible reaction in her diffuse old face, and the blue of her eyes was wonderfully clarified and augmented by her glasses, I was tempted to believe that she didn't hear or else had failed to understand. But that didn't wash. I changed the subject. I understood that despite the almost exclusive interest in music, she had from time to time supported scientific research. The papers reported that she had endowed a project for research in epilepsy. Immediately I tried to steer her into epilepsy. I mentioned the Freud essay in which the theory was developed that an epileptic fit was a dramatization of the death of one's father. This was why it made you stiff. But finding that my struggle to get off the hook was only giving me a bloody lip, I went for the bottom and lay there coldly silent. With all my heart I concentrated on the *Fatum*. *Fatum* signifies that in each human being there is something that is inaccessible to revision. This something can be taught *nothing*. Maybe it is founded in the Will to Power, and the Will to Power is nothing less than Being itself. Moved, or as the young would say, stoned out of my head, by the *Stabat Mater* (the glorious mother who would not stand up for *me*), I had been led to speak from the depths of my *Fatum*. I believe that I misunderstood old Mrs. Pergamon entirely. To speak of money to me was kindness, even magnanimity on her part—a man who knew Pergolesi was as good as rich and might almost be addressed as an equal. And in spite of me she endowed the schola cantorum. You don't penalize an institution because a kook at dinner speaks wildly to you. She was so very old that she had seen every sort of maniac there is. Perhaps I startled myself more than I did her.

She was being gracious, Miss Rose, and I had been trying to go beyond her, to pass her on a dangerous curve. A power contest? What might that mean? Why did I need power? Well, I may have needed it because from a position of power you can say anything. Powerful men give offense with impunity. Take as an instance what Churchill said about an M.P. named Driberg: "He is the man who brought pederasty into disrepute." And Driberg instead of being outraged was flattered, so that when another member of Parliament claimed the remark for himself and insisted that his was the name Churchill had spoken, Driberg said, *"You?* Why would Winston take notice of an insignificant faggot like *you!*" This quarrel amused London for several weeks. But then Churchill was Churchill, the descendant of Marlborough, his great biographer, and also the savior of his country. To be insulted by him guaranteed your place in history. Churchill was, however, a holdover from a more civilized age. A less civilized case would be that of Stalin. Stalin, receiving a delegation of Polish Communists in the Kremlin, said, "But what has become of that fine, intelligent woman Comrade Z?" The Poles looked at their feet. Because, as Stalin himself had had Comrade Z murdered, there was nothing to say.

This is contempt, not wit. It is Oriental despotism, straight, Miss Rose. Churchill was human, Stalin merely a colossus. As for us, here in America, we are a demotic, hybrid civilization. We have our virtues but are ignorant of style. It's only because American society has no place for style (in the sense of Voltairean or Gibbonesque style, style in the manner of Saint-Simon or Heine) that it is possible for a man like me to make such statements as he makes, harming no one but himself. If people are offended, it's by the "hostile intent" they sense, not by the keenness of the words. They classify me then as a psychological curiosity, a warped personality. It never occurs to them to take a full or biographical view. In the real sense of the term, biography has fallen away from us. We all flutter like new-hatched chicks between the feet of the great idols, the monuments of power.

So what are words? A lawyer, the first one, the one who represented me in the case against my brother's estate (the second one was Gerda's brother)—lawyer number one, whose name was Klaussen, said to me when an important letter had to be drafted, *"You* do it, Shawmut. You're the man with the words."

"And you're the whore with ten cunts!"

But I didn't say this. He was too powerful. I needed him. I was afraid.

But it was inevitable that I should offend him, and presently I did.

I can't tell you *why*. It's a mystery. When I tried to discuss Freud's epilepsy essay with Mrs. Pergamon I wanted to hint that I myself was subject to strange seizures that resembled falling sickness. But it wasn't just brain pathology, lesions, *grand mal* chemistry. It was a kind of perversely happy *gaieté de coeur*. Elements of vengefulness, or blasphemy? Well, maybe. What about demonic inspiration, what about energumens, what about Dionysus the god? After a distressing luncheon with Klaussen the lawyer at his formidable club, where he bullied me in a dining room filled with bullies, a scene from Daumier (I had been beaten down ten or twelve times, my suggestions all dismissed, and I had paid him a $25,000 retainer, but Klaussen hadn't bothered yet to master the elementary facts of the case)—after lunch, I say, when we were walking through the lobby of the club, where federal judges, machine politicians, paving contractors, and chairmen of boards conferred in low voices, I heard a great noise. Workmen had torn down an entire wall. I said to the receptionist, "What's happening?" She answered, "The entire club is being rewired. We've been having daily power failures from the old electrical system." I said, "While they're at it they might arrange to have people electrocuted in the dining room."

I was notified by Klaussen next day that for one reason or another he could no longer represent me. I was an incompatible client.

The intellect of man declaring its independence from worldly power—okay. But I had gone to Klaussen for protection. I chose him because he was big and arrogant, like the guys my brother's widow had hired. My late brother had swindled me. Did I want to recover my money or not? Was I fighting or doodling? Because in the courts you needed brazenness, it was big arrogance or nothing. And with Klaussen as with Mrs. Pergamon there was not a thing that Gerda could do—she couldn't send either of them flowers or ask them to lunch. Besides, she was already sick. Dying, she was concerned about my future. She remonstrated with me. "Did you have to needle him? He's a proud man."

"I gave in to my weakness. What's with me? Like, am I too good to be a hypocrite?"

"Hypocrisy is a big word. . . . A little lip service."

And again I said what I shouldn't have, especially given the state of her health: "It's a short step from lip service to ass kissing."

"Oh, my poor Herschel, you'll never change!"

She was then dying of leukemia, Miss Rose, and I had to promise her that I would put my case in the hands of her brother Hansl. She believed that for her sake Hansl would be loyal to me. Sure, his feeling for her was genuine. He loved his sister. But as a lawyer he was a disaster, not because he was disloyal but because he was in essence an inept conniver. Also he was plain crackers.

Lawyers, lawyers. Why did I need all these lawyers? you will ask. Because I loved my brother fondly. Because we did business, and business can't be done without lawyers. They have built a position for themselves at the very heart of money—strength at the core of what is strongest. Some of the cheerfulest passages in Walish's letter refer to my horrible litigation. He says, "I always knew you were a fool."

Himself, he took the greatest pains never to be one. Not that any man can ever be absolutely certain that his prudence is perfect. But to retain lawyers is clear proof that you're a patsy. There I concede that Walish is right.

My brother, Philip, had offered me a business proposition, and that, too, was my fault. I made the mistake of telling him how much money my music-appreciation book had earned. He was impressed. He said to his wife, "Tracy, guess who's loaded!" Then he asked, "What are you doing with it? How do you protect yourself against taxes and inflation?"

I admired my brother, not because he was a "creative businessman," as they said in the family—that meant little to me—but because . . . Well, there is in fact no "because," there's only the *given*, a lifelong feeling, a mystery. His interest in my finances excited me. For once he spoke seriously to me, and this turned my head. I told him, "I never even tried to make money, and now I'm knee deep in the stuff." Such a statement was a little disingenuous. It was, if you prefer, untrue. To take such a tone was also a mistake, for it implied that money wasn't so hard to make. Brother Philip had knocked himself out for it, while Brother Harry had earned heaps of it, incidentally, while fiddling. This, I now acknowledge, was a provocative booboo. He made a dark note of it. I even saw the note being made.

As a boy, Philip was very fat. We had to sleep together when we were children and it was like sharing the bed with a dugong. But since then he had firmed up quite a lot. In profile his face was large, with bags under the eyes, a sharp serious face upon a stout body. My late brother was a crafty man. He laid long-distance schemes. Over me he enjoyed the supreme advantage of detachment. My weakness was my fondness for him, contemptible in an adult male. He slightly resembled Spencer Tracy, but was more avid and sharp. He had a Texas tan, his hair was "styled," not barbered, and he wore Mexican rings on every one of his fingers.

Gerda and I were invited to visit his estate near Houston. Here he lived in grandeur, and when he showed me around the place he said to me, "Every morning when I open my eyes I say, 'Philip, you're living right in the middle of a park. You own a whole park.'"

I said, "It certainly is as big as Douglas Park in Chicago."

He cut me short, not wishing to hear about the old West Side, our dreary origins. Roosevelt Road with its chicken coops stacked on the sidewalks, the Talmudist horseradish grinder in the doorway of the fish store, or the daily drama of the Shawmut kitchen on Independence Boulevard. He abominated these reminiscences of mine, for he was thoroughly Americanized. On the other hand, he no more belonged on this Texas estate than I did. Perhaps no one belonged here. Numerous failed entrepreneurs had preceded him in this private park, the oilmen and land developers who had caused this monument to be built. You had the feeling that they must all have died in flophouses or on state funny-farms, cursing the grandiose fata morgana that Philip now owned, or seemed to own. The truth was that he didn't like it, either; he was stuck with it. He had bought it for various symbolic reasons, and under pressure from his wife.

He told me in confidence that he had a foolproof investment for me. People were approaching him with hundreds of thousands, asking to be cut into the deal, but he would turn them all down for my sake. For once he was in a position to do something for me.

Then he set his conditions. The first condition was that he was never to be questioned, that was how he did business, but I could be sure that he would protect me as a brother should and that there was nothing to fear. In the fragrant plantation gardens, he flew for one instant (no more) into Yiddish. He'd never let me lay my sound head in a sickbed. Then he flew out again. He said that his wife, who was the best woman in the world and the soul of honor, would respect his commitments and carry out his wishes with fanatical fidelity if anything were to happen to him. Her fanatical fidelity to him was fundamental. I didn't understand Tracy, he said. She was difficult to know but she was a true woman, and he wasn't going to have any clauses in our partnership agreement that would bind her formally. She would take offense at that and so would he. And you wouldn't believe, Miss Rose, how all these clichés moved me. I responded as if to an accelerator under his fat elegantly shod foot, pumping blood, not gasoline, into my mortal engine. I was wild with feeling and said yes to it all. Yes, yes! The plan was to create an auto-wrecking center, the biggest in Texas, which would supply auto parts to the entire South and to Latin America as well. The big German and Italian exporters were notoriously short of replacement parts; I had experienced this myself—I had once had to wait four months for a BMW front-wheel stabilizer unobtainable in the U.S. But it wasn't the business proposition that carried me away, Miss Rose. What affected me was that my brother and I should be really associated for the first time in our lives. As our joint enterprise could never in the world be Pergolesi, it must necessarily be business. I was unreasonably stirred by emotions that had waited a lifetime for expression; they must have worked their way into my heart at a very early age, and now came out in full strength to drag me down.

"What have you got to do with wrecking automobiles?" said Gerda. "And grease, and metal, and all that noise?"

I said, "What has the IRS ever done for music that it should collect half my royalties?"

My wife was an educated woman, Miss Rose, and she began to reread certain books and to tell me about them, especially at bedtime. We went through much of Balzac. *Père Goriot* (what daughters can do to a father), *Cousin Pons* (how an elderly innocent was dragged down by relatives who coveted his art collection) . . . One swindling relative after another, and all of them merciless. She related the destruction of poor César Birotteau, the trusting perfumer. She also read me selections from Marx on the obliteration of the ties of kinship by capitalism. But it never occurred to me that such evils could affect a man who had read about them. I had read about venereal diseases and had never caught any. Besides, it was now too late to take a warning.

On my last trip to Texas I visited the vast, smoking wrecking grounds, and on our way back to the mansion Philip told me that his wife had become a breeder of pit bulldogs. You may have read about these creatures, which have scandalized American animal lovers. They are the most terrifying of all dogs. Part terrier, part English bulldog, smooth-skinned, broad-chested, immensely muscular, they attack all strangers, kids as well as grownups. As they do not bark, no warning is given. Their intent is always to kill, and once they have begun to tear at you they can't be called off. The police, if they arrive in time, have to shoot them. In the pit, the dogs fight and die in silence. Aficionados bet millions of dollars on the fights (which are illegal, but what of it?). Humane societies and civil liberties groups don't quite know how to defend these murderous animals or the legal rights of their owners. There is a Washington lobby trying to exterminate the breed, and meantime enthusiasts go on experimenting, doing everything possible to create the worst of all possible dogs.

Philip took an intense pride in his wife. "Tracy is a wonder, isn't she?" he said. "There's terrific money in these animals. Trust her to pick up a new trend. Guys are pouring in from all over the country to buy pups from her."

He took me to the dog-runs to show the pit bulls off. As we passed, they set their paws on the wire meshes and bared their teeth. I didn't enjoy visiting the pens. My own teeth were on edge. Philip himself wasn't comfortable with the animals, by any means. He owned them, they were assets, but he wasn't the master. Tracy, appearing among the dogs, gave me a silent nod. The Negro employees who brought meat were tolerated. "But Tracy," Philip said, "she's their goddess."

I must have been afraid, because nothing satirical or caustic came to mind. I couldn't even make up funny impressions to take home to Gerda, with whose amusement I was preoccupied in those sad days.

But as a reverberator, which it is my nature to be, I tried to connect the breeding of these terrible dogs with the mood of the country. The pros and cons of the matter add some curious lines to the spiritual profile of the U.S.A. Not long ago, a lady wrote to the *Boston Globe* that it had been a failure of judgment in the Founding Fathers not to consider the welfare of cats and dogs in our democracy, people being what they are. The Founders were too lenient with human viciousness, she said, and the Bill of Rights ought to have made provision for the safety of those innocents who are forced to depend upon us. The first connection to come to mind was that egalitarianism was now being extended to cats and dogs. But it's not simple egalitarianism, it's a merging of different species: the line between man and other animals is becoming blurred. A dog will give you such simple heart's truth as you will never get from a lover or a parent. I seem to recall from the thirties (or did I read this in the memoirs of Lionel Abel?) how scandalized the French Surrealist André Breton was when he visited Leon Trotsky in exile. While the two men were discussing World Revolution, Trotsky's dog came up to be caressed and Trotsky said, "This is my only true friend." What? A dog the friend of this Marxist theoretician and hero of the October Revolution, the organizer of the Red Army? Symbolic surrealist acts, like shooting at random into a crowd in the street, Breton could publicly recommend, but to be sentimental about a dog like any bourgeois was shocking. Today's psychiatrists would not be shocked. Asked whom they love best, their patients reply in increasing numbers, "My dog." At this rate, a dog in the White House becomes a real possibility. Not a pit bulldog, certainly, but a nice golden retriever whose veterinarian would become Secretary of State.

I didn't try these reflections out on Gerda. Nor, since it would have been unsettling, did I tell her that Philip, too, was unwell. He had been seeing a doctor. Tracy had him on a physical-fitness program. Mornings he entered the annex to the master bedroom, in which the latest gymnastic equipment had been set up. Wearing overlong silk boxer shorts (I reckon that their theme was the whiskey sour, since they were decorated with orange slices resembling wheels), he hung by his fat arms from the shining apparatus, he jogged on a treadmill with an odometer, and he tugged at the weights. When he worked out on the Exercycle, the orange-slice wheels of his underpants extended the vehicular fantasy, but he was going nowhere. The queer things he found himself doing as a rich man, the false position he was in! His adolescent children were rednecks. The druidic Spanish moss vibrated to the shocks of rock music. The dogs bred for cruelty bided their time. My brother, it appeared, was only the steward of his wife and children.

Still, he wanted me to observe him at his exercises and to impress me with his strength. As he did push-ups, his dipping titties touched the floor before his chin did, but his stern face censored any comical comments I might be inclined to make. I was called upon to witness that under the fat there was a block of primal powers, a strong heart in his torso, big veins in his neck, and bands of muscle across his back. "I can't do any of that," I told him, and indeed I couldn't, Miss Rose. My behind is like a rucksack that has slipped its straps.

I made no comments, because I was a general partner who had invested $600,000 in the wreckage of rusty automobiles. Two miles behind the private park, there were cranes and compactors, and hundreds of acres were filled with metallic pounding and dust. I understood by now that the real power behind this enterprise was Philip's wife, a short round blonde of butch self-sufficiency, as dense as a meteorite and, somehow, as spacy. But no, it was I who was spacy, while she was intricately shrewd.

And most of my connubial ideas derived from the gentleness and solicitude of my own Gerda!

During this last visit with Brother Philip, I tried to

get him to speak about Mother. The interest he took in her was minimal. Family sentiment was not his dish. All that he had was for the new family; for the old family, nix. He said he couldn't recall Hammond, Indiana, or Independence Boulevard. "You were the only one I ever cared for," he said. He was aware that there were two departed sisters, but their names didn't come to him. Without half trying, he was far ahead of André Breton, and could never be overtaken. Surrealism wasn't a theory, it was an anticipation of the future.

"What was Chink's real name?" he said.

I laughed. "What, you've forgotten Helen's name? You're bluffing. Next you'll tell me you can't remember her husband, either. What about Kramm? He bought you your first pair of long pants. Or Sabina? She got you the job in the bucket shop in the Loop."

"They fade from my mind," he said. "Why should I keep those dusty memories? If I want details I can get you to fill me in. You've got such a memory hang-up —what use is it?"

As I grow older, Miss Rose, I don't dispute such views or opinions but tend instead to take them under consideration. True, I counted on Philip's memory. I wanted him to remember that we were brothers. I had hoped to invest my money safely and live on an income from wrecked cars—summers in Corsica, handy to London at the beginning of the musical season. Before the Arabs sent London real estate so high, Gerda and I discussed buying a flat in Kensington. But we waited and waited, and there was not a single distribution from the partnership. "We're doing great," said Philip. "By next year I'll be able to remortgage, and then you and I will have more than a million to cut up between us. Until then, you'll have to be satisfied with the tax write-offs."

I started to talk about our sister Chink, thinking my only expedient was to stir such family sentiments as might have survived in this atmosphere where the Spanish moss was electronicized by rock music (and, at the back, the pit bulldogs were drowning silently in the violence of their blood-instincts). I recalled that we had heard very different music on Independence Boulevard. Chink would play "Jimmy Had a Nickel" on the piano, and the rest of us would sing the chorus, or yell it out. Did Philip remember that Kramm, who drove a soda-pop truck (it was from affection, because he doted on Helen, that he called her Chink), could accurately pitch a case filled with bottles into a small opening at the very top of the pyramid? No, the pop truck wasn't exactly stacked like a pyramid, it was a ziggurat.

"What's a ziggurat?"

Assyrian or Babylonian, I explained, terraced, and not coming to a peak.

Philip said, "Sending you to college was a mistake, although I don't know what else you would have been fit for. Nobody else went past high school. . . . Kramm was okay, I guess."

Yes, I said, Chink got Kramm to pay my college tuition. Kramm had been a doughboy, did Philip remember that? Kramm was squat but powerful, full-faced, smooth-skinned like a Samoan, and wore his black hair combed flat to his head in the Valentino or George Raft style. He supported us all, paid the rent. Our dad, during the Depression, was peddling carpets to farm women in northern Michigan. *He* couldn't earn the rent. From top to bottom, the big household became Mother's responsibility, and if she had been a little tetched before, melodramatic, in her fifties she seemed to become crazed. There was something military about the way she took charge of

46

the house. Her command post was the kitchen. Kramm had to be fed because he fed us, and he was an enormous eater. She cooked tubs of stuffed cabbage and of chop suey for him. He could swallow soup by the bucket, put down an entire pineapple upside-down cake by himself. Mother shopped, peeled, chopped, boiled, fried, roasted, and baked, served and washed. Kramm ate himself into a stupor and then, in the night, he might come out in his pajama bottoms, walking in his sleep. He went straight to the icebox. I recalled a summer's night when I watched him cutting oranges in half and ripping into them with his teeth. In his somnambulism he slurped away about a dozen of them, and then I saw him go back to bed, following his belly to the right door.

"And gambled in a joint called the Diamond Horseshoe, Kedzie and Lawrence," said Philip. He did not, however, intend to be drawn into any reminiscences. He began, a little, to smile, but he remained basically gloomy, reserved.

Of course. He had entered upon one of his biggest swindles.

He changed the subject. He asked if I didn't admire the way Tracy ran this large estate. She was a magician. She didn't need interior decorators, she had done the whole place by herself. All the linens were Portuguese. The gardens were wonderful. Her roses won prizes. The appliances never gave trouble. She was a cordon bleu cook. It was true the kids were difficult, but that was how kids were nowadays. She was a terrific psychologist, and fundamentally the little bastards were well adjusted. They were just American youngsters. His greatest satisfaction was that everything was so American. It was, too—an all-American production.

For breakfast, if I called the kitchen persistently, I

could have freeze-dried coffee and a slice of Wonder bread. They were brought to my room by a black person who answered no questions. Was there an egg, a piece of toast, a spoonful of jam? Nothing. It wounds me desperately not to be fed. As I sat waiting for the servant to come with the freeze-dried coffee and the absorbent-cotton bread, I prepared and polished remarks that I might make to her, considering how to strike a balance between satire and human appeal. It was a waste of time to try to reach a common human level with the servants. It was obvious that I was a guest of no importance, Miss Rose. No one would listen. I could almost hear the servants being instructed to "come slack of former services" or "Put on what weary negligence you please"—the words of Goneril in *King Lear*. Also the room they had given me had been occupied by one of the little girls, now too big for it. The wallpaper, illustrated with Simple Simon and Goosey Gander, at the time seemed inappropriate (it now seems sharply pertinent).

And I was obliged to listen to my brother's praise of his wife. Again and again he told me how wise and good she was, how clever and tender a mother, what a brilliant hostess, respected by the best people who owned the largest estates. And a shrewd counselor (I could believe that!). Plus a warm sympathizer when he was anxious, an energetic lover, and she gave him what he had never had before—peace. And I, Miss Rose, with $600,000 sunk here, was constrained to go along, nodding like a dummy. Forced to underwrite all of his sustaining falsehoods, countersigning the bill of goods he sold himself, I muttered the words he needed to finish his sentences. (How Walish would have jeered!) Death breathing over both the odd brothers with the very fragrance of subtropical air—

magnolia, honeysuckle, orange-blossom, or whatever the hell it was, puffing into our faces. Oddest of all was Philip's final confidence (untrue!). For my ears only, he whispered in Yiddish that our sisters had shrieked like *papagayas* (parrots), that for the first time in his life he had quiet here, domestic tranquillity. Not true. There was amplified rock music.

After this lapse, he reversed himself with a vengeance. For a family dinner, we drove in two Jaguars to a Chinese restaurant, a huge showplace constructed in circles, or dining wells, with tables highlighted like symphonic kettledrums. Here Philip made a scene. He ordered far too many hors d'oeuvres, and when the table was jammed with dishes he summoned the manager to complain that he was being hustled, he hadn't asked for double portions of all these fried wontons, egg rolls, and barbecued ribs. And when the manager refused to take them back Philip went from table to table with egg rolls and ribs, saying, "Here! Free! Be my guest!" Restaurants always did excite him, but this time Tracy called him to order. She said, "Enough, Philip, we're here to eat, not raise everybody's blood pressure." Yet a few minutes later he pretended that he had found a pebble in his salad. I had seen this before. He carried a pebble in his pocket for the purpose. Even the kids were on to him, and one of them said, "He's always doing this routine, Uncle." It gave me a start to have them call me Uncle.

Indulge me for a moment, Miss Rose. I am covering the ground as quickly as I can. There's not a soul to talk to in Vancouver except ancient Mrs. Gracewell, and with her I have to ride in esoteric clouds. Pretending that he had cracked his tooth, Philip had shifted from the Americanism of women's magazines (lovely wife, beautiful home, the highest standard of normalcy) to that of the rednecks—yelling at the Orientals, ordering his children to get his lawyer on the table telephone. The philistine idiosyncrasy of the rich American brute. But you can no longer be a philistine without high sophistication, matching the sophistication of what you hate. However, it's no use talking about "false consciousness" or any of that baloney. Philly had put himself into Tracy's hands for full Americanization. To achieve this (obsolete) privilege, he paid the price of his soul. But then he may never have been absolutely certain that there is any such thing as a soul. What he resented about me was that I wouldn't stop hinting that souls existed. What was I, a Reform rabbi or something? Except at a funeral service, Philip wouldn't have put up with Pergolesi for two minutes. And wasn't I—never mind Pergolesi— looking for a hot investment?

When Philip died soon afterward, you may have read in the papers that he was mixed up with chop-shop operators in the Midwest, with thieves who stole expensive cars and tore them apart for export piece-meal to Latin America and the whole of the third world. Chop shops, however, were not Philip's crime. On the credit established by my money, the partnership acquired and resold land, but much of the property lacked clear title, there were liens against it. Defrauded purchasers brought suit. Big trouble followed. Convicted, Philip appealed, and then he jumped bail and escaped to Mexico. There he was kidnapped while jogging in Chapultepec Park. His kidnappers were bounty hunters. The bonding companies he had left holding the bag when he skipped out had offered a bounty for his return. Specialists exist who will abduct people, Miss Rose, if the sums are big enough to make the risks worthwhile. After Philip was brought back to Texas, the Mexican government began extradition proceedings on the ground that he was snatched illegally, which he was, certainly. My poor brother died while doing push-ups in a San Antonio prison yard during the exercise hour. Such was the end of his picturesque struggles.

After we had mourned him, and I took measures to recover my losses from his estate, I discovered that his personal estate was devoid of assets. He had made all his wealth over to his wife and children.

I could not be charged with Philip's felonies, but since he had made me a general partner I was sued by the creditors. I retained Mr. Klaussen, whom I lost by the remark I made in the lobby of his club about electrocuting people in the dining room. The joke was harsh, I admit, although no harsher than what people often think, but nihilism, too, has its no-nos, and professional men can't allow their clients to make such cracks. Klaussen drew the line. Thus I found myself after Gerda's death in the hands of her energetic but unbalanced brother, Hansl. He decided, on sufficient grounds, that I was an incompetent, and as he is a believer in fast action, he took dramatic measures and soon placed me in my present position. Some position! Two brothers in flight, one to the south, the other northward and faced with extradition. No bonding company will set bounty hunters on me. I'm not worth it to them. And even though Hansl had promised that I would be safe in Canada, he didn't bother to check the law himself. One of his student clerks did it for him, and since she was a smart, sexy girl it didn't seem necessary to review her conclusions.

Knowledgeable sympathizers when they ask who represents me are impressed when I tell them. They say, "Hansl Genauer? Real smart fellow. You ought to do all right."

Hansl dresses very sharply, in Hong Kong suits and shirts. A slender man, he carries himself like a concert violinist and has a manner that, as a manner, is fully convincing. For his sister's sake ("She had a wonderful life with you, she said to the last"), he was, or intended to be, my protector. I was a poor old guy, bereaved, incompetent, accidentally prosperous, foolishly trusting, thoroughly swindled. "Your brother fucked you but good. He and his wife."

"She was a party to it?"

"Try giving it a little thought. Has she answered any of your letters?"

"No."

Not a single one, Miss Rose.

"Let me tell you how I reconstruct it, Harry," said Hansl. "Philip wanted to impress his wife. He was scared of her. Out of terror, he wanted to make her rich. She told him she was all the family he needed. To prove that he believed her, he had to sacrifice his old flesh and blood to the new flesh and blood. Like, 'I give you the life of your dreams, all you have to do is cut your brother's throat.' He did his part, he piled up dough, dough, and more dough—I don't suppose he liked you anyway—and he put all the loot in her name. So that when he died, which was *never* going to happen . . ."

Cleverness is Hansl's instrument; he plays it madly, bowing it with elegance as if he were laying out the structure of a sonata, phrase by phrase, for his backward brother-in-law. What did I need with his fiddling? Isn't there anybody, dear God, on *my* side? My brother picked me up by the trustful affections as one would lift up a rabbit by the ears. Hansl, now in charge of the case, analyzed the betrayal for me, down to the finest fibers of its brotherly bonds, and this demonstrated that he was completely on my side—right? He examined the books of the partnership, which I had never bothered to do, pointing out Philip's misdeeds. "You see? He was leasing land from his wife, the nominal owner, for use by the wrecking company, and every year that pig paid himself a rent of ninety-eight thousand dollars. There went your profits. More deals of the same kind all over these balance sheets. While you were planning summers in Corsica."

"I wasn't cut out for business. I see that."

"Your dear brother was a full-time con artist. He might have started a service called Dial-a-Fraud. But then you also provoke people. When Klaussen handed over your files to me, he told me what offensive, wicked things you said. Why he decided he couldn't represent you anymore."

"But he didn't return the unused part of the fat retainer I gave him."

"*I'll* be looking out for you now. Gerda's gone, and that leaves me to see that things don't get worse—the one adult of us three. My clients who are the greatest readers are always in the biggest trouble. What they call culture, if you ask me, causes mostly confusion and stunts their development. I wonder if you'll ever understand why you let your brother do you in the way he did."

Philip's bad world borrowed me to live in. I had, however, approached him in the expectation of benefits, Miss Rose. I wasn't blameless. And if he and his people—accountants, managers, his wife—forced me to feel what they felt, colonized me with their realities, even with their daily moods, saw to it that I should suffer everything they had to suffer, it was after all *my* idea. I tried to make use of *them*.

I never again saw my brother's wife, his children, nor the park they lived in, nor the pit bulldogs.

"That woman is a legal genius," said Hansl.

Hansl said to me, "You'd better transfer what's left, your trust account, to my bank, where I can look after it. I'm on good terms with the officers over there. The guys are efficient, and no monkey business. You'll be taken care of."

I had been taken care of before, Miss Rose. Walish was dead right about "the life of feeling" and the people who lead it. Feelings are dreamlike, and dreaming is usually done in bed. Evidently I was forever looking for a safe place to lie down. Hansl offered to make secure arrangements for me so that I wouldn't have to wear myself out with finance and litigation, which were too stressful and labyrinthine and disruptive; so I accepted his proposal and we met with an officer of his bank. Actually the bank looked like a fine old institution, with Oriental rugs, heavy carved furniture, nineteenth-century paintings, and dozens of square acres of financial atmosphere above us. Hansl and the vice-president who was going to take care of me began with small talk about the commodity market, the capers over at City Hall, the prospects for the Chicago Bears, intimacies with a couple of girls in a Rush Street bar. I saw that Hansl badly needed the points he was getting for bringing in my account. He wasn't doing well. Though nobody was supposed to say so, I was soon aware of it. Many forms were put before me, which I signed. Then two final cards were laid down just as my signing momentum seemed irreversible. But I applied the brake. I asked the vice-president what these were for and he said, "If you're busy, or out of town, these will give Mr. Genauer the right to trade for you—buy or sell stocks for your account."

I slipped the cards into my pocket, saying that I'd

take them home with me and mail them in. We passed to the next item of business.

Hansl made a scene in the street, pulling me away from the great gates of the bank and down a narrow Loop alley. Behind the kitchen of a hamburger joint he let me have it. He said, "You humiliated me."

I said, "We didn't discuss a power of attorney beforehand. You took me by surprise, completely. Why did you spring it on me like that?"

"You're accusing me of trying to pull a fast one? If you weren't Gerda's husband I'd tell you to beat it. You undermined me with a business associate. You weren't like this with your own brother, and I'm closer to you by affection than he was by blood, you nitwit. I wouldn't have traded your securities without notifying you."

He was tearful with rage.

"For God's sake, let's move away from this kitchen ventilator," I said. "I'm disgusted with these fumes."

He shouted, "You're out of it! Out!"

"And you're *in* it."

"Where the hell else is there to be?"

Miss Rose, you have understood us, I am sure of it. We were talking about the vortex. A nicer word for it is the French one, *le tourbillon,* or whirlwind. I was not out of it, it was only my project to *get* out. It's been a case of disorientation, my dear. I know that there's a right state for each of us. And as long as I'm not in the right state, the state of vision I was meant or destined to be in, I must assume responsibility for the unhappiness others suffer because of my disorientation. Until this ends there can only be errors. To put it another way, my dreams of orientation or true vision taunt me by suggesting that the world in which I—together with others—live my life is a fabrication, an amusement park that, however, does not amuse. It resembles, if you are following, my brother's private park, which was supposed to prove by external signs that he made his way into the very center of the real. Philip had prepared the setting, paid for by embezzlement, but he had nothing to set in it. He was forced to flee, pursued by bounty hunters who snatched him in Chapultepec, and so forth. At his weight, at that altitude, in the smog of Mexico City, to jog was suicidal.

Now Hansl explained himself, for when I said to him, "Those securities can't be traded anyway. Don't you see? The plaintiffs have legally taken a list of all my holdings," he was ready for me. "Bonds, mostly," he said. "That's just where I can outfox them. They copied that list two weeks ago, and now it's in their lawyers' file and they won't check it for months to come. They think they've got you, but here's what we do: we sell those old bonds off and buy new ones to replace them. We change all the numbers. All it costs you is brokerage fees. Then, when the time comes, they find out that what they've got sewed up is bonds you no longer own. How are they going to trace the new numbers? And by then I'll have you out of the country."

Here the skin of my head became intolerably tight, which meant even deeper error, greater horror anticipated. And, at the same time, temptation. People had kicked the hell out of me with, as yet, no reprisals. My thought was: It's time *I* made a bold move. We were in the narrow alley between two huge downtown institutions (the hamburger joint was crammed in tight). An armored Brink's truck could hardly have squeezed between the close colossal black walls.

"You mean I substitute new bonds for the old, and I can sell from abroad if I want to?"

Seeing that I was beginning to appreciate the exquisite sweetness of his scheme, Hansl gave a terrific smile and said, "And you will. That's the dough you'll live on."

"That's a dizzy idea," I said.

"Maybe it is, but do you want to spend the rest of your life battling in the courts? Why not leave the country and live abroad quietly on what's left of your assets? Pick a place where the dollar is strong and spend the rest of your life in musical studies or what you goddamn well please. Gerda, God bless her, is gone. What's to keep you?"

"Nobody but my old mother."

"Ninety-four years old? And a vegetable? You can put your textbook copyright in her name and the income will take care of her. So our next step is to check out some international law. There's a sensational chick in my office. She was on the *Yale Law Journal.* They don't come any smarter. She'll find you a country. I'll have her do a report on Canada. What about British Columbia, where old Canadians retire?"

"Whom do I know there? Whom will I talk to? And what if the creditors keep after me?"

"You haven't got so much dough left. There isn't all that much in it for them. They'll forget you."

I told Hansl I'd consider his proposal. I had to go and visit Mother in the nursing home.

The home was decorated with the intention of making everything seem normal. Her room was much like any hospital room, with plastic ferns and fireproof drapes. The chairs, resembling wrought-iron garden furniture, were also synthetic and light. I had trouble with the ferns. I disliked having to touch them to see if they were real. It was a reflection on my relation to reality that I couldn't tell at a glance. But then Mother didn't know me, either, which was a more complex matter than the ferns.

I preferred to come at mealtimes, for she had to be fed. To feed her was infinitely meaningful for me. I took over from the orderly. I had long given up telling her, "This is Harry." Nor did I expect to establish rapport by feeding her. I used to feel that I had inherited something of her rich crazy nature and love of life, but it now was useless to think such thoughts. The tray was brought and the orderly tied her bib. She willingly swallowed the cream of carrot soup. When I encouraged her, she nodded. Recognition, nil. Two faces from ancient Kiev, similar bumps on the forehead. Dressed in her hospital gown, she wore a thread of lipstick on her mouth. The chapped skin of her cheeks gave her color also. By no means silent, she spoke of her family, but I was not mentioned.

"How many children have you got?" I said.

"Three: two daughters and a son, my son Philip."

All three were dead. Maybe she was already in communion with them. There was little enough of reality remaining in this life; perhaps they had made connections in another. In the census of the living, I wasn't counted.

"My son Philip is a clever businessman."

"Oh, I know."

She stared, but did not ask how I knew. My nod seemed to tell her that I was a fellow with plenty of contacts, and that was enough for her.

"Philip is very rich," she said.

"Is he?"

"A millionaire, and a wonderful son. He always used to give me money. I put it into Postal Savings. Have you got children?"

"No, I haven't."

"My daughters come to see me. But best of all is my son. He pays all my bills."

"Do you have friends in this place?"

"Nobody. And I don't like it. I hurt all the time, especially my hips and legs. I have so much misery that there are days when I think I should jump from the window."

"But you won't do that, will you?"

"Well, I think: What would Philip and the girls do with a mother a cripple?"

I let the spoon slip into the soup and uttered a high laugh. It was so abrupt and piercing that it roused her to examine me.

Our kitchen on Independence Boulevard had once been filled with such cockatoo cries, mostly feminine. In the old days the Shawmut women would sit in the kitchen while giant meals were cooked, tubs of stuffed cabbage, slabs of brisket. Pineapple cakes glazed with brown sugar came out of the oven. There were no low voices there. In that cage of birds you couldn't make yourself heard if you didn't shriek, too, and I had learned as a kid to shriek with the rest, like one of those operatic woman-birds. That was what Mother now heard from me, the sound of one of her daughters. But I had no bouffant hairdo, I was bald and wore a mustache, and there was no eyeliner on my lids. While she stared at me I dried her face with the napkin and continued to feed her.

"Don't jump, Mother, you'll hurt yourself."

But everyone here called her Mother; there was nothing personal about it.

She asked me to switch on the TV set so that she could watch *Dallas*.

I said it wasn't time yet, and I entertained her by

singing snatches of the *Stabat Mater*. I sang, *"Eja mater, fons amo-o-ris."* Pergolesi's sacred chamber music (different from his formal masses for the Neapolitan church) was not to her taste. Of course I loved my mother, and she had once loved me. I well remember having my hair washed with a bulky bar of castile soap and how pained she was when I cried from the soap in my eyes. When she dressed me in a pongee suit (short pants of Chinese silk) to send me off to a surprise party, she kissed me ecstatically. These were events that might have occurred just before the time of the Boxer Rebellion or in the back streets of Siena six centuries ago. Bathing, combing, dressing, kissing —these now are remote antiquities. There was, as I grew older, no way to sustain them.

When I was in college (they sent me to study electrical engineering but I broke away into music) I used to enjoy saying, when students joked about their families, that because I was born just before the Sabbath, my mother was too busy in the kitchen to spare the time and my aunt had to give birth to me.

I kissed the old girl—she felt lighter to me than wickerwork. But I wondered what I had done to earn this oblivion, and why fat-assed Philip the evildoer should have been her favorite, the true son. Well, he didn't lie to her about *Dallas*, or try for his own sake to resuscitate her emotions, to appeal to her maternal memory with Christian music (fourteenth-century Latin of J. da Todi). My mother, two-thirds of her erased, and my brother—who knew where his wife had buried him?—had both been true to the present American world and its liveliest material interests. Philip therefore spoke to her understanding. I did not. By waving my long arms, conducting Mozart's *Great Mass* or Handel's *Solomon*, I wafted myself away into the sublime. So for many years I had not made sense, had talked strangely to my mother. What had she to remember me by? Half a century ago I had refused to enter into *her* kitchen performance. She had belonged to the universal regiment of Stanislavski mothers. During the twenties and thirties those women were going strong in thousands of kitchens across the civilized world from Salonika to San Diego. They had warned their daughters that the men they married would be rapists to whom they must submit in duty. And when I told her that I was going to marry Gerda, Mother opened her purse and gave me three dollars, saying, "If you need it so bad, go to a whorehouse." Nothing but histrionics, of course.

"Realizing how we suffer," as Ginsberg wrote in "Kaddish," I was wickedly tormented. I had come to make a decision about Ma, and it was possible that I was fiddling with the deck, stacking the cards, telling myself, Miss Rose, "It was always me that took care of this freaked-in-the-brain, afflicted, calamitous, shrill old mother, not Philip. Philip was too busy building himself up into an imperial American." Yes, that was how I put it, Miss Rose, and I went even further. The consummation of Philip's upbuilding was to torpedo me. He got me under the waterline, a direct hit, and my fortunes exploded, a sacrifice to Tracy and his children. And now I'm supposed to be towed away for salvage.

I'll tell you the truth, Miss Rose, I was maddened by injustice. I think you'd have to agree not only that I'd been had but that I was singularly foolish, a burlesque figure. I could have modeled Simple Simon for the nursery-rhyme wallpaper of the little girl's room in Texas.

As I was brutally offensive to you without provocation, these disclosures, the record of my present state, may gratify you. Almost any elderly person, chosen at random, can provide such gratification to those he has offended. One has only to see the list of true facts, the painful inventory. Let me add, however, that while I, too, have reason to feel vengeful, I haven't experienced a Dionysian intoxication of vengefulness. In fact I have had feelings of increased calm and of enhanced strength—my emotional development has been steady, not fitful.

The Texas partnership, what was left of it, was being administered by my brother's lawyer, who answered all my inquiries with computer printouts. There were capital gains, only on paper, but I was obliged to pay taxes on them, too. The $300,000 remaining would be used up in litigation, if I stayed put, and so I decided to follow Hansl's plan even if it led to the *Götterdämmerung* of my remaining assets. All the better for your innocence and peace of mind if you don't understand these explanations. Time to hit back, said Hansl. His crafty looks were a study. That a man who was able to look so crafty shouldn't really be a genius of intrigue was the most unlikely thing in the world. His smiling wrinkles of deep cunning gave me confidence in Hansl. The bonds that the plaintiffs (creditors) had recorded were secretly traded for new ones. My tracks were covered, and I took off for Canada, a foreign country in which my own language, or something approaching it, is spoken. There I was to conclude my life in peace, and at an advantageous rate of exchange. I have developed a certain sympathy with Canada. It's no easy thing to share a border with the U.S.A. Canada's chief entertainment—it has no choice—is to watch (from a gorgeous setting) what happens in our country. The disaster is that there is no other show. Night after night they sit in darkness and watch us on the lighted screen.

"Now that you've made your arrangements, I can tell you," said Hansl, "how proud I am that you're hitting back. To go on taking punishment from those pricks would be a disgrace."

Busy Hansl really was crackers, and even before I took off for Vancouver I began to see that. I told myself that his private quirks didn't extend to his professional life. But before I fled, he came up with half a dozen unsettling ideas of what I had to do for him. He was a little bitter because, he said, I hadn't let him make use of my cultural prestige. I was puzzled and asked for an example. He said that for one thing I had never offered to put him up for membership in the University Club. I had had him to lunch there and it turned out that he was deeply impressed by the Ivy League class, the dignity of the bar, the leather seats, and the big windows of the dining room, decorated with the seals of the great universities in stained glass. He had graduated from De Paul, in Chicago. He had expected me to ask whether he'd like to join, but I had been too selfish or too snobbish to do that. Since he was now saving me, the least I could do was to use my influence with the membership committee. I saw his point and nominated him willingly, even with relish.

He next asked me to help him with one of his ladies. "They're Kenwood people, an old mail-order-house fortune. The family is musical and artistic. Babette is an attractive widow. The first guy had the Big C, and to tell the truth I'm a little nervous of getting in behind him, but I can fight that. I don't think I'll catch it, too. Now, Babette is impressed by you, she's heard you conduct and read some of your music criticism, watched you on Channel Eleven. Educated in Switzerland, knows languages, and this is a case where I can use your cultural clout. What I suggest is that you take us to Les Nomades—private dining without crockery noise. I gave her the best Italian food in town at the Roman Rooftop, but they not only bang the dishes there, they poisoned her with the sodium glutamate on the veal. So feed us at the Nomades. You can deduct the amount of the tab from my next bill. I always believed that the class you impressed people with you picked up from my sister. After all, you were a family of Russian peddlers and your brother was a lousy felon. My sister not only loved you, she taught you some style. Someday it'll be recognized that if that goddamn Roosevelt hadn't shut the doors on Jewish refugees from Germany, this country wouldn't be in such trouble today. We could have had ten Kissingers, and nobody will ever know how much scientific talent went up in smoke at the camps."

Well, at Les Nomades I did it again, Miss Rose. On the eve of my flight I was understandably in a state. Considered as a receptacle, I was tilted to the pouring point. The young widow he had designs on was attractive in ways that you had to come to terms with. It was fascinating to me that anybody with a Hapsburg lip could speak so rapidly, and I would have said that she was a little uncomfortably tall. Gerda, on whom my taste was formed, was a short, delicious woman. However, there was no reason to make comparisons.

When there are musical questions I always try earnestly to answer them. People have told me that I am comically woodenheaded in this respect, a straight man. Babette had studied music, her people were patrons of the Lyric Opera, but after she had asked for my opinion on the production of Monteverdi's *Coronation of Poppaea,* she took over, answering all her own questions. Maybe her recent loss had made her nervously talkative. I am always glad to let somebody else carry the conversation, but this Babette, in spite of her big underlip, was too much for me. A relentless talker, she repeated for half an hour what she had heard from influential relatives about the politics surrounding cable-TV franchises in Chicago. She followed this up with a long conversation on films. I seldom go to the movies. My wife had no taste for them. Hansl, too, was lost in all this discussion about directors, actors, new developments in the treatment of the relations between the sexes, the progress of social and political ideas in the evolution of the medium. I had nothing at all to say. I thought about death, and also about the best topics for reflection appropriate to my age, the on the whole agreeable openness of things toward the end of the line, the outskirts of the City of Life. I didn't too much mind Babette's chatter, I admired her taste in clothing, the curved white and plum stripes of her enchanting blouse from Bergdorf's. She was well set up. Conceivably her shoulders were too heavy, proportional to the Hapsburg lip. It wouldn't matter to Hansl; he was thinking about Brains wedded to Money.

I hoped I wouldn't have a stroke in Canada. There would be no one to look after me, neither a discreet, gentle Gerda nor a gabby Babette.

I wasn't aware of the approach of one of my seizures, but when we were at the half-open door of the checkroom and Hansl was telling the attendant that the lady's coat was a three-quarter-length sable wrap, Babette said, "I realize now that I monopolized the conversation, I talked and talked all evening. I'm so sorry. . . ."

"That's all right," I told her. "You didn't say a thing."

You, Miss Rose, are in the best position to judge the effects of such a remark.

Hansl next day said to me, "You just can't be trusted, Harry, you're a born betrayer. I was feeling sorry for you, having to sell your car and furniture and books, and about your brother who shafted you, and your old mother, and my poor sister passing, but you have no gratitude or consideration in you. You insult everybody."

"I didn't realize that I was going to hurt the lady's feelings."

"I could have married the woman. I had it wrapped up. But I was an idiot. I had to bring *you* into it. And now, let me tell you, you've made one more enemy."

"Who, Babette?"

Hansl did not choose to answer. He preferred to lay a heavy, ambiguous silence on me. His eyes, narrowing and dilating with his discovery of my enormity, sent daft waves toward me. The message of those waves was that the foundations of his good will had been wiped out. In all the world, I had had only Hansl to turn to. Everybody else was estranged. And now I couldn't count on him, either. It was not a happy development for me, Miss Rose. I can't say that it didn't bother me, although I could no longer believe in my brother-in-law's dependability. By the standards of stability at the strong core of American business society, Hansl himself was a freak. Quite apart from his disjunctive habits of mind, he was disqualified by the violinist's figure he cut, the noble hands and the manicured filbert fingernails, his eyes, which were like the eyes you glimpse in the heated purple corners of the small-mammal house that reproduces the gloom of nocturnal tropics. Would any Aramco official have become his client? Hansl had no reasonable plans but only crafty fantasies, restless schemes. They puffed out like a lizard's throat and then collapsed like bubble gum.

As for insults, I never intentionally insulted anyone. I sometimes think that I don't have to say a word for people to be insulted by me, that my existence itself insults them. I come to this conclusion unwillingly, for God knows that I consider myself a man of normal social instincts and am not conscious of any will to offend. In various ways I have been trying to say this to you, using words like seizure, rapture, demonic possession, frenzy, *Fatum*, divine madness, or even solar storm—on a microcosmic scale. The better people are, the less they take offense at this gift, or curse, and I have a hunch that you will judge me less harshly than Walish. He, however, is right in one respect. You did nothing to offend me. You were the meekest, the only one of those I wounded whom I had no reason whatsoever to wound. That's what grieves me most of all. But there is still more. The writing of this letter has been the occasion of important discoveries about myself, so I am even more greatly in your debt, for I see that you have returned me good for the evil I did you. I opened my mouth to make a coarse joke at your expense and thirty-five years later the result is a communion.

But to return to what I literally am: a basically unimportant old party, ailing, cut off from all friendships, scheduled for extradition, and with a future of which the dimmest view is justified (shall I have an extra bed put in my mother's room and plead illness and incompetency?).

Wandering about Vancouver this winter, I have considered whether to edit an anthology of sharp sayings. Make my fate pay off. But I am too demoralized to do it. I can't pull myself together. Instead, fragments of things read or remembered come to me persistently while I go back and forth between my house and the supermarket. I shop to entertain myself, but Canadian supermarkets unsettle me. They aren't organized the way ours are. They carry fewer brands. Items like lettuce and bananas are priced out of sight while luxuries like frozen salmon are comparatively cheap. But how would I cope with a big frozen salmon? I couldn't fit it into my oven, and how, with arthritic hands, could I saw it into chunks?

Persistent fragments, inspired epigrams, or spontaneous expressions of ill will come and go. Clemenceau saying about Poincaré that he was a hydrocephalic in patent-leather boots. Or Churchill answering a question about the queen of Tonga as she passes in a barouche during the coronation of Elizabeth II: "Is that small gentleman in the admiral's uniform the queen's consort?" "I believe he is her lunch."

Disraeli on his deathbed, informed that Queen Victoria has come to see him and is in the anteroom, says to his manservant, "Her Majesty only wants me to carry a message to dear Albert."

Such items might be delicious if they were not so persistent and accompanied by a despairing sense that I am no longer in control.

"You look pale and exhausted, Professor X."

"I've been exchanging ideas with Professor Y, and I feel absolutely drained."

Worse than this is the nervous word game I am unable to stop playing.

"She is the woman who put the 'dish' into 'fiendish.'"

"He is the man who put the 'rat' into 'rational.'"

"The 'fruit' in 'fruitless.'"

"The 'con' in 'icon.'"

Recreations of a crumbling mind, Miss Rose. Symptoms perhaps of high blood pressure, or minor tokens of private resistance to the giant public hand of the law (that hand will be withdrawn only when I am dead).

No wonder, therefore, that I spend so much time with old Mrs. Gracewell. In her ticktock Meissen parlor with its uncomfortable chairs I am at home. Forty years a widow and holding curious views, she is happy in my company. Few visitors want to hear about the Divine Spirit, but I am seriously prepared to ponder the mysterious and intriguing descriptions she gives. The Divine Spirit, she tells me, has withdrawn in our time from the outer, visible world. You can see what it once wrought, you are surrounded by its created forms. But although natural processes continue, Divinity has absented itself. The wrought work is brightly divine but Divinity is not now active within it. The world's grandeur is fading. And this is our human setting, devoid of God, she says with great earnestness. But in this deserted beauty man himself still lives as a God-pervaded being. It will be up to him—to us—to bring back the light that has gone from these molded likenesses, if we are not prevented by the forces of darkness. Intellect, worshipped by all, brings us as far as natural science, and this science, although very great, is incomplete. Redemption from *mere* nature is the work of feeling and of the awakened eye of the Spirit. The body, she says, is subject to the forces of gravity. But the soul is ruled by levity, pure.

I listen to this and have no mischievous impulses. I shall miss the old girl. After much monkey business, dear Miss Rose, I am ready to listen to words of ultimate seriousness. There isn't much time left. The federal marshal, any day now, will be setting out from Seattle.

What Kind
of Day Did
You Have?

Dizzy with perplexities, seduced by a restless spirit, Katrina Goliger took a trip she shouldn't have taken. What was the matter with her, why was she jumping around like this? A divorced suburban matron with two young kids, was she losing ground, were her looks going or her options shrinking so fast that it made her reckless? Looks were not her problem; she was pretty enough, dark hair, nice eyes. She had a full figure, a little on the plump side, but she handled it with some skill. Victor Wulpy, the man in her life, liked her just as she was. The worst you could say of her was that she was clumsy. Clumsiness, however, might come out as girlishness if it was well managed. But there were few things which Trina managed well. The truth, to make a summary of it, was that she was passably pretty, she was awkward, and she was wildly restless.

In all fairness, her options were increasingly limited

73

by Wulpy. It wasn't that he was being capricious. He had very special difficulties to deal with—the state of his health, certain physical disabilities, his advanced age, and, in addition to the rest, his prominence. He was a major figure, a world-class intellectual, big in the art world, and he had been a bohemian long before bohemianism was absorbed into everyday life. The civilized world knew very well who Victor Wulpy was. You couldn't discuss modern painting, poetry—any number of important topics—without referring to him.

Well, then, towards midnight, and in the dead of winter—Evanston, Illinois, where she lives at the bottom of a continental deep freeze—Katrina's phone rings and Victor asks her—in effect he tells her—"I have to have you here first thing in the morning."

"Here" is Buffalo, New York, where Victor has been lecturing.

And Katrina, setting aside all considerations of common sense or of self-respect, says, "I'll get an early flight out."

If she had been having an affair with a younger man, Katrina might have passed it off with a laugh, saying, "That's a real brainstorm. It would be a gas, wouldn't it, and just what this zero weather calls for. But what am I supposed to do with my kids on such short notice?" She might also have mentioned that her divorced husband was suing for custody of the little girls, and that she had a date downtown tomorrow with the court-appointed psychiatrist who was reporting on her fitness. She would have mixed these excuses with banter, and combined them with a come-on: "Let's do it Thursday. I'll make it up to you." With Victor refusal was not one of her options. It was almost impossible, nowadays, to say no to him.

Poor health was a euphemism. He had nearly died last year.

Various forces—and she wasn't altogether sorry—robbed her of the strength to resist. Victor was such a monument, and he went back so far in modern cultural history. You had to remember that he had begun to publish in *transition* and *Hound and Horn* before she was born. He was beginning to have an avant-garde reputation while she was still in her playpen. And if you thought he was now tired out and had no more surprises up his sleeve, you were thinking of the usual three-score and ten, not of Victor Wulpy. Even his bitterest detractors, the diehard grudgers, had to admit that he was still first-rate. And about how many Americans had leaders of thought like Sartre, Merleau-Ponty, and Hannah Arendt said, *"Chapeau bas!* This is a man of genius"—Merleau-Ponty being especially impressed with Victor's essays on Karl Marx.

Besides, Victor was personally so impressive—he had such a face, such stature; without putting it on, he was so commanding that he often struck people as being a king, of an odd kind. A New York-style king, thoroughly American—good-natured, approachable, but making it plain that he was a sovereign; he took no crap from anybody. But last year—it was that time of life for him, the mid-seventies—he went down with a crash. It happened at Harvard, and he was taken to Mass. General for surgery. The doctors there had dragged him from the edge of the grave. Or maybe he had spurned the grave himself, wrapped in bandages as he was and with pipes up his nose and drugged to the limit. Seeing him on his back, you would never have believed that he would walk through the door again. But he did just that.

Suppose, however, that Victor had died, what would Katrina have done? To think of it confused her. But Katrina's sister, Dorothea, who never spared anybody, spelled out the consequences of Victor's death. Dorothea, in plain truth, couldn't let the subject alone. "This has been the main event of your life. This time, kid, you really came out swinging." (An odd figure for Katrina, who was pretty and plump and seldom so much as raised her voice.) "You're going to be up against it when it finally happens. You must have known you could only have a short run." Katrina knew all that Dotey had to say. The résumé ran as follows: You dumped your husband to have this unusual affair. Sexual excitement and social ambition went together. You aimed to break into high cultural circles. I don't know what you thought *you* had to offer. If you took Daddy's word for it, and he'd repeat it from the next world, you're just an average Dumb Dora from north-suburban Chicagoland.

Quite true, the late Billy Weigal had called his daughters Dumb Dora One and Dumb Dora Two. He sent them down to the state university at Champaign-Urbana, where they joined a sorority and studied Romance languages. The girls wanted French? Good. Theater arts? Sure, why not. Old Doc Weigal pretended to think that it was all jibber-jabber. He had been a politician, mainly a tax fixer with high connections in the Chicago Democratic machine. His wife, too, was a mental lightweight. It was part of the convention that the womenfolk be birdbrains. It pleased his corrupt, protective heart. As Victor pointed out (all higher interpretation came from him), this was plain old middle-class ideology, the erotic components of which were easy to make out. Ignorance in women, a strong stimulus for men who considered themselves rough. On an infinitely higher level, Baudelaire had advised staying away from learned ladies. Bluestockings and bourgeois ladies caused sexual paralysis. Artists could trust only women of the people.

Anyway, Katrina had been raised to consider herself a nitwit. That she knew she was not one was an important secret postulate of her feminine science. And she didn't really object to Dorothea's way of discussing her intricate and fascinating problem with Victor. Dorothea said, "I want to get you to look at it from every angle." What this really meant was that Dotey would try to shaft her from every side. "Let's start with the fact that as Mrs. Alfred Goliger nobody in Chicago would take notice of you. When Mr. Goliger invited people to look at his wonderful collections of ivory, jade, semiprecious stones, and while he did all the talking, he only wanted you to serve the drinks and eats. And to the people with whom he tried to make time, the Lyric Opera types, the contemporary arts crowd, the academics, and those other shits, you were just a humdrum housewife. Then all of a sudden, through Wulpy, you're meeting all the Motherwells and Rauschenbergs and Ashberys and Frankenthalers, and you leave the local culture creeps groveling in the dust. However, when your old wizard dies, what then? Widows are forgotten pretty fast, except those with promotional talent. So what happens to girl friends?"

Arriving at Northwestern University to give his seminars on American painting, Victor had been lionized by the Goligers. Alfred Goliger, who, flying to Bombay and to Rio, had branched out from gems to antiques and *objets d'art* and bought estate jewelry and also china, sterling, pottery, statuary in all continents, longed to be a part of the art world. He wasn't one of your hobbled husbands; he did pretty much as he liked in Brazil and India. He misjudged Katrina if he thought that in her he had a homebody who spent her time choosing wallpapers and attending PTA meetings. Victor, the perfect lion, relaxing among Evanston admirers while he drank martinis and ate hors d'oeuvres, took in the eager husband, aggressively on the make, and then considered the pretty wife—in every sense of the word a dark lady. He perceived that she was darkest where darkness counted most. Circumstances had made Katrina look commonplace. She did what forceful characters do with such imposed circumstances; she used them as camouflage. Thus she approached Wulpy like a nearsighted person, one who has to draw close to study you. She drew so near that you could feel her breath. And then her lowering, almost stubborn look rested on you for just that extra beat that carried a sexual message. It was the incompetency with which she presented herself, the nearsighted puzzled frown, that made the final difference. Her first handshake informed him of a disposition, an inclination. He saw that all her preparations had been set. With a kind of engraved silence about the mouth under the wide bar of his mustache, Wulpy registered all this information. All he had to do was give the countersign. He intended to do just that.

At first it was little more than the fooling of a visiting fireman, an elderly, somewhat spoiled celebrity. But Wulpy was too big a man for crotchets. He was a disciplined intellectual. He stood for something. At the age of seventy, he had arranged his ideas in well-nigh final order: none of the weakness, none of the drift that made supposedly educated people contemptible. How can you call yourself a modern thinker if you lack the realism to identify a weak marriage quickly, if you don't know what hypocrisy is, if you haven't come to terms with lying—if, in certain connections, people can still say about you, "He's a sweetheart!"? Nobody would dream of calling Victor "a sweetheart." Wickedness? No, well-seasoned judgment. But whatever his first intentions might have been, the affair became permanent. And how do you assess a woman who knows how to bind such a wizard to her? She's got to be more than a dumpy suburbanite sexpot with clumsy ankles. And this is something more than the cruel absurdity, the decline and erotic enslavement, of a distinguished man grown (how suddenly!) old.

The divorce was ugly. Goliger was angry, vengeful. When he moved, he stripped the house, taking away his Oriental treasures, the jade collection, the crystal, the hangings, the painted gilded elephants, the bone china, even some of the valuable jewelry he had given her and which she hadn't had the foresight to put in the bank. He was determined to evict her from the house, too, a fine old house. He could do that if he obtained custody of the kids. The kids took little notice of the disappearance of the Indian and Venetian objects, although Trina's lawyer argued in court that they were disorientated. Dorothea said about her nieces, "I'll be interested to find out what gives with those two mysterious characters. As for Alfred, this is all-out war." She thought that Katrina was too absentminded to be a warrior. "Are you taking notice, or not?"

"Of course I'm taking notice. He was always flying to an auction. Never at home. What did *he* do, away in India?"

Katrina was still at the dinner table when Victor's call came. Her guest was Lieutenant Krieggstein, a member of the police force. He arrived late, because of the fierce weather, and told a story about skidding into a snowdrift and waiting for a tow truck. He had almost lost his voice and said it would take him an hour to thaw. A friend of the family, he needed no permission to bring up wood from the cellar and build a fire. The house had been built in the best age of Chicago architecture (made like a Stradivarius, said Krieggstein), and the curved tiles of the fireplace ("the old craftsmanship!") were kingfisher blue.

"I've seen rough weather before, but this beats everything," he said, and he asked for Red Devil sauce to sprinkle on his curry and drank vodka from a beer mug. His face still burned with the frost, and his eyes went on watering at the table. He said, "Oh, what a luxury that fire is on my back."

"I hope it doesn't set off your ammunition."

The Lieutenant carried at least three guns. Were all plain-clothes ("soft-clothes") men armed to the teeth, or did he have more weapons because he was a little guy? He set himself up as gracious but formidable. Just challenge him and you'd see fatal action. Victor said about him that he was just this side of sanity but was always crossing the line. "A lone cowhand on both sides of the Rio Grande simultaneously." On the whole, he took an indulgent view of Krieggstein.

It was nearly midnight in Buffalo. Katrina hadn't expected Victor to call just yet. Thoroughly familiar with his ways, Katrina knew that her old giant must have had a disappointing evening, had probably thrown himself disgusted on the bed in the Hilton, more than half his clothing on the floor and a pint of Black Label nearby to "keep the auxiliary engines going." The trip was harder than he was willing to admit. Beila, his wife, had advised him not to take it, but her opinions didn't count. A subordinate plant manager didn't tell the chairman of the board what to do. He was off to see Katrina. Lecturing, of course, was his pretext. "I promised those guys," he said. Not entirely a pretext, however. Greatly in demand, he got high fees. Tonight he had spoken at the state university, and tomorrow he was speaking to a group of executives in Chicago. Buffalo was a combined operation. The Wulpys' youngest daughter, Vanessa, who was an undergraduate there, was having problems. For Victor, family problems could never be what they were for other people—he wouldn't *have* them. Vanessa was being provocative and he was irritated.

Well, when the phone rang, Katrina said, "There's Victor. A little early. This may take a while." With Krieggstein you needn't stand on ceremony. Dinner had ended, and if she was too long on the phone he could let himself out. A large heavy beauty, shapely (only just within the limits), Katrina left the dining room as rapidly as her style of movement allowed. She released the catch of the swinging kitchen door. Of course Krieggstein meant to stay and to eavesdrop. Her affair was no secret and he considered himself her confidant. He had every qualification for this: he was a cop, and cops saw it all; he was a Pacific-war hero; and he was her scout's-honor friend. Listening, he turned his thick parboiled face to the fire, made his plump legs comfortable, crossed his short arms over his cardigan.

"How has it been, Victor?" said Katrina. How tired winter travel had made him was what she had to determine from the pitch of his voice and his choice of words. This must have been an exceptionally hard trip. It was strenuous labor for a man of his size, and with a surgically fused knee, to pole his way upon a walking stick against the human tides of airports. Wearing his Greek sea captain's cap, he was all the more conspicuous. He made his way everywhere with a look of willing acceptance and wit. He was on good terms with his handicaps (a lifelong, daily familiarity with pain) and did not complain about going it alone. Other famous old men had helpers. She had heard that Henry Moore kept no fewer than six assistants. Victor had nobody. His life had assumed a crazy intensity that could not be shared. Secrecy was necessary, obviously. At the heart of so much that was obvious was an unyielding mystery: Why *did* he? Katrina's answer was Love. Victor wouldn't say, declined to give an answer. Perhaps he hadn't yet found the core of the question.

Katrina thought him mysterious-looking, too. Beneath the bill of the Greek or Lenin-style cap there was a sort of millipede tangle about the eyes. His eyes were long, extending curiously into the temples. His cheeks were as red in sickness as in health; he was almost never pale. He carried himself with admirable, nonposturing, tilted grace, big but without heaviness. Not a bulky figure. He had style. You could, if you liked, call him an old bohemian, but such classifications did not take you far. No category could hold Victor.

The traveling-celebrity bit was very tiring. You flew in and you were met at the airport by people you didn't know and who put you under a strain because they wanted to be memorable individually, catch your attention, ingratiate themselves, provoke, flatter—it all came to the same thing. Driving from the airport, you were locked in a car with them for nearly an hour. Then there were drinks—a cocktail hubbub. After four or five martinis you went in to dinner and were seated between two women, not always attractive. You had to remember their names, make conversation, give them equal time. You might as well be running for office, you had to shake so many hands.

You ate your prime rib and drank wine, and before you had unfolded your speech on the lectern, you were already tuckered out. You shouldn't fight all this, said Victor; to fight it only tired you more. But normally Victor thrived on noise, drink, and the conversation of strangers. He had so much to say that he overwhelmed everybody who approached him. In the full blast of a cocktail party he was able to hear everything and to make himself heard; his tenor voice was positively fifelike when he made an important point, and he was superarticulate.

If after his lecture a good discussion developed, he'd be up half the night drinking and talking. That was what he loved, and to be abed before midnight was a defeat. So he was either uncharacteristically fatigued or the evening had been a drag. Stupid things must have been said to him. And here he was, a man who had associated with André Breton, Duchamp, the stars of his generation, weary to the bone, in frozen Buffalo (you could picture Niagara Falls more than half iced over), checking in with a girl friend in Evanston, Illinois. Add to the list of bad circumstances his detestation of empty hours in hotel rooms. Add also that he had probably taken off his pants, as she had seen him do in this mood, and thrown them at the wall, plus his big shoes, and his shirt made into a ball. He had his dudgeons, especially when there hadn't been a single sign of intelligence or entertainment. Now for comfort (or was it out of irritation) he telephoned Katrina. Most likely he had had a couple of drinks, lying naked, passing his hand over the hair of his chest, which sometimes seemed to soothe him. Except for his socks, he would then resemble the old men that Picasso had put into his late erotic engravings. Victor himself had written about the painter-and-model series done at Mougins in 1968, ferocious scribbles of satyr artists and wide-open odalisques. Through peepholes aged wrinkled kings spied on gigantic copulations. (Victor was by turns the painter-partner and the aged king.) Katrina's pretty lopsided-ness might have suited Picasso's taste. (Victor, by the way, was no great admirer of Picasso.)

"So Buffalo wasn't a success?"

"Buffalo! Hell, I can't see any reason why it exists."

"But you said you had to stop to see Vanessa."

"That's another ordeal I can do without. We're having breakfast at seven."

"And your lecture?"

"I read them my paper on Marx's *The Eighteenth Brumaire*. I thought, for a university crowd . . ."

"Well, tomorrow will be more important, more interesting," said Katrina.

Victor had been invited to address the Executives Association, an organization of bankers, economists, former presidential advisers, National Security Council types. Victor assured her that this was a far more important outfit than the overpublicized Trilateral Commission, which, he said, was a front organization using ex-Presidents and other exploded stars to divert attention from real operations. The guys who were bringing him to Chicago wanted him to talk about "Culture and Politics, East and West." Much they cared about art and culture, said Victor. But they sensed that it had to be dealt with; challenging powers were ascribed to it, nothing immediate or worrisome, but one ought to know what intellectuals were up to. "They've listened to professors and other pseudo experts," said Victor, "and maybe they believe they should send for an old Jewish character. Pay him his price and he'll tell you without fakery what it's all about." The power of big-shot executives wouldn't overawe him. Those people, he said, were made of

Styrofoam. He was gratified nevertheless. They had asked for the best, and that was himself—a realistic judgment, and virtually free from vanity. Katrina estimated that he would pick up a ten-thousand-dollar fee. "I don't expect the kind of dough that Kissinger gets, or Haig, although I'll give better value," he told her. He didn't mention a figure, though. Dotey, no bad observer, said that he'd talk freely about anything in the world but money—*his* money.

Dotey's observations, however, were commonplace. She spoke with what Katrina had learned to call *ressentiment*—from behind a screen of grievances. What could a person like Dotey understand about a man like Victor, whom she called "that gimpy giant"? What if this giant should have been in his time one of the handsomest men ever made? What if he should still have exquisite toes and fingers; a silken scrotum that he might even now (as he held the phone) be touching, leading out the longest hairs—his unconscious habit when he lay in bed? What, moreover, if he should be a mine of knowledge, a treasury of insights in all matters concerning the real needs and interests of modern human beings? Could a Dorothea evaluate the *release* offered to a woman by such an extraordinary person, the independence? Could she feel what it meant to be free from so much *junk?*

"By the way, Victor," said Katrina. "Do you remember the notes you dictated over the phone for use, maybe, tomorrow? I typed them up for you. If you need them, I'll have them with me when I meet you at O'Hare in the morning."

"I've had a different thought," said Victor. "How would it be if you were to fly here?"

"Me? Fly to Buffalo?"

"That's right. You join me, and we'll go on to Chicago together."

Immediately all of Katrina's warmest expectations were reversed, and up from the bottom there seeped instead every kind of dreariness imaginable. While Victor was in the air in the morning, she wouldn't be preparing, treating herself to a long bath, then putting on her pine-green knitted Vivanti suit and applying the Cabochard, his favorite perfume. She would be up until two A.M., improvising, trying to make arrangements, canceling her appointment downtown, setting her clock for five A.M. She hated to get up while it was still night.

There must be a sensible explanation for this, but Katrina couldn't bring herself to ask what it was—like "What's wrong? Are you sick?" She had unbearable questions to put to herself, too: Will I have to take him to the hospital? . . . Why me? His daughter is there. Does he need emergency surgery? Back to all the horrible stuff that had happened at Mass. General? A love that began with passionate embraces ending with barium X-rays, heavy drugs, bad smells? The grim wife coming back to take control?

Don't go so fast, Katrina checked herself. She regrouped and reentered her feelings at a different place. He was completely by himself and was afraid that he might start to crumble in his plane seat: a man like Victor, who was as close to being a prince as you could be (in what he described as "this bungled age"), such a man having to telephone a girl—and to Victor, when you came right down to it, she was *a* girl, one of many (although she was pretty sure she had beaten the rest of the field). He had to appeal to a girl ("I've had a different thought") and expose his weakness to her.

What was necessary now was to speak as usual, so that when he said, "I had the travel desk make a reservation for you, if you want to use it—are you there?" she answered, "Let me find a pen that writes." A perfectly good pen hung on a string. What she needed was to collect herself while she thought of an alternative. She wasn't clever enough to come up with anything, so she began to print out the numbers he gave her. Heavyhearted? Of course she was. She was forced to consider her position from a "worst case" point of view. A North Shore mother of two, in a bad, a deteriorating marriage, had begun to be available sexually to visitors. Selectively. It was true that a couple of wild mistakes had occurred. But then, a godsend, Victor turned up.

In long discussions with her analyst (whom she no longer needed), she had learned how central her father was in all this, in the formation or deformation of her character. Until she was ten years old she had known nothing but kindness from her daddy. Then, with the first hints of puberty, her troubles began. Exasperated with her, he said she was putting on a guinea-pig look. He called her a con artist. She was doing the farmer's-daughter-traveling-salesman bit. "That puzzled expression, as if you can't remember whether a dozen is eleven or thirteen. And what do you suppose happens with the thirteenth egg, hey? Pretty soon you'll let a stranger lead you into the broom-closet and take off your panties." Well! Thank you, Daddy, for all the suggestions you planted in a child's mind. Predictably she began to be sly and steal pleasure, and she did play the farmer's daughter, adapting and modifying until she became the mature Katrina. In the end (a blessed miracle) it worked out for the best, for the result was just what had attracted Victor—an avant-garde personality who happened to be crazy about just this erotic mixture. Petty bourgeois sexuality, and retrograde petty bourgeois at that, happened to turn Victor on. So here was this suburban broad, the cliché of her father's loaded forebodings: call her what you liked—voluptuary, luxurious beauty, confused sexpot, carnal idiot with piano legs, her looks (mouth half open or half shut) meaning everything or nothing. Just this grace-in-clumsiness was the aphrodisiac of one of the intellectual captains of the modern world. She dismissed the suggestion (Dotey's suggestion) that it was his decline that had brought her into his life, that she appeared when he was old, failing, in a state of desperation or erotic bondage. And it was true that any day now the earth would open underfoot and he'd be gone.

Meanwhile, if he wasn't so powerful as he once had been (as if some dust had settled on his surface), he was powerful still. His color was fresh and his hair vigorous. Now and then for an instant he might look pinched, but when he sat with a drink in his hand, talking away, his voice was so strong and his opinions so confident that it was inconceivable that he should ever disappear. The way she sometimes put it to herself was he was more than her lover. He was also retraining her. She had been admitted to his master class. Nobody else was getting such instruction.

"I've got all the numbers now."

"You'll have to catch the eight o'clock flight."

"I'll park at the Orrington, because while I'm gone for the day I don't want the car sitting in front of the house."

"Okay. And you'll find me in the VIP lounge. There should be time for a drink before we catch the one P.M. flight."

"Just as long as I'm back by midafternoon. And I can bring the notes you dictated."

"Well," said Victor, "I *could* have told you they were indispensable."

"I see."

"I ask you to meet me, and it sounds like an Oriental proposition, as if the Sultan were telling his concubine to come out beyond the city walls with the elephants and the musicians. . . ."

"How nice that you should mention elephants," said Katrina, alert at once.

"Whereas it's just Chicago-Buffalo-Chicago."

That he should refer by a single word to her elephant puzzle, her poor attempt to do something on an elephant theme, was an unusual concession. She had stopped mentioning it because it made Victor go cross-eyed with good-humored boredom. But now he had dropped a hint that ordering her to fly to Buffalo was just as tedious, just as bad art, as her floundering attempt to be creative with an elephant.

Katrina pushed this no further. She said, "I wish I could attend your talk tomorrow. I'd love to hear what you'll say to those executives."

"Completely unnecessary," Victor said. "You hear better things from me in bed than I'll ever say to those guys."

He did say remarkable things during their hours of high intimacy. God only knows how much intelligence he credited her with. But he was a talker, he *had* to talk, and during those wide-ranging bed conversations (monologues) when he let himself go, he didn't stop to explain himself; it was blind trust, it was *faute de mieux,* that made him confide in her. As he went on, he was more salty, scandalous, he was murderous. Reputations were destroyed when he got going, and people torn to bits. So-and-so was a plagiarist who didn't know what to steal, X who was a philosopher was a chorus boy at heart, Y had a mind like a lazy Susan, six spoiled appetizers and no main course. Abed, Victor and Katrina smoked, drank, touched each other (tenderness from complicity), laughed;

they *thought*—my God, they thought! Victor carried her into utterly foreign spheres of speculation. He lived for ideas. And he didn't count on Katrina's comprehension; he couldn't. Incomprehension darkened his life sadly. But it was a fixed condition, a given. And when he was wicked she understood him well enough. He wasn't wasting his wit on her, as when he said about Fonstine, a rival who tried to do him in, "He runs a Procrustean flophouse for bum ideas"; Katrina made notes later, and prayed that she was being accurate. So as usual Victor had it right— she did hear better things in bed than he could possibly say in public. When he took an entire afternoon off for such recreation, he gave himself over to it entirely—he was a day-long deep loller. When on the other hand he sat down to his papers, he was a day-long worker, and she didn't exist for him. Nobody did.

Arrangements for tomorrow having been made, he was ready to hang up. "You'll have to phone around to clear the decks," he said. "The TV shows nasty weather around Chicago."

"Yes, Krieggstein drove into a snowdrift."

"Didn't you say you were having him to dinner? Is he still there? Let him make himself useful."

"Like what?"

"Like walking the dog. There's a chore he can spare you."

"Oh, he'll volunteer to do that. Well, good night, then. And we'll have a wingding when you get here."

Hanging up, she wondered whether she hadn't said "wingding" too loudly (Krieggstein) and also whether Victor might not be put off by such dated words, sorority sex slang going back to the sixties. Hints from the past wouldn't faze him—what did he care about her college sex life? But he was unnervingly fastidious about language. As others were turned off by gross-ness, he was sensitive to bad style. She got into trouble in San Francisco when she insisted that he see *M*A*S*H*. "I've been to it, Vic. You mustn't miss this picture." Afterwards, he could hardly bear to talk to her, an unforgettable disgrace. Eventually she made it up with him, after long days of coolness. Her conclusion was, "I can't afford to be like the rest."

Now back to Krieggstein: how different a corner within the human edifice Krieggstein occupied. "So you have to go out of town," he said. At the fireside, somber and solid, he was giving his fullest attention to her problem. She often suspected that he might be an out-and-out kook. If he *was* a kook, how had he become her great friend? Well, there was a position to fill and nobody else to fill it with. And he was, remember, a true war hero. It was no easy matter to figure out who or what Sammy Krieggstein really was. Short, broad, bald, rugged, he apparently belonged to the police force. Sometimes he said he was on the vice squad, and sometimes homicide or narcotics; and now and then he wouldn't say at all, as if his work were top-secret, superclassified. "This much I'll tell you, dear—there are times on the street when I could use the good old flamethrower." He had boxed in the Golden Gloves tournament, way back before the Pacific war, and had scar tissue on his face to prove it. Still earlier he had been a street fighter. He made himself out to be very tough—a terrifying person who was also a gentleman and a tender friend. The first time she invited him for a drink he asked for a cup of tea, but he laid out all his guns on the tea table. Under his arm he carried a magnum, in his belt was stuck a flat small gun, and he had another pistol strapped to his leg. He had entertained the little girls with these weapons. Perfectly safe, he said. "Why should we give the whole weapon monopoly to the wild element on the streets?" He told Katrina when he took her to Le Perroquet about stabbings and disembowelments, car chases and shootouts. When a bruiser in a bar recently took him for a poor schnook, he showed him one of the guns and said, "All right, pal, how would you like a second asshole right between your eyes." Drawing a theoretical conclusion from this anecdote, Krieggstein said to Katrina, "You people"—his interpretations were directed mainly at Victor—"ought to have a better idea than you do of how savage it is out there. When Mr. Wulpy wrote about *The House of the Dead*, he referred to 'absolute criminals.' In America we are now far out on a worse track. A hundred years ago Russia was still a religious country. We haven't got the saints that are supposed to go with the sinners. . . ." The Lieutenant valued his acquaintance with the famous man. He himself, in his sixties, was working on a Ph.D. in criminology. On any topic of general interest Krieggstein was prepared to take a position immediately.

Victor called him the Santa Claus of threats. He was amused by him. He also said, "Krieggstein belongs to the Golden Age of American Platitudes."

"What do you mean by that, Victor?"

"I'm thinking first of all about the ladies he takes out, the divorcees he's so attentive to. He sends them candy and flowers, Gucci scarves, Jewish New Year's cards. He keeps track of their birthdays."

"I see. Yes, he does that."

"He's part Whitehat, part Heavy. He tries to be like one of those Balzac characters, like what's-his-name—Vautrin."

"Only, what is he *really?*" said Katrina. For Victor, what a Krieggstein was really wasn't worth thinking about. Yet when she returned to the dining room, the flapping of the double-hinged door at her back was also the sound of her dependency. She *needed* somebody, and here was Krieggstein who offered himself. At least he gave the appearance of offering. Not many went as far as *that*. Didn't even make the gesture. Here she was thinking of her sister Dorothea.

"Bad moment, eh?" said Krieggstein gravely. "You have to go. Is he sick again?"

"He didn't say that."

"He wouldn't." Krieggstein, contracted with seriousness, had a look of new paint over old—rust painted over in red.

"I have to go."

"You certainly must, if it's like that. But it's not so bad, is it? You're lucky to have that old Negro lady taking care of the little girls the way she took care of you and your sister."

"That sounds better than it really is. By now Ysole ought to be completely trustworthy. You would think . . ."

"Isn't she?"

"The old woman is very complex, and as she grows older she's even harder to interpret. She always was satirical and sharp."

"She's taking sides; you've told me so before. She disapproves of the divorce. She keeps an eye on you. You suspect she takes money from Alfred and gives him information. But she had no children of her own."

"She was fond of us when we were kids. . . ."

"But transferred her loyalty to your children? I haven't got what it takes to track her motives with."

Katrina thought: But whom am I having this conversation with? Krieggstein's bare head, bare face, by firelight had the shapes you saw in Edward Lear's books of nonsense verse—distorted eggs. He meant to wear an expression of Churchillian concern—the Hinge of Fate. He was saying it wouldn't be a good idea to lose your head. The big artists, big minds, didn't peter out like average guys. Think of Casals in his nineties, or Bertrand Russell, ex cetera. Even Francisco Franco on his deathbed. When they told the old fellow that some General García was there to say goodbye to him, he said, "Why, is García going on a trip?"

Katrina wanted to smile at this. There were too many densities to permit a smile—crowds of anxious difficulties threatening to riot.

The Lieutenant said, "You can be sure I'll help all I can. *Anything* you need done." Krieggstein, always tactfully and with respect, hinted that he would like to figure more personally in her life. The humblest of suitors, he was a suitor nonetheless. This, too, took skillful managing, and Trina didn't always know what to do with him.

She said, "I have to call off a date with the court psychiatrist."

"A second time?"

"Alfred has dragged Victor into it. He said our relationship was harming the kids. This headshrink was very rude to me. Parents are criminals to these people. He was so rude that Dorothea suspected he was fixed."

"Sometimes the shrinkers prove their impartiality by being rough on both parties," said the Lieutenant. "Still, it's a realistic suspicion. Did you mention to your lawyer what your sister suggested?"

"He wouldn't answer. Lawyers level only among themselves. If ever."

"This doctor may be ethical. That's still another cause of confusion. As a buddy used to say on Guadalcanal, the individual in the woodpile may be

Honesty in person—I could take this appointment for you. I have all the right credentials."

"Oh, please don't do that!" said Katrina.

"Objectively, I could make a wonderful case for you."

"If you'd only call his appointment secretary and set a time later in the week."

Dorothea was forever warning Trina against Krieggstein, whom she had met at one of the gun-display tea parties. "I wouldn't have him around. I think he's bananas. Is he really a cop, or some imaginary Kojak?"

"Why shouldn't he be real?" said Katrina.

"He could be a night watchman. No—if he worked nights he wouldn't be dating so many lonely middle-aged women. Still taking them to the senior prom. Have you had him checked out? Does he have a permit for those three guns?"

"The guns are nothing."

"Maybe he's a transit cop. I'm sure he's a nut case."

Krieggstein was asking Katrina, "Did you tell the psychiatrist that you were writing a book for children?"

"I didn't. It never occurred to me."

"You see? You don't do yourself justice—put your best foot forward."

"What would really help, Sam, would be to walk the dog. Poor old thing, she hasn't been out."

"Oh, of course," said Krieggstein. "I should have thought of that."

The snow creaked under his weight as he led big Sukie across the wooden porch. The new street lamps were graceful, beautiful, everybody agreed, golden and pure. In summer, however, their light confused the birds, who thought the sun had risen and wore themselves out twittering. In winter the lights seemed to have descended from outer space. Packed into his storm coat, Krieggstein followed the stout, slow dog. Victor called him a "fantast." Who else would use such a word? "A fantast lacking in invention," he said. But the Lieutenant was a safe escort. He took Trina to see Yul Brynner at McCormick Place. The three guns in fact made her feel safe. She was protected. He was her loyal friend.

She found herself affirming this to Dorothea later, after he was gone. She and her sister often had a midnight chat on the telephone.

After her husband died, Dorothea sold the big house in Highland Park and moved into fashionable Oldtown, bringing with her the Chinese bridal bed she and Winslow had bought at Gump's in San Francisco. The bedroom was small. A single window opened on the back alley. But she wouldn't part with her Chinese bed, and now she lay with her telephone inside the carved frame. To Katrina all that carving was like the crown of thorns. No wonder Dotey complained of insomnia and migraines. And *she* was setting *Katrina* straight? "You're locked into this futureless love affair, isolated, and the only man safe enough to see is this dumdum cop. Now you're hopping off to Buffalo."

"Krieggstein is a decent fellow."

"He's three-quarters off the screen."

Poodle-haired, thin, restless, with what Daddy used to call "neurasthenic stick" arms and legs, and large black eyes ready to soar out of her face, Dorothea was a spiky person, a sharp complainer.

"The children will go to school as usual with the older kid next door. Ysole comes at ten."

"You have to rush away and tumble through the clouds because the great man says you must. You claim you have no choice, but I think you like it. You remind me of that woman from Sunday school—'her foot abides not in her house.' A year's study in France was a wonderful privilege for you and me after graduation, but it was damaging, too, if you ask me. Dad was getting rid of some of the money he raked in through the tax assessor's office, and it was nicer to make Parisian demoiselles of us than to launder his dough in the usual ways. He was showing off. We were lost in Paris. Nobody to pay us any attention. Today I could really use those dollars."

O Dotey! bragging and deploring in the same breath. Dotey's husband had owned a small plastics factory. It was already going under when he died. So now she had to hustle plastic products. Her son was working for an MBA but not at a first-rate school. A woman in her situation needed a good address, and the rent she paid in Oldtown was outrageous. "For this kind of dough they could exterminate the rats. But I signed a two-year lease, and the landlord laughs at me." Forced into the business world, she sounded more and more like Father. But she hated the hustling. It was death to Dorothea to have to go anywhere, to have to do anything. To get out of bed in the morning was more than she could bear. Filtering her coffee, she cursed blindly, the soaring eyes filled with rage when the kettle whistled. To drag the comb through her hair she had to muster all her strength. As she herself said, "Like the lady in Racine: *Tout me nuit, et conspire à me nuire.*" (Taking a Chicago dig at her French education, a French dig at Chicago.) "Only Phèdre is you, baby, sick with love."

Dorothea drove herself, trembling, out of the house. Think how hard it was for her to call on chainstore buyers and institutional purchasing agents. She even managed to get on the tube to promote her product, wangling invitations from UHF ethnic and Moral Majority stations as a Woman Executive. Sometimes she seemed to be fainting under her burdens, purple lids closing. On the air, however, she was unfailingly vivacious and put on a charming act. And when she was aroused, she was very tough. "Let Wulpy go home if he's sick. Why doesn't his wife come fetch him?"

"Don't forget, I almost lost Victor last year," said Katrina.

"You almost . . . almost lost *him."*

"It's true you had surgery the same week, and I had to be away, but you weren't on the critical list, Dotey."

"I wasn't referring to me but to his wife, that poor woman, and what she suffered from you and other lady friends. . . . If she had to leave the room, this dingaling broad from Evanston would rush in and throw herself on the sick man."

No use telling Dotey not to be so rude and vulgar. Katrina listened to her with a certain passivity, even with satisfaction—it amounted, almost, to pleasure. You might call it perturbation-pleasure. Dotey continued: "It isn't right that the man should use his mighty prestige on a poor lady from the suburbs. It's shooting fish in a barrel. You'll tell me that you have the magical secret, how to turn him on. . . ."

"I don't think that it's what I *do*, Dotey. It happens simply to be *me*. He even loves my varicose veins, which I would try to hide from somebody else. Or my uneven gum line, and that was my lifelong embarrassment. And when my eyes are puffy, even that draws him."

"Christ, that's it then," said Dorothea, testy. "You hold the lucky number. With you he gets it up."

Katrina thought: Why should we talk so intimately if there isn't going to be any sympathy? It was sad. But on a more reasonable view you couldn't blame Dorothea for being irritable, angry, and envious. She had a failing business to run. She needed a husband. She had no prospects to speak of. She hates the fact that I'm now completely out of her league, Katrina told herself. Over these four years I've met people like John Cage, Bucky Fuller, de Kooning. I come home and tell her how I chatted with Jackie Onassis or Françoise de la Renta. All she has to tell me is how hard it is to push her plastic bags, and how nasty and evil-minded those purchasing agents are.

Dorothea had lost patience. When she thought that the affair with Victor was a flash in the pan, she had been more tolerant, willing to listen. Katrina had even persuaded her to read some of Victor's articles. They had started with an easy one, "From Apollinaire to E. E. Cummings," but then went on to more difficult texts, like "Paul Valéry and the Complete Mind," "Marxism in Modern French Thought." They didn't tackle Marx himself, but they had French enough between them to do Valéry's *Monsieur Teste,* and they met for lunch at Old Orchard Shopping Center to discuss this strange book. First they looked at clothes, for with so many acres of luxurious merchandise about them it would have been impossible to concentrate immediately on *Teste.* Katrina had always tried to widen her horizons. For many years she had taken flying lessons. She was licensed to pilot a single-engine plane. After a lapse of twenty years she had tried to resume piano lessons. She had studied the guitar, she kept up her French at the center on Ontario Street. Once, during the worst of times, she had taken up foreign sports cars, driving round and round the north suburbs with no destination. She had learned lots of Latin, for which she had no special use. At one time she considered going into law, and had passed the aptitude test with high marks. Trying to zero in on some kind of perfection. And then in a booth at Old Orchard, Katrina and Dorothea had smoked cigarettes and examined Valéry: What was the meaning of the complete mind, "man as full consciousness"? Why did it make Madame Teste happy to be studied by her husband, as happy to be studied as to be loved? Why did she speak of him as "the angel of pure consciousness"? To grasp Valéry was hard enough. Wulpy *on* Valéry was utterly inaccessible to Dorothea, and she demanded that Trina explain. "Here he compares Monsieur Teste to Karl Marx—what does he mean by that?"

"Well," said Katrina, trying hard, "let's go back to this statement. It says, 'Minds that come from the void into this strange carnival and bring lucidity from outside . . .'"

Then Dotey cried, "*Which* void!" She wore the poodle hairdo as a cover for or an admission of the limitations of her bony head. But even this may have been a ruse, as she was really very clever in her way. Only her bosom was filled with a boiling mixture of sisterly feelings, vexation, resentment. She would bear with Katrina for a while and then she would say, "What is it with you and the intelligentsia? Because we went to the Pont Royal bar and none of those philosophers tried to pick us up? Or are you competing intellectually with the man's wife?"

No, Beila Wulpy had no such pretensions. The role of the great man's wife was what she played. She did it with dignity. Dark and stout, beautiful in her way, she reminded you of Catherine of Aragon—abused majesty. Although she was not herself an intellectual, she knew very well what it was to be one—the real thing. She was a clever woman.

Katrina tried to answer. "The strange carnival is the history of civilization as it strikes a detached mind. . . ."

"We don't play in this league," said Dotey at last. "It's not for types like us, Trina. And your brain is not the organ he's interested in."

"And I believe I'm equal to this, too, in a way of my own," said Katrina, obstinate. Trying to keep the discussion under control. "Types like us" wounded her, and she felt that her eyes were turning turbid. She met the threat of tears, or of sobs, by sinking into what she had always called her "flesh state": her cheeks grew thick, and she felt physically incompetent, gross. Dotey spoke with a harshness acquired from her City Hall father: "I'm just a broad who has to hustle plastic bags to creeps who proposition me." Katrina understood well enough that when Dotey said, "I'm a broad," she was telling her, "That's what you are, too." Then Dotey said, "Don't give me the 'strange carnival' bit." She added, "What about your elephant?"

This was a cheap shot. Katrina had been trying for some time to write a children's story about an elephant. She hoped to make some money by it, and to establish her independence. It had been a mistake to mention this to Dotey. She had done it because it was a story often told in the family. "That old elephant thing that Dad used to tell us? I'm going to put it to use." But for one reason and another she hadn't yet worked out the details. It was mean of Dotey to get at her through the elephant. The Valéry discussions at Old Orchard had ended with this dig.

But of course she had to tell Dotey that she was flying to Buffalo, and Dotey, sitting upright with the telephone in her carven Chinese bed, said, "So if any hitch develops, what you'd like is that I should cover for you with Alfred."

"I don't expect it to come to that. Just to be on the safe side, give me a number where I can reach you during the afternoon."

"I have to be all over the city. Competitors are trying to steal my chemist from me. Without him I'll have to fold. I'm near the breaking point, and I can do without extra burdens. And listen now, Trina, do you really care so much? Suppose the court does give Alfred the kids."

"I won't accept that."

"You might not mind too much. Mother's interest in you and me was minimal. She cared more about the pleats in her skirt. To this day, down on Bay Harbor Island, she's like that. You'll say you aren't Mother, but things do rub off."

"What has this got to do with Mother?"

"I'm only reckoning the way people actually do. You aren't getting anywhere with those kids. The house is a burden. Alfred took away all the pretty things. It eats up too much money in maintenance. Suppose Alfred did get custody? You'd move East with all the painters and curators. It would be nothing but arts and letters. Victor's set . . ."

"There isn't any set."

"There are crowds of people after him. You could insist on being together more openly, because Victor would *owe* you if you lost the kids. While he lasted . . ."

"In the midst of such conversations, Dotey, I think how often I've heard women say, 'I wish I had a sister.'"

Dorothea laughed. "Women who have sisters don't say it! Well, my way of being a good sister is to come in and turn on all the lights. You put off having children until you were almost too old. Alfred was upset about it. He's a quick-acting decisive type. Jewelers have to be. In his milieu he's somebody. Glance at a diamond, quote you a price. You didn't want kids by him? You tried to keep your options open? You were waiting for the main chance? Naturally Alfred will do you in if he can."

That's right, Katrina commented silently, scare me good. I'll never regret what I've done. She said, "I'd better go and set the alarm clock."

"I'll give you a couple of numbers where you might find me late in the afternoon," said Dorothea.

At five-thirty the alarm went off. Katrina never had liked this black winter hour. Her heart was low as she slid back the closet door and began to dress. To go with the green suit she chose a black cashmere sweater and matching hose. She rolled backwards clumsily on the chaise longue, legs in the air, to pull the hose on. Her boots were of ostrich skin and came from the urban cowboy specialty shop on South State Street which catered to Negro dudes and dudesses. The pockmarked leather, roughly smooth and beautiful, was meant for slimmer legs than her own. What did that matter? They—she herself—gave Victor the greatest possible satisfaction.

She had set aside fifteen minutes for the dog. In the winter Ysole wouldn't walk her. At her age a fall on the ice was all she needed. ("Will *you* take care of me if I break my hip?" asked the old woman.) But Katrina liked taking Sukie out. It was partly as Dorothea had said: "Her feet abide not in her house." But the house, from which Alfred had removed the best carpets and chairs, the porcelain elephants from India and the curly gilt Chinese lions, did give Katrina vacancy heartaches. However, she had never really liked housekeeping. She needed action, and there was some action even in dog walking. You could talk to other dog owners. Astonishing, the things they sometimes said—the kinky proposals that were made. Since she need not take them seriously, she was in a position simply to enjoy them. As for Sukie, she had had it. The vet kept hinting that a sick, blind dog should be put down. Maybe Krieggstein would do her a favor—take the animal to the Forest Preserve and shoot her. Would the little girls grieve? They might or might not. You couldn't get much out of those silent kids. They studied their mother without comment. Krieggstein said they were great little girls, but Katrina doubted that they were the sort of children a friend of the family could dote on. One who belonged to the Golden Age of Platitudes, maybe. One of Krieggstein's odder suggestions was that the girls be enrolled in a martial arts course; Katrina should encourage them to be more aggressive. Also he tried to persuade Katrina to let him take them to the police pistol-practice range. She said they'd be scared out of their wits by the noise. He insisted on the contrary that it would do them a world of good. Dorothea referred to her nieces as "those mystery kids."

You couldn't hurry the dog. Black-haired, swaybacked, gentle, she sniffed every dog stain in the snow. She circled, then changed her mind. Where to do it? Done in the wrong place, it would unsettle the balance of things. All have their parts to play in the great symphony of the instincts (Victor). And even on a shattering cold day, gritting ice underfoot, the dog took her time. A hoarse sun rolled up. For a few minutes the circling snow particles sparkled, and then a wall of cloud came down. It would be a gray day.

Katrina woke the girls and told them to dress and

come downstairs for their granola. Mother had to go to a meeting. Kitty from next door would come at eight to walk them to school. The girls seemed hardly to hear her. In what ways are they like me? Katrina sometimes wondered. Their mouths had the same half-open (or half-closed) charm. Victor didn't like to speak of kids. He especially avoided discussing her children. But he did make theoretical observations about the younger generation. He said they had been given a warrant to ravage their seniors with guilt. Kids were considered pitiable because their parents were powerless nobodies. As soon as they were able, they distanced themselves from their elders, whom they considered to be failed children. You would have thought that such opinions would depress Victor. No, he was spirited and cheerful. Not sporadically, either; he had a level temper.

When Katrina, ready to go, came into the kitchen in her fleece-lined coat, the girls were still sitting over their granola. The milk had turned brown while they dawdled. "I'm leaving a list on the bulletin board, tell Ysole. I'll see you after school." No reply. Katrina left the house half unwilling to admit how good it was to go away, how glad she would be to reach O'Hare, how wonderful it would be to make a flight even though Victor, waiting in Buffalo, might be sick.

The jet engines sucked and snarled up the frozen air; the huge plane lifted; the gray ground skidded away and you rose past hangars, over factories, ponds, bungalows, football fields, the stitched incisions of railroad tracks curving through the snow. And then the skyscraper community to the south. On an invisible sidewalk beneath, your little daughters walking to school might hear the engines, unaware that their Mummy overflew them. Now the gray water of the great lake appeared below with all its stresses, wind patterns, whitecaps. Goodbye. Being above the clouds always made Katrina tranquil. Then *bing!* the lucid sunlight coming through infinite space (refrigerated blackness, they said) filled the cabin with warmth and color. In a book by Kandinsky she had once picked up in Victor's room, she had learned that the painter, in a remote part of Russia where the interiors of houses were decorated in an icon style, had concluded that a painting, too, ought to be an interior, and that the artist should induce the viewer to enter in. Who wouldn't rather? she thought. Drinking coffee above the state of Michigan, Katrina had her single hour of calm and luxury. The plane was almost empty.

There were even some thoughts about her elephant project. Would she or wouldn't she finish it?

In Katrina's story the elephant, a female, had been leased as a smart promotional idea to push the sale of Indian toys on the fifth floor of a department store. The animal's trainer had had trouble getting her into the freight elevator. After testing the floor with one foot and finding it shaky, she had balked, but Nirad, the Indian mahout, had persuaded her at last to get in. Once in the toy department she had had a heavenly time. Sales were out of sight. Margey was the creature's name, but the papers, which were full of her, called her Largey. The management was enthusiastic. But when the month ended and Margey-Largey was led again to the freight elevator and made the hoof test, nothing could induce her to enter. Now there was an elephant in the top story of a department store on Wabash Avenue, and no one could think of a way to get her out. There were management conferences and powwows. Experts were called in. Legions of inventive cranks flooded the lines with suggestions. Open the roof and lift out the animal with a crane? Remove a wall and have her lowered by piano movers? Drug her and stow her unconscious in the freight elevator? But how could you pick her up when she was etherized? The Humane Society objected. The circus from which Margey-Largey had been rented had to leave town and held the department store to its contract. Nirad the mahout was frantic. The great creature was in misery, suffered from insomnia. Were there no solutions? Katrina wasn't quite inventive enough to bring it off. Inspiration simply wouldn't come. Krieggstein wondered whether the armed forces might not have a jumbo-sized helicopter. Or if the store had a central gallery or well like Marshall Field's. Katrina after two or three attempts had stopped trying to discuss this with Victor. You didn't pester him with your nonsense. There was a measure of the difference between Victor and Krieggstein.

If he had been sick in earnest, Victor would have canceled the lecture, so he must have sent for her because he longed to see her (the most desirable maximum), or simply because he needed company. These reasonable conclusions made her comfortable, and for about an hour she rode through the bright sky as if she *were* inside a painting. Then, just east of Cleveland, the light began to die away, which meant that the plane was descending. Darkness returned. Beneath her was Lake Erie—an open toilet, she had heard an environmentalist call it. And now the jet was gliding into gray Buffalo, and she was growing agitated. Why was she sent for? Because he was sick and old, in spite of the immortality that he seemed wrapped in, and it was Katrina's fault that he was on the road. He did it for her sake. He didn't travel with assistants (like Henry Moore or other dignitaries of the same rank) because a sexual romance imposed secrecy; because Alfred was gunning for her—Alfred who had always outclassed and outsmarted her and who was incensed by this turnaround. And if Alfred were to win his case, Victor would have Katrina on his hands. But would he accept her? But it would never come to that.

After landing in Buffalo, she stopped in the ladies' room and when she looked herself over she was far from satisfied with the thickness of her face and her agitated eyes. She put on lipstick (Alfred's rage was burning and smoking on the horizon and she was applying lipstick). She did what she could with her comb and went out to get directions to the first-class lounge.

Victor never flew first-class—why waste money? He only used the facilities. The executives in first were not his type. He had always lived like an artist, and therefore belonged in the rear cabin. Owing to his bum knee, he did claim early seating, together with nursing infants and paraplegics. No display of infirmity, but he needed an aisle seat for his rigid leg. What was true was that he assumed a kind of presidential immunity from all inconveniences. For some reason this was especially galling to Dorothea, and she took a Who-the-hell-is-he! tone when she said, "He takes everything for granted. When he came to Northwestern—that fatal visit!—he borrowed a jalopy and wouldn't even put out fifty bucks for a battery, but every day phoned some sucker to come with cables and give him a jump. And here's a man who must be worth upwards of a million in modern paintings alone."

"I don't know," said Katrina. (At her stubbornest she lowered her eyes, and when she looked as if she were submitting, she resisted most.) "Victor *really* believes in equality. But I don't think that special consideration, in his case, is out of line."

When Victor appeared at a party, true enough, people cleared a path for him, and a hassock was brought and a drink put in his hands. As he took it, there was no break in his conversation. Even his super-rich friends were glad to put themselves out for him. Cars were sent. Apartments (in places like the Waldorf) were available, of which he seldom availed himself. An old-style Villager, he kept a room to write in on Sullivan Street, among Italian neighbors, and while he was working he would pick up a lump of provolone and scraps from the breadbox, drink whiskey or coffee from his Pyrex measuring cup, lie on his bed (the sheets were maybe changed annually) to refine his thoughts, passing them through his mind as if the mind were a succession of high-energy chambers. It was the thinking that mattered. He had those thinking dark eyes shining inside the densely fringed lids, big diabolical brows, authoritative not unkindly. The eyes were set, or *let* into his cheeks, at an odd angle. The motif of the odd angle appeared in many forms. And on Sullivan Street he required no special consideration. He bought his own salami and cheese, cigarettes, in the Italian grocery, carried them to his third-floor walk-up (rear), working until drink time, perfectly independent. Uptown, he might accept a lift in a limousine. In the soundproof glass cabinet of a Rolls, Katrina had once heard him talking during a half-hour ride downtown with a billionaire Berliner. (Escaped from the Nazis in the thirties with patents for synthetic rubber, he had bought dozens of Matisses, cheap.) Victor was being serious with him, and Katrina had tried to keep track of the subjects covered between Seventy-sixth Street and Washington

Square: the politics of modern Germany from the Holy Roman Empire through the Molotov-Ribbentrop Pact; what surrealist communism had *really* been about; Kiesler's architecture; Hans Hofmann's influence; what limits were set by liberal democracy for the development of the arts. Three or four other wonderful topics she couldn't remember. Various views on the crises in economics, cold war, metaphysics, sexaphysics. The clever, lucky old Berlin Jew, whose head was like a round sourdough loaf, all uneven and dusted with flour, had asked the right questions. It wasn't as if Victor had been singing for his ride. He didn't do that sort of thing.

Dorothea tried, and tried too hard, to find the worst possible word for Victor. She would say, "He's a Tartuffe."

"You called me Madame Bovary," said Katrina. "What kind of a pair does that make us?"

Dotey, you got your B.A. fair and square. Now stick to plastic bags.

Such comments, tactfully censored, seemed to swell out Katrina's lips. You often saw a sort of silent play about her mouth. Interpreted, it told you that Victor was a real big shot, and that she was proud of—well, of their special intimacy. He confided in her. She knew his true opinions. They were conspirators. She was with him in his lighthearted, quick-moving detachment from everything that people (almost all of them) were attached to. In a public-opinion country, he made his own opinions. Katrina was enrolled as his only pupil. She paid her tuition with joy.

This at least was one possible summary of their relations, the one she liked best.

Passing down the glass-walled corridors of the airport, Katrina didn't like the look of the sky—a kind of colic in the clouds, and snow gusts spitting and twisting on the fields of concrete. Traffic, however, was normal. Planes were rolling in, trundling towards the runways. The look of the sky was wicked, but you didn't want to translate your anxieties into weather conditions. Anyway, the weather was shut out when you entered the VIP lounge. First-class lounges were always inner rooms, low-lighted, zones of quiet and repose. Drinks were free, and Victor, holding a glass, rested his legs on a coffee table. His stick was wedged beside him in sofa cushions. The action of the whiskey wasn't sufficient, for his yellow-green corduroy car coat was zippered and buttoned for warmth. As she kissed him the Cabochard fragrance puffed from her dress, scarf, throat—she could smell it herself. Then they looked each other in the face to see what was up. She wouldn't have said that he was sick—he didn't look it, and he didn't have about him the sick flavor that had become familiar to her during his illness. *That* at least! So there was no cause for panic. He was, however, out of sorts, definitely—something was working at him, like vexation, disgust. She knew the power of his silent glooms. Several objects had been deposited at the side of the sofa. His duffel bag she knew; heavy canvas, stained, it might have contained a plumber's tools, but there was something else with it, just around the corner.

Well, I was sent for, and I came. Was I needed, or was it extreme tetchiness?

"Right on the dot," she said, turning her watch on the wrist.

"Good."

"All I have to do is make it back."

"I see no reason why you shouldn't. It didn't give you a lot of trouble to arrange, did it?"

"Only ducking a date with the court psychiatrist, and chancing the usual heat from Alfred."

"Such behavior in this day and age," said Victor. "Why does your husband have to interpose himself as if *he* were a principal, and behave like a grand-opera lunatic?"

"Well, you know, Victor. Alfred always had lots of assurance, but rivalry with you was more than his self-esteem could bear."

Victor was not the type to be interested in personality troubles. Insofar as they were nothing but personal, he cared for nobody's troubles. That included his own.

"What have you got there, with your duffel bag?"

"I'll tell you as soon as we've ordered you some whiskey." Early drinking was unusual; it meant he needed an extra boost. When his arm was raised, the signal couldn't be overlooked, and the hostess came right over. In the old Mediterranean or in Asia you might have found examples of Victor's physical type. He towered. He also tilted, on account of the leg. Katrina had never determined exactly what was the matter with it, medically. For drainage it was punctured in two places, right through the flesh. Sometimes there was a deposit around the holes, and it was granular, like brown sugar. That took getting used to, just a little. He made jokes about his size. He said he was too big for the subtler human operations. He would point out the mammoths, they hadn't made it, and he would note how many geniuses were little guys. But that was just talk. At heart he was pleased with the way he was. Nothing like a mammoth. He was still one of the most dramatic-looking men in the world, and besides, as she had reason to know, his nervous reactions were very fine. A face like Victor's might have been put on the cover of a book about the ancient world: the powerful horizontal planes— forehead, cheekbones, the intelligent long eyes, the brows kinky with age now, and with tufts that could be wicked. His mouth was large, and the cropped mustache was broad. By the way the entire face expanded when he spoke emphatically you recognized that he was a kind of tyrant in thought. His cheekbones were red, like those of an actor in makeup; the sharp color hadn't left him even when he was on the critical list. It seemed a mistake that he should be dying. Besides, he was so big that you wondered what he was doing in a bed meant for ordinary patients, but when he opened his eyes, those narrow visual canals, the message was, "I'm dying!" Still, only a couple of months later he was back in circulation, eating and drinking, writing critical pieces—in full charge. A formidable person, Victor Wulpy. Even the way he gimped was formidable, not as if he was dragging his leg but as if he were kicking things out of the way. All of Victor's respect was reserved for people who lived out their *idea*. For whether or not you were aware of it, you had one, high or low, keen or stupid. He came on like the king of something—of the Jews perhaps. By and by, you became aware of a top-and-bottom contrast in Victor; he was not above as he was below. In the simplest terms, his shoes were used up and he wore his pants negligently, but when his second drink had warmed him and he took off the corduroy coat, he uncovered one of his typical shirts. It resembled one of Paul Klee's canvases, those that were filled with tiny rectilinear forms—green, ruby, yellow, violet, washed out but still beautiful. His large trunk was one warm artwork. After all, he was a chieftain and pundit in the art world, a powerful man; even his oddities (naturally) had power. Kingly, artistic, democratic, he had been around forever. He was withering, though. But women were after him, even now.

His voice strengthened by the drink, he began to

talk. He said, "Vanessa says her teachers put heat on her to bring me for a lecture, but it was mostly her own idea. Then she didn't attend. She had to play chamber music."

"Did you meet her Cuban boyfriend?"

"I'm coming to that. He's a lot better than the others."

"So there's no more religion?"

"After all the noise about becoming a rabbi, and the trouble of getting her into Hebrew Union College, she dropped out. Her idea seems to have been to boss Jews—adult Jews—in their temples and holler at them from the pulpit. Plenty of them are so broken-down that they would not only acquiesce but brag about it. Nowadays you abuse people and then they turn around and take ads in the paper to say how progressive it is to be kicked in the face."

"Now she's fallen in love with this Cuban student. Are they still Catholics, under Castro? She books you for a lecture and plays a concert the same night."

"Not only that," said Victor. "She has me carry her violin to Chicago for repairs. It's a valuable instrument, and I have to bring it to Bein and Fushi in the Fine Arts Building. Can't let it be botched in Buffalo. A Guarnerius."

"So you met for breakfast?"

"Yes. And then I was taken to meet the boy's family. He turns out to be a young Archimedes type, a prodigy. They're refugees, probably on welfare. Fair enough, that among all the criminals the Cubans stuck us with there should be a genius or two. . . ."

"By the way, are you sure he's such a genius?"

"You can't go by me. He got a fat four-year scholarship in physiology. His brothers are busboys, if that. And that's where Nessa is meddling. The mother is in a state."

"Then she gave you her violin—an errand to do?"

"I accepted to avoid something worse. I paid a fair price for the instrument and by now it's quintupled in value. I want an appraisal from Bein and Fushi, just in case it enters Nessa's head to sell the fiddle and buy this Raul from his mother. Elope. Who knows what. . . . We can go to Bein together."

More errands for Katrina. Victor had sent Vanessa away to avoid a meeting with his lady friend, his Madame Bovary.

"We can lay the fiddle under a seat. I suppose that left-wing students came to your talk."

"Why so? I had a bigger crowd than that. The application of *The Eighteenth Brumaire* to American politics and society . . . the farce of the Second Empire. Very timely."

"It doesn't sound too American to me."

"What, more exotic than Japanese electronics, German automobiles, French cuisine? Or Laotian exiles settled in Kansas?"

Yes, she could see that, and see also how the subject would appear natural to Victor Wulpy from New York, of East Side origin, a street boy, sympathetic to mixed, immigrant and alien America; broadly tolerant of the Cuban boyfriend; exotic himself, with a face like his, and the Greek cap probably manufactured in Taiwan.

Victor had gone on talking. He was telling her now about a note he had received at the hotel from a fellow he had known years ago—a surprise that did not please him. "He takes the tone of an old chum. Wonderful to meet again after thirty years. He happens to be in town. And good old Greenwich Village —I hate the revival of these relationships that never were. Meantime, it's true, he's become quite a celebrity."

"Would I know the name?"

"Larry Wrangel. He had a recent success with a film called *The Kronos Factor*. Same type as *2001* or *Star Wars*."

"Of course," said Katrina. "That's the Wrangel who was featured in *People* magazine. A late-in-life success, they called him. Ten years ago he was still making porno movies. Interesting." She spoke cautiously, having disgraced herself in San Francisco. Even now she couldn't be sure that Victor had forgiven her for dragging him to see *M*A*S*H*. Somewhere in his mental accounts there was a black mark still. Bad taste approaching criminality, he had once said. "He must be very rich. The piece in *People* said that his picture grossed four hundred million. Did he attend your lecture?"

"He wrote that he had an engagement, so he might be a bit late, and could we have a drink afterwards. He gave a number, but I didn't call."

"You were what—tired? disgruntled?"

"In the old days he was bearable for about ten minutes at a time—just a character who longed to be taken seriously. The type that bores you most when he's most earnest. He came from the Midwest to study philosophy at NYU and he took up with the painters at the Cedar bar and the writers on Hudson Street. I remember him, all right—a little guy, quirky, shrewd, offbeat. I think he supported himself by writing continuity for the comic books—Buck Rogers, Batman, Flash Gordon. He carried a scribbler in his zipper jacket and jotted down plot ideas. I lost track of him and I don't care to find the track again—Trina, I was disturbed by some discoveries I made about my invitation from the Executives Association."

"What is this about the Executives?"

"I found out that a guy named Bruce Beidell is the main adviser to the speakers committee, and it turns out that he was the one who set up the invitation, and saw to it that I'd be told. He knows I don't like him. He's a rat, an English Department academic who became a culture politician in Washington. In the early Nixon years he built big expectations on Spiro Agnew; he used to tell me that Agnew was always studying serious worthy books, asking him for bigger and better classics. Reading! To read Beidell's mind you'd need a proctoscope. Suddenly I find that he'll be on the panel tonight, one of the speakers. And that's not all. It's even more curious. The man who will introduce me is Ludwig Felsher. The name won't mean much to you, but he's an old old-timer. Before 1917 there was a group of Russian immigrants in the U.S., and Lenin used some of these people after the revolution to do business for him—Armand Hammer types who made ingenious combinations of big money with Communist world politics and became colossally rich. Felsher brought over masterpieces from the Hermitage to raise currency for the Bolsheviks. Duveen and Berenson put in a cheap bid for those treasures." Victor had been personally offended by Berenson and detested him posthumously.

"So you're in bad company. You never do like to share the platform."

He used both hands to move his leg to a more comfortable position. After this labor he was very sharp. "I've been among pimps before. I can bear it. But it's annoying to appear with these pricks. For a few thousand bucks: contemptible. I know this Felsher. From GPU to KGB, and his standing with American capitalists is impeccable. He's old, puffy, bald, red in the face, looks like an unlanced boil. No matter who you are, if you've got enough dough you'll get bear hugs from the Chief Executive. You've made campaign contributions, you carry unofficial messages to Moscow, and you're hugged in the Oval Office."

Fretful. Fallen among thieves. That was why he had sent for her, not because he suddenly suspected a metastasis.

"I'll hate seeing Beidell. Nothing but a fish bladder in his head, and the rest of him all malice and intrigue. Why are these corporation types so dumb?"

Katrina encouraged him to say more. She crossed her booted legs and offered him a listening face. Her chin was supported on bent fingers.

"Under these auspices. I don't mind telling you my teeth are on edge," he said.

"But, Victor, you could turn the tables on them all. You could let them have it."

Naturally he could. If he had a mind to. It would take a lot out of him, though. But he was not one of your (nowadays) neurotic, gutless, conniving intellectual types. From those he curtly dissociated himself. Katrina saw him in two aspects, mainly. In one aspect Victor reminded her comically of the huge bad guy in a silent Chaplin movie, the bully who bent gas lamps in the street to light his cigar and had huge greasepaint eyebrows. In the other he was a person of intensest delicacy and of more shadings than she would ever be able to distinguish. More and more often since he became sick, he had been saying that he needed to save his strength for what mattered. And did those executives matter? They didn't matter a damn. The Chase Manhattan, World Bank, National Security Council connections meant zilch to him, he said. He hadn't sought *them* out. And it wasn't as if they didn't know his views. He had more than once written, on the subject announced for tonight, that true personality did not exist at the top of either hierarchy, East *or*

West. Between them the superpowers had the capacity to kill everybody, but there was no evidence of human capacities in the top leadership. On both sides power was in the hands of comedians and pseudo persons. The neglect, abasement, dismissal of art was a primary cause of this degeneration. If Victor were fired up, the executives would hear bold and unusual things from him about the valuing of life, bound up with the valuing of art. But he was ailing, he was tarnished, ruffled. This was Victor *himself. He* was thinking he shouldn't even *be* here. Why was he in the Buffalo airport in midwinter? In this lounge? Bound for Chicago? He was not at the exact center of his own experiences on a day like this. He felt peripheral, at times dim. There were sensations which should absolutely be turned off. And he couldn't do that, either. He felt himself being held hostage by oblique, unidentifiable forces.

He said, "One agreeable recollection I do have of this man Wrangel. He played the fiddle in reverse. Being left-handed, he had the instrument restrung, the sound posts moved. Back then, it was important to have your little specialty. He went a long way, considering the small scale of his ingenuity. Became a big-time illusionist."

The attendant had brought Katrina a small bottle of Dewar's. Pouring it, she held the glass to the light to look at the powerful spirit of the spirit, like a spiral, finer than smoke. Then she said, "It may do some good to look at the notes I typed for you."

"Yes, let's."

She used reading glasses; Victor had no need of them. In some respects he hadn't aged at all. For a big man he was graceful, and for an old one he was youthful. Krieggstein might be right, and the excitement of thought did prevent decay—her policeman

119

friend must have overheard this somewhere, or picked it up in the "Feminique" section of the *Tribune*. On his own he couldn't make such observations.

The fixtures in the lounge were like those in the cabin of a plane, and Victor had to hold up the paper to catch the slanted ceiling-light beam. "A quick once-over," he said. "I don't expect much. 'Why people have taken to saying that truth is stranger'—or did I say 'stronger'?—'than fiction. Because liberal democracy makes for enfeebled forms of self-consciousness—who was the fellow who said that speaking for himself he would never exchange the public world, for all its harshness and imperfections, for the stuffiness of a private world? Weak self-conceptions, poor fictions. Lack of an *Idea*. Collective preemption of *Ideas* by professional groups (lawyers, doctors, engineers). They make a simulacrum of "standards," and this simulacrum becomes the morality of their profession. All sense of individual cheating disappears. First step towards "stability," for them, is to cancel individual moral judgments. Leadership can then be assumed by fictional personages.'"

"Would you say our leaders are fictional personages?" said Katrina.

"Wouldn't you?"

Victor didn't look well now. The red in his cheeks was an irritable red, and there were other dangerous signs of distemper. He stared at her in that way he had of seeming, once more, to review her credentials. It was humiliating. But she joined him in his doubts and was sorry for him. It was best for him now to talk. Even when he had to forgo the certainty of being understood. He lowered his head like a bull deciding whether or not to gore, and then he went on talking. She liked it best when his talk was mischievous and mean—when he said that a man had no brain but a fish bladder in his skull. Seriousness was more worri-some, and at present he was being serious. He told Katrina now that he didn't think these were useful notes. He had said the same things in his Marx lecture and said them better. Marx connected individual wakefulness with class struggle. When social classes found themselves prevented from acting politically, and class struggle fell into abeyance, temporarily, consciousness also became confused—waking, sleep-ing, dreaming, all mixed up.

Did he still consider himself a Marxist? Katrina wanted to know. She was scared by her own temerity, but even more afraid of being dumb. "I ask because you speak of class struggle. But also because you consider the Communist countries such a failure."

He said that, well, he had trained his mind on hard Marxist texts in his formative years and was perma-nently influenced—and why not? After reading *The Eighteenth Brumaire* again, he was convinced that Marx had America's present number. Here Victor, his leg extended like one of Admiral Nelson's cannon under wraps, gave a characteristically dazzling glance from beneath the primeval tangle of his brows and said that the Buffalo talk and the Chicago one would be connected. When wage earners, the middle class, the professions, lose track of their true material interests, they step outside history, so to speak, and then nonclass interests take over, and when that happens society itself collapses into neuroses. An era of playacting begins. Vast revolutionary changes are concealed by the trivialities of the actors. Clowns and ham actors govern, or seem to. Superficially, it looks like farce. The deeper reality is anything but.

He was such an exceptional being altogether that because of the vast difference (to lesser people, Katrina meant), he himself might strike you as an actor. The interval of serious conversation had made him look more like himself—it had revived him. Katrina now admitted, "I was worried about you, Vic."

"Why? Because I asked you to come? I'm sore at those guys in Chicago and I wanted to tell you about it. I felt frustrated and depleted."

He can tell me things he's too dignified to say otherwise. He can be the child, Katrina concluded. Which not even my own kids will be with me. As a mother I seem to be an artificial product. Would that be because I can't put any sex into being a mother? She said to Victor, "My guess was that the bleak weather and the travel were getting you down."

Oh, as for bleakness. Examining her, he established that "bleak" was a different thing for him. Nor did he mean low spirits when he said "depleted." He wasn't low, he was higher than he liked, very high, in danger of being disconnected. He was superlucid, which he always wanted to be, but this lucidity had its price: clear ideas becoming ever more clear the more the ground opened under your feet—illumination increasing together with your physiological progress towards death. I never expected to live forever, but neither did I expect *this*. And there was no saying what *this* was, precisely. It was both definite and cloudy. And here Katrina gave him support, materially. Katrina, a lady with a full body, sat on her swelling bottom line. She wore a knitted dark-green costume. She had strong legs in black boots. Where the ostrich quills once grew, the surface of the leather was bubbled. Very plain to him in her figure were the great physical forces of the human trunk and the weight of the backswell, the separation of the thighs. The composure of her posture had a whore effect on him—did she know this or not? Was she aware that her neatness made him horny? He kept it from her, so that she had no idea of the attraction of her hands, especially the knuckle folds and the tips of what he called, to himself only, her touch-cock fingers. Katrina was his manifest Eros, this worried, comical lady for whom he had such complex emotions, for the sake of which he put up with so many idiocies, struggled with so many irritations. She could irritate him to the point of heartbreak, so that he asked was it worth it, and why didn't he spin off this stupid cunt; and couldn't he spend his old age better, or had his stars run out of influence altogether? He used to be able to take his business where he liked. That pagan availability was closing out. At first she had been his lump of love. He counted the stages. At first, just fun. The next stage was laughable, as he recognized through her that his erotic epoch might after all be the Victorian, with its special doodads. Then there seemed to be a kind of Baudelairean phase,

> . . . *tu connais la caresse*
> *Qui fait revivre les morts* . . .

Only he didn't in fact buy that. His wasn't an example of clinically disturbed sexuality. He felt detached from all such fancy stuff. She *did* in fact have the touch that brought back the dead—his dead. But there was no witchery or sadic darkness about it. Evidently, whether he liked it or not, his was a common sexual type. He was beyond feeling the disgrace of its commonness. She kept him going, and he had to confess that he wouldn't know what to do at all if he didn't keep going. Therefore he went flying around. He was not ready to succumb. He paid no more attention to death than to a litter of puppies pulling at the cuffs of his pants.

About bleak winter, he was saying to Katrina, "I have trouble staying warm. I've heard that capsicum helps. For the capillaries. Last night was bad. I put my feet in hot water. I had to wear double socks and still was cold."

"I can take care of that."

Wonderful, what powers women will claim.

"And Vanessa, this morning—what was she like?"

"Well," he said, "what these kids really want is to make you obey the same powers that *they* have to serve. The older generation, it happens, cooperates with them. The Cuban mother was puzzled. I could read it in her eyes—'What in hell are you people *up* to?'"

"Oh, you met her."

"You bet I did. This morning I was sitting in her kitchen, and the boy was our interpreter. The kid's IQ must be out of sight. The woman says she has nothing against Vanessa. Nessa has made herself part of the family. She's moved in on them. She peels potatoes and washes pots. She and the boy don't go to restaurants and movies because he has no money and won't let her pay. So they study day and night, and they're both on the dean's list. But my daughter is just meddling. She abducted the genius of the family who was supposed to be the salvation of his siblings and his mama."

"But she says she loves him, and looks at you with those long eyes she inherited from you."

"She's a little bitch. I found out that she was giving her mother sex advice. How a modern wife can please a husband better. And you have to find new ways to humor an old man. She told Beila all about some homosexual encyclopedia. She said not to buy it, but gave her the address of a shop where she could read some passages on foreplay."

Katrina saw nothing funny in this. She was stabbed with anger. "Were you approached? That way?"

"By Beila? Everybody would have to go mad altogether."

No, not Beila. You had only to think about it to see how impossible it would be. Beila carried herself with the pride of the presiding woman, the wife. Her rights were maintained with Red Indian dignity. She was a gloomy person. (Victor had made her gloomy—one could understand that.) She was like the wife of a Cherokee chieftain, or again Catherine of Aragon. There was something of each type of woman in the gaudy-gloomy costumes she designed for herself. Tremendous, her silent air of self-respect. For such a proud person to experiment along lines suggested by a gay handbook was out of the question, totally. Still, Katrina felt the hurt of it. Disrespect. Ill will. It was disrespectful also of Beila. Beila was long-suffering. At heart, Beila was a generous woman. Katrina really did know the score.

"So there's the new generation," said Victor. "When you consider the facts, they seem sometimes to add up to an argument for abortion. My youngest child! The wildest of all three. Now she's abandoned her plan to be a rabbi and she looks more Jewish than ever, with those twists of hair beside her ears."

Curious how impersonal Victor could be. Categories like wife, parent, child never could affect his judgment. He could discuss a daughter like any other subject submitted to his concentrated, radiant consideration—with the same generalizing detachment. It wasn't unkindness. It wasn't ordinary egotism. Katrina didn't have the word for it.

Anyway, they were together in the lounge, and to have him to herself was one of her best pleasures. He was always being identified on New York streets, buttonholed by readers, bugged by painters (and there were millions of people who painted), but here in this sequestered corner Katrina did not expect to be molested. She was wrong. A man appeared; he entered obviously looking for someone. That someone could only be Victor. She gave a warning signal—lift of the head—and Victor cautiously turned and then said in a low voice, somewhat morose, "It's him—I mean the character who wrote me the note."

"Oh-oh."

"He's a determined little guy. . . . That's quite a fur coat he's wearing. It must have been designed by F.A.O. Schwarz." It seemed to sweeten his temper to have said this. He smiled a little.

"That is an expensive garment," said Katrina.

It was a showy thing, beautifully made but worn without a manner. In circles of fur, something like the Michelin tire circles, it reached almost to the floor. Larry Wrangel was slight, slender, his bald head was unusually long. The grizzled side hair, unbrushed, looked as if he had slept on it when it was damp. A long soiled white scarf, heavy silk, drooped over the fur. Under the scarf a Woolworth's red bandanna was knotted. The white fur must have been his travel coat. For it wouldn't have been of any use in Southern California. His tanned face was lean, the skin stretched—perhaps a face lift? Katrina speculated. His scalp was spotted with California freckles. The dark eyebrows were nicely arched. His mouth was thin, shy and also astute.

Victor said as they were shaking hands, "I couldn't get back to you last night."

"I didn't really expect it."

Wrangel pulled over one of the Swedish-modern chairs and sat forward in his rolls of white fur. Not removing the coat was perhaps his way of dealing with the difference in their sizes—bulk against height.

He said, "I guessed you would be surrounded, and also bushed by late evening. Considering the weather, you had a good crowd."

Wrangel did not ignore women. As he spoke he inspected Katrina. He might have been trying to determine why Victor should have taken up with this one. Whole graduating classes of girls on the make used to pursue Victor.

Katrina quickly reconciled herself to Wrangel—a little, smart man, not snooty with her, no enemy. He was eager only to have a talk, long anticipated, a serious first-class talk. Victor, unwell, feeling damaged, was certainly thinking how to get rid of the man.

Wrangel was chatting rapidly, wanting to strike the right offering and losing no time. He tried the old Cedar bar and the Artists' Club on Eighth Street. He spoke of Baziotes and of Arshile Gorky, of Gorky's loft on Union Square. He mentioned Parker Tyler, and Tyler's book on Pavel Tchelitchew, naming also Edith Sitwell, who had been in love with Tchelitchew (Wulpy grimaced at Edith Sitwell and said, "Tinkle poems, like harness bells"). Wrangel laughed, betraying much tension in his laughter. Shyness and shrewdness made him seem to squint and even to jeer. He wished to be expansive, to make himself agreeable. He didn't have the knack for it. An expert in pleasing Victor, Katrina could have told him where he was going wrong. Victor's attitude was one of thinly dissimulated impatience. Trina felt that he was being too severe. The fellow should be given a chance. He's being put down extra hard because he's a celebrity.

On closer inspection, the white furs which should

have been immaculate were spotted by food and drink; nor was there any reason (he was so rich!) why the silk scarf should be so unclean. She took a liking to Wrangel, though. He made a point of including her in the conversation. If he mentioned a name like Chiaromonte or Barrett, he would say, aside, "A top intellectual in that circle," or, "The fellow who introduced Americans to German phenomenology."

But Victor wouldn't have any of this nostalgia, and he said, "What are you doing in Buffalo anyway? This is a hell of a season to leave California."

"I have a screwy kind of motive," said Wrangel. "Clinical psychologists, you see, often send me suggestions for films, inspired by the fantasies of crazy patients. So once a year I make a swing of selected funny farms. And here in Buffalo I saw some young fellows who were computer bugs—institutionalized."

"That's a new wrinkle," said Victor. "I would have thought that you didn't need to leave California, then."

"The maddest mad are on the Coast? Do you think so?"

"Well, not now, maybe," Victor said. Then he made one of his characteristic statements: "It takes a serious political life to keep reality real. So there are sections of the country where brain softening is accelerated. And Southern California from the first has been set up for the maximum exploitation of whatever goes wrong with the American mind. They farm the kinks as much as they do lettuces and oranges."

"Yes, I suppose so," said Wrangel.

"As for the part played by intellectuals . . . Well, I suppose in this respect there's not much difference between California and Massachusetts. They're in the act together with everybody else. I mean intellectuals. Impossible for them to hold out. Besides, they're so badly educated they can't even identify the evils. Even Vespasian when he collected his toilet tax had to justify himself: *Pecunia non olet*. But we've come to a point where it's *only* money that doesn't stink."

"True, intellectuals are in shameful shape. . . ."

Katrina observed that Wrangel's eyes were iodine-colored. There was an iodine tinge even to the whites.

"The main money people despise the intelligentsia, I mean especially the fellows that bring the entertainment industry suggestions for deepening the general catalepsy. Or the hysteria."

Wrangel took this meekly enough. He seemed to have thought it all through for himself and then passed on to further considerations. "The banks, of course . . ." he said. "It can take about twenty million bucks to make one of these big pictures, and they need a profit in the neighborhood of three hundred percent. But as for money, I can remember when Jackson Pollock was driving at top speed in and out of the trees at East Hampton while loving up a girl in his jeep. He wouldn't have been on welfare and food stamps, if he had lived. He played with girls, with art, with death, and wound up with dollars. What do those drip canvases fetch now?" Wrangel said this in a tone so moderate that he got away with it. "Sure the investment golems think of me as a gold mine, and they detest me. I detest them right back, in spades." He said to Katrina, "Did you hear Victor's lecture last night? It was the first time in forty years that I actually found myself taking notes like a student."

Katrina couldn't quite decide what opinion Victor was forming of this Wrangel. When he'd had enough, he would get up and go. No boring end-men would ever trap him in the middle. As yet there was no sign that he was about to brush the man off. She was glad of that, she found Wrangel entertaining; and she was as discreet as could be in working the band of her watch forward on her wrist. Tactful, she drew back her sleeve to see the time. Very soon now the kids would be having their snack. Silent Pearl, wordless Soolie. She had failed to get a rise out of them with the elephant story. A lively response would have helped her to finish it. But you simply couldn't get them to react. Not even Lieutenant Krieggstein with his display of guns impressed them. Krieggstein may have confused them when he pulled up his trousers and showed the holster strapped to his stout short leg. Then, too, he sometimes wore his wig and sometimes not. That also might have been confusing.

Victor had decided to give Wrangel a hearing. If this proved to be a waste of time, he would start forward, assemble his limbs, take his stick upside down like a polo mallet, and set off, as silent as Pearl, as wordless as Soolie. Since he loved conversation, his cutting out would be a dreadful judgment on the man. "You gave me a lot to think about during the night," said Wrangel. "Your comments on the nonrevolution of Louis Napoleon and his rabble of deadbeats, and especially the application of that to the present moment—what you called the proletarianized present." He took out a small notebook, which Trina identified as a Gucci product, and read out one of his notes. " 'Proletarianization: people deprived of everything that formerly defined humanity to itself as human.' "

Never mind the fellow's thoughts of the night, Victor was trying to adjust himself to the day, shifting his frame, looking for a position that didn't shoot pains down the back of his thigh. Since the operation, his belly was particularly tender, distended and lumpy, and the small hairs stuck him like burning darts. As if turned inwards. The nerve endings along the scar were like the tip of a copper wire with the strands undone. For his part, Wrangel seemed fit—youthfully elderly, durably fragile, probably a vegetarian. As he was trying to fix Wrangel's position, somewhere between classics of thought (Hegel) and the funny papers, there came before Victor the figures of Happy Hooligan and the Captain from *The Katzenjammer Kids* with the usual detached colors, streaks of Chinese vermilion and blocks of forest green. Looking regal, feeling jangled, Victor sat and listened. Wrangel's eyes were inflamed; it must really have been a bad night for him. He had a wry, wistful, starveling expression on his face, and his silk banner made you think of the scarf that had broken Isadora's neck. His main pitch was now beginning. He had read *The Eighteenth Brumaire,* and he could prove it. Why had the French Revolution been made in the Roman style? All the revolutionists had read Plutarch. Marx noted that they had been inspired by "old poetry." "Ancient traditions lying like a nightmare on the brains of the living."

"I see that you boned up on your Marx."

"It's marvelous stuff." Wrangel refused to take offense. All of Katrina's sympathies were with him. He was behaving well. He said, "Now let's see if I can put it together with *your* conjectures. It's still a struggle with the burden of history. *Le mort saisit le vif.* And you suggest that the modern avant-garde hoped to be free from this death grip of tradition. Art becoming an activity in which life brings raw material to the artists, and the artist using his imagination to bring forth a world of his own, owing nothing to the old humanism."

"Well, okay. What of it?" said Victor.

Katrina's impression was that Wrangel was pleased with himself. He thought he was passing his orals.

"Then you said that the parody of a revolution in 1851—history as farce—might be seen as a prelude to today's politics of deception—government by comedians who use mass-entertainment techniques. Concocted personalities, pseudo events."

Worried for him now, Katrina moved to the edge of her seat. She thought it might be necessary to rise soon, get going, break it up. "So you fly around the country and talk to psychiatrists," she said.

Her intervention was not welcome, although Wrangel was polite. "Yes."

"A sound approach to popular entertainment," said Victor. "Enlist the psychopaths."

"Try leaving them out, at any level," said Wrangel, only slightly stiff. He said, "In Detroit I'm seeing a party named Fox. He has published a document by a certain D'Amiens, who is sometimes also Boryshinski. The author is supposed to have disappeared without a trace. He had made the dangerous discovery that the planet is controlled by powers from other worlds. All this according to Mr. Fox's book. These other-world powers have programmed the transformation and control of the human species through something called CORP-ORG-THINK. They work through a central data bank and they already have control of the biggest corporations, banking circles, and political elites. Some of their leading people are David Rockefeller, Whitney Stone of Stone and Webster, Robert Anderson of Arco. And the overall plan is to destroy our life-support system, and then to evacuate the planet. The human race will be moved to a more suitable location."

"And what becomes of this earth?" said Katrina.

"It becomes hell, the hell of the unfit whom CORP plans to leave behind. When the long reign of Quantification begins, says Boryshinski, mankind will accept a purely artificial mentality, and the divine mind will be overthrown by the technocratic mind."

"Does this sound to you like a possible film?" said Katrina.

"If they don't ask too much for the rights, I might be interested."

"How would you go about saving us—in the picture, I mean?" Victor said. "Maybe Marx suggests some angle that you can link up with the divine mind."

Katrina hoped that Wrangel would stand up to Victor, and he did. Being deferential got you nowhere; you had to fight him if you wanted his good opinion. Wrangel said, "I'd forgotten how grand a writer Marx was. What marvelous images! The ghosts of Rome surrounding the cradle of the new epoch. The bourgeois revolution storming from success to success. 'Ecstasy the everyday spirit.' 'Men and things set in sparkling brilliants.' But a revolution that draws its poetry from the past is condemned to end in depression and dullness. A real revolution is not imitative or histrionic. It's a *real* event."

"Oh, all right," said Victor. "You're dying to tell me what *you* think. So why don't you tell me and get it over with."

"My problem is with class struggle," said Wrangel, "the destiny of social classes. You argue that class paralysis produces these effects of delusion—lying, cheating, false appearances. It all seems real, but what's really real is the unseen convulsion under the apparitions. You're imposing European conceptions of class on Americans."

Katrina's thought was: Ah, he wants to play with the big boys. She was afraid he might be hurt.

"And what's your idea?" said Victor.

"Well," said Wrangel, "I have a friend who says

that the created souls of people, of the Americans, have been removed. The created soul has been replaced by an artificial one, so there's nothing real that human beings can refer to when they try to judge any matter for themselves. They live mainly by *rationales*. They have made-up guidance systems."

"That's the artificial mentality of your Boryshinski," said Victor.

"It has nothing to do with Boryshinski. Boryshinski came much later."

"Is this friend of yours a California friend? Is he a guru?" said Victor.

"I wish we had had time for a real talk," said Wrangel. "You always set a high value on ideas, Victor. I remember that. Well, I've considered this from many sides, and I am convinced that most ideas are trivial. A thought of the real is also an image of the real; if it's a true thought, it's a true picture and is accompanied also by a true feeling. Without this, our ideas are corpses. . . ."

"Well, by God!" Victor took up his stick, and Katrina was afraid that he might take a swipe at Wrangel, whack him with it. But no, he planted the stick before him and began to rise. It was a complicated operation. Shifting forward, he braced himself upon his knuckles. He lifted up the bum leg; his color was hectic. Remember (Katrina remembered) that he was almost always in pain.

Katrina explained as she was picking up the duffel bag and the violin case, "We have a plane to catch."

Wrangel answered with a sad smile. "I see. Can't fight flight schedules, can we?"

Victor righted his cap from the back and made for the door, stepping wide in his crippled energetic gait.

Outside the lounge Katrina said, "We still have about half an hour to kill."

"Driven out."

"He was terribly disappointed."

"Sure he was. He came East just to take me on. Maybe his guru told him that he was strong enough, at last. He gave himself away when he mentioned Parker Tyler and Tchelitchew. Tchelitchew, you see, attacked me. He said *he* had a vision of the world, whereas the abstract painting that I advocated was like a crazy lady expecting a visit from the doctor and smearing herself with excrement to make herself attractive—like a love potion. Wrangel was trying to stick me with this insult."

Threatening weather, the wicked Canadian north wind crossing the border in white gusts, didn't delay boarding. The first to get on the plane was Victor. His special need, an aisle seat at the back, made this legitimate. It depressed Katrina to enter the empty dark cabin. The sky looked dirty, and she was anxious. Their seats were in the tail, next to the rest rooms. She stowed the violin overhead and the zipper bag under the seat. Victor lowered himself into place, arranged his body, leaned backwards, and shut his eyes. Either he was very tired or he wanted to be alone with his thoughts.

The plane filled up. It was some comfort that despite the mean look of the weather, practical-minded people never doubted that they would lift off from Buffalo and land in Chicago—business as usual. In the hand of God, but also routine. Katrina, who looked sensible along with the rest of the passengers, didn't know what to do about her anxious doubts, couldn't collect them in a single corner and turn the key on them. In one respect Dotey was dead right: Katrina jumped at any chance to rush off and be with Victor. Victor, even if he was ailing, even if no life

with him was really possible—he couldn't last long—
was entirely different from other people. Other people mostly stood in a kind of bleakness. They had the
marks of privation upon them. There was a lack of
space and air about them, they were humanly bare,
whereas Victor gave off a big light. Strange little
Wrangel may have been a pretentious twerp. He
wanted to exchange serious thoughts; he might be
puffing himself up absurdly, a faker, as Victor suspected. But when he had talked about ecstasy as the
everyday spirit or men and things set in brilliants, she
had understood exactly what he was saying. She had
understood even better when he said that when the
current stopped, the dullness and depression were
worse than ever. To spell it out further, she herself
could never generate any brilliancy. If she had somebody to get her going, she could join in and perhaps
make a contribution. This contribution would be
feminine and sexual. It would be important, it might
even be indispensable, but it would not be inventive.
She could, however, be inventive in deceit. And she
had made an effort to branch out with the elephant
story. She had, nevertheless, had that serious setback
with $M*A*S*H$. The movie house itself had been part
of her misfortune. They were surrounded by hippies,
not very young ones, and in the row ahead there was a
bearded guy slurping popsicles and raising himself to
one cheek, letting off loud farts. Victor said, "There's
change from the general for the caviar it's eaten."
Katrina hadn't yet figured out *that* one. Then Victor
stood up and said, "I won't sit in this stink!" When
they reached the street, the disgrace and horror of
being *exposed* by $M*A*S*H$ and associated with San
Francisco degenerates made Katrina want to throw
herself in front of a cable car rushing downhill from
the Mark Hopkins.

Now she made a shelf of her hand on her brow and looked away from Victor, who was staring out at the field. Was there anything she could do about that goddamn elephant? Suppose a man turned up who hypnotized ball players and could do the same with an animal. They were now discovering new mental powers in the bigger mammals. Whales, for example, sang to one another; they were even thought to be capable of rhyming. Whales built walls out of air bubbles and could encircle and entrap millions of shrimp. What if an eccentric zoologist were to visit the management with a new idea? Meanwhile the management had to send for fodder while the elephant dropped whole pyramids of dung. The creature was melancholy and wept tears as big as apricots. The mahout demanded mud. If Margey didn't have a good wallow soon, she'd go berserk and wreck the entire fifth floor. Abercrombie & Fitch (were they still in Chicago?) offered to send over a big-game hunter. For them it would be terrific publicity to shoot her. Humane people would be outraged. Suppose a pretty high-school girl were to come forward with the solution? And what if she were to be a Chinese girl? In Chinese myth, elephants and not men had once been the masters of the world. And then?

Victor's mind was also at work, although you couldn't say that he was thinking. Something soft and heavy seemed to have been spread over his body. It resembled the lead apron laid over you by X-ray technicians. Victor was stretched under this suave deadly weight and feeling as you felt when waking from a deep sleep—unable to lift your arm. On the field, in the winter light, the standing machines were paler than the air, and the entire airport stood in a frame of snow, looking like a steel engraving. It reminded him of the Lower East Side in—oh, about

1912. The boys (ancients today, those who were alive) were reading the Pentateuch. The street, the stained pavement, was also like a page of Hebrew text, something you might translate if you knew how. Jacob lay dreaming of a ladder which rose into heaven. *V'hinei malachi elohim*—behold the angels of God going up and down. This had caused Victor no surprise. What age was he, about six? It was not a dream to him. *Jacob* was dreaming, while Victor was awake, reading. There was no "long ago." It was all now. The cellar classroom had a narrow window at sidewalk level, just enough to permit a restricted upward glance showing fire escapes under snow, the gold shop sign of the Chinese laundry hanging from the ironwork, and angels climbing up and down. This did not have to be interpreted. It came about in a trance, as if under the leaden weight of the flexible apron. Now the plane was starting its takeoff run, and soon the No Smoking sign would be turned off. Victor would have liked to smoke, but the weight of his hands made any movement impossible.

It wasn't like him to cherish such recollections, although he had them, and they had lately been more frequent. He began now to remember that his mother had given him the windpipe of a goose after drying it in the Dutch oven of the coal stove, and that he had cut a notch in the windpipe with his father's straight razor and made a whistle of it. When it was done, he disliked it. Even when dry it had kept its terrible red color, and it was very harsh to the touch and had left an unpleasant taste in his mouth. This was not exactly Marx's nightmare of history from which mankind had to be liberated. The raw fowl taste was nasty. The angels on the fire escape, however, were very pleasing, and his consciousness of them, while it was four thousand years old, had also been exactly contemporary. Different ideas of time and space had not yet been imposed upon him. One comprehensive light contained everybody. Among the rest—parents, patriarchs, angels, God—there was yourself. Victor did not feel bound to get to the bottom of this; it was only a trance, probably an effect of fatigue and injury. He gave a side thought to Mass. General, where a tumor had been lifted out of a well of blood in his belly, and he reminded himself that he was still a convalescent— reminded himself also that Baudelaire had believed the artist to be always in a spiritually convalescent state. (This really was Baudelaire Day; just a while ago it had been the touch that brought the dead to life.) Only just returned from the shadow of death, the convalescent inhaled with delight the close human odors of the plane. Pollution didn't matter, the state of a convalescent being the state of a child drunk with impressions. Genius *must* be the recovery of the powers of childhood by an act of the creative *will*. Victor knew all this like the palm of his hand or the nose on his face. By combining the strength of a man (analytic power) with the ecstasy of a child you could discover the New. What God's Revelation implied was that the Jews (his children) would obstinately will (with mature intelligence) the divine adult promise. This would earn them the hatred of the whole world. They were always archaic, *and* they were always contemporary—we could sort that out later.

But now suppose that this should *not* be convalescence but something else, and that he should be on the circuit not because he was recovering but because he was losing ground. Falling apart? This was where Katrina entered the picture. Hers was the touch that resurrected, or that reunited, reintegrated his otherwise separating physical powers. He asked himself: That she turns me on, does that mean that I love her, or does it simply mean that she belongs to the class of women that turn me on? He didn't like the question he was asking. But he was having many difficult sensations, innumerable impressions of winter, winters of seven decades superimposed. The winter world even brought him a sound, not for the ear but for some other organ. And none of this was clearly communicable, nor indeed worth communicating. It was simply part of the continuing life of every human being. Everybody was filled with visions that had been repressed, and amassed involuntarily, and when you were sick they were harder to disperse.

"I can tell you, now that we're in the air, Victor, that I am *relieved*. I wasn't sure we'd get back." The banking plane gave them a single glimpse of Lake Erie slanting green to the right, and then rose into dark-gray snow clouds. It was a bumpy flight. The headwind was strong. "Have I ever told you about my housekeeper's husband? He's a handsome old Negro who used to be a dining car waiter. Now he gambles. Impressive to look at. Ysole's afraid of him."

"Why are we discussing him?"

"I wonder if I shouldn't have a talk with her husband about Ysole. If she takes money from Alfred, if she should testify against me in the case, it would be serious. His lawyer could bring out that she *raised* me, and therefore has my number."

"Would she want to harm you as much as that?"

"Well, she's always been somewhat cracked. She used to call herself a conjure-woman. She's shrewd and full of the devil."

"I wonder why we're flying at this altitude. By now we should have been above the clouds," said Victor.

They had fifteen minutes of open sky and then dropped back again into the darkness. "Yes, why are we so low?" said Katrina. "We're not getting any-where."

The seat-belt sign went on and the pilot announced, "Owing to the weather, O'Hare Airport is closed, briefly. We will be landing in Detroit in five minutes."

"I *can't* be stuck in Detroit!" said Katrina.

"Easy, Katrina. In Chicago it isn't even one o'clock. We'll probably sit on the ground awhile and take right off again."

Suddenly fields were visible beneath—warehouses, hangars, highways, water. The landing gear came into position as Katrina, watching from the ground, had often seen it do, when the belly of the Boeing opened and the black bristling innards descended. Victor was able to stop one of the busy stewardesses, and she told them that it was a bad scene in Chicago. "Blitzed by snow."

When they disembarked they found themselves immediately in a crowd of grounded passengers. Once you got into such a crowd your fear was that you'd never get out. How lucky that Victor was not fazed. He was going forward in that rising-falling gait of his, his brows resembling the shelf mushrooms that grow on old tree trunks. For her part, Katrina was para-lyzed by tension. Signs signified little. BAGGAGE CLAIM: there was no baggage. She was carrying Vanessa's precious fiddle. TERMINAL: Why should Victor limp all the way to the terminal only to be sent back to some gate? "There should be agents here to give informa-tion."

"No way. They're not organized for this," said Victor. "And we can't get near the phones. They're lined up ten deep. Let's see if we can find two seats and try to figure out what to do."

It was slow going. Alternate blasts of chill from the

gates and heat from the blowers caught them about the legs and in the face. They found a single seat, and Victor sat himself down. He had that superlative imperturbability in the face of accident and local disturbances that Katrina was welcome to share if she could. Beila seemed to have learned how to do it. Trina had not acquired the knack. Victor laid his heel on the duffel bag. The violin case he took between his legs. With his stick he improvised a barrier to keep people from tripping over him.

Going off to gather information, Katrina found a man in a blue-gray uniform who looked as if he might be a flight engineer. He was leaning, arms crossed, against the wall. She noticed how well shined his black shoes were, and that he had a fresh complexion. She thought that he should be able to direct her. But when she said, "Excuse me," he refused to take notice of her, he turned his face away. She said, "I wonder if you could tell me. My flight is grounded. Where can I find out what's happening?"

"How would I know!"

"Because you're in uniform, I thought . . ."

He put his hand to her chest and pushed her away. "What are you *doing?*" she said. She felt her eyes flooding, growing turbid, smarting. "What's the *matter* with you?" What followed was even worse. While he looked into her face, not downwards, his heel ground her instep. He was stomping her foot. And this was not being done in anger. It didn't seem anger at all; it was a different kind of intensity. She tried to read the name on the bar clipped to his chest, but he was gone before she could make it out. She thought: I've put myself in a position where people can hurt me and get away with it. As if I came out of Evanston to do wrong and it's written all over me. It might have been a misogynist, or other psychopath in uniform. A bitter hot current came from low underneath, going through her bowels like fainting heat, then moved up her chest and into her throat and cheeks. Hurt as she was, she conjectured that it might have been disrespect for his profession that put him in a fury, an engineer being approached like a cabin steward. Or he might have been putting out waves of hate magnetism and praying for somebody to approach, to give the works to. Victor, if he had been there, would have hit the guy on the head with his stick. Sick or well, he had presence of mind.

While she waited in a flight information line, Katrina concentrated on shrinking down the incident and restoring scale. He was just a person from a nice family in the suburbs probably, average comfortable people, judging from the way he wore his uniform—what Victor, when he got going, called the "animal human average" and, quoting one of his writers, "the dark equivocal crowd saturated with falsity." He liked such strong expressions. Good thing she had on the ostrich boots. Otherwise the man might have broken something.

When her turn came, the woman behind the counter had little information to give. New flights would be announced as soon as O'Hare opened its runways. "There'll be a rush for seats. Maybe I'd better buy first-class tickets," said Katrina.

"I can't reserve for you. The computer has no information, no matter how I punch it."

"Still, I'll buy two open first-class flights. On my credit card. They can be turned in if I don't use them."

As she approached Victor from the side, he looked pleasant enough in his cap—silent, bemused, amused. It was in the lower face that the signs of aging were most advanced, in the shortening of his jaw and the sharpening of its corners. In profile the signs were more noticeable, touched off more worry, inspired more sorrow. Katrina did not think that her full face, the just-repainted mouth, and the carriage of her bosom gave it away, but she was in low spirits: his condition, the jam of passengers, the spite of the man who had stomped her, the agony of being stuck here. From the front Victor was as "rich" in looks as ever. Yet she could not borrow much strength from him. There were Wulpy fans even here in Detroit who would have rushed out to the airport in a fleet of cars if they had known that he was here. They were better qualified to appreciate him than a woman who had twisted his arm to see $M*A*S*H$. These fans from the city would talk, drink, or take him home. All she could do was to stand on Square One—a woman from Evanston, not vivid with desperation but dull with it, without a particle of invention to her.

You seldom saw Victor in a flap. He wasn't greatly disturbed—not yet anyway. "Aren't you getting hungry? I am," he said.

"We should eat, I suppose."

"I guess we could find a fast-food spot."

"Something more substantial than a hamburger."

". . . Not to spoil tonight's banquet," he said.

Their march through the concourse began. Normally Victor was a fair walker, patient with his infirmity. But a solid mass like this was daunting. Movement was further complicated by baggage carts, sweepers, and wheelchairs, and Katrina soon said, "We aren't getting anywhere. It's after one o'clock in Chicago."

Victor said, "I wouldn't panic just yet. The housekeeper is there. Your sister. Your friend the cop."

"My sister isn't exactly in sympathy."

"You often say how critical she is. Still, she may not let you down."

"Even through bad times, I stood by her. Last summer she drove up with a shovel in the trunk of her car and said she was on her way to the cemetery to dig up her husband. She said she just had to see him again. I took her into the garden and made her drunk. Then she told me I had let her down, that I had gone to Boston to be with you when *she* was having surgery. They removed that tumor from the cervix."

Victor, far from shocked, nodded as she spoke—grieving wives, hysterical sisters. To read about such matters in a well-written book might have been of interest; to hear about them, no. Katrina could not convey how awful it had been to get her sister plastered—the damp heat, Dotey's thin face sweating. Because of the smell of clay underfoot you were reminded of graves. Just try to picture Dotey with neurasthenic stick arms, digging. She would have passed out in a matter of minutes.

Victor was filled with scenes from world history, fully documented knowledge of evil, battles, deportations to the murder camps from the *Umschlagplatz* in Warsaw, the terrible scenes during the evacuation from Saigon, and certainly he could imagine Dorothea trying to dig up her husband's corpse. But when to turn your imagination to phenomena of this class remained unclear. He had written about the "inhuman" as an element of the Modern, about the feebleness, meanness, drunkenness of modern man and of the consequences of this for art and for politics. His reputation was based upon the analyses he had made of Modernist extremism. He was the teacher of famous painters and writers. She had pored over his admirable books, yet she, you see, had to deal with him on the personal level. And on the personal level, well, he had more to say about art as a remedy for the bareness, as a cover for modern nakedness, than about the filling of *personal* gaps, or deficiencies. Yet even there he was not entirely predictable. He never ran out of surprises.

"I see you favoring your left foot. Does the boot pinch?"

"It was stepped on."

"You bumped into somebody?"

"A nice fair-haired young man rushed away from me when I stopped to get information, but before he rushed away he stomped me."

Victor stopped, looking at her from his height. "Why didn't you report him?"

"He disappeared."

"More and more new kinds of crazies coming at you. How changed everything is! . . . It was women and children first when the *Titanic* went down. Middle-class gallantry is gone with the Biedermeier."

"There's no real damage. It just aches some. But, Vic, think of the time lost to eat bad food. Is there nothing we can do to get out of here?"

"I might try to telephone the guy in charge of tonight's arrangements. Let me look in my wallet." Hooking his cane over his shoulder, he examined his hip-pocket army-navy billfold. "Yes. Continental Bank. Horace Kinglake. Why don't we phone him? If he wants me to speak tonight, he'd better organize our rescue. Why don't you call him, Katrina?"

"You want me to do the talking?"

"Why not? He must have top-level contacts with United or American. I hope you brought your telephone credit card."

"I did," said Katrina.

"Airports used to have good central services. Even Grand Central had telephone operators. Let's see if we can get hold of a phone." They had just begun to move forward when Victor stopped Katrina, saying, "I see our buddy Wrangel. He's coming toward us."

"He's sure to see us. You're pretty conspicuous."

"What if he does? . . . He did say he was flying to Detroit, didn't he?"

"When you walked out, I was embarrassed," said Katrina.

"He had no business to pursue me to the lounge."

"A different way to view it is that he came all the way from California to hear your lecture and to engage in conversation."

"To settle an old score, I think. This is a day when events have a dream tendency," said Victor. "There's a line about *'les revenants qui vous raccrochent en plein jour.'*"

"You'd better give me the card with that Kinglake's number."

Victor, curiously, didn't try to avoid Wrangel, and Wrangel, to Katrina's surprise, was terribly pleased to find them in the concourse. He might justifiably have been a little huffy. Not at all. In his own shy way he was delighted. "You didn't say you were going to Detroit, too."

"We weren't. We're grounded by the bad weather in Chicago."

"Oh, you have to wait. In that case why don't you have lunch with me?"

"I wish we could," said Katrina. "But we have to get to a telephone. It's urgent."

"Phoning would be much easier from a restaurant. Just a minute ago I passed a decent-looking bar and grill."

It was a big dark place, under a low ceiling, Tudor decor. As soon as the hostess appeared, Katrina saw money changing hands. It looked like a ten-dollar bill that Wrangel slipped the woman. Why not, if *The Kronos Factor* had grossed four hundred million? A leather booth was instantly available. Victor occupied the corner, laying his leg along the settee on the left. "Shall we drink?" said Wrangel. "Shall we order before you make your call? Miss," he said to the hostess, "please let this lady use your telephone. What shall we get for you, my dear?"

"A turkey sandwich, white meat, on toast."

"Duck *à l'orange,*" said Victor. In a lounge as dark as this, where you couldn't see what you were eating, Katrina would have chosen a simpler meal for him as well. Amber light descended from a fixture upon Wrangel's head and on the thick white furs.

"Better make that call person-to-person," Victor advised Katrina.

It was good advice, for Horace Kinglake was hard to reach. The call went through many transfers. By his voice when he said "Kinglake," she recognized that he was an adroit, managerial type. From Victor she had picked up a certain contempt for polished executives. Still, it was comforting to talk even to a man whose courtesies were artificial. "Stuck in Detroit? Oh, we can't have that, can we? Some two hundred acceptances have come in. An audience from all parts of the country. It would be a disaster if Mr. Wulpy. . . I am really concerned. And so sorry. Wasn't there an earlier flight?" Cursing Victor, probably, for this last-minute fuck-up.

"Is the Chicago weather so ferocious?" Katrina asked for facts to go with her forebodings.

But Mr. Kinglake was taking her call in a private dining room, and what would a senior executive in his seventieth-story offices know about weather in the streets? He had heard some reports of a freak storm.

"We'll get Mr. Wulpy here, regardless. I'll put my ace troubleshooter on this. Give me about half an hour."

"You can reach us at this number in Detroit. . . . I wonder, is O'Hare closed down for the day?"

"There is Midway and also Meigs Field."

Half reassured, she went back to the booth. A woman in her position, taking chances, playing outlaw in order to be at Victor's side—the big man's consort; but when she had seen him in profile (just after the flight engineer had stomped her instep, and when she had felt that there were unsobbed sobs in her chest), she had had a new view of the deterioration he had suffered since he had taken up with her.

The double shot of booze he had drunk apparently had done him good. He held a thick wide glass in his hand—a refill. This was what his system needed, food and drink and a booth to rest in. He could well have afforded to bring her here himself, and to slip the hostess ten bucks and to have the use of the telephone. But he would never have done that. It would have been a sacrifice of principle. And this was why he had been glad to see Wrangel. Wrangel had got him off his feet. The duck à l'orange would be awful. A servitor, an aide, was necessary to satisfy his psyche. Also somebody to pick up the tab. She admitted that this was important to him.

Trina made her report, and Victor said, "Well, we can just take it easy until he calls back. I'll talk to him myself, about tonight's program. Sit down, kid, and have a drink." Katrina shared the corner beside him. Vanessa's fiddle stood upright behind them. Katrina was grateful to Wrangel just then. She needed help with Victor. He seemed to her unstable, off center. The term often used in *Psychology Today* was "labile." He was labile. And he was more pleased than not to have Wrangel's company now. He seemed to have forgotten the poisonous dig about Tchelitchew. Katrina thought it likely that Wrangel had never heard about Tchelitchew's offensive statement. Of course, Victor believed that movies of the kind made by Wrangel infected the mental life of the country (and the international community), but they weren't considering Wrangel's movies just now. Evidently, though, they had been talking about erotic films, for Wrangel was saying that he hadn't personally been involved in that business. "Productions of that kind don't need scriptwriters."

"No?" said Victor. "Just interracial couples balling away?"

"I wonder if you can get the waitress to bring me a Bloody Mary," said Katrina.

"Certainly," said Wrangel. "Now, to fill you in on my career since the Village days, I had many kinds of writing jobs. One of the more curious was with the crew in Texas that helped to put together the memoirs of President Johnson."

"How did that come about?" said Katrina.

"Out of the Bread Loaf Conference, where I met some Washington journalists. Also Robert Frost—and a few gentleman types from Harvard. And I was recommended by Dick Goodwin, so there I was in Austin on Johnson's staff of writers. He had retired by then."

"How was that done—the work?" said Victor.

"It began with a course of brainwashing. We used to gather atop the Federal Building in Austin built by LBJ toward the end of his administration. He had his own suite, and he landed by helicopter, from his ranch, and came down from the rooftop to spend the day with us. He repeated his version of every event until it was grafted on our minds. You often come across these legend builders who hypnotize you by repetition. You become the receptacle of their story. Robert Frost was another of those authorized-version fellows. They do all of the talking, and they repeat themselves until your mind begins to reject alternative versions. Johnson brought us to his ranch, too. He drove over the pastures in his Lincoln, and the bodyguards followed in their Lincoln. When he needed more to drink, he rolled down his window and the guards pulled up alongside and poured him more whiskey. Most of us were intimidated by him—easier to do with a person like me, Victor, than with you."

"Oh, it's been tried. Once at Berenson's villa. The famous mummy was brought out—another Litvak, like myself. I was raised to respect my elders, but I didn't care to have so many cultural flourishes made over me."

"The Latin quotations . . ." Katrina reminded him.

"The *lacrimae rerum*. Wow! If it could have been done by ass-kissing his patrons and patronesses, B.B. would have dried away a good many tears. Then he said that he understood I was a considerable person in the bohemian life of New York. And I said that to call me a bohemian was like describing John the Baptist as a hydrotherapist. I had hoped to get the discussion around to modern painting, but of course that never happened."

A friendly chat. It was now half past two. At noon Katrina had been afraid that Victor might hit Wrangel on the head with his stick for saying, "Most ideas are trivial." How well they were getting along now.

"You didn't mean that you were any kind of John the Baptist?" said Wrangel.

"No, it just drove me wild to be patronized."

For the moment, Victor was being charming. "Most people know better than to lack charm," he had once told Katrina. "Even harsh people have their own harsh charm. Some are *all* charm, like Franklin D. Roosevelt. Some repudiate all charm, like Stalin. When all-charm and no-charm met at Yalta, no-charm won hands down." Victor in his heart of hearts dismissed charm. Style, yes; style was essential; but charm tended to blur your thoughts. And if Victor was now charming with Wrangel, joking about John the Baptist, it was because he wanted to prevent Wrangel from bringing out his Gucci appointment book with its topic sentences on *The Eighteenth Brumaire*.

It was plainly Wrangel's purpose to resume—to develop a serious conversation. It was the drive for serious conversation that had made him cross the continent from L.A. to Buffalo. Trina was beginning to see a certain efficiency and toughness in Wrangel. It was not by accident that he had earned so many millions. While he seemed "humbly happy" in Victor's company, he was also opinionated, obstinate. In the past, and even today, Victor had dismissed him—not a mind of the A category—and Wrangel was determined to win a higher rating. He thought he deserved it. That was Katrina's view. The shy, astute man in the Arctic fox coat had Victor Wulpy to himself—a failing Victor, but Wrangel would not know that, since Victor carried himself so firmly, and after a few slugs of Scotch he sat up as princely as ever. He was, however, very far from himself. He was in one of those badly lighted (on purpose) no-man's-land restaurants that airports specialize in; he had eaten all the sesame sticks and crackers on the table, and when he put one of his hands under the back of Katrina's sweater she felt an icy pang through her silk slip.

The food was served just as Victor was called to the phone, and Wrangel asked the waiter to take it back to the kitchen and keep it warm.

Tilting to the right to avoid the hanging ornaments, fixtures with gilt chains, Victor followed the hostess to the telephone.

"Do you know," said Katrina, partly to forestall a conversation about Victor, "I was interested to hear that you started out by inventing plots for science comics. You must be very quick at it. I've been trying and trying to do a children's story about an elephant stuck on the top floor of a Chicago department store, and you have no idea how it drags and bothers me. When the animal was taken up in the freight elevator, she tested the floor, and she was reluctant to trust it. Her mahout—the trainer—sweet-talked her into it. She was a great success in the store, but when it came time to go down and she tested the elevator again with her foot, she wouldn't enter."

"They're stuck with her? How to get her out?" He gave one of his intense but restricted smiles. "What have you thought of?"

"Piano movers; the fire department; drugging the elephant; hypnotism; dismantling a wall; a wooden ramp down the staircase."

"A builders' crane?" said Wrangel.

"Sure, but the roof would have to be opened."

"Of course it would. Even if there were a hatch. But look here—suppose they braced the floor of the elevator from beneath. Temporary steel beams. She goes in. Maybe some person she trusts is inside and gives her hay mixed with marshmallows while the supports are being removed by mechanic commandos at top speed. So they get her down and parade her on Michigan Boulevard."

"Oh, that's a perfectly angelic solution!" said Katrina.

"As long as the floor is firm when she tests it."

"Fabulous! Do elephants have a weakness for marshmallows? You are a wizard plotter. I think I may be able to handle it now. Totally inexperienced, you see."

"I'd be only too happy to help. If you get stuck, this card of mine has all the numbers where I can be reached."

"That's awfully decent. Thanks."

"And it's a very bright idea for a kids' book. Charming. I hope it goes over big."

Trina for a moment considered telling him what a difference an independent success would make to her. He looked now, despite his own success and celebrity, like a man who had had very bad times, ugly defeats, choking disappointments, and so she was tempted to talk openly to him. It would bring some light and warmth into this dark frozen day, some emotional truth. But it wouldn't be prudent to open up. He had helped with the elephant. However, there was Victor to think of. This Wrangel might be eager to make use of what she would tell him about herself to obtain privileged knowledge of Victor, for which he perhaps had an unusual, a ravenous, a kinky appetite.

"Victor is a marvelous man," said Wrangel. "I always admired him enormously. I was just a kid when I met him, and he couldn't possibly take me seriously. For a long time I've had a relationship to him of which he couldn't be aware. I made a study of him, you see. I've put a tremendous lot of thought into him. I'm afraid I have to confess that he's been an obsession. I've read all his books, collected his articles."

"He thinks you came East on purpose, to talk to him."

"It's true, and I'm not surprised that he guessed it. He was sick last year, wasn't he?"

"Near death."

"I can see he's not his old self."

"I hope you don't have some idea about straightening out his thinking, Mr. Wrangel."

"Who, me? Do I think he'd listen to *me*? I know better than that."

"And I don't want you to think that if you tell me your opinions I'm going to transmit them."

"Why would I do that? It would be just as easy to send him my opinions in writing. Believe it or not, Miss Gallagher, it's more a matter of affection."

"Although you haven't even seen him in thirty years?"

"The psyche has a different calendar," he said. "Anyway, you haven't got it quite right. Anybody who knows Victor naturally wants to talk about him. There's so much to him."

"There are a hundred people you could discuss him with—the famous painters he influenced, or types like Clement Greenberg or Kenneth Burke or Harold Rosenberg—or any of the big-time art theorists. Plus a whole regiment of other people's wives."

"You must be a musician, Miss Gallagher. You carry a violin."

"It belongs to Victor's youngest daughter and we're taking it to Chicago for repair. If I were a violinist, why would I write a story about an elephant? I understand that you used to fiddle yourself."

"Did Victor remember my left-handed fooling—my trick instrument?"

"Anyway, what were you going to say about Victor, Mr. Wrangel?"

"Victor was meant to be a great man. Very, very smart. A powerful mind. A subtle mind. Completely independent. Not really a Marxist, either. I went to visit Sidney Hook last week, who used to be my teacher at NYU, and we were talking about the radicals of the older generation in New York. Sidney pooh-poohed them. They never had been serious, never organized themselves to take control as the European left did. They were happy enough, talking. Talk about Lenin, talk about Rosa Luxemburg, or German fascism, or the Popular Front, or Léon Blum, or Trotsky's interpretation of the Molotov-Ribbentrop Pact, or about James Burnham or whomever. They spent their lives discussing everything. If they felt their ideas were correct, they were satisfied. They were a bunch of mental hummingbirds. The flowers were red enough, but there couldn't have been any nectar. Still, it was enough if they were very ingenious, and if they drew a big, big picture—the very biggest picture. Now apply this to what Victor said one plane hop back, in Buffalo, that it takes a serious political life to keep reality real. . . ."

Katrina pretended that he was saying this to the wrong party. "I don't have any theoretical ability at all," she said, and she bent towards him as if to call attention to her forehead, which couldn't possibly have had real thoughts behind it. She was the farmer's daughter who couldn't remember how many made a dozen. But she saw from Wrangel's silent laugh—his skin was so taut, had he or hadn't he had a face lift in California?—saw from the genial scoff lines around his mouth that she wasn't fooling him for a minute.

"Victor was one of those writers who took command of a lot of painters, told them what they were doing, what they should do. Society didn't care about art anyway, it was busy with other things, and art became the plaything of intellectuals. Real painters, real painting, those are very rare. There are masses of educated people, and they'll tell you that they're all for poetry, philosophy, or painting, but they don't know them, don't do them, don't really care about them, sacrifice nothing for them, and really can't spare them the time of day—can't read, can't see, and can't hear. Their real interests are commercial, professional, political, sexual, financial. They don't live by art, with art, through art. But they're willing in a way to be imposed upon, and that's what the pundits do. They do it to the artists as well. The brush people are led by the word people. It's like some General Booth with a big brass band leading artists to an abstract heaven."

"You have clever ways of expressing yourself, Mr. Wrangel. Are you saying that Victor is nothing but a promoter?"

"Not for a minute. He's a colorful, powerful, intricate man. Unlike the other critic crumb-bums, he has a soul. Really. As for being a promoter, I can't see how he could hold the forefront if he didn't do a certain amount of promoting and operating. Well, what's the status of innocence, anyway, and can you get anywhere without hypocrisy? I'm not calling Victor a hypocrite; I'm saying that he has no time to waste on patsies, and he's perfectly aware that America is one place where being a patsy won't kill you. We can afford confusion of mind, in a safe, comfortable country. Of course, it's been fatal to art and culture. . . ."

"Is this your way of asking *me* how corrupt Victor is?" Katrina asked. Heavy distress, all the more distressing because of its mixed elements, came over her. Should she tell Wrangel off? Was it disloyal to listen to him? But she was fascinated and hungry for

more. And Victor himself would have thought her a
patsy for raising the question of loyalty at all. Too big
for trivial kinds of morality, he waved them off. And
Wrangel was taking advantage of Victor's brief absence, crowding in as many comments as he could. He
was very smart, and she now felt like a dope for
bothering him with her elephant.

He was trying to impress her, strutting a little (was
he trying also to make time with her?), but his passion
for understanding Victor was genuinely a passion.

"Victor is a promoter. He did well by himself,
solidly. But he hasn't faked anything. He really
studied the important questions of art—art and technology, art and science, art in the era of the mass life.
He understands how the artistic faculties are ham-
pered in America, which isn't really an art land. Here
art isn't serious. Not in the way a vaccine for herpes is
serious. And even for professionals, critics, curators,
editors, art is just *blah!* And it should be like the air
you breathe, the water you drink, basic, like nutrition
or truth. Victor knows what the real questions are,
and if you ask him what's the matter here he would
tell you that without art we can't judge what life is, we
can't sort anything out at all. Then the 'practical
sphere' itself, where 'planners,' generals, opinion-
makers, and Presidents operate, is no more real than
the lint under your bed. But even Victor's real interest
is politics. Sometimes his politics are idiotic, too, as
they were during the French student crisis, when he
agreed with Sartre that we were on the verge of an
inspiring and true revolution. He got carried away.
His politics would have made bad art. In politics
Victor is still something of a sentimentalist. Some
godlike ideas he has, and a rich appreciation of human
complexities. But he couldn't be engrossed in the
colors of the sky around Combray, as Proust was.

He's not big on hawthorn blossoms and church steeples, and he'll never get killed crossing the street because he's having visions."

Katrina said, "In Victor's place, I don't know how I'd feel about such a close study."

"Shall I tell you something? There was more than one hint of Victor Wulpy in the adventures of Buck Rogers."

This little guy, the celebrity covered by *People*—opinionated, sensitive, emotional—was definitely an oddball. Under the flame-shaped bulbs with their incandescent saffron threads, delicacy, obstinacy, and bliss were mingled in his face.

He began now to tell her about his son, an only child. "By my second wife," he said. "A younger woman. My Hank is now twenty-one. A problem from the beginning. He was born to startle. Some kids are dropping acid, stealing cars—that was the least of it. If he signed checks with my name, I could handle it by keeping my checking account low. He made the house so terrible that he drove his mother out. She couldn't take it, and she's now living with someone else. Illegal dealings started when Hank was about fourteen. Chased on the highway by the police. He held out money on dope dealers and they tried to kill him. No communication between me and the boy—too much sea-noise in his head. He's in a correctional prison now where I'm not allowed to visit. There the recidivists are treated like infants. Their diet is infantile—farina—and they're forced to wear diapers. The theory must be that the problem lies in infancy, so there's a program of compulsory regression. That's how human life is interpreted by psychological specialists."

"Heartbreaking," said Katrina.

"Oh, I can't afford to be heartbroken. He's my

crazy Absalom. His mother is finished with him. She'll talk to me. To him, never. He resembles her physically: fair-haired and slight, the boy is. A born mechanic, and a genius with engines, only he'd take apart my Porsche and leave the parts lying on the ground."

"Does he hate you?"

"He doesn't use such language."

Why, the boy may kill him in the end, Katrina thought. The one who's loyal may be the one who pays with his life.

"Enough of that," said Wrangel. "Getting back to Victor. It wasn't by his opinions that he influenced my attitudes towards art, but by the way he was. I don't really *like* his ideas. In the old days I would compare him mentally to Franklin D. Roosevelt, whom I personally admired although critical of his policies."

Like Roosevelt! Of course! Both handicapped men. Katrina made some rapid comparisons. Beila was like Eleanor Roosevelt. She, Trina, was like Missy Le-Hand. Katrina remembered hearing that Missy Le-Hand, with whom Roosevelt had had a love affair, fell ill and crept away to die, and Roosevelt, busy with the war, had no time to think about her, didn't ask what had become of her. FDR was as cold as he was great. Victor, too, talked about the coldness and isolation of people—the mark of the Modern. The Modern truth was severe. Making love to a middle-class woman, it was necessary to indulge her sentiments of warmth, but to a hard judgment these had no historical reality. There was monstrousness and horror in Modern man. Useless to deny dehumanization. That was how Victor would talk, when he lay in bed like one of Picasso's naked old satyrs. But you, spread beside him—the full woman, perhaps the fat woman, woman-smelling— you perhaps knew more about him than he knew himself.

160

They now saw Victor working his way back to the booth, and Wrangel signaled to the waitress to serve their lunch. The glazed orange duck looked downright dangerous. Circles of fat swam in the spiced gravy. Famished, Victor attacked his food. His whiskey glass was soon fingerprinted with grease. He tore up his rolls over the dish and spooned up the fatty sops. He was irritable. Wrangel tried to make conversation, as a host should do. Victor gave him a gloomy if not sinister look—a glare, to be more accurate—when Wrangel began to point out connections between cartoons and abstract ideas. When people spoke of ideas as "clear," didn't they mean reductive? Human beings, in reduction, represented as *things*. Acceptable enough when they were funny. But suppose the intention wasn't funny, as shorthand representations of the human often were, then you got an abstract condensation of the Modern theme. Take Picasso and Daumier as caricaturists (much deference in this to Victor, the expert). It might be fair to say that Daumier treated a social subject: the middle class, the courtroom. Picasso didn't. In Picasso you had the flavor of nihilism that went with increased abstraction. Wrangel in his rolls of fur and his chin supported by silk scarf and cotton bandanna was nervous, insecure of tone, twitching.

"What's this about reason?" said Victor. "First you tell me that ideas are trivial, they're dead, and then what do you do but discuss ideas with me?"

"There's no contradiction, is there, if I say that abstract ideas and caricature go together?"

"I have little interest in discussing this," said Victor. "It'll keep until you get back to California, won't it?"

"I suppose it will."

"Well, then, stow it. Skip it. Stuff it."

"It's a pity that my success in sci-fi should be held against me. Actually I've had a better than average training in philosophy."

"Well, I'm not in the mood for philosophy. And I don't want to discuss the nihilism that goes with reason. I figure you've done enough to fuck up the consciousness of millions of people with this mish-mash of astrophysics and divinity that has made you so famous. Your trouble is that you'd like to sneak up on real seriousness. Well, you've already made your contribution. Your statement is on record."

"You yourself have written about 'divine sickness,' Victor. I would suppose that any creature, regardless of his worldly status, had one ticket good for a single admission if he has suffered—if he paid his price."

But Victor wouldn't hear him out. He made a face so satirical, violent, so killing that Katrina would have turned away from it if it hadn't been so extraordinary —an aspect of Victor never manifested before. He drew his lips over his teeth to imitate bare gums. He gabbled in pantomime, not a sound coming out. He let out his tongue like a dog panting. He squeezed his eyes so tight that you couldn't see anything except the millipede brows and lashes. He put his thumbs to the sides of his head and waggled his fingers. Then he slid himself out of the booth, took up the duffel, and started for the door. Katrina, too, stood up. She held Vanessa's fiddle in her arms, saying, "I'd apologize for him if you didn't also know him. He's in very bad shape, Mr. Wrangel, you can see that for yourself. Last year we nearly lost him. And he's in pain every day. Try to remember that. I'm sorry about this. Don't let him get to you."

"Well, this is a lesson. Of course, it makes me very sad. Yes, I see he's in bad shape. Yes, it's a pity."

It had cut him up, and Katrina's heart went out to

Wrangel. "Thank you," she said, drawing away, turning. She hoped she didn't look too clumsy from the rear.

Victor was waiting for her in the concourse and she spoke to him angrily. "That was bad behavior. I didn't like being a party to it."

"When he started on me with Daumier and Picasso, I couldn't stand it, not a minute more of it."

"You feel rotten and you took it out on him."

He conceded this in silence.

"You didn't behave well with me, either. You never said a word about your conversation with Kinglake, and whether we're getting out of here or not."

"He's sending a corporate plane for us. He says it can get through."

"Now, you know I'm in trouble if I'm stuck in Detroit overnight."

"You're not going to be stuck. A plane is coming for us."

Once more, thousands of people. Nothing he could think of accounted for the sorrow she was feeling in the crowd-crazed concourse. Victor stopped beside the blazing window of a costume jewelry boutique and stared down into her face. He was speaking to her. She could not hear. Her ears seemed plugged.

"You should have told me sooner. You know my anxiety about being stuck."

"Why *should* I put up with a guy like Wrangel?" he said. "Thousands of people zero in on me. They come to clean up their act, or make a bid to change their act altogether. They want better clichés to live by. A man like Wrangel has to achieve another 'self' because he's in a position he never expected to reach. When he turned up in the Village long ago, he made himself striking by restringing his violin or by being a comic-strip plot spinner whose *real* life was with Hegel and

Pascal. Now he's become a big pop symbol, so he's completely lost. Wears Arctic fox. All right, if you don't stand up to the real conditions of life and stand up to them with strength and shrewdness, you are condemned to live by one poor fiction or another, of which you are the commonplace interpreter. Their commonplaces sting these guys without mercy, and drive them to try to be original. See how hard Wrangel was trying. He wanted me to adopt him and be his spiritual uncle or something—too old for a father. A while back I got a letter from a guy, an artist, who works in fire extinguishers. He said he was guarding the human soul from the arsonists of evil. He would never paint anything except fire extinguishers. He demanded my blessing. *I* have no Secret Service to protect me. I have to fend 'em off myself."

"All right. . . . Now, what are we supposed to do until the plane arrives?"

"There's a hotel on these premises, upstairs, out of this madhouse. Kinglake has reserved a room for us."

"Thank God! I can't face any more shoving and pushing up and down the corridors," said Katrina. "What kind of plane are they sending?"

"A plane. How should I know? You're overreacting. This is not such an awful crisis. The Negro woman wouldn't desert the kids, and there's your sister."

"I've been trying to tell you. My sister is half bonkers."

"I had words with Kinglake about Felsher, the man who is supposed to introduce me. I said he was an old Stalinist bum, and he'd give a low tone to the occasion. It's too late to change the program, but I put my objection on record."

"Can we go up to the room, Victor? You have a rest. I have to use the phone."

They made their way to the hotel desk. They were expected. Victor signed the card and he refused a bellhop. "We don't want help. Nothing to carry. We're just waiting for our plane." Why should it cost a buck to put the key in the lock?

When he came into the room, Victor pitched himself heavily on the bed and Katrina removed his shoes. They must have been size sixteen. Nevertheless, his feet were delicate in shape. A human warmth was released from these shoes when she pulled them off. She stacked pillows behind his head. As he made himself comfortable, he was aware again of the bristling of nerve ends in the belly. Surgical damage. The frayed ends of copper wires. Hair-darts ingrown.

"I'm calling my sister. Don't worry, I'll tell the operator to cut in."

She went down the list of numbers Dotey had given her. People answered who were rude and hung up—behavior was getting worse and worse. At last she reached her sister, who said she was on the far South Side, fifteen miles from home, twenty-five from Evanston. Hazardous driving. "Too bad about all this snow," she said. It was, however, satisfaction and not sympathy that her voice expressed.

"Did you call Evanston? Is Ysole there?"

"Ysole wanted me to tell her where you were. She didn't believe you were in Schaumburg. She said that Krieggstein phoned in several times. He does stand by you, doesn't he? He's in love with you, Trina."

"He's a friend to me."

"Where are you, by the way?"

"We had to land in Detroit."

"Detroit! Jesus! I heard that O'Hare was closing. Can you get back?"

"A little late. Not too much. Did Ysole say that Alfred had called? By now the psychiatrist has told the lawyer about the canceled appointment, and if his lawyer has heard, so has mine."

"You encourage Krieggstein too much," said Dotey.

"I'm one of many. He courts ten ladies at a time."

"So he says. It's you he's fascinated by. After Victor goes, he'll close in. You may be too beat to resist him."

"You're being very ugly to me, Dorothea."

Victor had pulled a pillow over the top of his head like a cowl. His eyes were closed, and he said, "Don't tangle with her. Bottle up your feelings."

"Let's conclude. I'm tying up a customer's line," said Dotey.

"I count on you to stand by. . . ."

"To go to Evanston tonight is out of the question. I've accepted a dinner invitation."

"You didn't mention that last night."

"I'm sitting with business associates," Dotey was saying. "You can reach me at home between six and eight."

"All right," said Katrina. Very quietly, obedient to Victor, she put down the phone.

"Be a sweetheart and turn off the air conditioning, Katrina. I hate this fucking false airflow in hotels. The motor gets me down. These places more and more resemble funeral parlors."

Katrina's face as she turned the switch was blotched with the stings her sister had inflicted on her. "Dotey has like an instinct against me. When I'm in trouble she's always ready to give me more lumps."

"You'll manage without her. We'll fly back in an executive jet. You'll go to Evanston in a limousine." To these words of comfort Victor added, "The kids love a snowfall. They're out playing, and they're happy. I'd give you odds." Even he was somewhat

166

surprised by the gentleness of his tone. He was in a melting mood. It seemed to him that even when making faces at Wrangel he hadn't felt harsh—playful rather. How to see such an occurrence: Chief Iffucan, the Indian in his caftan, the old man with henna hackles. Barbarous charm. It was possible for Wulpy to take such a view. The irritation of his scars had abated. He did not listen to Katrina's next conversation, which was with Ysole. What he was led to consider (again, a frequent subject) was the limits he had never until lately reckoned with. Now he touched limits on every side: "Thou hast appointed his bounds that he cannot pass." For the representative of American energy and action these omnipresent touchable bounds were funny-lamentable. What was a *weak* "barbarian"? Newfangled men needed strength. Philosophers of action must be able to act. Of course, Wulpy had had his intimations of helplessness (the Biblical "appointed bounds" didn't count, those were from another life—the *yivrach katzail,* "he fleeth as a shadow," he had studied as a boy). The bad leg had not been a limitation. It had been an aid to ascendancy. As perhaps the foot of Oedipus had been. But no longer than three years ago he had had his mother lying in the back seat of his beat-up Pontiac, serving for the afternoon as an ambulance. An old cousin had telephoned to say that his mother was virtually speechless in the nursing home where he kept her. He had finally gone to inspect this unspeakable tenement. He packed her bag and checked her out of there. That afternoon, a day of killing heat, he drove from one joint to another and tried to place her. He visited nursing homes, locking her in the car (bad neighborhoods) while he climbed stairs—the torment of getting two feet on each tread—to look at bedrooms, enter kitchens and bathrooms, and discuss terms with a bedlam population of "administrators," otherwise "dollar psychotics," who tore the money from you. (Not that he didn't fight for every buck. "Licensed abuse," he told them. "A horrible rip-off.") At four o'clock he had still not found the right place for her, that semiconscious regal monument in the back seat of his jalopy. And while he drove around Astoria and Jackson Heights, Katrina—in fantasy—drove her car behind him, tailgating him between red walls of dead brick. This imaginary Katrina wore nothing but a coat, under which she was naked, in a state of sexual readiness. When he parked and hobbled into a building, he imagined that she had pulled up behind, invisibly, and that she was streaming under the buckled Aquascutum coat. That this was a commonplace fantasy, he knew well. But he accepted it. Apparently he needed to imagine the woman-slime odor—that swamp-smell—and the fever that came with it was peculiarly his. At last Wulpy had found a good place, or maybe just gave up, and his mother was carried in while he wrote the check. The old girl seemed indifferent by now. In a matter of months she was dead, leaving Victor with his ideas and his travels, his erotic activities—the whole vivid stir: an important man, making important statements, publishing important articles. Shortly after his mother died, he himself entered Mass. General. There he escaped death, but became aware that it was necessary to consider the appointed bounds. Something like a great river was going to change its course. A Mississippi was about to find a new bed. Whole cities would drown. Mansions would float across the Gulf of Mexico, lifted from their foundations, and come aground on the sands of Venezuela.

"Where are you anyway, Trina?" said Ysole.

"I had to attend a meeting in Schaumburg, and I'm stuck out here."

"All right," said Ysole. "Give me that suburban number where you're at." When Katrina made no answer, Ysole said, "You never would tell the truth if you could lie instead."

Look at it this way: There was a howling winter space between them. The squat Negro woman with her low deformed hips who pressed the telephone to her ear, framed in white hair, was far shrewder than Katrina and was (with a black nose and brown mouth formed by nature for amusement) amused by her lies and antics. Katrina considered. Suppose that I told her, "I'm in a Detroit motel with Victor Wulpy. And right now he's getting out of bed to go to the bathroom." What use could such facts be to her? Ysole said, "Your friend the cop and your sister both checked in with me."

"If I'm not home by five, when Lilburn comes, give him a drink, and have dinner there, too."

"This is our regular night for bingo. We go to the church supper."

"I'll pay you fifty bucks, which is more than you can win at the church."

Ysole said no.

Katrina again felt: Everybody has power over me. Alfred, punishing me, the judge, the lawyers, the psychiatrist, Dotey—even the kids. They all apply standards nobody has any use for, except to stick you with. That's what drew me to Victor, that he wouldn't let anybody set conditions for him. Let others make the concessions. That's how I'd like to be. Except that I haven't got his kind of ego, which is a whole mountain of ego. Now it's Ysole's turn. "Are you holding me up, Ysole?" she said.

"Trina, I wouldn't stay for five hundred. I had to fight Lilburn for this one night of the week. When do you figure to get home?"

"As fast as I can."

"Well, the kids will be all right. I'll lock the doors, and they can watch TV."

They hate us, said Trina to herself, after Ysole had hung up. They hate us terribly.

She needed Visine to ease the burning of her eyes. In the winter she was subject to eye inflammation. She thought it was because exhaust gases clung closer to the ground in zero weather and the winter air stank more. She opened her purse and sat on the edge of the bed raking through keys, compacts, paper tissues, dollar bills, credit cards, emery boards.

"You got nowhere with the telephone, I see," said Victor. He was now standing above her, and he passed his hand through her hair. There was always some skepticism mixed with his tenderness when he approached her, as if he were sorry for her, sorry for all that she would never understand, that he would never do. Then he made a few distracted observations —unusual for him. Again he mentioned the air-conditioning unit. He couldn't find the switch that turned it off. It reminded him of the machinery he had heard for the first time when he was etherized as a kid for surgery on his leg. Unconscious, he saw a full, brilliant moon. An old woman tried to climb over a bar—the diameter of this throbbing moon. If she had made it he would have died. "Those engines may have been my own heartbeats. Invisible machinery has affected me ever since. And you know how much invisible machinery there is in a place like this—all the jets, all the silicon-chip computers. . . . Now, Katrina, do something for me. Reach under my belt. Put your delicious hand down there. I need a touch from you. It's one of the few things I can count on."

She did it. It was not too much to ask of a woman of

mature years. A matter between human friends. Signs of eagerness were always instantaneous. Never failing.

"What about a quickie, Trina?"

"But the phone will ring."

"All the better, under pressure."

"In these boots?"

"Just pull down your things."

Victor lowered himself towards her. To all that was exposed he applied his cheeks, warmth to warmth, to her thighs, on her belly with its faint trail of hairs below the navel. The telephone was silent. It didn't ring. They were winning, winning, winning, winning. They won!

That was what Victor said to her. "We got some of our own back."

"We were due for *one* break," said Katrina. "Dizzy luck. I'm spinning around."

"Let's stay put awhile. Don't get up. There's a Russian proverb: If late for an appointment, walk slower. We're best off just as we are. Kinglake would have rung us if the plane weren't on its way."

"Do you think it's after sundown, Victor?"

"How would we know from here? We're on the inside of the inside of the inside. Why worry? You'll be only a little late. They have to get me there. No Wulpy, no festival. It's a test for *them,* a challenge they've accepted."

They rested on the edge of the bed, legs hanging. He took Katrina's hand, kissed her fingers. He was a masterful, cynical man, but with her at times like these he put aside his cynicism. She took it as a sign—how much he cared for her. He much enjoyed talking when they lay together like this. She could recall many memorable things he had said on such occasions: "You could write better than Fonstine"—

171

one of his enemies—"if you took off your shoes and pounded the keyboard with your rosy heels. Or just by lifting your skirts and sitting on the machine with your beautiful bottom. The results would be more inspiring."

Victor now mentioned Wrangel. "He wanted to establish a relationship."

"He has great respect—admiration for you," said Katrina. "He said that to him when he came to the Village in the fifties—just a kid—you were in a class with Franklin D. Roosevelt. Meant to be a great man."

"I was sure he would do lots of talking while I was on the telephone. Well, not to be modest about it, Katrina . . ." (And what was there to be modest about? They lay together at the foot of the bed, bare between the waist and the knees. His arm was still under her shoulders.) "In some respects I can see . . . I thought what I would do with power. It gave me an edge over intellectuals who never tried to imagine power. This was why they couldn't *think*. I have more iron in me. My ideas had more authority because I conceived what I would do in authority. It's my nature. . . ." He paused. "It *was* my nature. I'm going to have to part with my nature presently. All the more reason to increase the dispassionate view I always preferred."

"Talking like this, just after sex?" said Katrina.

"I would have done well in a commanding situation. I have the temperamental qualifications. Don't flinch from being a reprobate. Naturally political, and I have a natural contempt for people in private life who have no power-stir. Let it be in thought, let it be in painting. It has to be a powerful reading of the truth of existence. Metaphysical passion. You get as much truth as you have the courage to approach."

Having nobody but me to tell this to. This was one of Katrina's frequent thoughts—she was disappointed for his sake. If there had been a pad to the right of her she might have taken notes. She did have *some* idea what he was saying.

"Some of the sharpest pains we feel come from the silence imposed on the deepest inward mining that we do. The most unlikely-looking people may be the most deep miners. I've often thought, 'He, or she, is intensely at work, digging in a different gallery, but the galleries are far apart, in parallels which never meet, and the diggers are deaf to one another's work.' It must be one of the wickedest forms of human suffering. And it could explain the horrible shapes often taken by what we call 'originality.'"

"Was there nothing Wrangel said that had any value?"

"I might have been interested by his guru. I had a sense of secondhand views. I don't think Wrangel had any hot news for me. If this is something like the end of time—for this civilization—everything already is quite clear and intelligible to alert minds. In our *real* thoughts, and I don't mean what we say—what's said is largely hokum—in the real thoughts, alert persons recognize what is happening. There may have been something in what Wrangel said—still echoing his guru—about the connections made by real thoughts: a true thought may have a true image corresponding to it. Do you know why communication broke down with Wrangel? It was uncomfortable to hear a California parody of things that I had been thinking myself. I've been very troubled, Katrina. And the ideas I've developed over sixty years don't seem to help me to cope with the trouble. I made an extreme commitment to lucidity. . . ."

"But aren't you lucid?"

"That's my *mental* lucidity. I've been having lucid impressions—like dreams, visions—instead of lucid ideas."

"What's this about?"

"Well, there's shared knowledge that we don't talk about. That deaf deep mining."

"Like what?"

"Cryptic persistent suggestions: the dead are not really *dead*. Or, we don't create thoughts, as that movie drip suggested. A thought *is* real, already created, and a real thought can pay you a visit. I think I understand why this happens to me. After so many years in the arts, you begin to assume that the value of life is bound up with the value of art. And there is no rational basis for this. Then you begin to suspect that it's the 'rational' that lacks real meaning. Rationality would argue back that it's the weakening of the organism that suggests this. A stupid argument." Victor refrained from speaking of the erotic side of this—magical, aesthetic, erotic—or of what this final flare-up of eroticism might mean. It might mean that he was paying out from his last fibers for lucidity of impression and for sexual confirmation of the fact that he still existed. But full strength, strong fibers, only made you more capable of lying to yourself, of maintaining the *mauvaise foi,* the false description of your personal reality. He didn't mention to Katrina the underground music which signified (had signified to Mark Antony) that the god Hercules was going away.

He changed the subject. He said to Katrina, "It's a real laugh that Wrangel should mix me up in his mind with FDR."

Roosevelt, too, was dying at a moment when to have strength was more necessary than ever. And hadn't there been a woman with him at Warm Springs when he had his brain hemorrhage?

"Didn't it ever occur to you?" said Katrina.

"It occurred, but I didn't encourage the thought. Stalin made a complete fool of the man. Those trips to Teheran and Yalta must have been the death of him. They were ruinous physically. I'm certain that Stalin meant to hasten his death. Terrible journeys. Roosevelt felt challenged to demonstrate his vigor. Stalin didn't budge. Roosevelt let himself be destroyed, proving his strength as chief of a great power, and also his 'nobility.'"

Katrina, who had moved her round face closer—a girl posing for a "sweetheart snapshot," cheek to cheek—said, "Aren't you cold? Wouldn't you like me to pull the covers over you? No? At least slide your fingers under me to warm up."

To encourage him she turned on her side. A gambit she could always count on—the smooth shape of her buttocks, their crème de Chantilly whiteness. He always laughed when she offered herself this way, and put out his big, delicate hands. Something of a tough guy he really was, and particularly with age distortion—the wrecked Picasso Silenus reaching towards the nude beauty. She felt a sort of aristocratic delicacy from him even when he was manipulating these round forms of hers. It was really a bit crazy, the pride she took in her bottom. He matched up the freckles on each cheek—she had two prominent birthmarks—as if they were eyes. "Now you're squinting. Now you're cross-eyed. Now you're planning a conspiracy." Victor paused and said, "This is what little Wrangel was saying about cartoons and abstractions, isn't it? Making these faces?" Then he smoothed her gently and said, "It's no figure of speech to say that your figure leaves me speechless."

It was at this moment that the telephone began to ring, again and again—merciless. It was the desk.

Their plane was just now landing. The limousine had started out. They were to be downstairs in five minutes.

They waited in the cold, under the bright lights. Victor had his stick and the mariner's cap—the broad mustache, the wonderful face, the noble ease in all circumstances. The Thinker Prince. Never quite up to his great standard, she felt just a little clumsy beside him. She was in charge of the damned fiddle, too. To hold an instrument she couldn't play. It turned her into a native bearer. She should set it on her head. And there they were on the edges of Detroit, standing on one of its crusts of light. Just like the other blasted cities of the northern constellation— Buffalo, Cleveland, Chicago, St. Louis—all those fields of ruin that looked so golden and beautiful by night.

"*This* is no limousine," said Victor, irritated, when the car stopped. "It's a goddamn compact Honda."

But he made no further fuss about it. Opening the door of the car and taking a grip on the edge of the roof, he began to install himself in the front seat. First there was the stiff leg to get in, over on the driver's end, by the brake, and then he eased in his head and his huge back so that, as he turned, the car was crammed to the top. Then he descended into the seat with patient, clever labor. It was like a difficult intromission. But as soon as he was in place, and while Katrina was settling herself in the back, he was already talking. Nerving himself for the approaching lecture, tuning up? "Did you ever get through the Céline book I gave you?"

"The *Journey?* I did, finally."

"It's not agreeable, but it is important. It's one of those French things I've had on my mind."

"Like the Baudelaire?"

"Right." The driver had taken off swiftly by a dark side road, along fences. Victor made an effort to turn in the small seat; he wanted to look at her. Apparently he wished to make a statement not only in words but also with his face. "Didn't you think Céline was truly terrifying? He uses the language that people everywhere really use. He expresses the ideas and feelings they really share."

"Last time we spoke about it you said those were the ideas that made France collapse in 1940. And that the Germans also had those same ideas."

"I don't think that was exactly what I said. Talking about nihilism . . ."

Why had he asked her to read that book? Towards the end of it—a nightmare—a certain adventurer named Robinson refused to tell a woman that he loved her, and this "loving" woman, enraged, had shot him dead. Not even when she pointed the gun at him in the taxicab could she make him say the words "I love you." The "loving" woman was really a maniac, while the man, the "lover," although he was himself a crook, a deadbeat, a murderer, had one shred of honor left, and that, too, was in the terminal stage. Better dead than carried off for life by this loony ogress whom he would have to pretend to "love." It wasn't so much the book that had shocked Katrina—a book was only a book—but the fact that he, Victor, had told her to read it. Of course, he was always pushing the widest possible perspective of historical reality. The whole universe was his field of operations. A cosmopolitan in the fullest sense, a giant of comprehension, he was located in the central command post of comprehension. "Face the destructive facts. No palliatives," was the kind of thing he said.

"That book was next door to the murder camps," she said.

"I don't deny it."

"Well, back at the hotel you said that alert people everywhere were recognizing the same facts. But same isn't quite the way it was in the Céline book. Not even for you, Victor."

There was no time to answer. The car had stopped at the small private-aircraft building. When the driver ran from the front seat to open her door, she thought his face was distorted. Maybe it was only the cold that made him grimace. Extricating himself from the car, Victor again caught at the roof and hopped backwards, drawing out the bad leg.

They entered the overilluminated shack. At the counter, where phones were jingling, Trina gave the name Wulpy to the dispatcher. The man said, "Yes, your Cessna is on the ground. It'll taxi up in a few minutes."

She passed the news to Victor, who nodded but went on talking. "I'll grant you, the French had been had by their ideology. An ideology is a spell cast by the ruling class, a net of binding falsehoods, and the discovery of this can throw people into a rage. That's why Céline is violent."

"People? *Some* people."

You have a love affair and then you ask your ladylove to read a book to discredit love, and it's the most extreme book you can select. That's some valentine.

Her ostrich boots gave her no sense of elegance as she preceded him into the Cessna. She felt clumsy and thick, every graceless thing that a woman can be, and she carried Vanessa's instrument across her chest. By the light of the lurid revolving bubble on the fuselage, she watched Victor being assisted into the plane. The

two-man crew received Victor and Katrina with particular consideration. This was how the personnel
were trained for these executive ferrying jobs. Passengers were guests. Would they care for coffee? And
fresh doughnuts, or powdered bismarcks? Or would
they prefer whiskey? The afternoon papers hadn't
been available when they left Chicago. They did,
however, have *Barron's* and the *Wall Street Journal*.
The seats were luxurious—as much leg room as you
liked, excellent reading lights. Here was the panel
with its many switches. Neither of the passengers
cared to read just now.

The pilot said, "We'll be landing at Midway, and
you'll get a helicopter ride to Meigs."

"Well, this is more like it," said Victor. "You see?"
She translated "You see?" as an assertion that he had
not misled her. He had sent for her, and he was
returning her to Chicago. He had the power to make
good all assurances. He raised his whiskey glass. We'll
drink to you and me. Something like a smile passed
over his face, but he was also ruffled, moody. His
eyes, those narrow canals, were black with mortal
injury. None of these powers—summoning special
machines, commanding special privileges—really
seemed to mean a thing. Doodads for a canary's cage.
"Oh, yes, you're a pilot yourself," he remembered.

"Not one of these planes," said Katrina. She held
up her wristwatch to the light. Ysole would have left
the house by now.

Suddenly the silence of the cabin was torn by a
furious roar. Nothing could be heard. The plane
bumped across the icy seams of the field. Then came
the clean run and they were (thank God!) airborne.
Their course would take them southwest across Lake
Michigan. It was just as well in this weather that the
water should be invisible. The parlorlike neatness of

the cabin was meant to give a sense of safety. She tasted the coffee—it was freeze-dried, it was not hot. When she bit into the jelly doughnut, she liked the fragrance of the fried dough but not the cold jelly that gushed out.

He may have had no special intention in giving her the Céline book to read. If so, why did he bring it up now? And what of the dowager Beila, to whom Vanessa had recommended the book on homosexual foreplay? They *were* a bookish family, weren't they. But this was to misread Beila completely. You could no more think of her that way than you could think of Queen Victoria. And Victor did not encourage discussions of Beila. Sometimes he spoke of "wives of a certain kind." "Perfect happiness for wives of a certain kind is to immobilize their husbands." The suggestion was that a man in his seventies who had barely survived Mass. General and had a bad leg was a candidate for immobilization. You could as easily immobilize Niagara Falls. A perfectly objective judgment of Beila, removing all rivalry and guilt, was that she behaved with dignity. When it looked as if Victor was not going to make it at Mass. General, Beila had asked him whether he wanted to see Katrina, who was hiding in one of the waiting rooms. Victor did want to see her, and Beila had sent for her, and had withdrawn from the room also, to let them take leave of each other. Then Katrina and Victor had gripped hands. He seemed unable to speak. She wept with heartbreak. She told him that she would always love him. He held her hand fast and said, "This is it, kid." His tongue was impeded, but he was earnest and clear, she remembered. And since then, she thought how important it was that her claim to access should be affirmed, and that his feeling for her should be acknowledged. It wasn't just another adultery. She wasn't one of his casual women. Before death, his emotions were open, and she came—when she rushed in she was bursting. Her suffering was conceded its rights. Their relationship was certified; it took a sort of formal imprint from the sickroom. Last farewells. He was dying. When he released her hand, meaning that it was time to go—too much for him, perhaps, too painful—and she went out sobbing, she saw the distant significant figure of Beila down the corridor, watching or studying her.

Well, what had Beila's generosity achieved, when Victor was on his feet again? It only made matters simpler for the lovers. Then this creepy, rabbinical, fiddling, meddling, and bratty daughter advised a mother in her late sixties to learn to tickle and to suck, use advanced techniques of lewdness. ("For two cents I'd throw her fiddle right into the lake! Little bitch!") Beila needed all the dignity she could muster. And especially with a husband whose description might be: "Others abide our judgment, thou art free!" Finally Victor himself bringing up the ultimate, hellish judgment on "love"—that love was something *"dégueulasse."* Like spoiled meat; dogs would walk away from it, but "lovers" poured out some "tenderness sauce" and then it became a dainty dish to set before the king—handing Katrina such a book to read.

That wasn't what he had been like in Mass. General, with death on top of him.

It occurred to her that his aim was to desensitize her feelings so that when he died—and he felt it coming—she would suffer less.

But he did play rough. A few years ago he had suggested that Joe So-and-so, a nice young poet, very pretty, too, no ball of fire, though, was attentive to her. "Do you think you might like him?" That may have been a test. Just as possibly it was an attempt to get rid of her, and his estimation of So-and-so's talent (no secret that there *was* no talent) also told Katrina how he ranked her on a realistic scale—a dumpy sexpot, varicose veins, uneven gum line, crème de Chantilly inner thighs but otherwise no great shakes. Her oddities happened to suit him, Victor. But there were idiosyncrasies, and then there were real standards. Since his miraculous recovery he had made no offensive matchmaking suggestions. He even seemed to suspect, jealously, that she was looking around, in the glamour world to which he had introduced her. She wouldn't have been surprised if, by insulting Wrangel and trying to make her a party to the insult, Victor had tried to eliminate this celebrity producer as a rival. He was a very cunning man, Victor. This afternoon's sex, for instance, had it been desire or had it been payola? No, no; even Dotey said, "You're his only turn-on." That was the truth. She brought Victor to life again. The *"caresse qui fait revivre les morts."* The man's sexual resurrection.

The door of the cockpit was open. Beyond the shoulders of the pilots were the lights of the instrument panel. The copilot occasionally glanced back at the passengers. Then he said, "It's getting a little bumpy. Better fasten those belts." A patch of rough air? It was far worse than that. The plane was knocked, thumped like a speeding speedboat by the waves. Victor, who had been savagely silent, finally took notice. He reached for Katrina's hand. The pilots now closed the door to the cockpit. Underfoot, plastic cups, liquor bottles, doughnuts were sliding leftwards.

"You realize how tilted we are, Victor?"

"They must be trying to climb out of this turbulence. In a big plane you wouldn't notice. We've both flown through worse weather."

"I don't believe that."

The overhead light became dimmer and dimmer. Various shades of darkness were what you saw in Katrina's face. On Victor's cheekbones the red color seemed laid on with a brush. "They couldn't be having a power failure—what do you think, Victor?"

"I don't believe that." As was his custom, he sketched out a summary. It included Katrina and took the widest possible overview. They were in a Cessna because he had accepted a lecture invitation, a trip not strictly necessary and which (for himself he took it calmly) might be fatal. For Katrina it was even less than necessary. For her he was sorry. She was here because of him. But then it came home to him that he didn't understand a life so different from his own. Why did anybody want to live such a life as she lived? I know why I did mine. Why does she do hers? It was a wicked question, even put comically, for it had its tinge of comedy. But when he had put the question he felt exposed, without any notice at all, to a kind of painful judgment. Supposedly, his life had had real scale, it produced genuine ideas, and these had caused significant intellectual and artistic innovations. All of that was serious. Katrina? Not serious. Divorcing, and then pursuing a prominent figure—the pursuit of passion, high pleasure? Such old stuff—*not* serious! Nevertheless, they were together now, both leaning far over in the banking plane; same destiny for them both. He was her reason for being here, and she was (indirectly) his. Vanessa, for female reasons, put Katrina in a rage, but her knees (sexual even now) gripped the violin protectively. He had often said, conceded, that the obscurest and most powerful question, deeper than politics, was that of an understanding between man and woman. And he knew very well that Katrina had formed absurd visions of what she would do with him—take him away from Beila, then serve him for the rest of his life, then achieve unbelievable social elevation, preside over a salon, then become known after his death as a legendary woman of wide knowledge and great subtlety. This mixed Katrina, a flutter of images, both commonplace and magical. Before her this man of words *was,* at times, speechless. He doted on her *because! Because* she was just within the line separating grace from clumsiness, *because* of the sensual effect, on him, of her fingers, *because* of the pathos of her knees holding the violin. She held him better than any fiddle. And now will you tell me what *any* of this has to do with the *ideas* of Victor Wulpy! What had made him really angry with Wrangel was that he had said most ideas were trivial —meaning, principally, that Victor's own ideas were trivial. And if Victor could not explain Katrina's sexual drawing power, the Eros that (only just) kept him from disintegrating, Wrangel did have a point, didn't he? Katrina, as a subject for thought, was the least trivial of all. Of all that might be omitted in thinking, the worst was to omit your own being. You had lost, then. You heard the underground music of your ancestor Hercules growing fainter as he abandoned you. All you were left with was lucidity, final superlucidity, which was delayed until you reached the border of death. Any minute now he might discover what the other side of the border was like.

He had heard planes making stress noises before, but nothing like the crackling of metal about him now, as if the rivets were going to pop like old-time collar buttons. Wings after all were very slight. Even in calm blue daylight, when they quivered, you thought: A pair of ironing boards, that's all.

"Victor, we're banking the other way. . . . I've never seen it so bad."

No comment. No denying the obvious. The plane tumbled like a playing card.

"If we go down . . ."

"It'll be my fault. *I* got you into this."

There was a moment of level flight. Victor wondered why his heart rate had not increased. He didn't hold his breath, he was not sweating, when the plane dropped again.

"You don't even mind too much," said Katrina.

"Of course I mind."

"Now listen, Victor. If it's death any minute, if we're going to end in the water . . . I'm going to ask you to tell me something."

"Don't start that, Katrina."

"It's very simple. I just want you to say it. . . ."

"Come off it, Katrina. With so much to think about, at a time like this, you ask me *that*? Love?" Temper made his voice fifelike again. His mouth expanded, the mustache widening also. He was about to speak even more violently.

She cut him off. "Don't be awful with me now, Victor. If we're going to crash, why shouldn't you say it? . . ."

"You grab this opportunity to twist my arm."

"If we don't love each other, what are we doing? How did we get here?"

"We got here because you're a woman and I'm a man, and that's how we got here."

An odd thought, he had: Atheists accept extreme unction. The wife urges, and the dying man nods. Why not?

In the next interval they felt the controlled lift of the aircraft. They had found smoother air again and were sailing more calmly. Katrina, still in suspense, began to think about gathering her storm-scattered spirits.

"We may be okay," said Victor.

She felt that she was less okay than she had ever been. My God! what a lot of ground I lost, she was thinking.

The cockpit door slid back, and the copilot said, "All right? That was a bad patch. But we're coming up on South Chicago in a minute." A spatter of words, an incomprehensible crackle, came from the control tower at Midway.

Victor was silent, but he looked good-humored. What a man he was for composure! And he didn't hold ridiculous things against you. He was really very decent that way. *M*A*S*H,* for instance. He couldn't say, "I love you." It would have been *mauvaise foi.* Death staring you in the face was no excuse. She was going back and forth over her words, his words, while the plane made its approach and its landing. She was mulling all of it over even when they whirled off in the helicopter, under the slapping blades. The way girls were indoctrinated: Don't worry, dear, love will solve your problems. Make yourself deserving, and you'll be loved. People are crazy, but they're not *too* crazy. So you won't actually be murdered. You'll be okay. And with this explanation from a dopey mother (and Mother really was stupid), you went into action.

Victor said to her, "You see how these executives do things?"

"What is it, about six o'clock? I'll be two hours late back to Evanston."

"After they drop me, they can run you home. I'll tell them to. Do me a favor and take the fiddle home with you."

"All right, I will." Tomorrow she'd have to bring it to Bein and Fushi.

She didn't like the look of him at Meigs Field. Another time it might have excited her to land here.

The blues of the ground lights were so bright, and the revolving reds so vivid and clear against the snow. But Victor was very slow getting out of the machine, which made her sore at heart. A fellow shook hands with him. That was Mr. Kinglake, who handed them into a big car. They came out between the aquarium and the museum and proceeded, all power and luxury like a funeral livery, to Randolph Street, and north on Michigan Boulevard to the 333 Building. Victor, keeping his own counsel all this while, squeezed her fingers before he got out.

"Tomorrow?" he said.

"Sure, tomorrow. And *merde* for luck. Don't let those people throw you."

"Not to worry. I'm on top of this," said Victor.

So he was. He had gotten her back to Chicago, too.

In the cushioned warmth of the limousine, northward bound, Katrina, as she pictured Victor in the swift, rich men's gilded elevator rushing upward, upward, felt a clawing at her heart and innards—pity for the man, which he didn't feel for himself. Really, he did not. Pressed for time. He had too much to think about. All that unfinished mental business to keep him busy forever and ever. He wouldn't have liked it that she should feel clawed around the heart for his sake.

And then, had it been right to turn on a man of his stature and stick him with a cliché? But one good thing about Victor was that he was very light on your venial sins, especially the feminine ones. Still, in that case, he might have obliged her, might have spoken the words she wanted to hear. He didn't need to worry that she might make use of them later, against him.

The lake came very close to the road along the Outer Drive and made mad charges on the pilings and the beaches, rushing horribly white out of the hundreds of miles of darkness they had just crossed in the Cessna.

At Howard Street the white mausoleums and enormous Celtic crosses faced the water. It was a shame to spoil such fine real estate with graves. She disliked this stretch of the road and said to the driver, "This is a favorite speed trap for the cops." He didn't wish to answer. "Now please take me to the Orrington," she said.

She drove her car home from the garage, and had to park in a rut some distance from the curb because her driveway hadn't been cleared.

The house was dark. Nobody there. Her first fear was that Alfred had come and taken the girls away. She let herself into the warm hallway, pushing the handsome heavy white door against the resistance of a living creature: Sukie, of course, the poor old thing, not too deaf to hear the scratch of Katrina's key.

Lighted, the living room showed that Soolie and Pearl had been cutting composition paper after school. Probably Ysole had ordered them to do it. Their habit was to force you to give them commands. But where had they gone? Katrina looked in the kitchen for a message. Nothing on the bulletin board. Nothing on the dining room table. She rang Alfred's number. If he was there, he didn't answer. She telephoned Dorothea and after two rings there came Dotey's little recording, which Katrina had never heard with such dislike—Dotey being playful: "When the vibrations of the gong subside, kindly leave your name and message." The gong, to go with the bed, was also Chinese. Katrina said, "Dotey, where the hell are my kids?" Immediately she depressed the button, and when the dial tone resumed, she dialed Lieutenant Krieggstein. No one there. She considered next whether to try her lawyer. He sharply disliked being bothered at home. Just now this was not a consideration. What did matter was that she had nothing to tell him except that she feared her children had been abducted by their father while she was gone. . . . Gone where? Flying with her lover.

Sukie had followed her to the kitchen and pressed against her, needing to be taken out. Absentmindedly tender, Katrina stroked the animal's black neck. The fur was thick, but it was flimsy to the touch. Might as well walk her while I think what to do, Katrina decided, and clipped the leash to Sukie's collar. All the neighbors had been shoveled out; only the Goliger house was still under snow. The dog relieved herself at once. Obviously, no one had thought of her all day. Katrina went to the corner in her slow, hip-rich gait, the hat pushed back from her forehead—so very tired she hardly noticed the cold. Her face was aching with the strains of the day. Had Ysole taken the girls home with her? To the church bingo? That was the least likely conjecture of all.

Turning back from the corner, she saw a car parking in front of her house. Because its lights shone into her eyes, she couldn't identify it. She began trotting in her ostrich-skin boots, pulling the dog by the leash, saying, "Come on, girl. Come on."

The children were being lifted over the snow heaps and set down on the sidewalk. She recognized Krieggstein by his fedora. Also his storm coat, bulky and hampering, and his movements.

"Where did you go? Where have you been? There was no message."

"I took the children to dinner."

"Soolie. Pearl. . . . What kind of day did you have?" said Katrina.

They answered nothing at all, but Krieggstein said, "We had a great outing at Burger King. They don't fry like the other fast-food joints, they grill their meat. Then we stopped at Baskin-Robbins and bought a quart of chocolate marshmallow mousse. Good stuff."

"Did you just walk in and find them?"

"No, I took over from your Negro woman. You called her, didn't you?"

"Of course I did."

"I arranged to come by," said Krieggstein. "Didn't she tell you that?"

"She let me think she was taking off at five o'clock."

"Her idea of a joke," said Krieggstein. "I asked her to tell you that I'd be here."

"Oh, thank you, Sam."

In the hallway he helped her off with her coat. They removed it from her weary body.

Katrina's mind at that moment made an important connection. Why should Victor declare, "I love you"? For her sake, he went on the road. Would he have made such a journey for any other reason? If he was like FDR, whose death Stalin had hastened by forcing him to come to Yalta, to Teheran, why would a woman who claimed to love him impose such hardships on him?

"Whose violin is this?" said Krieggstein. "I never saw a fiddle here before."

He was taking off his storm coat, pulling down his gun-bulging jacket, smoothing his parboiled face, rubbing his frost-red eyes.

She had been right when she had said in the Cessna, "You don't even mind too much." Victor had denied it. But he could do nothing else. Her guess was that he longed to be dying. Dying would illuminate. There were ideas closely associated with dying which only dying could reveal. He probably felt that he had postponed too long; although he loved her, he couldn't postpone much longer.

"Did you call the psychiatrist?" she said.

"I did better than that, Trina. The receptionist said you were going to be charged for the hour anyway, so I went and had a talk with the guy."

"*Me* charged? *Alfred* will be charged. Did he talk to you?"

"Give me some credit. You don't make the grade of police lieutenant by dumb bungling. I gave him an impression of stability. He and I speak the same language. Working on my Ph.D. in criminology, we understood each other. I said you couldn't come because you had a female-type emergency. You had to go to the gynecologist. I came instead, as a friend of the family. *I* know what bad mothers are. My experiences as police officer: cocaine mothers, nymphomaniacs, armed prostitutes, alcoholic mothers. He could take it from me what a stable person you are."

"I'll go to the kitchen. The girls want their dessert."

They had set out the bowls and spoons. She took the scoop to the chocolate marshmallow mousse. They didn't say, "Where have you been, Mother?" She was not called upon for any alibis. Their small faces with identical bangs communicated nothing. They did have curious eyes, science-fiction eyes that dazzled and also threatened from afar. Wrangel might have seen that, too. Emissaries from another planet, grown from seeds that dropped from outer space, little invaders with iridium in their skulls. Victor was right, you know, about the way that *Star Wars* flicks corrupted everybody, implanted mistrust of your own flesh and blood. Well, okay, but now I see how to extricate my elephant.

She returned to Krieggstein to thank him, and to get rid of him. He wanted to stay and bask in her gratitude. "How good it was of you to stand by me," she said. "Ysole gave me a scare, and I thought that Alfred would come and snatch the kids."

"I'd do anything for you, Katrina," said Krieggstein. "Just now you're all wrapped up in Victor—how is he, by the way?—and I don't expect anything for my loyalty. No strings attached. . . ."

Well, Katrina had to admit that Dotey was right on target. Krieggstein was presenting himself as a successor, humble but determined. Maybe he *was* a cop, and not a loony with guns. Give him the benefit of the doubt. Let's assume he was the real thing. He was getting his degree in criminology. He was going to be chief of police, head of the FBI, he might make J. Edgar Hoover himself look insignificant—he was off the wall, nevertheless. Since Alfred had removed all the art objects, the house had felt very bare, but with a man like Krieggstein she'd learn what bareness could really be.

"Right now, the most considerate thing you could do, Sam, would be to slip out of the house and let me be. I'll just lock the door and I'll take a bath. I have to have a bath, then send the kids to bed and take a sleeping pill."

"Sorry," said Krieggstein. "In the present state of your emotions I have no business to say anything of an intimate nature. . . ."

She rose, and handed him his storm coat. "Anything of an intimate nature now, Sam, and I'll break down completely." She put her hands over her ears, saying, "I'll go to pieces under your very eyes."

Zetland:
By a
Character
Witness

YES, I KNEW THE GUY. WE WERE BOYS IN Chicago. He was wonderful. At fourteen, when we became friends, he had things already worked out and would willingly tell you how everything had come about. It went like this: First the earth was molten elements and glowed in space. Then hot rains fell. Steaming seas were formed. For half the earth's history, the seas were azoic, and then life began. In other words, first there was astronomy, and then geology, and by and by there was biology, and biology was followed by evolution. Next came prehistory and then history—epics and epic heroes, great ages, great men; then smaller ages with smaller men; then classical antiquity, the Hebrews, Rome, feudalism, papacy, renascence, rationalism, the industrial revolution, science, democracy, and so on. All this Zetland got out of books in the late twenties, in the Midwest. He was a clever kid. His bookishness pleased everyone. Over pale-blue eyes, which sometimes looked strained, he wore big goggles. He had full lips and big boyish teeth, widely spaced. Sandy hair, combed straight back, exposed a large forehead. The skin of his round face often looked tight. He was short, heavyish, strongly built but not in good health. At seven years old he had had peritonitis and pneumonia at the same time, followed by pleurisy, emphysema, and TB. His recovery was complete, but he was never free from minor ailments. His skin was peculiar. He was not allowed to be in the sun for long. Exposure to sunlight caused cloudy brown subcutaneous bruises, brownish iridescences. So, often, while the sun shone, he drew the shades and read in his room by lamplight. But he was not at all an invalid. Though he played only on cloudy days, his tennis was good, and he swam a thoughtful breaststroke with frog motions and a froggy underlip. He played the fiddle and was a good sight reader.

The neighborhood was largely Polish and Ukrainian, Swedish, Catholic, Orthodox, and Evangelical Lutheran. The Jews were few and the streets tough. Bungalows and brick three-flats were the buildings. Back stairs and porches were made of crude gray lumber. The trees were cottonwood elms and ailanthus, the grass was crabgrass, the bushes lilacs, the flowers sunflowers and elephant-ears. The heat was corrosive, the cold like a guillotine as you waited for the streetcar. The family, Zet's bullheaded father and two maiden aunts who were "practical nurses" with housebound patients (dying, usually), read Russian novels, Yiddish poetry, and were mad about culture. He was encouraged to be a little intellectual. So, in short pants, he was a junior Immanuel Kant. Musical (like Frederick the Great or the Esterhazys), witty (like Voltaire), a sentimental radical (like Rousseau), bereft of gods (like Nietzsche), devoted to the heart and to the law of love (like Tolstoy). He was earnest (the early shadow of his father's grimness), but he was playful, too. Not only did he study Hume and Kant but he discovered dada and surrealism as his voice was changing. The mischievous project of covering the great monuments of Paris in mattress ticking appealed to him. He talked about the importance of the ridiculous, the paradox of playful sublimity. Dostoyevsky, he lectured me, had it right. The intellectual (petty bourgeois-plebeian) was a megalomaniac. Living in a kennel, his thoughts embraced the universe. Hence the funny agonies. And remember Nietzsche, the *gai savoir*. And Heine and the "Aristophanes of Heaven." He was a learned adolescent, was Zetland.

Books in Chicago were obtainable. The public library in the twenties had many storefront branches along the car lines. Summers, under flipping guttapercha fan blades, boys and girls read in the hard chairs. Crimson trolley cars swayed, cowbellied, on the rails. The country went broke in 1929. On the public lagoon, rowing, we read Keats to each other while the weeds bound the oars. Chicago was nowhere. It had no setting. It was something released into American space. It was where trains arrived; where mail orders were dispatched. But on the lagoon, with turning boats, the water and the sky clear green, pure blue, the boring power of a great manufacturing center arrested (there was no smoke, the mills were crippled—industrial distress benefited the atmosphere), Zet recited "Upon the honeyed middle of the night . . ." Polack children threw rocks and crab apples from the shore.

Studying his French, German, math, and music. In his room a bust of Beethoven, a lithograph of Schubert (also with round specs) sitting at the piano, moving his friends' hearts. The shades were drawn, the lamp burned. In the alley, peddlers' horses wore straw hats to ward off sunstroke. Zet warded off the prairies, the real estate, the business and labor of Chicago. He boned away at his Kant. Just as assiduously, he read Breton and Tristan Tzara. He quoted, "The earth is blue, like an orange." And he propounded questions of all sorts. Had Lenin really expected democratic centralism to work within the Bolshevik party? Was Dewey's argument in *Human Nature and Conduct* unassailable? Was the "significant form" position fruitful for painting? What was the future of primitivism in art?

Zetland wrote surrealist poems of his own:

Plum lips suck the green of sleeping hills . . .

or:

Foaming rabbis rub electrical fish!

The Zetland apartment was roomy, inconvenient, in the standard gloomy style of 1910. Built-in buffets and china closets, a wainscot in the dining room with Dutch platters, a gas log in the fireplace, and two stained-glass small windows above the mantelpiece. A windup Victrola played "Eli, Eli," the *Peer Gynt* Suite. Chaliapin sang "The Flea" from *Faust,* Galli-Curci the "Bell Song" from *Lakmé,* and there were Russian soldiers' choruses. Surly Max Zetland gave his family "everything," he said. Old Zetland had been an immigrant. His start in life was slow. He learned the egg business in the poultry market on Fulton Street. But he rose to be assistant buyer in a large department store downtown: imported cheeses, Czech ham, British biscuits and jams—fancy goods. He was built like a fullback, with a black cleft in the chin and a long mouth. You would wear yourself out to win this mouth from its permanent expression of disapproval. He disapproved because he *knew life*. His first wife, Elias's mother, died in the flu epidemic of 1918. By his second wife old Zetland had a feebleminded daughter. The second Mrs. Zetland died of cancer of the brain. The third wife, a cousin of the second, was much younger. She came from New York; she had worked on Seventh Avenue; she had a *past*. Because of this *past* Max Zetland gave way to jealousy and made nasty scenes, breaking dishes and shouting brutally. *"Des histoires,"* said Zet, then practicing his French. Max Zetland was a muscular man who weighed two hundred pounds, but these were only scenes—not dangerous. As usual, the morning after, he stood at the bathroom mirror and shaved with his painstaking brass Gillette, made neat his reprehending face, flattened his hair like an American executive, with military brushes. Then, Russian style, he drank his tea through a sugar cube, glancing at the *Tribune,* and went off to his position in the Loop, more or less *in Ordnung*. A normal day. Descending the back stairs, a short cut to the El, he looked through the window of the first floor at his Orthodox parents in the kitchen. Grandfather sprayed his bearded mouth with an atomizer—he had asthma. Grandmother made orange-peel candy. Peels dried all winter on the steam radiators. The candy was kept in shoeboxes and served with tea.

Sitting in the El, Max Zetland wet his finger on his tongue to turn the pages of the thick newspaper. The tracks looked down on small brick houses. The El ran like the bridge of the elect over the damnation of the slums. In those little bungalows Poles, Swedes, micks, spics, Greeks, and niggers lived out their foolish dramas of drunkenness, gambling, rape, bastardy, syphilis, and roaring death. Max Zetland didn't even have to look; he could read about it in the *Trib*. The little trains had yellow cane seats. Hand-operated gates of bent metal, waist-high, let you out of the car. Tin pagoda roofs covered the El platforms. Each riser of the long staircase advertised Lydia Pinkham's Vegetable Compound. Iron loss made maidens pale. Max Zetland himself had a white face, white-jowled, a sarcastic bear, but acceptably pleasant, entering the merchandising palace on Wabash Avenue, neat in his office, smart on the telephone, fluent except for a slight Russian difficulty with initial aitches, releasing a mellow grumble when he spoke, his mind factual, tabular, prices and contracts memorized. He held in the smoke of his cigarettes as he stood by his desk. The smoke drifted narrowly from his nose. With a lowered face, he looked about. He judged with furious Jewish snobbery the laxity and brainlessness of the golf-playing goy who could afford to walk in knickers on the restricted fairway, who could be what he seemed, who had no buried fury, married no lascivious New York girls, had no idiot orphans, no house of death. Max Zetland's hard paunch subdued by the cut of his jacket, the tense muscles of his calves showing through trouser legs, the smoke-retentive nose, the rage of taciturnity—well, in the business world one must be a nice fellow. He was an executive in a great retail organization and he *was* a nice fellow. He was a short-headed man whose skull had no great depth. But his face was broad, heavily masculine, self-consciously centered between the shoulders. His hair was parted in the middle and brushed flat. There was a wide space between his front teeth, which Zet inherited. Only the unshavable pucker in his father's chin was a sign of pathos, and this hint of the pitiful Max Zetland was defied by the Russian military stoutness of his bearing, by his curt style of smoking, by the snap with which he drank a glass of schnapps. Among friends his son had various names for him. The General, the Commissar, Osipovich, Ozymandias, he often called him. "My name is Ozymandias, king of kings: Look on my works, ye Mighty, and despair!"

Before his third marriage, Ozymandias the widower would come home from the Loop with the *Evening American,* printed on peach-colored paper. He took a glass of whiskey before dinner and saw his daughter. Perhaps she was not feebleminded, only temporarily retarded. His bright son tried to tell him that Casanova was hydrocephalic until he was eight and considered an imbecile, and that Einstein was a backward child. Max hoped she might be taught to sew. He started with table manners. Meals, for a time, were horrible. She was unteachable. In her the family face was compressed, reduced, condensed into a cat's face. She stammered, she tottered, her legs were long and undeveloped. She picked up her skirt in company, she trickled on the toilet without closing the door. The kid gave away all the weaknesses of the breed. Relatives were sympathetic, but this sympathy of aunts and cousins Max sensed to be self-congratulatory. He coldly rejected it, looking straight before him and lengthening his straight mouth. When people spoke sympathetically to him about his daughter, he seemed to be considering the best way to put them to death.

Father Zetland read Russian and Yiddish poetry. He preferred the company of musical people and artists, bohemian garment workers, Tolstoyans, followers of Emma Goldman and of Isadora Duncan, revolutionists who wore pince-nez, Russian blouses, Lenin or Trotsky beards. He attended lectures, debates, concerts, and readings; the utopians amused him; he respected brains and was sold on high culture. It was obtainable in Chicago, in those days.

Facing Humboldt Park, on California Avenue, the Chicago anarchists and Wobblies had their forum; the Scandinavians had their fraternal lodges, churches, a dance hall; the Galician Jews a synagogue; the Daughters of Zion their charity day nursery. On Division Street, after 1929, little savings banks crashed. One became a fish store. A tank for live carp was made of the bank marble. The vault became an icebox. A movie house turned into a funeral parlor. Nearby, the red carbarn rose from slummy weeds. The vegetarians had a grand photo of old Count Tolstoy in the window of the Tolstoy Vegetarian Restaurant. What a beard, what eyes, and what a nose! Great men repudiated the triviality of ordinary and merely human things, including what was merely human in themselves. What was a nose? Cartilage. A beard? Cellulose. A count? A caste figure, a thing produced by epochs of oppression. Only Love, Nature, God are good and great.

In one-hundred-percent-industrial contemporary Chicago, where shadows of loveliness were lacking, a flat wheel of land meeting a flat wheel of fresh water, intelligent boys like Zet, though fond of the world, too, were not long detained by surface phenomena. No one took Zet fishing. He did not go to the woods, was not taught to shoot, nor to clean a carburetor, nor even to play billiards or to dance. Zet concentrated on his books—his astronomy, geology, etc. First the blazing mass of matter, then the lifeless seas, then pulpy creatures crawling ashore, simple forms, more complex forms, and so on; then Greece, then Rome, then Arabian algebra, then history, poetry, philosophy, painting. Still wearing knickers, he was invited by neighborhood study groups to speak on the élan vital, on the differences between Kant and Hegel. He was professorial, Germanic, the *Wunderkind,* Max Zetland's secret weapon. Old Zet would be the *man* of the family and young Zet its *genius.*

"He wanted me to be a John Stuart Mill," said Zet. "Or some shrunken little Itzkowitz of a prodigy— Greek and calculus at the age of eight, damn him!" Zet believed he had been cheated of his childhood, robbed of the angelic birthright. He believed all that old stuff about the sufferings of childhood, the lost paradise, the crucifixion of innocence. Why was he sickly, why was he myopic, why did he have a greenish color? Why, grim old Zet wanted him to be all marrow, no bone. He caged him in reprehending punitive silence, he demanded that he dazzle the world. And he never—but never—approved of anything.

To be an intellectual was the next stage of human development, the historical fate of mankind, if you prefer. Now the masses were reading, and we were off in all directions, Zet believed. The early phases of this expansion of mind could not fail to produce excesses, crime, madness. Wasn't that, said Zet, the meaning of books like *The Brothers Karamazov,* the decay produced by rationalism in the feudal peasant Russian? And parricide the first result of revolution? The resistance to the modern condition and the modern theme? The terrible wrestling of Sin and Freedom? The megalomania of the pioneers? To be an intellectual was to be a parvenu. The business of these parvenus was to purge themselves of their first wild impulses and of their crazy baseness, to change themselves, to become disinterested. To love truth. To become great.

Naturally Zetland was sent to college. College was waiting for him. He won prizes in poetry, essay contests. He joined a literary society, and a Marxist study group. Agreeing with Trotsky that Stalin had betrayed the October Revolution, he joined the Spartacus Youth League, but as a revolutionist he was fairly vague. He studied logic under Carnap, and later with Bertrand Russell and Morris R. Cohen.

The best of it was that he got away from home and lived in rooming houses, the filthier the better. The best was a whitewashed former coalbin on Woodlawn Avenue. Soft coal, still stored in the adjoining shed, trickled between the whitewashed planks. There was no window. On the cement floor was a rag rug, worried together out of tatters and coming unbound. An old oak library table with cigarette burns and a shadeless floorlamp were provided. The meters for the whole house were over Zet's cot. Rent was $2.50 a week. The place was jolly—it was bohemian, it was European. Best of all, it was Russian! The landlord, Perchik, said that he had been game-beater for Grand Duke Cyril. Abandoned in Kamchatka when the Japanese War began, he trudged back across Siberia. With him Zet had Russian conversations. Long in the teeth, Perchik wore a meager beard, and the wires of his dime-store specs were twisted. In the back he had built a little house out of pop bottles, collected in a coaster in the alleys. Rags and garbage were burned in the furnace, and the fumes blew through the hot-air registers. The landlord sang old ballads and hymns, falsetto. Really, the place couldn't have been better. Disorderly, dirty, irregular, free, and you could talk all night and sleep late. Just what you wanted for thought, for feeling, for invention. In his happiness, Zet entertained the Perchik house with his charades, speeches, jokes, and songs. He was a laundry mangle, a time clock, a tractor, a telescope. He did *Don Giovanni* in all parts and voices—*"Non sperar, se non m'uccidi . . . Donna folle, indarno gridi."* He reproduced the harpsichord background in the recitatives or the oboe weeping when the Commendatore's soul left his body. To follow up he might do Stalin addressing a party congress, a Fuller brush salesman in German, or a submarine commander sinking an *amerikanische* freighter. Zet also was practically useful. He helped people to move. He minded kids for married graduate students. He cooked for the sick. He looked after people's dogs and cats when they went out of town, and shopped for old women in the house when it snowed. Now he was something between the stout boy and the nearsighted young man with odd ideas and exotic motives. Loving, virtually Franciscan, a simpleton for God's sake, easy to cheat. An ingenu. At the age of nineteen he had a great deal of Dickensian heart. When he earned a little money mopping floors at Billings Hospital, he shared it with clinic patients, bought them cigarettes and sandwiches, lent them carfare, walked them across the Midway. Sensitive to suffering and to symbols of suffering and misery, his eyes filled when he went into some Depression grocery. The withered potatoes, the sprouting onions, the unhappy face of the storekeeper got him. His cat had a miscarriage, and he wept about that, too, because the mother cat was grieving. I flushed the stillborn cats down the boardless grimy toilet in the cellar. He made me testy, carrying on like that. Practicing his feelings on everyone, I said. He warned me not to be hard-hearted. I said he exaggerated everything. He accused me of a lack of sensibility. It was an odd argument for two adolescents. I suppose the power of Americanization faltered during the Depression. We broke away, and seized the opportunity to be more *foreign*. We were a laughable pair of university highbrows who couldn't have a spat without citing William James and Karl Marx, or

Villiers de l'Isle-Adam or Whitehead. We decided that we were the tender-minded and tough-minded of William James, respectively. But James had said that to know everything that happened in one city on a single day would crush the toughest mind. No one could be as tough as he needed to be. "You'll be barren of sympathy if you don't look out," Zet said. That was the way he talked. His language was always elegant. Lord knows where his patrician style came from—Lord Bacon, perhaps, plus Hume and a certain amount of Santayana. He debated with his friends in the whitewashed cellar. His language was very pure and musical.

But then he was musical. He didn't walk down the street without practicing a Haydn quartet, or Borodin or Prokofiev. Overcoat buttoned at the neck, he hauled his briefcase and made the violin stops inside his fuzz-lined gloves and puffed the music in his throat and cheeks. In good heart, with bad color, the color of yellow grapes, he did the cello in his chest and the violins high in the nose. The trees were posted in the broom-swept, dust-mixed snow and were bound to the subpavement soil and enriched by sewer seepage. Zetland and the squirrels enjoyed the privileges of motility.

Heat overpowered him when he entered Cobb Hall. Its interior was Baptist brown, austere, varnished, very like old churches. The building was kept very hot, and he felt the heat on his face immediately. It struck him on the cheeks. His goggles fogged up. He dropped the slow movement of his Borodin quartet and sighed. After the sigh he wore an intellectual, not a musical, expression. He now was ready for semiotics, symbolic logic—the reader of Tarski, Carnap, Feigl, and Dewey. A stoutish young man whose color was poor, whose sandy hair, brushed flat, had greenish lights, he sat in the hard seminar chair and fetched out his cigarettes. Playing parts, he was here a Brain. With Skinny Jones in his raveled sweater and missing front teeth, with Tisewitch whose eyebrows were kinky, with Dark Devvie—a lovely, acid, pale girl—and Miss Krehayn, a redhead and hard stutterer, he was a leading logical positivist.

For a while. In the way of mental work, he could do anything, but he was not about to become a logician. He was, however, attracted by rational analysis. The emotional struggles of mankind were never resolved. The same things were done over and over, with passion, with passionate stupidity, insectlike, the same emotional struggles repeated in daily reality—urge, drive, desire, self-preservation, aggrandizement, the search for happiness, the search for justification, the experience of coming to be and of passing away, from nothingness to nothingness. Very boring. Frightening. Doom. Now, mathematical logic could extricate you from all this nonsensical existence. "See here," said Zet in his soiled canvas Bauhaus chair, the dropped glasses shortening his short nose. "As propositions are either true or false, whatever *is* is right. Leibnitz was no fool. Provided that you really know that what is, indeed *is*. Still, I haven't entirely made up my mind about the religious question, as a true positivist should."

Just then from straight-ruled Chicago, blue with winter, brown with evening, crystal with frost, the factory whistles went off. Five o'clock. The mousegray snow and the hutchy bungalows, the furnace blasting, and Perchik's shovel gritting in the coalbin. The radio boomed through the floors, to us below. It was the *Anschluss*—Schuschnigg and Hitler. Vienna was just as cold as Chicago now; much gloomier.

"Lottie is expecting me," said Zetland.

Lottie was pretty. She was also, in her own way, theatrical—the party girl, the pagan beauty with hibiscus in her teeth. She was a witty young woman, and she loved an amusing man. She visited his coalbin. He stayed in her room. They found an English basement together which they furnished with an oak table and rose velvet junk. They kept cats and dogs, a squirrel, and a pet crow. After their first quarrel Lottie smeared her breasts with honey as a peace gesture. And before graduation she borrowed an automobile and they drove to Michigan City and were married. Zet had gotten a fellowship in philosophy at Columbia. There was a wedding and goodbye party for them on Kimbark Avenue, in an old flat. After being separated for five minutes, Zet and Lottie ran the whole length of the corridor, embracing, trembling, and kissing. "Darling, suddenly you weren't there!"

"Sweetheart, I'm always there. I'll always be there!"

Two young people from the sticks, overdoing the thing, acting out their love in public. But there was more to it than display. They adored each other. Besides, they had already lived as man and wife for a year with all their dogs and cats and birds and fishes and plants and fiddles and books. Ingeniously, Zet mimicked animals. He washed himself like a cat and bit fleas on his haunch like a dog, and made goldfish faces, wagging his fingertips like fins. When they went to the Orthodox church for the Easter service, he learned to genuflect and make the sign of the cross Eastern style. Charlotte kept time with her head when he played the violin, just a bit off, his loving metronome. Zet was forever acting something out and Lottie was also demonstrative. There is probably no way for human beings to avoid playacting, Zet said.

As long as you know where the soul is, there is no harm in being Socrates. It is when the soul can't be located that the play of being someone turns desperate.

So Zet and Lottie were not simply married but delightfully married. Instead of a poor Macedonian girl whose muttering immigrant mother laid spells and curses on Zet and whose father sharpened knives and scissors, and went up and down alleys ringing a hand bell, Zet had *das Ewig-Weibliche,* a natural, universal, gorgeous power. As for Lottie, she said, "There's no one in the world like Zet." She added, "In every way." Then she dropped her voice, speaking from the side of her mouth with absurd Dietrich charm, in tough Chicago style, saying, "I'm not exactly inexperienced, I want you to know." That was no secret. She had lived with a fellow named Huram, an educational psychologist, who had a mended harelip, over which he grew a mustache. Before that there had been someone else. But now she was a wife and overflowed with wifely love. She ironed his shirts and buttered his toast, lit his cigarette, and gazed like a little Spanish virgin at him, all aglow. It amused some, this melting and *Schwärmerei*. Others were irritated. Father Zetland was enraged.

The couple departed from La Salle Street Station for New York, by day coach. The depot looked archaic, mineral. The steam foamed up to the sooty skylights. The El pillars vibrated on Van Buren Street, where the hockshops and the army-navy stores and the two-bit barbershops were. The redcap took the valises. Zet tried to say something to Ozymandias about the kingly airs of the black porters. The aunts were also there. They didn't easily follow when Zet made one of his odd statements about the black of the station and the black of the redcaps and their ceremonious African style. The look that went between the old girls agreed that he was not making sense, poor Elias. They blamed Lottie. Excited at starting out in life, married, a fellow at Columbia University, he felt that his father was casting his own glumness on him, making him heavy-hearted. Zet had grown a large brown mustache. His big boyish teeth, wide-spaced, combined oddly with these mature whiskers. The low, chesty, almost burly figure was a shorter version of his father's. But Ozymandias had a Russian military posture. He did not believe in grinning and ducking and darting and mimicry. He stood erect. Lottie cried out affectionate things to everyone. She wore an apple-blossom dress and matching turban and apple-blossom high-heeled shoes. The trains clashed and huffed, but you could hear the rapid stamping of Lottie's gaudy heels. Her Oriental eyes, her humorous peasant nose, her pleasant bosom, her smooth sexual rear with which Zet's hand kept contact all the while, drew the silent, harsh attention of Ozymandias. She called him "Pa." He strained cigarette smoke between his teeth with an expression that passed for a smile. Yes, he managed to look pleasant through it all. The Macedonian in-laws didn't show up at all. They were on a streetcar and caught in a traffic jam.

On this sad, jolly occasion Ozymandias restrained himself. He looked very European despite the straw summer skimmer he was wearing, with a red-white-and-blue band. The downtown buyer, well trained in dissembling, subdued the snarls of his heart and by pressing down his chin with the black hole in it cooled his rage. Temporarily he was losing his son. Lottie kissed her father-in-law. She kissed the aunts, the two practical nurses who read Romain Rolland and Warwick Deeping beside the wheelchair and the death-bed. Their opinion was that Lottie might be more fastidious in her feminine hygiene. Aunt Masha thought the herringy odor was due to dysmenorrhea. Virginal, Aunt Masha was unfamiliar with the odor of a woman who had been making love on a warm day. The young people took every opportunity to strengthen each other.

Imitating their brother, the aunts, too, gave false kisses with inexperienced lips. Lottie then cried with joy. They were leaving Chicago, the most boring place in the world, and getting rid of surly Ozymandias and of her mother the witch and her poor daddy the knife grinder. She was married to Zet, who had a million times more charm and warmth and brains than anyone else.

"Oh, Pa! Goodbye!" Zet emotionally took his iron father in his arms.

"Do right. Study. Make something of yourself. If you get in trouble, wire for money."

"Dear Pa, I love you. Masha, Dounia, I love you, too," said Lottie, now red-faced with tears. She gave them all sobbing kisses. Then at the coach window, waving, the young people embraced and the train slid off.

As the Pacemaker departed, Father Zetland shook his fist at the observation car. He stamped his feet. At Lottie, who was ruining his son, he cried, "You wait! I'll get you. Five years, ten years, but I'll get you." He shouted, "You bitch—you nasty cunt."

Russian in his rage, he cried out *"Cont!"* His sisters did not understand.

Zet and Lottie swam into New York City from the skies—that was how it felt in the Pacemaker, rushing along the Hudson at sunrise. First many blue twigs overhanging the water, then a rosy color, and then the heavy flashing of the river under the morning sun.

They were in the dining car, their eyes heavy. They were drained by a night of broken sleep in the day coach, and they were dazzled. They drank coffee from cups as heavy as soapstone, and poured from New York Central pewter. They were in the East, where everything was better, where objects were diffcrent. Here there was deeper meaning in the air.

After changing at Harmon to an electric locomotive, they began a more quick and eager ride. Trees, water, sky, and the sky raced off, floating, and there came bridges, structures, and at last the tunnel, where the air brakes gasped and the streamliner was checked. There were yellow bulbs in wire mesh, and subterranean air came through the vents. The doors opened, the passengers, pulling their clothing straight, flowed out and got their luggage, and Zet and Lottie, reaching Forty-second Street, refugees from arid and inhibited Chicago, from Emptyland, embraced at the curb and kissed each other repeatedly on the mouth. They had come to the World City, where all behavior was deeper and more resonant, where they could freely be themselves, as demonstrative as they liked. Intellect, art, the transcendent, needed no excuses here. Any cabdriver understood, Zet believed.

"Ah, darling, darling—thank God," said Zet. "A place where it's normal to be a human being."

"Oh, Zet, amen!" said Lottie with tremors and tears.

At first they lived uptown, on the West Side. The small, chinging trolleys still rolled on slant Broadway. Lottie chose a room described as a studio, at the rear of a brownstone. There was a studio bedroom, and the bathroom was also the kitchen. Covered with a heavy, smooth board, the tub became the kitchen table. You could reach the gas ring from the bath. Zet liked that. Frying your eggs while you sat in the water. You could hear the largo of the drain as you drank your coffee, or watch the cockroaches come and go about the cupboards. The toaster spring was tight. It snapped out the bread. Sometimes a toasted cockroach was flung out. The ceilings were high. There was little daylight. The fireplace was made of small tiles. You could bring home an apple crate from Broadway and have a ten-minute fire, which left a little ash and many hooked nails. The studio turned into a Zet habitat, a Zet-and-Lottie place: dark, dirty portieres, thriftshop carpets, upholstered chairs with bald arms that shone, said Zetland, like gorilla hide. The window opened on an air shaft, but Zet had lived even in Chicago behind drawn shades or in a whitewashed coalbin. Lottie bought lamps with pink porcelain shades flounced at the edges like ancient butter dishes. The room had the agreeable dimness of a chapel, the gloom of a sanctuary. When I visited Byzantine churches in Yugoslavia, I thought I had found the master model, the archetypal Zet habitat.

The Zetlands settled in. Crusts, butts, coffee grounds, dishes of dog food, books, journals, music stands, odors of Macedonian cookery (mutton, yogurt, lemon, rice), and white Chilean wine in bulbous bottles. Zetland reconnoitered the philosophy department, brought home loads of books from the library, and put himself to work. His industry might have pleased Ozymandias. But nothing, he would say, could really please the old guy. Or perhaps his ultimate pleasure was never to be pleased, and never to approve. With an M.A. of her own in sociology, Lottie went to work in an office. Look at her, said Zet, such an impulsive young woman, and so efficient, such a crack executive secretary. See how steady she was, how uncomplaining about getting up in the dark, and what a dependable employee this Balkan Gypsy had turned out to be. He found a sort of sadness in this, and he was astonished. Office work would have killed him. He had tried that. Ozymandias had found jobs for him. But routine and paperwork paralyzed him. He had worked in the company warehouse helping the zoologist to see what ailed the filberts and the figs and the raisins, keeping parasites in check. That was interesting, but not for long. And one week he had worked in the shops of the Field Museum, learning to make plastic leaves for habitats. Dead animals, he learned, were preserved in many poisons and that, he said, was how he felt about being an employee—a toxic condition.

So it was Lottie who worked, and the afternoons were very long. Zet and the dog waited for her at five o'clock. At last she came, with groceries, hurrying westward from Broadway. In the street Zet and Miss Katusha ran toward her. Zet called out, "Lottie!" and the brown dog scrabbled on the pavement and whined. Lottie was wan from the subway, and warm, and made contralto sounds in her throat when she was kissed. She brought home hamburger meat and yogurt, bones for Katusha, and small gifts for Zetland. They were still honeymooners. They were ecstatic in New York. They had the animal ecstasies of the dog for emphasis or analogy. They made friends in the building with a pulp writer and his wife—Giddings and Gertrude. Giddings wrote Westerns: the Balzac of the Badlands, Zet named him. Giddings called him the Wittgenstein of the West Side. Zetland thus had an audience for his cheerful inventions. He read aloud funny sentences from the *Encyclopedia of Unified Sciences* and put H. Rider Haggard, Giddings's favorite novelist, into the language of symbolic logic. Evenings, Lottie became again a Macedonian Gypsy, her mama's daughter. Mama was a necromancer from Skoplje, said Zetland, and made spells with cats' urine and snakes' navels. She knew the erotic secrets of antiquity. Evidently Lottie knew them, too. It was established that Lottie's female qualities were rich, and deep and sweet. Romantic Zetland said fervent and grateful things about them.

From so much sweetness, this chocolate life, nerves glowing too hotly, came pangs of anxiety. In its own way the anxiety was also delicious, he said. He explained that he had two kinds of ecstasy, sensuous and sick. Those early months in New York were too much for him. His lung trouble came back, and he ran a fever; he ached, passed urine painfully, and he lay in bed, the faded wine-colored pajamas binding him at the crotch and under the plump arms. His skin developed its old irritability.

It was his invalid childhood all over again for a few weeks. It was awful that he should fall into it, a grown man, just married, but it was delectable, too. He remembered the hospital very well, the booming in his head when he was etherized and the horrible open wound in his belly. It was infected and wouldn't heal. He drained through a rubber tube which an ordinary diaper pin secured. He understood that he was going to die, but he read the funny papers. All the kids in the ward had to read were funny papers and the Bible: Slim Jim, Boob McNutt, Noah's Ark, Hagar, Ishmael ran into each other like the many colors of the funnies. It was a harsh Chicago winter, there were golden icon rays at the frosted windows in the morning, and the streetcars droned and ground, clanged. Somehow he had made it out of the hospital, and his aunts nursed him at home with marrow broth and scalded milk and melted butter, soda biscuits as big as playing cards. His illness in New York brought back the open wound with its rotten smell and the rubber tube which a diaper pin kept from falling into his belly, and bedsores and his having to learn again at the age of eight how to walk. A very early and truthful sense of the seizure of matter by life energies, the painful, difficult, intricate chemical-electrical transformation and organization, gorgeous, streaming with radiant colors, and all the scent and the stinking. This combination was too harsh. It whirled too much. It troubled and intimidated the soul too much. What were we here for, of all strange beings and creatures the strangest? Clear colloid eyes to see with, for a while, and see so finely, and a palpitating universe to see, and so many human messages to give and to receive. And the bony box for thinking and for the storage of thoughts, and a cloudy heart for feelings. Ephemerids, grinding up other creatures, flavoring and heating their flesh, devouring this flesh. A kind of being filled with death-knowledge, and also filled with infinite longings. These peculiar internal phrases were not intentional. That was just it, they simply came to Zetland, naturally, involuntarily, as he was consulting with himself about this tangle of bright and terrifying qualities.

So Zet laid aside his logic books. They had lost their usefulness. They joined the funny papers he had put away when he was eight years old. He had no more use for Rudolf Carnap than for Boob McNutt. He said to Lottie, "What other books are there?" She went to the shelf and read off the titles. He stopped her at *Moby Dick,* and she handed him the large volume. After reading a few pages he knew that he would never be a Ph.D. in philosophy. The sea came into his inland, Lake Michigan soul, he told me. Oceanic cold was just the thing for his fever. He felt polluted, but he read about purity. He had reached a bad stage of limited selfhood, disaffection, unwillingness to be; he was sick; he wanted *out*. Then he read this dazzling book. It rushed over him. He thought he would drown. But he didn't drown; he floated.

The creature of flesh and blood, and ill, went to the toilet. Because of his intestines he shuffled to sit on the board and over the porcelain, over the sewer-connected hole and its water—the necessary disgrace. And when the dizzy floor tiles wavered under his sick eyes like chicken wire, the amethyst of the ocean was also there in the bevels of the medicine-chest mirror, and the white power of the whale, to which the bathtub gave a fleeting gauge. The cloaca was there, the nausea, and also the coziness of bowel smells going back to childhood, the old brown colors. And the dismay and sweetness of ragged coughing and the tropical swampiness of the fever. But also there rose up the seas. Straight through the airshaft, west, and turn left at the Hudson. The Atlantic was there.

The real business of his life was with comprehensive vision, he decided. He had been working in philosophy with the resemblance theory of universals. He had an original approach to the predicate "resemble." But that was finished. When sick, he was decisive. He had the weak sweats and was coughing up blue phlegm with his fist to his mouth and his eyes swelling. He cleared his throat and said to Lottie, who sat on the bed holding his tea for him during this coughing fit, "I don't think I can go on in the philosophy department."

"It's really worrying you, isn't it? You were talking philosophy in your sleep the other night."

"Was I?"

"Talking in your sleep about epistemology or something. I don't understand that stuff, you know that."

"Ah, well, it's not really for me, either."

"But, honey, you don't have to do anything you don't like. Switch to something else. I'll back you all the way."

"Ah, you're a dear woman. But we'll have to get along without the fellowship."

"What's it worth? Those cheap bastards don't give you enough to live on anyway. Zet, dear, screw the money. I can see you've gone through a change of heart because of that book."

"Oh, Lottie, it's a miracle, that book. It takes you out of this human world."

"What do you mean, Zet?"

"I mean it takes you out of the universe of mental projections or insulating fictions of ordinary social practice or psychological habit. It gives you elemental liberty. What really frees you from these insulating social and psychological fictions is the other fiction, of art. There really is no human life without this poetry. Ah, Lottie, I've been starving on symbolic logic."

"I've *got* to read that book now," she said.

But she didn't get far with it. Sea books were for men, and anyway she wasn't bookish; she was too impulsive to sit long with any book. That was Zet's department. He would tell her all she needed to know about *Moby Dick*.

"I'll have to go and talk to Professor Edman."

"As soon as you're strong enough, go on down and quit. Just quit. All the better. What the hell do you want to be a professor for? Oh, that dog!" Katusha had gotten into a barking duel with an animal in the next yard. "Shut up, you bitch! Sometimes I really hate that lousy dog. I feel her barking right in the middle of my head."

"Give her to the Chinese laundryman; he likes her."

"Likes her? He'd cook her. Now look, Zet, don't

you worry about a thing. Screw that logic. Okay? You can do a hundred things. You know French, Russian, German, and you're a real brain. We don't need much to live on. No fancy stuff for me. I shop on Union Square. So what?"

"With that beautiful Macedonian body," said Zet, "Klein's is just as good as *haute couture*. Blessings on your bust, your belly, and your bottom."

"If your fever goes down by the weekend, we'll go to the country, to Giddings and Gertrude."

"Pa will be upset when he hears I've dropped out of Columbia."

"So what? I know you love him, but he's such a grudger, you can't please him anyway. Well, screw him, too."

They moved downtown in 1940 and lived on Bleecker Street for a dozen years. They were soon prominent in Greenwich Village. In Chicago they had been bohemians without knowing it. In the Village Zet was identified with the avant-garde in literature and with radical politics. When the Russians invaded Finland, radical politics became absurd. Marxists debated whether the workers' state could be imperialistic. This was too nonsensical for Zetland. Then there was the Nazi-Soviet pact, there was the war. Constantine was born during the war—Lottie wanted him to have a Balkan name. Zetland wanted to enter the service. When he behaved with spirit, Lottie was always for him, and she supported him against his father, who of course disapproved.

A Silver
Dish

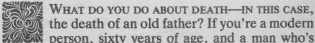WHAT DO YOU DO ABOUT DEATH—IN THIS CASE, the death of an old father? If you're a modern person, sixty years of age, and a man who's been around, like Woody Selbst, what do you do? Take this matter of mourning, and take it against a contemporary background. How, against a contemporary background, do you mourn an octogenarian father, nearly blind, his heart enlarged, his lungs filling with fluid, who creeps, stumbles, gives off the odors, the moldiness or gassiness, of old men. I *mean!* As Woody put it, be realistic. Think what times these are. The papers daily give it to you—the Lufthansa pilot in Aden is described by the hostages on his knees, begging the Palestinian terrorists not to execute him, but they shoot him through the head. Later they themselves are killed. And still others shoot others, or shoot themselves. That's what you read in the press, see on the tube, mention at dinner. We

know now what goes daily through the whole of the human community, like a global death-peristalsis.

Woody, a businessman in South Chicago, was not an ignorant person. He knew more such phrases than you would expect a tile contractor (offices, lobbies, lavatories) to know. The kind of knowledge he had was not the kind for which you get academic degrees. Although Woody had studied for two years in a seminary, preparing to be a minister. Two years of college during the Depression was more than most high-school graduates could afford. After that, in his own vital, picturesque, original way (Morris, his old man, was also, in his days of nature, vital and picturesque), Woody had read up on many subjects, subscribed to *Science* and other magazines that gave real information, and had taken night courses at De Paul and Northwestern in ecology, criminology, existentialism. Also he had traveled extensively in Japan, Mexico, and Africa, and there was an African experience that was especially relevant to mourning. It was this: on a launch near the Murchison Falls in Uganda, he had seen a buffalo calf seized by a crocodile from the bank of the White Nile. There were giraffes along the tropical river, and hippopotamuses, and baboons, and flamingos and other brilliant birds crossing the bright air in the heat of the morning, when the calf, stepping into the river to drink, was grabbed by the hoof and dragged down. The parent buffaloes couldn't figure it out. Under the water the calf still threshed, fought, churned the mud. Woody, the robust traveler, took this in as he sailed by, and to him it looked as if the parent cattle were asking each other dumbly what had happened. He chose to assume that there was pain in this, he read brute grief into it. On the White Nile, Woody had the impression that he had gone back to the pre-Adamite past, and he brought reflections on this impression home to South Chicago. He brought also a bundle of hashish from Kampala. In this he took a chance with the customs inspectors, banking perhaps on his broad build, frank face, high color. He didn't look like a wrongdoer, a bad guy; he looked like a good guy. But he liked taking chances. Risk was a wonderful stimulus. He threw down his trenchcoat on the customs counter. If the inspectors searched the pockets, he was prepared to say that the coat wasn't his. But he got away with it, and the Thanksgiving turkey was stuffed with hashish. This was much enjoyed. That was practically the last feast at which Pop, who also relished risk or defiance, was present. The hashish Woody had tried to raise in his backyard from the Africa seeds didn't take. But behind his warehouse, where the Lincoln Continental was parked, he kept a patch of marijuana. There was no harm at all in Woody, but he didn't like being entirely within the law. It was simply a question of self-respect.

After that Thanksgiving, Pop gradually sank as if he had a slow leak. This went on for some years. In and out of the hospital, he dwindled, his mind wandered, he couldn't even concentrate enough to complain, except in exceptional moments on the Sundays Woody regularly devoted to him. Morris, an amateur who once was taken seriously by Willie Hoppe, the great pro himself, couldn't execute the simplest billiard shots anymore. He could only conceive shots; he began to theorize about impossible three-cushion combinations. Halina, the Polish woman with whom Morris had lived for over forty years as man and wife, was too old herself now to run to the hospital. So Woody had to do it. There was Woody's mother, too—a Christian convert—needing care; she was over eighty and frequently hospitalized. Everybody had diabetes and pleurisy and arthritis and cataracts and cardiac pacemakers. And everybody had lived by the body, but the body was giving out.

There were Woody's two sisters as well, unmarried, in their fifties, very Christian, very straight, still living with Mama in an entirely Christian bungalow. Woody, who took full responsibility for them all, occasionally had to put one of the girls (they had become sick girls) in a mental institution. Nothing severe. The sisters were wonderful women, both of them gorgeous once, but neither of the poor things was playing with a full deck. And all the factions had to be kept separate—Mama, the Christian convert; the fundamentalist sisters; Pop, who read the Yiddish paper as long as he could still see print; Halina, a good Catholic. Woody, the seminary forty years behind him, described himself as an agnostic. Pop had no more religion than you could find in the Yiddish paper, but he made Woody promise to bury him among Jews, and that was where he lay now, in the Hawaiian shirt Woody had bought for him at the tilers' convention in Honolulu. Woody would allow no undertaker's assistant to dress him, but came to the parlor and buttoned the stiff into the shirt himself, and the old man went down looking like Ben-Gurion in a simple wooden coffin, sure to rot fast. That was how Woody wanted it all. At the graveside, he had taken off and folded his jacket, rolled up his sleeves on thick freckled biceps, waved back the little tractor standing by, and shoveled the dirt himself. His big face, broad at the bottom, narrowed upward like a Dutch house. And, his small good lower teeth taking hold of the upper lip in his exertion, he performed the final duty of a son. He was very fit, so it must have been emotion, not the shoveling, that made him redden so. After the funeral, he went home with

Halina and her son, a decent Polack like his mother, and talented, too—Mitosh played the organ at hockey and basketball games in the Stadium, which took a smart man because it was a rabble-rousing kind of occupation—and they had some drinks and comforted the old girl. Halina was true blue, always one hundred percent for Morris.

Then for the rest of the week Woody was busy, had jobs to run, office responsibilities, family responsibilities. He lived alone; as did his wife; as did his mistress: everybody in a separate establishment. Since his wife, after fifteen years of separation, had not learned to take care of herself, Woody did her shopping on Fridays, filled her freezer. He had to take her this week to buy shoes. Also, Friday night he always spent with Helen—Helen was his wife de facto. Saturday he did his big weekly shopping. Saturday night he devoted to Mom and his sisters. So he was too busy to attend to his own feelings except, intermittently, to note to himself, "First Thursday in the grave." "First Friday, and fine weather." "First Saturday; he's got to be getting used to it." Under his breath he occasionally said, "Oh, Pop."

But it was Sunday that hit him, when the bells rang all over South Chicago—the Ukrainian, Roman Catholic, Greek, Russian, African Methodist churches, sounding off one after another. Woody had his offices in his warehouse, and there had built an apartment for himself, very spacious and convenient, in the top story. Because he left every Sunday morning at seven to spend the day with Pop, he had forgotten by how many churches Selbst Tile Company was surrounded. He was still in bed when he heard the bells, and all at once he knew how heartbroken he was. This sudden big heartache in a man of sixty, a practical, physical, healthy-minded, and experienced man, was deeply unpleasant. When he had an unpleasant condition, he believed in taking something for it. So he thought: What shall I take? There were plenty of remedies available. His cellar was stocked with cases of Scotch whisky, Polish vodka, Armagnac, Moselle, Burgundy. There were also freezers with steaks and with game and with Alaskan king crab. He bought with a broad hand—by the crate and by the dozen. But in the end, when he got out of bed, he took nothing but a cup of coffee. While the kettle was heating, he put on his Japanese judo-style suit and sat down to reflect.

Woody was moved when things were *honest*. Bearing beams were honest, undisguised concrete pillars inside highrise apartments were honest. It was bad to cover up anything. He hated faking. Stone was honest. Metal was honest. These Sunday bells were very straight. They broke loose, they wagged and rocked, and the vibrations and the banging did something for him—cleansed his insides, purified his blood. A bell was a one-way throat, had only one thing to tell you and simply told it. He listened.

He had had some connections with bells and churches. He was after all something of a Christian. Born a Jew, he was a Jew facially, with a hint of Iroquois or Cherokee, but his mother had been converted more than fifty years ago by her brother-in-law, the Reverend Doctor Kovner. Kovner, a rabbinical student who had left the Hebrew Union College in Cincinnati to become a minister and establish a mission, had given Woody a partly Christian upbringing. Now, Pop was on the outs with these fundamentalists. He said that the Jews came to the mission to get coffee, bacon, canned pineapple, day-old bread, and dairy products. And if they had to listen to sermons, that was okay—this was the Depression and you couldn't be too particular—but he knew they sold the bacon.

The Gospels said it plainly: "Salvation is from the Jews."

Backing the Reverend Doctor were wealthy fundamentalists, mainly Swedes, eager to speed up the Second Coming by converting all Jews. The foremost of Kovner's backers was Mrs. Skoglund, who had inherited a large dairy business from her late husband. Woody was under her special protection.

Woody was fourteen years of age when Pop took off with Halina, who worked in his shop, leaving his difficult Christian wife and his converted son and his small daughters. He came to Woody in the backyard one spring day and said, "From now on you're the man of the house." Woody was practicing with a golf club, knocking off the heads of dandelions. Pop came into the yard in his good suit, which was too hot for the weather, and when he took off his fedora the skin of his head was marked with a deep ring and the sweat was sprinkled over his scalp—more drops than hairs. He said, "I'm going to move out." Pop was anxious, but he was set to go—determined. "It's no use. I can't live a life like this." Envisioning the life Pop simply *had* to live, his free life, Woody was able to picture him in the billiard parlor, under the El tracks in a crap game, or playing poker at Brown and Koppel's upstairs. "You're going to be the man of the house," said Pop. "It's okay. I put you all on welfare. I just got back from Wabansia Avenue, from the relief station." Hence the suit and the hat. "They're sending out a caseworker." Then he said, "You got to lend me money to buy gasoline—the caddie money you saved."

Understanding that Pop couldn't get away without

his help, Woody turned over to him all he had earned at the Sunset Ridge Country Club in Winnetka. Pop felt that the valuable life lesson he was transmitting was worth far more than these dollars, and whenever he was conning his boy a sort of high-priest expression came down over his bent nose, his ruddy face. The children, who got their finest ideas at the movies, called him Richard Dix. Later, when the comic strip came out, they said he was Dick Tracy.

As Woody now saw it, under the tumbling bells, he had bankrolled his own desertion. Ha ha! He found this delightful; and especially Pop's attitude of "That'll teach you to trust your father." For this was a demonstration on behalf of real life and free instincts, against religion and hypocrisy. But mainly it was aimed against being a fool, the disgrace of foolishness. Pop had it in for the Reverend Doctor Kovner, not because he was an apostate (Pop couldn't have cared less), not because the mission was a racket (he admitted that the Reverend Doctor was personally honest), but because Doctor Kovner behaved foolishly, spoke like a fool, and acted like a fiddler. He tossed his hair like a Paganini (this was Woody's addition; Pop had never even heard of Paganini). Proof that he was not a spiritual leader was that he converted Jewish women by stealing their hearts. "He works up all those broads," said Pop. "He doesn't even know it himself, I swear he doesn't know how he gets them."

From the other side, Kovner often warned Woody, "Your father is a dangerous person. Of course, you love him; you should love him and forgive him, Voodrow, but you are old enough to understand he is leading a life of wice."

It was all petty stuff: Pop's sinning was on a boy level and therefore made a big impression on a boy.

And on Mother. Are wives children, or what? Mother often said, "I hope you put that brute in your prayers. Look what he has done to us. But only pray for him, don't see him." But he saw him all the time. Woodrow was leading a double life, sacred and profane. He accepted Jesus Christ as his personal redeemer. Aunt Rebecca took advantage of this. She made him work. He had to work under Aunt Rebecca. He filled in for the janitor at the mission and settlement house. In winter, he had to feed the coal furnace, and on some nights he slept near the furnace room, on the pool table. He also picked the lock of the storeroom. He took canned pineapple and cut bacon from the flitch with his pocketknife. He crammed himself with uncooked bacon. He had a big frame to fill out.

Only now, sipping Melitta coffee, he asked himself: Had he been so hungry? No, he loved being reckless. He was fighting Aunt Rebecca Kovner when he took out his knife and got on a box to reach the bacon. She didn't know, she couldn't prove that Woody, such a frank, strong, positive boy, who looked you in the eye, so direct, was a thief also. But he was also a thief. Whenever she looked at him, he knew that she was seeing his father. In the curve of his nose, the movements of his eyes, the thickness of his body, in his healthy face, she saw that wicked savage Morris.

Morris, you see, had been a street boy in Liverpool —Woody's mother and her sister were British by birth. Morris's Polish family, on their way to America, abandoned him in Liverpool because he had an eye infection and they would all have been sent back from Ellis Island. They stopped awhile in England, but his eyes kept running and they ditched him. They slipped away, and he had to make out alone in Liverpool at the age of twelve. Mother came of better people. Pop, who slept in the cellar of her house, fell in love with her. At sixteen, scabbing during a sea-men's strike, he shoveled his way across the Atlantic and jumped ship in Brooklyn. He became an Ameri-can, and America never knew it. He voted without papers, he drove without a license, he paid no taxes, he cut every corner. Horses, cards, billiards, and women were his lifelong interests, in ascending order. Did he love anyone (he was so busy)? Yes, he loved Halina. He loved his son. To this day, Mother be-lieved that he had loved her most and always wanted to come back. This gave her a chance to act the queen, with her plump wrists and faded Queen Victo-ria face. "The girls are instructed never to admit him," she said. The Empress of India speaking.

Bell-battered Woodrow's soul was whirling this Sunday morning, indoors and out, to the past, back to his upper corner of the warehouse, laid out with such originality—the bells coming and going, metal on naked metal, until the bell circle expanded over the whole of steel-making, oil-refining, power-producing mid-autumn South Chicago, and all its Croatians, Ukrainians, Greeks, Poles, and respectable blacks heading for their churches to hear Mass or to sing hymns.

Woody himself had been a good hymn singer. He still knew the hymns. He had testified, too. He was often sent by Aunt Rebecca to get up and tell a churchful of Scandihoovians that he, a Jewish lad, accepted Jesus Christ. For this she paid him fifty cents. She made the disbursement. She was the book-keeper, fiscal chief, general manager of the mission. The Reverend Doctor didn't know a thing about the operation. What the Doctor supplied was the fervor. He was genuine, a wonderful preacher. And what about Woody himself? He also had fervor. He was drawn to the Reverend Doctor. The Reverend Doctor taught him to lift up his eyes, gave him his higher life. Apart from this higher life, the rest was Chicago—the ways of Chicago, which came so natural that nobody thought to question them. So, for instance, in 1933 (what ancient, ancient times!), at the Century of Progress World's Fair, when Woody was a coolie and pulled a rickshaw, wearing a peaked straw hat and trotting with powerful, thick legs, while the brawny red farmers—his boozing passengers—were laughing their heads off and pestered him for whores, he, although a freshman at the seminary, saw nothing wrong, when girls asked him to steer a little business their way, in making dates and accepting tips from both sides. He necked in Grant Park with a powerful girl who had to go home quickly to nurse her baby. Smelling of milk, she rode beside him on the streetcar to the West Side, squeezing his rickshaw puller's thigh and wetting her blouse. This was the Roosevelt Road car. Then, in the apartment where she lived with her mother, he couldn't remember that there were any husbands around. What he did remember was the strong milk odor. Without inconsistency, next morning he did New Testament Greek: The light shineth in darkness—*to fos en te skotia fainei*—and the darkness comprehended it not.

And all the while he trotted between the shafts on the fairgrounds he had one idea, nothing to do with these horny giants having a big time in the city: that the goal, the project, the purpose was (and he couldn't explain why he thought so; all evidence was against it)—God's idea was that this world should be a love world, that it should eventually recover and be entirely a world of love. He wouldn't have said this to a soul, for he could see himself how stupid it was—personal and stupid. Nevertheless, there it was at the center of his feelings. And at the same time, Aunt

Rebecca was right when she said to him, strictly private, close to his ear even, "You're a little crook, like your father."

There was some evidence for this, or what stood for evidence to an impatient person like Rebecca. Woody matured quickly—he had to—but how could you expect a boy of seventeen, he wondered, to interpret the viewpoint, the feelings, of a middle-aged woman, and one whose breast had been removed? Morris told him that this happened only to neglected women, and was a sign. Morris said that if titties were not fondled and kissed, they got cancer in protest. It was a cry of the flesh. And this had seemed true to Woody. When his imagination tried the theory on the Reverend Doctor, it worked out—he couldn't see the Reverend Doctor behaving in that way to Aunt Rebecca's breasts! Morris's theory kept Woody looking from bosoms to husbands and from husbands to bosoms. He still did that. It's an exceptionally smart man who isn't marked forever by the sexual theories he hears from his father, and Woody wasn't all that smart. He knew this himself. Personally, he had gone far out of his way to do right by women in this regard. What nature demanded. He and Pop were common, thick men, but there's nobody too gross to have ideas of delicacy.

The Reverend Doctor preached, Rebecca preached, rich Mrs. Skoglund preached from Evanston, Mother preached. Pop also was on a soapbox. Everyone was doing it. Up and down Division Street, under every lamp, almost, speakers were giving out: anarchists, Socialists, Stalinists, single-taxers, Zionists, Tolstoyans, vegetarians, and fundamentalist Christian preachers—you name it. A beef, a hope, a way of life or salvation, a protest. How was it that the accumulated gripes of all the ages took off so when transplanted to America?

And that fine Swedish immigrant Aase (Osie, they pronounced it), who had been the Skoglunds' cook and married the eldest son, to become his rich, religious widow—she supported the Reverend Doctor. In her time she must have been built like a chorus girl. And women seem to have lost the secret of putting up their hair in the high basketry fence of braid she wore. Aase took Woody under her special protection and paid his tuition at the seminary. And Pop said . . . But on this Sunday, at peace as soon as the bells stopped banging, this velvet autumn day when the grass was finest and thickest, silky green: before the first frost, and the blood in your lungs is redder than summer air can make it and smarts with oxygen, as if the iron in your system was hungry for it, and the chill was sticking it to you in every breath . . . Pop, six feet under, would never feel this blissful sting again. The last of the bells still had the bright air streaming with vibrations.

On weekends, the institutional vacancy of decades came back to the warehouse and crept under the door of Woody's apartment. It felt as empty on Sundays as churches were during the week. Before each business day, before the trucks and the crews got started, Woody jogged five miles in his Adidas suit. Not on this day still reserved for Pop, however. Although it was tempting to go out and run off the grief. Being alone hit Woody hard this morning. He thought: Me and the world; the world and me. Meaning that there always was some activity to interpose, an errand or a visit, a picture to paint (he was a creative amateur), a massage, a meal—a shield between himself and that troublesome solitude which used the world as its reservoir. But Pop! Last Tuesday, Woody had gotten into the hospital bed with Pop because he kept pulling out the intravenous needles. Nurses stuck them back, and then Woody astonished them all by climbing into bed to hold the struggling old guy in his arms. "Easy, Morris, Morris, go easy." But Pop still groped feebly for the pipes.

When the tolling stopped, Woody didn't notice that a great lake of quiet had come over his kingdom, the Selbst Tile warehouse. What he heard and saw was an old red Chicago streetcar, one of those trams the color of a stockyard steer. Cars of this type went out before Pearl Harbor—clumsy, big-bellied, with tough rattan seats and brass grips for the standing passengers. Those cars used to make four stops to the mile, and ran with a wallowing motion. They stank of carbolic or ozone and throbbed when the air compressors were being charged. The conductor had his knotted signal cord to pull, and the motorman beat the foot gong with his mad heel.

Woody recognized himself on the Western Avenue line and riding through a blizzard with his father, both in sheepskins and with hands and faces raw, the snow blowing in from the rear platform when the doors opened and getting into the longitudinal cleats of the floor. There wasn't warmth enough inside to melt it. And Western Avenue was the longest car line in the world, the boosters said, as if it was a thing to brag about. Twenty-three miles long, made by a draftsman with a T square, lined with factories, storage buildings, machine shops, used-car lots, trolley barns, gas stations, funeral parlors, six-flats, utility buildings, and junkyards, on and on from the prairies on the south to Evanston on the north. Woodrow and his father were going north to Evanston, to Howard

Street, and then some, to see Mrs. Skoglund. At the end of the line they would still have about five blocks to hike. The purpose of the trip? To raise money for Pop. Pop had talked him into this. When they found out, Mother and Aunt Rebecca would be furious, and Woody was afraid, but he couldn't help it.

Morris had come and said, "Son, I'm in trouble. It's bad."

"What's bad, Pop?"

"Halina took money from her husband for me and has to put it back before old Bujak misses it. He could kill her."

"What did she do it for?"

"Son, you know how the bookies collect? They send a goon. They'll break my head open."

"Pop! You know I can't take you to Mrs. Skoglund."

"Why not? You're my kid, aren't you? The old broad wants to adopt you, doesn't she? Shouldn't I get something out of it for my trouble? What am I—outside? And what about Halina? She puts her life on the line, but my own kid says no."

"Oh, Bujak wouldn't hurt her."

"Woody, he'd beat her to death."

Bujak? Uniform in color with his dark-gray work clothes, short in the legs, his whole strength in his tool-and-die-maker's forearms and black fingers; and beat-looking—there was Bujak for you. But, according to Pop, there was big, big violence in Bujak, a regular boiling Bessemer inside his narrow chest. Woody could never see the violence in him. Bujak wanted no trouble. If anything, maybe he was afraid that Morris and Halina would gang up on him and kill him, screaming. But Pop was no desperado murderer. And Halina was a calm, serious woman. Bujak kept his savings in the cellar (banks were going out of business). The worst they did was to take some of his money, intending to put it back. As Woody saw him, Bujak was trying to be sensible. He accepted his sorrow. He set minimum requirements for Halina: cook the meals, clean the house, show respect. But at stealing Bujak might have drawn the line, for money was different, money was vital substance. If they stole his savings he might have had to take action, out of respect for the substance, for himself—self-respect. But you couldn't be sure that Pop hadn't invented the bookie, the goon, the theft—the whole thing. He was capable of it, and you'd be a fool not to suspect him. Morris knew that Mother and Aunt Rebecca had told Mrs. Skoglund how wicked he was. They had painted him for her in poster colors—purple for vice, black for his soul, red for Hell flames: a gambler, smoker, drinker, deserter, screwer of women, and atheist. So Pop was determined to reach her. It was risky for everybody. The Reverend Doctor's operating costs were met by Skoglund Dairies. The widow paid Woody's seminary tuition; she bought dresses for the little sisters.

Woody, now sixty, fleshy and big, like a figure for the victory of American materialism, sunk in his lounge chair, the leather of its armrests softer to his fingertips than a woman's skin, was puzzled and, in his depths, disturbed by certain blots within him, blots of light in his brain, a blot combining pain and amusement in his breast (how did *that* get there?). Intense thought puckered the skin between his eyes with a strain bordering on headache. Why had he let Pop have his way? Why did he agree to meet him that day, in the dim rear of the poolroom?

"But what will you tell Mrs. Skoglund?"

"The old broad? Don't worry, there's plenty to tell her, and it's all true. Ain't I trying to save my little laundry-and-cleaning shop? Isn't the bailiff coming for the fixtures next week?" And Pop rehearsed his pitch on the Western Avenue car. He counted on Woody's health and his freshness. Such a straightforward-looking body was perfect for a con.

Did they still have such winter storms in Chicago as they used to have? Now they somehow seemed less fierce. Blizzards used to come straight down from Ontario, from the Arctic, and drop five feet of snow in an afternoon. Then the rusty green platform cars, with revolving brushes at both ends, came out of the barns to sweep the tracks. Ten or twelve streetcars followed in slow processions, or waited, block after block.

There was a long delay at the gates of Riverview Park, all the amusements covered for the winter, boarded up—the dragon's-back high-rides, the Bobs, the Chute, the Tilt-a-Whirl, all the fun machinery put together by mechanics and electricians, men like Bujak the tool-and-die-maker, good with engines. The blizzard was having it all its own way behind the gates, and you couldn't see far inside; only a few bulbs burned behind the palings. When Woody wiped the vapor from the glass, the wire mesh of the window guards was stuffed solid at eye level with snow. Looking higher, you saw mostly the streaked wind horizontally driving from the north. In the seat ahead, two black coal heavers, both in leather Lindbergh flying helmets, sat with shovels between their legs, returning from a job. They smelled of sweat, burlap sacking, and coal. Mostly dull with black dust, they also sparkled here and there.

There weren't many riders. People weren't leaving the house. This was a day to sit legs stuck out beside the stove, mummified by both the outdoor and the indoor forces. Only a fellow with an angle, like Pop, would go and buck such weather. A storm like this was out of the compass, and you kept the human scale by having a scheme to raise fifty bucks. Fifty soldiers! Real money in 1933.

"That woman is crazy for you," said Pop.

"She's just a good woman, sweet to all of us."

"Who knows what she's got in mind. You're a husky kid. Not such a kid, either."

"She's a religious woman. She really has religion."

"Well, your mother isn't your only parent. She and Rebecca and Kovner aren't going to fill you up with their ideas. I know your mother wants to wipe me out of your life. Unless I take a hand, you won't even understand what life is. Because they don't know— those silly Christers."

"Yes, Pop."

"The girls I can't help. They're too young. I'm sorry about them, but I can't do anything. With you it's different."

He wanted me like himself, an American.

They were stalled in the storm, while the cattle-colored car waited to have the trolley reset in the crazy wind, which boomed, tingled, blasted. At Howard Street they would have to walk straight into it, due north.

"You'll do the talking at first," said Pop.

Woody had the makings of a salesman, a pitchman. He was aware of this when he got to his feet in church to testify before fifty or sixty people. Even though Aunt Rebecca made it worth his while, he moved his own heart when he spoke up about his faith. But occasionally, without notice, his heart went away as he spoke religion and he couldn't find it anywhere. In its absence, sincere behavior got him through. He had to rely for delivery on his face, his voice—on behavior. Then his eyes came closer and closer together.

And in this approach of eye to eye he felt the strain of hypocrisy. The twisting of his face threatened to betray him. It took everything he had to keep looking honest. So, since he couldn't bear the cynicism of it, he fell back on mischievousness. Mischief was where Pop came in. Pop passed straight through all those divided fields, gap after gap, and arrived at his side, bent-nosed and broad-faced. In regard to Pop, you thought of neither sincerity nor insincerity. Pop was like the man in the song: he wanted what he wanted when he wanted it. Pop was physical; Pop was digestive, circulatory, sexual. If Pop got serious, he talked to you about washing under the arms or in the crotch or of drying between your toes or of cooking supper, of baked beans and fried onions, of draw poker or of a certain horse in the fifth race at Arlington. Pop was elemental. That was why he gave such relief from religion and paradoxes, and things like that. Now, Mother *thought* she was spiritual, but Woody knew that she was kidding herself. Oh, yes, in the British accent she never gave up she was always talking to God or about Him—please God, God willing, praise God. But she was a big substantial bread-and-butter down-to-earth woman, with down-to-earth duties like feeding the girls, protecting, refining, keeping pure the girls. And those two protected doves grew up so overweight, heavy in the hips and thighs, that their poor heads looked long and slim. And mad. Sweet but cuckoo—Paula cheerfully cuckoo, Joanna depressed and having episodes.

"I'll do my best by you, but you have to promise, Pop, not to get me in Dutch with Mrs. Skoglund."

"You worried because I speak bad English? Embarrassed? I have a mockie accent?"

"It's not that. Kovner has a heavy accent, and she doesn't mind."

"Who the hell are those freaks to look down on me? You're practically a man and your dad has a right to expect help from you. He's in a fix. And you bring him to her house because she's bighearted, and you haven't got anybody else to go to."

"I got you, Pop."

The two coal trimmers stood up at Devon Avenue. One of them wore a woman's coat. Men wore women's clothing in those years, and women men's, when there was no choice. The fur collar was spiky with the wet, and sprinkled with soot. Heavy, they dragged their shovels and got off at the front. The slow car ground on, very slow. It was after four when they reached the end of the line, and somewhere between gray and black, with snow spouting and whirling under the street lamps. In Howard Street, autos were stalled at all angles and abandoned. The sidewalks were blocked. Woody led the way into Evanston, and Pop followed him up the middle of the street in the furrows made earlier by trucks. For four blocks they bucked the wind and then Woody broke through the drifts to the snowbound mansion, where they both had to push the wrought-iron gate because of the drift behind it. Twenty rooms or more in this dignified house and nobody in them but Mrs. Skoglund and her servant Hjordis, also religious.

As Woody and Pop waited, brushing the slush from their sheepskin collars and Pop wiping his big eyebrows with the ends of his scarf, sweating and freezing, the chains began to rattle and Hjordis uncovered the air holes of the glass storm door by turning a wooden bar. Woody called her "monk-faced." You no longer see women like that, who put no female touch on the face. She came plain, as God made her. She said, "Who is it and what do you want?"

"It's Woodrow Selbst. Hjordis? It's Woody."

"You're not expected."

"No, but we're here."

"What do you want?"

"We came to see Mrs. Skoglund."

"What for do you want to see her?"

"Just tell her we're here."

"I have to tell her what you came for, without calling up first."

"Why don't you say it's Woody with his father, and we wouldn't come in a snowstorm like this if it wasn't important."

The understandable caution of women who live alone. Respectable old-time women, too. There was no such respectability now in those Evanston houses, with their big verandas and deep yards and with a servant like Hjordis, who carried at her belt keys to the pantry and to every closet and every dresser drawer and every padlocked bin in the cellar. And in High Episcopal Christian Science Women's Temperance Evanston, no tradespeople rang at the front door. Only invited guests. And here, after a ten-mile grind through the blizzard, came two tramps from the West Side. To this mansion where a Swedish immigrant lady, herself once a cook and now a philanthropic widow, dreamed, snowbound, while frozen lilac twigs clapped at her storm windows, of a new Jerusalem and a Second Coming and a Resurrection and a Last Judgment. To hasten the Second Coming, and all the rest, you had to reach the hearts of these scheming bums arriving in a snowstorm.

Sure, they let us in.

Then in the heat that swam suddenly up to their mufflered chins Pop and Woody felt the blizzard for what it was; their cheeks were frozen slabs. They stood beat, itching, trickling in the front hall that *was* a hall, with a carved newel post staircase and a big stained-glass window at the top. Picturing Jesus with the Samaritan woman. There was a kind of Gentile closeness to the air. Perhaps when he was with Pop, Woody made more Jewish observations than he would otherwise. Although Pop's most Jewish characteristic was that Yiddish was the only language he could read a paper in. Pop was with Polish Halina, and Mother was with Jesus Christ, and Woody ate uncooked bacon from the flitch. Still, now and then he had a Jewish impression.

Mrs. Skoglund was the cleanest of women—her fingernails, her white neck, her ears—and Pop's sexual hints to Woody all went wrong because she was so intensely clean, and made Woody think of a waterfall, large as she was, and grandly built. Her bust was big. Woody's imagination had investigated this. He thought she kept things tied down tight, very tight. But she lifted both arms once to raise a window and there it was, her bust, beside him, the whole unbindable thing. Her hair was like the raffia you had to soak before you could weave with it in a basket class—pale, pale. Pop, as he took his sheepskin off, was in sweaters, no jacket. His darting looks made him seem crooked. Hardest of all for these Selbsts with their bent noses and big, apparently straightforward faces was to look honest. All the signs of dishonesty played over them. Woody had often puzzled about it. Did it go back to the muscles, was it fundamentally a jaw problem—the projecting angles of the jaws? Or was it the angling that went on in the heart? The girls called Pop Dick Tracy, but Dick Tracy was a good guy. Whom could Pop convince? Here Woody caught a possibility as it flitted by. Precisely because of the way Pop looked, a sensitive person might feel remorse for condemning unfairly or judging unkindly. Just because of a face? Some must have bent over backward.

Then he had them. Not Hjordis. She would have put Pop into the street then and there, storm or no storm. Hjordis was religious, but she was wised up, too. She hadn't come over in steerage and worked forty years in Chicago for nothing.

Mrs. Skoglund, Aase (Osie), led the visitors into the front room. This, the biggest room in the house, needed supplementary heating. Because of fifteen-foot ceilings and high windows, Hjordis had kept the parlor stove burning. It was one of those elegant parlor stoves that wore a nickel crown, or miter, and this miter, when you moved it aside, automatically raised the hinge of an iron stove lid. That stove lid underneath the crown was all soot and rust, the same as any other stove lid. Into this hole you tipped the scuttle and the anthracite chestnut rattled down. It made a cake or dome of fire visible through the small isinglass frames. It was a pretty room, three-quarters paneled in wood. The stove was plugged into the flue of the marble fireplace, and there were parquet floors and Axminster carpets and cranberry-colored tufted Victorian upholstery, and a kind of Chinese étagère, inside a cabinet, lined with mirrors and containing silver pitchers, trophies won by Skoglund cows, fancy sugar tongs and cut-glass pitchers and goblets. There were Bibles and pictures of Jesus and the Holy Land and that faint Gentile odor, as if things had been rinsed in a weak vinegar solution.

"Mrs. Skoglund, I brought my dad to you. I don't think you ever met him," said Woody.

"Yes, Missus, that's me, Selbst."

Pop stood short but masterful in the sweaters, and his belly sticking out, not soft but hard. He was a man of the hard-bellied type. Nobody intimidated Pop. He never presented himself as a beggar. There wasn't a cringe in him anywhere. He let her see at once by the way he said "Missus" that he was independent and that he knew his way around. He communicated that he was able to handle himself with women. Handsome Mrs. Skoglund, carrying a basket woven out of her own hair, was in her fifties—eight, maybe ten years his senior.

"I asked my son to bring me because I know you do the kid a lot of good. It's natural you should know both of his parents."

"Mrs. Skoglund, my dad is in a tight corner and I don't know anybody else to ask for help."

This was all the preliminary Pop wanted. He took over and told the widow his story about the laundry-and-cleaning business and payments overdue, and explained about the fixtures and the attachment notice, and the bailiff's office and what they were going to do to him; and he said, "I'm a small man trying to make a living."

"You don't support your children," said Mrs. Skoglund.

"That's right," said Hjordis.

"I haven't got it. If I had it, wouldn't I give it? There's bread lines and soup lines all over town. Is it just me? What I have I divvy with. I give the kids. A bad father? You think my son would bring me if I was a bad father into your house? He loves his dad, he trusts his dad, he knows his dad is a good dad. Every time I start a little business going I get wiped out. This one is a good little business, if I could hold on to that little business. Three people work for me, I meet a payroll, and three people will be on the street, too, if I close down. Missus, I can sign a note and pay you in two months. I'm a common man, but I'm a hard worker and a fellow you can trust."

Woody was startled when Pop used the word "trust." It was as if from all four corners a Sousa band blew a blast to warn the entire world: "Crook! This is a crook!" But Mrs. Skoglund, on account of her religious preoccupations, was remote. She heard nothing. Although everybody in this part of the world, unless he was crazy, led a practical life, and you'd have nothing to say to anyone, your neighbors would have nothing to say to you, if communications were not of a practical sort, Mrs. Skoglund, with all her money, was unworldly—two-thirds out of this world.

"Give me a chance to show what's in me," said Pop, "and you'll see what I do for my kids."

So Mrs. Skoglund hesitated, and then she said she'd have to go upstairs, she'd have to go to her room and pray on it and ask for guidance—would they sit down and wait. There were two rocking chairs by the stove. Hjordis gave Pop a grim look (a dangerous person) and Woody a blaming one (he brought a dangerous stranger and disrupter to injure two kind Christian ladies). Then she went out with Mrs. Skoglund.

As soon as they left, Pop jumped up from the rocker and said in anger, "What's this with the praying? She has to ask God to lend me fifty bucks?"

Woody said, "It's not you, Pop, it's the way these religious people do."

"No," said Pop. "She'll come back and say that God wouldn't let her."

Woody didn't like that; he thought Pop was being gross and he said, "No, she's sincere. Pop, try to understand: she's emotional, nervous, and sincere, and tries to do right by everybody."

And Pop said, "That servant will talk her out of it. She's a toughie. It's all over her face that we're a couple of chiselers."

"What's the use of us arguing," said Woody. He drew the rocker closer to the stove. His shoes were wet through and would never dry. The blue flames fluttered like a school of fishes in the coal fire. But Pop went over to the Chinese-style cabinet or étagère and tried the handle, and then opened the blade of his penknife and in a second had forced the lock of the curved glass door. He took out a silver dish.

"Pop, what is this?" said Woody.

Pop, cool and level, knew exactly what this was. He relocked the étagère, crossed the carpet, listened. He stuffed the dish under his belt and pushed it down into his trousers. He put the side of his short thick finger to his mouth.

So Woody kept his voice down, but he was all shook up. He went to Pop and took him by the edge of his hand. As he looked into Pop's face, he felt his eyes growing smaller and smaller, as if something were contracting all the skin on his head. They call it hyperventilation when everything feels tight and light and close and dizzy. Hardly breathing, he said, "Put it back, Pop."

Pop said, "It's solid silver; it's worth dough."

"Pop, you said you wouldn't get me in Dutch."

"It's only insurance in case she comes back from praying and tells me no. If she says yes, I'll put it back."

"How?"

"It'll get back. If I don't put it back, you will."

"You picked the lock. I couldn't. I don't know how."

"There's nothing to it."

"We're going to put it back now. Give it here."

"Woody, it's under my fly, inside my underpants. Don't make such a noise about nothing."

"Pop, I can't believe this."

"For cry-ninety-nine, shut your mouth. If I didn't

trust you I wouldn't have let you watch me do it. You don't understand a thing. What's with you?"

"Before they come down, Pop, will you dig that dish out of your long johns."

Pop turned stiff on him. He became absolutely military. He said, "Look, I order you!"

Before he knew it, Woody had jumped his father and begun to wrestle with him. It was outrageous to clutch your own father, to put a heel behind him, to force him to the wall. Pop was taken by surprise and said loudly, "You want Halina killed? Kill her! Go on, you be responsible." He began to resist, angry, and they turned about several times, when Woody, with a trick he had learned in a Western movie and used once on the playground, tripped him and they fell to the ground. Woody, who already outweighed the old man by twenty pounds, was on top. They landed on the floor beside the stove, which stood on a tray of decorated tin to protect the carpet. In this position, pressing Pop's hard belly, Woody recognized that to have wrestled him to the floor counted for nothing. It was impossible to thrust his hand under Pop's belt to recover the dish. And now Pop had turned furious, as a father has every right to be when his son is violent with him, and he freed his hand and hit Woody in the face. He hit him three or four times in midface. Then Woody dug his head into Pop's shoulder and held tight only to keep from being struck and began to say in his ear, "Jesus, Pop, for Christ sake remember where you are. Those women will be back!" But Pop brought up his short knee and fought and butted him with his chin and rattled Woody's teeth. Woody thought the old man was about to bite him. And because he was a seminarian, he thought: Like an unclean spirit. And held tight. Gradually Pop stopped threshing and struggling. His eyes stuck out and his mouth was open, sullen. Like a stout fish. Woody released him and gave him a hand up. He was then overcome with many many bad feelings of a sort he knew the old man never suffered. Never, never. Pop never had these groveling emotions. There was his whole superiority. Pop had no such feelings. He was like a horseman from Central Asia, a bandit from China. It was Mother, from Liverpool, who had the refinement, the English manners. It was the preaching Reverend Doctor in his black suit. You have refinements, and all they do is oppress you? The hell with that.

The long door opened and Mrs. Skoglund stepped in, saying, "Did I imagine, or did something shake the house?"

"I was lifting the scuttle to put coal on the fire and it fell out of my hand. I'm sorry I was so clumsy," said Woody.

Pop was too huffy to speak. With his eyes big and sore and the thin hair down over his forehead, you could see by the tightness of his belly how angrily he was fetching his breath, though his mouth was shut.

"I prayed," said Mrs. Skoglund.

"I hope it came out well," said Woody.

"Well, I don't do anything without guidance, but the answer was yes, and I feel right about it now. So if you'll wait, I'll go to my office and write a check. I asked Hjordis to bring you a cup of coffee. Coming in such a storm."

And Pop, consistently a terrible little man, as soon as she shut the door, said, "A check? Hell with a check. Get me the greenbacks."

"They don't keep money in the house. You can cash it in her bank tomorrow. But if they miss that dish, Pop, they'll stop the check, and then where are you?"

As Pop was reaching below the belt, Hjordis brought in the tray. She was very sharp with him. She said, "Is this a place to adjust clothing, Mister? A men's washroom?"

"Well, which way is the toilet, then?" said Pop.

She had served the coffee in the seamiest mugs in the pantry, and she bumped down the tray and led Pop down the corridor, standing guard at the bathroom door so that he shouldn't wander about the house.

Mrs. Skoglund called Woody to her office and after she had given him the folded check said that they should pray together for Morris. So once more he was on his knees, under rows and rows of musty marbled-cardboard files, by the glass lamp by the edge of the desk, the shade with flounced edges, like the candy dish. Mrs. Skoglund, in her Scandinavian accent—an emotional contralto—raising her voice to Jesus-uh Christ-uh, as the wind lashed the trees, kicked the side of the house, and drove the snow seething on the windowpanes, to send light-uh, give guidance-uh, put a new heart-uh in Pop's bosom. Woody asked God only to make Pop put the dish back. He kept Mrs. Skoglund on her knees as long as possible. Then he thanked her, shining with candor (as much as he knew how), for her Christian generosity and he said, "I know that Hjordis has a cousin who works at the Evanston YMCA. Could she please phone him and try to get us a room tonight so that we don't have to fight the blizzard all the way back? We're almost as close to the Y as to the car line. Maybe the cars have even stopped running."

Suspicious Hjordis, coming when Mrs. Skoglund called to her, was burning now. First they barged in, made themselves at home, asked for money, had to have coffee, probably left gonorrhea on the toilet seat. Hjordis, Woody remembered, was a woman who wiped the doorknobs with rubbing alcohol after guests had left. Nevertheless, she telephoned the Y and got them a room with two cots for six bits.

Pop had plenty of time, therefore, to reopen the étagère, lined with reflecting glass or German silver (something exquisitely delicate and tricky), and as soon as the two Selbsts had said thank you and goodbye and were in midstreet again up to the knees in snow, Woody said, "Well, I covered for you. Is that thing back?"

"Of course it is," said Pop.

They fought their way to the small Y building, shut up in wire grille and resembling a police station—about the same dimensions. It was locked, but they made a racket on the grille, and a small black man let them in and shuffled them upstairs to a cement corridor with low doors. It was like the small-mammal house in Lincoln Park. He said there was nothing to eat, so they took off their wet pants, wrapped themselves tightly in the khaki army blankets, and passed out on their cots.

First thing in the morning, they went to the Evanston National Bank and got the fifty dollars. Not without difficulties. The teller went to call Mrs. Skoglund and was absent a long time from the wicket. "Where the hell has he gone?" said Pop.

But when the fellow came back, he said, "How do you want it?"

Pop said, "Singles." He told Woody, "Bujak stashes it in one-dollar bills."

But by now Woody no longer believed Halina had stolen the old man's money.

Then they went into the street, where the snow-removal crews were at work. The sun shone broad, broad, out of the morning blue, and all Chicago would be releasing itself from the temporary beauty of those vast drifts.

"You shouldn't have jumped me last night, Sonny."

"I know, Pop, but you promised you wouldn't get me in Dutch."

"Well, it's okay. We can forget it, seeing you stood by me."

Only, Pop had taken the silver dish. Of course he had, and in a few days Mrs. Skoglund and Hjordis knew it, and later in the week they were all waiting for Woody in Kovner's office at the settlement house. The group included the Reverend Doctor Crabbie, head of the seminary, and Woody, who had been flying along, level and smooth, was shot down in flames. He told them he was innocent. Even as he was falling, he warned that they were wronging him. He denied that he or Pop had touched Mrs. Skoglund's property. The missing object—he didn't even know what it was—had probably been misplaced, and they would be very sorry on the day it turned up. After the others were done with him, Dr. Crabbie said that until he was able to tell the truth he would be suspended from the seminary, where his work had been unsatisfactory anyway. Aunt Rebecca took him aside and said to him, "You are a little crook, like your father. The door is closed to you here."

To this Pop's comment was "So what, kid?"

"Pop, you shouldn't have done it."

"No? Well, I don't give a care, if you want to know. You can have the dish if you want to go back and square yourself with all those hypocrites."

"I didn't like doing Mrs. Skoglund in the eye, she was so kind to us."

"Kind?"

"Kind."

"Kind has a price tag."

Well, there was no winning such arguments with Pop. But they debated it in various moods and from various elevations and perspectives for forty years and more, as their intimacy changed, developed, matured.

"Why did you do it, Pop? For the money? What did you do with the fifty bucks?" Woody, decades later, asked him that.

"I settled with the bookie, and the rest I put in the business."

"You tried a few more horses."

"I maybe did. But it was a double, Woody. I didn't hurt myself, and at the same time did you a favor."

"It was for me?"

"It was too strange of a life. That life wasn't *you*, Woody. All those women . . . Kovner was no man, he was an in-between. Suppose they made you a minister? Some Christian minister! First of all, you wouldn't have been able to stand it, and second, they would throw you out sooner or later."

"Maybe so."

"And you wouldn't have converted the Jews, which was the main thing they wanted."

"And what a time to bother the Jews," Woody said. "At least *I* didn't bug them."

Pop had carried him back to his side of the line, blood of his blood, the same thick body walls, the same coarse grain. Not cut out for a spiritual life. Simply not up to it.

Pop was no worse than Woody, and Woody was no better than Pop. Pop wanted no relation to theory, and yet he was always pointing Woody toward a position—a jolly, hearty, natural, likable, unprincipled position. If Woody had a weakness, it was to be unselfish. This worked to Pop's advantage, but he criticized Woody for it, nevertheless. "You take too much on yourself," Pop was always saying. And it's true that Woody gave Pop his heart because Pop was so selfish. It's usually the selfish people who are loved the most. They do what you deny yourself, and you love them for it. You give them your heart.

Remembering the pawn ticket for the silver dish, Woody startled himself with a laugh so sudden that it made him cough. Pop said to him after his expulsion from the seminary and banishment from the settlement house, "You want in again? Here's the ticket. I hocked that thing. It wasn't so valuable as I thought."

"What did they give?"

"Twelve-fifty was all I could get. But if you want it you'll have to raise the dough yourself, because I haven't got it anymore."

"You must have been sweating in the bank when the teller went to call Mrs. Skoglund about the check."

"I was a little nervous," said Pop. "But I didn't think they could miss the thing so soon."

That theft was part of Pop's war with Mother. With Mother, and Aunt Rebecca, and the Reverend Doctor. Pop took his stand on realism. Mother represented the forces of religion and hypochondria. In four decades, the fighting never stopped. In the course of time, Mother and the girls turned into welfare personalities and lost their individual outlines. Ah, the poor things, they became dependents and cranks. In the meantime, Woody, the sinful man, was their dutiful and loving son and brother. He maintained the bungalow—this took in roofing, pointing, wiring, insulation, air-conditioning—and he paid for heat and light and food, and dressed them all out of Sears, Roebuck and Wieboldt's, and bought them a TV, which they watched as devoutly as they prayed. Paula took courses to learn skills like macramémaking and needlepoint, and sometimes got a little job as recreational worker in a nursing home. But she wasn't steady enough to keep it. Wicked Pop spent most of his life removing stains from people's clothing. He and Halina in the last years ran a Cleanomat in West Rogers Park—a so-so business resembling a laundromat—which gave him leisure for billiards, the horses, rummy and pinochle. Every morning he went behind the partition to check out the filters of the cleaning equipment. He found amusing things that had been thrown into the vats with the clothing—sometimes, when he got lucky, a locket chain or a brooch. And when he had fortified the cleaning fluid, pouring all that blue and pink stuff in from plastic jugs, he read the *Forward* over a second cup of coffee, and went out, leaving Halina in charge. When they needed help with the rent, Woody gave it.

After the new Disney World was opened in Florida, Woody treated all his dependents to a holiday. He sent them down in separate batches, of course. Halina enjoyed this more than anybody else. She couldn't stop talking about the address given by an Abraham Lincoln automaton. "Wonderful, how he stood up and moved his hands, and his mouth. So real! And how beautiful he talked." Of them all, Halina was the soundest, the most human, the most honest. Now that Pop was gone, Woody and Halina's son, Mitosh, the organist at the Stadium, took care of her needs over and above Social Security, splitting expenses. In Pop's opinion, insurance was a racket. He left Halina nothing but some out-of-date equipment.

Woody treated himself, too. Once a year, and sometimes oftener, he left his business to run itself, arranged with the trust department at the bank to take care of his gang, and went off. He did that in style, imaginatively, expensively. In Japan, he wasted little time on Tokyo. He spent three weeks in Kyoto and stayed at the Tawaraya Inn, dating from the seventeenth century or so. There he slept on the floor, the Japanese way, and bathed in scalding water. He saw the dirtiest strip show on earth, as well as the holy places and the temple gardens. He visited also Istanbul, Jerusalem, Delphi, and went to Burma and Uganda and Kenya on safari, on democratic terms with drivers, Bedouins, bazaar merchants. Open, lavish, familiar, fleshier and fleshier but (he jogged, he lifted weights) still muscular—in his naked person beginning to resemble a Renaissance courtier in full costume—becoming ruddier every year, an outdoor type with freckles on his back and spots across the flaming forehead and the honest nose. In Addis Ababa he took an Ethiopian beauty to his room from the street and washed her, getting into the shower with her to soap her with his broad, kindly hands. In Kenya he taught certain American obscenities to a black woman so that she could shout them out during the act. On the Nile, below Murchison Falls, those fever trees rose huge from the mud, and hippos on the sandbars belched at the passing launch, hostile. One of them danced on his spit of sand, springing from the ground and coming down heavy, on all fours. There, Woody saw the buffalo calf disappear, snatched by the crocodile.

Mother, soon to follow Pop, was being lightheaded these days. In company, she spoke of Woody as her boy—"What do you think of my Sonny?"—as though he was ten years old. She was silly with him, her behavior was frivolous, almost flirtatious. She just didn't seem to know the facts. And behind her all the others, like kids at the playground, were waiting their turn to go down the slide: one on each step, and moving toward the top.

Over Woody's residence and place of business there had gathered a pool of silence of the same perimeter as the church bells while they were ringing, and he mourned under it, this melancholy morning of sun and autumn. Doing a life survey, taking a deliberate look at the gross side of his case—of the other side as well, what there was of it. But if this heartache continued, he'd go out and run it off. A three-mile jog—five, if necessary. And you'd think that this jogging was an entirely physical activity, wouldn't you? But there was something else in it. Because, when he was a seminarian, between the shafts of his World's Fair rickshaw, he used to receive, pulling along (capable and stable), his religious experiences while he trotted. Maybe it was all a single experience repeated. He felt truth coming to him from the sun. He received a communication that was also light and warmth. It made him very remote from his horny Wisconsin passengers, those farmers whose whoops and whore cries he could hardly hear when he was in one of his states. And again out of the flaming of the sun would come to him a secret certainty that the goal set for this earth was that it should be filled with good, saturated with it. After everything preposterous, after dog had eaten dog, after the crocodile death had pulled everyone into his mud. It wouldn't conclude as Mrs. Skoglund, bribing him to round up the Jews and hasten the Second Coming, imagined it, but in another way. This was his clumsy intuition. It went no further. Subsequently, he proceeded through life as life seemed to want him to do it.

There remained one thing more this morning, which was explicitly physical, occurring first as a sensation in his arms and against his breast and, from the pressure, passing into him and going into his breast.

It was like this: When he came into the hospital room and saw Pop with the sides of his bed raised, like a crib, and Pop, so very feeble, and writhing, and toothless, like a baby, and the dirt already cast into his face, into the wrinkles—Pop wanted to pluck out the intravenous needles and he was piping his weak death noise. The gauze patches taped over the needles were soiled with dark blood. Then Woody took off his shoes, lowered the side of the bed, and climbed in and held him in his arms to soothe and still him. As if he were Pop's father, he said to him, "Now, Pop. Pop." Then it was like the wrestle in Mrs. Skoglund's parlor, when Pop turned angry like an unclean spirit and Woody tried to appease him, and warn him, saying, "Those women will be back!" Beside the coal stove, when Pop hit Woody in the teeth with his head and then became sullen, like a stout fish. But this struggle in the hospital was weak—so weak! In his great pity, Woody held Pop, who was fluttering and shivering. From those people, Pop had told him, you'll never find out what life is, because they don't know what it is. Yes, Pop—well, what is it, Pop? Hard to comprehend that Pop, who was dug in for eighty-three years and had done all he could to stay, should now want nothing but to free himself. How could Woody allow the old man to pull the intravenous needles out? Willful Pop, he wanted what he wanted when he wanted it. But what he wanted at the very last Woody failed to follow, it was such a switch.

After a time, Pop's resistance ended. He subsided and subsided. He rested against his son, his small body curled there. Nurses came and looked. They disapproved, but Woody, who couldn't spare a hand to wave them out, motioned with his head toward the door. Pop, whom Woody thought he had stilled, only had found a better way to get around him. Loss of heat was the way he did it. His heat was leaving him. As can happen with small animals while you hold them in your hand, Woody presently felt him cooling. Then, as Woody did his best to restrain him, and thought he was succeeding, Pop divided himself. And when he was separated from his warmth, he slipped into death. And there was his elderly, large, muscular son, still holding and pressing him when there was nothing anymore to press. You could never pin down that self-willed man. When he was ready to make his move, he made it—always on his own terms. And always, always, something up his sleeve. That was how he was.

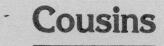

Cousins

JUST BEFORE THE SENTENCING OF TANKY METZ-
ger in a case memorable mainly to his immediate family, I wrote a letter—I was induced,
pressured, my arm was twisted—to Judge Eiler of the
Federal Court. Tanky and I are cousins, and Tanky's
sister Eunice Karger kept after me to intercede,
having heard that I knew Eiler well. He and I became
acquainted years ago when he was a law student and I
was presiding over a television program on Channel
Seven which debated curious questions in law. Later I
was toastmaster at a banquet of the Chicago Council
on Foreign Relations, and a picture in the papers
showed Eiler and me in dinner jackets shaking hands
and beaming at each other.

So when Tanky's appeal was turned down, as it
should have been, Eunice got me on the telephone.
First she had a cry so passionate that it shook me up in
spite of myself. When her control returned she said

that I must use my influence. "Lots of people say that you're friends with the judge."

"Judges aren't that way. . . ." I corrected myself: "Some judges may be, but Eiler isn't."

Eunice only pressed harder. "Please, Ijah, don't brush me off. Tanky could get up to fifteen years. I'm not in a position to spell out the entire background. About his associates, I mean. . . ." I knew quite well what she meant; she was speaking of his mob connections. Tanky had to keep his mouth shut if he didn't want the associates to order his execution.

I said, "I more or less get the point."

"Don't you feel for him?"

"How could I not."

"You've led a very different life from the rest, Ijah, but I've always said how fond you were of the Metzgers."

"It's true."

"And loved our father and our mother, in the old days."

"I'll never forget them."

She lost control again, and why she sobbed so hard, no expert, not even the most discerning, could exactly specify. She didn't do it from weakness. That I can say with certainty. Eunice is not one of your fragile vessels. She is forceful like her late mother, tenacious, determined. Her mother had been honorably direct, limited and primitive.

It was a mistake to say, "I'll never forget them," for Eunice sees herself as her mother's representative here among the living, and it was partly on Shana's account that she uttered such sobs. Sounds like this had never come over this quiet office telephone line of mine. What a disgrace to Shana that her son should be a convicted felon. How would the old woman have coped with such a wound! Still refusing to surrender her mother to death, Eunice (alone!) wept for what Shana would have suffered.

"Remember that my mother idolized you, Ijah. She said you were a genius."

"That she did. It was an intramural opinion. The world didn't agree."

Anyway, here was Eunice pleading for Raphael (Tanky's real name). For his part, Tanky didn't care a damn about his sister.

"Have you been in touch, you two?"

"He doesn't answer letters. He hasn't been returning calls. Ijah! I want him to know that I care!"

Here my feelings, brightened and glowing in the recollection of old times, grew dark and leaden on me. I wish Eunice wouldn't use such language. I find it hard to take. Nowadays "We Care" is stenciled on the walls of supermarkets and loan corporations. It may be because her mother knew no English and also because Eunice stammered when she was a kid that it gives her great satisfaction to be so fluent, to speak as the most advanced Americans now speak.

I couldn't say, "For Christ's sake don't talk balls to me." Instead I had to comfort her because she was heartsick—a layer cake of heartsickness. I said, "You may be sure he knows how you feel."

Gangster though he may be.

No, I can't swear that Cousin Raphael (Tanky) actually is a gangster. I mustn't let his sister's clichés drive me (madden me) into exaggeration. He associates with gangsters, but so do aldermen, city officials, journalists, big builders, fundraisers for charitable institutions—the mob gives generously. And gangsters aren't the worst of the bad guys. I can name greater evildoers. If I had been a Dante, I'd have worked it all out in full detail.

I asked Eunice pro forma why she had approached

me. (I didn't need to be a clairvoyant to see that Tanky had put her up to it.) She said, "Well, you are a public personality."

She referred to the fact that many years ago I invented the famous-trials TV program, and appeared also as moderator, or master of ceremonies. I was then in a much different phase of existence. Having graduated near the top of my law-school class, I had declined good positions offered by leading firms because I felt too active, or kinetic (hyperkinetic). I couldn't guarantee my good behavior in any of the prestigious partnerships downtown. So I dreamed up a show called *Court of Law*, in which significant, often notorious, cases from the legal annals were retried by brilliant students from Chicago, Northwestern, De Paul, or John Marshall. Cleverness, not institutional rank, was where we put the accent. Some of our most diabolical debaters were from the night schools. The opportunities for dialectical subtlety, imposture, effrontery, eccentric display, nasty narcissism, madness, and other qualifications for the practice of law were obvious. My function was to pick entertaining contestants (defense and prosecution), to introduce them, to keep up the pace—to set the tone. With the help of my wife (my then wife, who was a lawyer, too), I chose the cases. She was attracted by criminal trials with civil rights implications. My preference was for personal oddities, mysteries of character, ambiguities of interpretation—less likely to make a good show. But I proved to have a knack for staging these dramas. Before the program I always gave the contestants an early dinner at Fritzel's on Wabash Avenue. Always the same order for me—a strip steak, rare, over which I poured a small pitcher of Roquefort salad dressing. For dessert, a fudge sundae, with which I swallowed as much cigarette ash as chocolate.

I wasn't putting on an act. This early exuberance and brashness I later chose to subdue; it presently died down. Otherwise I might have turned into "a laff riot," in the language of *Variety,* a zany. But I saw soon enough that the clever young people whom I would lead in debate (mainly hustlers about to take the bar exam, already on the lookout for clients and avid for publicity) were terribly pleased by my odd behavior. The Fritzel dinner loosened up the participants. During the program I would guide them, goad them, provoke, pit them against one another, override them. At the conclusion, my wife Sable (Isabel: I called her Sable because of her dark coloring) would read the verdict and the decision of the court. Many of our debaters have since become leaders of the bar, rich celebrities. After our divorce, Sable married first one and then another of them. Eventually she made it big in communications—on National Public Radio.

Judge Eiler, then a young lawyer, was more than once a guest on the program.

So to my cousins I remained thirty years later the host and star of *Court of Law,* a media personality. Something magical, attributes of immortality. Almost as though I had made a ton of money, like a Klutznik or a Pritzker. And now I learned that to Eunice I was not only a media figure, but a mystery man as well. "In the years when you were gone from Chicago, didn't you work for the CIA, Ijah?"

"I did not. For five years, out in California, I was in the Rand Corporation, a think tank for special studies. I did research and prepared reports and analyses. Much the kind of thing the private group I belong to here now does for banks. . . ."

I wanted to dispel the mystery—scatter the myth of Ijah Brodsky. But of course words like "research" and "analysis" only sounded to her like spying.

A few years ago, when Eunice came out of the hospital after major surgery, she told me she had no one in all the world to talk to. She said that her husband, Earl, was "not emotionally supportive" (she wanted to say that he was close-fisted). Her daughters had left home. One was in the Peace Corps and the other, about to graduate from medical school, was too busy to see her. I asked Eunice out to dinner—drinks first in my apartment on Lake Shore Drive. She said, "All these dark old rooms, dark old paintings, these Oriental rugs piled one on top of the other, and books in foreign languages—and living alone" (meaning that I didn't have horrible marital fights over an eight-dollar gas bill). "But you must have girls—lady friends?"

She was hinting at the "boy question." Did the somber luxury I lived in disguise the fact that I had turned queer?

Oh, no. Not that, either. Just singular (to Eunice). Not even a different drummer. I do no marching.

But, to return to our telephone conversation, I finally got it out of Eunice that she had called me at the suggestion of Tanky's lawyer. She said, "Tanky is flying in tonight from Atlantic City"—gambling— "and asked to meet you for dinner tomorrow."

"Okay, say that I'll meet him at the Italian Village on Monroe Street, upstairs in one of the little private rooms, at seven P.M. To ask the headwaiter for me."

I hadn't really talked with Tanky since his discharge from the army, in 1946, when conversation was still possible. Once, at O'Hare about ten years ago, we ran into each other when I was about to board a plane and he was on the incoming flight. He was then a power in his union. (Just what this signified I have lately learned from the papers.) Anyway, he spotted me in the crowd and introduced me to the man he was traveling with. "I want you to meet my famous cousin, Ijah Brodsky," he said. At which moment I was gifted with a peculiar vision: I saw how we might have appeared to a disembodied mind above us both. Tanky was built like a professional football player who had gotten lucky and in middle age owned a ball club of his own. His wide cheeks were like rosy Meissen. He sported a fair curly beard. His teeth were large and square. What are the right words for Tanky at this moment?: voluminous, copious, full of vitamins, potent, rich, insolent. By way of entertainment he was putting his cousin on display—bald Ijah with the eyes of an orangutan, his face flat and round, transmitting a naiveté more suited to a brute from the zoo—long arms, orange hair. I was someone who emitted none of the signals required for serious consideration, a man who was not concerned with the world's work in any category which made full sense. It passed through my thoughts that once, early in the century, when Picasso was asked what young men in France were doing, he answered, *"La jeunesse, c'est moi."* But I had never been in a position to illustrate or represent *anything*. Tanky, in fun, was offering me to his colleague as an intellectual, and while I don't mind being considered clever, I confess I do feel the disgrace of being identified as an intellectual.

By contrast, consider Tanky. He had done well out of his rackets. He was one of those burly people who need half an acre of cloth for a suit, who eat New York sirloin strip steaks at Eli's, put together million-dollar deals, fly to Palm Springs, Las Vegas, Bermuda. Tanky was saying, "In our family, Ijah was the genius. One of them, anyway; we had a couple or three."

I was no longer the law-school whiz kid for whom a brilliant future had been predicted—so much was true. The tone of derision was justified, insofar as I had enjoyed being the family's "rose of expectancy."

As for Tanky's dark associate, I have no idea who he may have been—maybe Tony Provenzano, or Sally (Bugs) Briguglio, or Dorfman of the Teamsters union insurance group. It was not Jimmy Hoffa. Hoffa was then in jail. Besides, I, like millions of others, would have recognized him. We knew him personally, for after the war Tanky and I had both been employed by our cousin Miltie Rifkin, who at that time operated a hotel in which Hoffa was supposed to have an interest. Whenever Hoffa and his gang came to Chicago, they stayed there. I was then tutoring Miltie's son Hal, who was too fast and foxy to waste time on books. Longing to see action, Hal was only fourteen when Miltie put him in charge of the hotel bar. It amused his parents one summer to let him play manager, so that when liquor salesmen approached him, Miltie could say, "You'll have to see my son Hal; he does the buying. Ask for the young fellow who looks like Eddie Cantor." They would find a fourteen-year-old boy in the office. I was there to oversee Hal, while teaching him the rules governing the use of the ablative (he was a Latin School pupil). I kept an eye on him. A smart little kid of whom the parents were immensely proud.

Necessarily I spent much time in the bar, and so became acquainted with the Hoffa contingent. Goons, mostly, apart from Harold Gibbons, who was highly urbane and in conversation, at least with me, bookish in his interests. The others were very tough indeed, and Cousin Miltie made the mistake of trying to hold his own with them, man to man, a virile brute. He was not equal to this self-imposed challenge. He could be harsh, he accepted nihilism in principle, but the high-powered executive will simply was not there.

Miltie couldn't say, as Caesar did to a sentry who had orders not to let him pass, "It's easier for me to kill you than to argue." Hoffas are like that.

Tanky, then just out of the service, was employed by Miltie to search out tax-delinquent property for him. It was one of Miltie's side rackets. Evictions were common. So it was through Miltie Rifkin that Cousin Tanky (Raphael) met Red Dorfman, the one-time boxer who acted as broker between Hoffa and organized crime in Chicago. Dorfman, then a gym teacher, inherited Tanky from his father, from Red, the old boxer. A full set of gang connections was part of the legacy.

These were some of the people who dominated the world in which it was my intention to conduct what are often called "higher activities." To "long for the best that ever was": this was not an abstract project. I did not learn it over a seminar table. It was a constitutional necessity, physiological, temperamental, based on sympathies which could not be acquired. Human absorption in faces, deeds, bodies, drew me towards metaphysics. I had these peculiar metaphysics as flying creatures have their radar. Maturing, I found the metaphysics in my head. And school, as I have just told you, had little to do with it. As a commuting university student sitting for hours on the elevated trains that racketed, bobbled, squealed, pelted at top speed over the South Side slums, I boned up on Plato, Aristotle, or St. Thomas for Professor Perry's class.

But never mind these preoccupations. Here in the Italian Village was Tanky, out on a $500,000 bond, waiting to be sentenced. He didn't look good. He didn't have fast colors after all. His big face was swelled out by years of brutal business. The amateur internist in me diagnosed hypertension—250 over 165

271

were the numbers I came up with. His inner man was toying with a stroke as the alternative to jail. Tanky kept the Edwardian beard trimmed, for his morale, and that very morning, as this was no time to show white hairs, the barber might have given it a gold rinse. The kink of high vigor had gone out of it, however. Tanky wouldn't have cared for my sympathy. He was well braced, a man ready to take his lumps. The slightest hint that I was sorry would have irritated him. Experienced sorry-feelers will understand me, though, when I say that there was a condensed mass of troubles on his side of the booth. This mass emitted signals for which I lacked the full code.

An old-time joint opposite the First National, where I have my office on the fifty-first floor (those upswept incurves rising, rising), the Italian Village is one of the few restaurants in the city with private recesses for seduction or skulduggery. It dates back to the twenties and is decorated like a saint's day carnival in Little Italy, with strings of electric bulbs and wheels of lights. It also suggests a shooting gallery. Or an Expressionist stage set. Prohibition fading away, the old Loop was replaced by office buildings, and the Village became a respectable place, known to all the stars of the musical world. Here visiting divas and great baritones gorged on risotto after singing at the Lyric. Signed photos of artists hung on the walls. Still, the place retained its Al Capone atmosphere—redsauce blood, the footsmell of cheeses, the dishes of invertebrates raked up from sea mud.

Little was said of a personal nature. I worked across the street? Tanky said. Yes. Had he asked what my days were like, I would have begun by saying that I was up at six to play indoor tennis to start the blood circulating, and that when I got to the office I read the

New York Times, the *Wall Street Journal,* the *Economist,* and *Barron's,* and scanned certain printouts and messages prepared by my secretary. Having noted the outstanding facts, I put them all behind me and devoted the rest of the morning to my private interests.

But Cousin Tanky did not ask how my days were spent. He mentioned our respective ages—I am ten years his senior—and said that my voice had deepened as I grew older. Yes. My basso profundo served no purpose except to add depth to small gallantries. When I offer a chair to a lady at a dinner party, she is enveloped in a deep syllable. Or when I comfort Eunice, and God knows she needs it, my incoherent rumble seems to give assurance of stability.

Tanky said, "For some reason you keep track of all the cousins, Ijah."

The deep sound I made in reply was neutral. I didn't think it would be right, even by so much as a hint, to refer to his career in the union or to his recent trial.

"Tell me what happened to Miltie Rifkin, Ijah. He gave me a break when I got out of the army."

"Miltie now lives in the Sunbelt. Married to the switchboard operator from the hotel."

Now, Tanky might have given *me* fascinating information about Miltie, for I know that Cousin Miltie had been dying to draw Hoffa deeper into the hotel operation. Hoffa had such reservoirs of money behind him, all those billions in the pension fund. Miltie was stout, near obese, with a handsome hawk face, profile-proud, his pampered body overdressed, bedizened, his glance defiant and contentious. A clever money-maker, he was, in his fits—choleric by temperament—dangerously quick to throw punches. It was insane of him to fight so much. His former wife,

Libby, weighing upwards of two hundred and fifty pounds, hurrying about the hotel on spike heels, was what we used to call a "suicide blonde" (dyed by her own hand). Catering, booking, managing, menacing, bawling out the *garde-manger,* firing housekeepers, hiring bartenders, Libby was all made up like a Kabuki performer. In trying to restrain Miltie (they were less man and wife than business partners), she had her work cut out for her. Several times Miltie complained to Hoffa about one of his goons, whose personal checks were not clearing. The goon—his name escapes me, but for parking purposes he had a Clergy sticker on the windshield of his Chrysler—knocked Miltie down in the lobby, then choked him nearly to death. This occurrence came to the attention of Robert F. Kennedy, who was then out to get Hoffa, and Kennedy issued a subpoena for Cousin Miltie to testify before the McClellan Committee. To give evidence against Hoffa's people would have been madness. Libby cried out when word came that a subpoena was on its way: "Now see what you've done. They'll chop you to bits!"

Miltie fled. He drove to New York, where he loaded his Cadillac on the *Queen Elizabeth.* He didn't flee alone. The switchboard operator kept him company. They were guests in Ireland of the American ambassador (linked through Senator Dirksen and the senator's special assistant, Julius Farkash). While staying at the U.S. Embassy, Miltie bought land for what was to have become the new Dublin airport. He bought, however, in the wrong location. After which, he and his wife-to-be flew to the Continent in a transport plane carrying the Cadillac. They did crossword puzzles during the flight. Landing in Rome . . .

I spared Tanky these details, many of which he probably knew. Besides, the man had seen so much action that they wouldn't have been worth mentioning. It would have been an infraction of something to speak of Hoffa or to refer to the evasion of a subpoena. Tanky, of course, had been forced to say no to the usual federal immunity offer. It would have been fatal to accept it. One understands this better now that the FBI wiretaps and other pieces of evidence in the Williams-Dorfman trial have been made public. Messages like: "Tell Merkle that if he doesn't sell us the controlling interest in his firm on our terms, we'll waste him. Not only him. Say that we'll also hack up his wife and strangle his kids. And while you're at it, pass the word to his lawyer that we'll do the same to him and his wife, and his kids."

Tanky personally was no killer. He was Dorfman's man of business, one of his legal and financial team. He was, however, sent to intimidate people who were slow to cooperate or repay. He crushed his cigar on the fine finish of desks, and broke the framed photographs of wives and children (which I think in some cases a good idea). Millions of dollars had to be involved. He didn't get violent over trifles.

And naturally it would have been offensive to speak of Hoffa, for Tanky might be one of the few who knew how Hoffa had disappeared. I myself, reading widely (with the motives of a concerned cousin), was persuaded that Hoffa had entered a car on his way to a "reconciliation" meeting in Detroit. He was immediately knocked on the head and probably murdered in the back seat. His body was shredded in one machine, and incinerated in another.

Much knowledge of such happenings was in Tanky's looks, in the puffiness of his face—an edema of deadly secrets. This knowledge made him dangerous. Because of it he would go to prison. The organization, convinced that he was steadfast, would take care of him. What he needed from me was nothing but a private letter to the judge. "Your honor, I submit this statement to you on behalf of the defendant in *U.S.* v. *Raphael Metzger*. The family have asked me to intercede as a friend of the court, and I do so fully convinced that the jury has done its job well. I shall try to persuade you, however, to be lenient in sentencing. Metzger's parents were decent, good people. . . ." Adding, perhaps, "I knew him in his infancy," or "I was present at his circumcision."

These are not matters to bring to the court's attention: that he was a whopping kid; that nothing so big was ever installed in a high chair; or that he still wears the expression he was born with, one of assurance, of cheerful insolence. His is a case of the Spanish proverb:

*Genio y figura
Hasta la sepultura*

The divine or, as most would prefer to say, the genetic stamp visible even in corruption and ruin. And we belong to the same genetic pool, with a certain difference in scale. My frame is much narrower. Nevertheless, some of the same traits are there, creases in the cheeks, a turn at the end of the nose, and most of all, a tendency to fullness in the underlip —the way the mouth works towards the sense-world. You could identify these characteristics also in family pictures from the old country—the Orthodox, totally different human types. Yet the cheekbones of bearded men, a band of forehead under a large skullcap, the shock of a fixed stare from two esoteric eyes, are recognizable still in their descendants.

Cousins in an Italian restaurant, looking each other over. It was no secret that Tanky despised me. How could it be a secret? Cousin Ijah Brodsky, speaking strange words, never really making sense, acting from peculiar motives, obviously flaky. Studied the piano, was touted as some kind of prodigy, made a sensation in the Kimball Building (the Noah's Ark of stranded European music masters), worked at Compton's Encyclopedia, edited a magazine, studied languages—Greek, Latin, Russian, Spanish—and also linguistics.

I had taken America up in the wrong way. There was only one language for a realist, and that was Hoffa language. Tanky belonged to the Hoffa school —in more than half its postulates, virtually identical with the Kennedy school. If you didn't speak real, you spoke phony. If you weren't hard, you were soft. And let's not forget that at one time, when his bosses were in prison, Tanky, their steward, managed an institution that owns more real estate than the Chase Manhattan Bank.

But to return to Cousin Ijah: music, no; linguistics, no; he next distinguished himself at the University of Chicago Law School, after he had been disappointed in the university's metaphysicians. He didn't practice law, either; that was just another phase. A star who never amounted to anything. He fell in love with a concert harpist who had only eight fingers. Unrequited, it didn't pan out; she was faithful to her husband. Ijah's wife, who organized the TV show, had been as shrewd as the devil. She couldn't make anything of him, either. Ambitious, she dismissed him when it became plain that Ijah was not cut out for a team player, lacked the instincts of a go-getter. She was like Cousin Miltie's wife, Libby, and thought of herself as one of an imperial pair, the dominant one.

What was Tanky to make of someone like Ijah? Ijah was *not* passive. Ijah *did* have a life plan. But this plan was incomprehensible to his contemporaries. In fact, he didn't appear to have any contemporaries. He had contacts with the living. Not quite the same thing.

The principal characteristic of our existence is *suspense*. Nobody—nobody at all—can say how it's going to turn out.

What was curious and comical to Tanky was that Ijah should be so highly respected and connected. This deep-toned Ijah, a member of so many upperclass clubs and associations, was a gentleman. Tanky's cousin a *gentleman!* Ijah's bald head with the reasonably composed face was in the papers. He obviously made pretty good money (peanuts to Tanky). Maybe he would be reluctant to disclose to a federal judge that he was closely related to a convicted felon. If that was what Tanky thought, he was mistaken.

Years ago, Ijah was a kind of wild-ass type. His TV show was like a Second City act, a Marx Brothers routine. It went on in a fever of absurdities.

Ijah's conduct is much different now. Today he's quiet, he's a gentleman. What does it take to be a gentleman? It used to require hereditary lands, breeding, conversation. Towards the end of the last century, Greek and Latin did it, and I have some of each. If it comes to that, I enjoy an additional advantage in that I don't have to be anti-Semitic or strengthen my credentials as a civilized person by putting down Jews. But never mind that.

"Your Honor, it may be instructive to hear the real facts in a case you have tried. On the bench, one seldom learns what the wider human circumstances are. As Metzger's cousin, I can be *amicus curiae* in a larger sense.

"I remember Tanky in his high chair. Tanky is what he was called on the Schurz High football squad. To his mother he was R'foel. She called him Folya, or Folka, for she was a village woman, born behind the

Pale. A tremendous infant, strapped in, struggling with his bonds. A powerful voice and a strong color. Like other infants he must have fed on Pablum or farina, but Cousin Shana also gave him more potent things to eat. She cooked primitive dishes like calves' foot jelly in her kitchen, and I remember eating stewed lungs, which had a spongy texture, savory but chewy, much gristle. The family lived on Hoyne Street in a brick bungalow with striped awnings, alternating broad bands of white and cantaloupe. Cousin Shana was a person of great force, and she kept house as it had been kept for hundreds of years. She was a wide woman, a kind of human blast furnace. Her style of conversation was exclamatory. She began by saying, in Yiddish, "Hear! Hear! Hear! Hear!" And then she told you her opinion. It may be that persons of her type have become extinct in America. She made an immense impression on me. We were fond of each other, and I went to the Metzgers' because I was at home there, and also to see and hear primordial family life.

"Shana's aunt was my grandmother. My paternal grandfather was one of a dozen men who had memorized the whole of the Babylonian Talmud (or was it the Jerusalem one? here I am ignorant). All my life I have asked, "Why do that?" But it was done.

"Metzger's father sold haberdashery in the Boston Store down in the Loop. In the Austro-Hungarian Empire he had been trained as a cutter and also as a designer of men's clothing. A man of many skills, he was always nicely dressed, stocky, bald except for a lock at the front, combed to swerve to the right. Some men are mutely bald; his baldness was expressive; stressful lumps would form in his skin, which dissolved with the return of calm. He said little; he grinned and beamed instead, and if there is a celestial meridian of good nature, it intersected his face. He had guileless abbreviated teeth with considerable spaces between them. What else? He was a stickler for respect. Nobody was to take his amiability for granted. When his temper rose, failure to find words gave him a stifled look, while large lumps came up under his scalp. One seldom saw this, however. He suffered from a tic of the eyelids. Also, to show his fondness (to boys) he used harmless Yiddish obscenities—a sign that he took you into his confidence. You would be friends when you were old enough.

"Just one thing more, Your Honor, if you care about the defendant's personal background. Cousin Metzger, his father, enjoyed stepping out in the evening, and he often came to play cards with my father and my stepmother. In winter they drank tea with raspberry preserves; in summer I was sent to the drugstore to buy a quart brick of three-layered ice cream—vanilla, chocolate, and strawberry. You asked for 'Neapolitan.' It was a penny-ante poker game and often went on past midnight."

"I understand you're a friend of Gerald Eiler," said Tanky.

"Acquaintance. . . ."

"Ever been to his house?"

"About twenty years ago. But the house is gone, and so is his wife. I also used to meet him at parties, but the host who gave them passed away. About half of that social circle is in the cemetery."

As usual, I gave more information than my questioner had any use for, using every occasion to transmit my sense of life. My father before me also did this. Such a habit can be irritating. Tanky didn't care who was in the cemetery.

"You knew Eiler before he was on the bench?"

"Oh, long before. . . ."

"Then you might be just the guy to write to him about me."

By sacrificing an hour at my desk I might spare Tanky a good many years of prison. Why shouldn't I do it for old times' sake, for the sake of his parents, whom I held in such affection. I *had* to do it if I wanted to continue these exercises of memory. My souvenirs would stink if I let Shana's son down. I had no space to work out whether this was a moral or a sentimental decision.

I might also write to Eiler to show off the influence I so queerly had. Tanky's interpretation of my motives would make a curious subject. Did I want to establish that, bubble brain though I seemed to him, there were sound reasons why a letter from me might carry weight with a veteran of the federal judiciary like Eiler? Or prove that *I* had lived right? He would never concede me that. Anyway, with a long sentence hanging over him, he was in no mood to study life's mysteries. He was sick, deadly depressed.

"It's pretty snazzy across the street over at First National."

Below, in the plaza, is the large Chagall mosaic, costing millions, the theme of which is the Soul of Man in America. I often doubt that old Chagall had the strength necessary to take such a reading. He is too levitational. Too many fancies.

I explained: "The group I'm with advises bankers on foreign loans. We specialize in international law— political economy and so forth."

Tanky said, "Eunice is very proud of you. She sends me clippings about how you're speaking to the Council on Foreign Relations. Or you're sitting in the same box with the governor at the opera. Or were the escort of Mrs. Anwar Sadat when she got an honorary degree. And you play tennis, indoors, with *politicians.*"

How was it that Cousin Ijah's esoteric interests gave him access to these prominent people—art patrons, politicians, society ladies, dictators' widows? Tanky came down heavy on the politicians. About politicians he knew more than I ever would, knew the *real* guys; he had done business with the machine people, he had cash-flow relations with them. He could tell *me* who took from whom, which group owned what, who supplied the schools, hospitals, the county jail and other institutions, who milked public housing, handed out the franchises, made the sweetheart deals. Unless you were a longtime insider, you couldn't find the dark crossings used by the mob and the machine. They were occasionally revealed. Very recently two hit men tried to kill a Japanese dope supplier in his car. Tokyo Joe Eto is his name. He was shot three times in the skull and ballistics experts are unable to explain why not a single bullet penetrated the brain. Having nothing more to lose, Tokyo Joe named the killers, one of whom proved to be a deputy on the county sheriff's payroll. Were other city or county payrollers moonlighting for the Mafia? Nobody proposed to investigate. Cousin Tanky knew the answers to many such questions. Hence the gibing look he gave me in the booth. But even that look was diluted, much below full strength. Facing the shades of the prison house, he was not well. We had our share of wrongdoers in the family, but few who made it to the penitentiary. He didn't mean to discuss this with me, however. All he wanted was that I should use such influence as I might have. It was worth a try. Another iron in the fire. As for my motive in agreeing to intercede, it was too obscure to be worth the labor of examination. Sentiment. Eccentric foolery. Vanity.

"Okay, Raphael. I'll try a letter to the judge."

I did it for Cousin Metzger's tic. For the three bands of Neapolitan ice cream. For the furious upright growth of Cousin Shana's ruddy hair, and the avid veins of her temples and in the middle of her forehead. For the strength with which her bare feet advanced as she mopped the floor and spread the pages of the *Tribune* over it. It was also for Cousin Eunice's stammer, and for the elocution lessons that cured it, for the James Whitcomb Riley recitations she gave to the captive family and the determination of the "a-a-a-a" with which she stood up to the challenge of "When the Frost Is on the Punkin." I did it because I had been present at Cousin Tanky's circumcision and heard his cry. And because his cumbersome body was now wrapped in defeat. The curl had gone out of his beard. He looked like Death's sparring partner and his cheeks were battered under the eyes. And if he thought that *I* was the sentimentalist and *he* the nihilist, he was mistaken. I myself have some experience of evil and of the dissolution of the old bonds of existence; of the sores that have broken out on the body of mankind, which I, however, have the impulse to touch with my own hands.

I wrote the letter because the cousins are the elect of my memory.

"Raphael Metzger's parents, Your Honor, were hard-working, law-abiding people, not so much as a traffic violation on their record. Over fifty years ago, when the Brodskys came to Chicago, the Metzgers sheltered them for weeks. We slept on the floor, as penniless immigrants did in those days. We children were clothed and bathed and fed by Mrs. Metzger. This was before the birth of the defendant. Admittedly, Raphael Metzger became a tough guy. Still, he has committed no violent crimes and it is possible, with such a family background, that he may yet become a useful citizen. In pre-sentencing hearings, doctors have testified that he suffers from emphysema and also from high blood pressure. If he has to serve a sentence in one of the rougher prisons, his health may be irreparably damaged."

This last was pure malarkey. A good federal prison is like a sanatorium. I have been told by more than one ex-convict: "They made a new man out of me in jail. They fixed my hernia and operated my cataracts, they gave me false teeth and fitted me with a hearing aid. On my own, I could never afford it."

A veteran like Eiler has received plenty of clemency letters. Thousands of them are sent by civic leaders, by members of the Congress, and, sure as shooting, by other federal judges, all of them using the low language of high morals—payola letters putting in a good word for well-connected constituents or political buddies, or old friends in the rackets. You can leave it to Judge Eiler to read between the lines.

I may even have been effective. Tanky got a short sentence. Eiler certainly understood that Tanky was acting on instructions from the higher-ups. If there were kickbacks, he didn't keep much of the money. Presumably a few bucks did stick to his fingers, but he never would have owned four large homes, like some of his bosses. I take it, too, that the judge was aware of secret investigations then going on and of indictments being prepared by grand juries. The government was after bigger game. These are not matters which Eiler will ever discuss with me. When we meet, we talk music or tennis, sometimes foreign trade. We gossip about the university. But Eiler was aware that a stiff sentence might have endangered Tanky's life. He would have been suspected of giving information to get out sooner. It is generally agreed that Tanky's patron, Dorfman, was killed last year after his conviction in the Nevada bribery case because he would have been sent to prison for life and he might therefore well have chosen to make a deal with the authorities. Dorfman was shot in the head last winter by two men, executed with smooth skill in a parking lot. The TV cameras took many close-ups of the bloodstained slush. Nobody bothered to wash it away, and in my fantasy the rats came at night to lap it. Expecting to die, Dorfman made no arrangement to protect himself. He hired no bodyguards. A free-for-all shoot-out between bodyguards and hit-men might have brought reprisals against his family. So he silently endured the emotions of a doomed man, as he waited for the inevitable hit.

A word about how people think of such things in Chicago, about this life to which all have consented. Buy cheap, sell dear is the very soul of business. The foundations of political stability, of democracy, according even to its eminent philosophers, are swindle and fraud. Now, smoothness in fraud arranges immunity for itself. The top executives, the lawyers at the nucleus of power, the spreaders of the most fatal nets—*they* are never shredded and incinerated, *they* never leave the blood of their brains in parking lots. Therefore Chicagoans accord a certain respect to those four-mansion crooks who risk their lives in crimes of high visibility. We are looking at the fear of death that defines your essential bourgeois. The Chicago public doesn't examine its attitudes as closely as this, but there you are: the mob big shot has prepared his soul for execution. He *must.* For such elementary reminders that justice in some form still exists the plain man is grateful. (I am having a moment of impotent indignation; let's drop it.)

I have to relate that I was embarrassed by the

delivery of a case of Lafite-Rothschild prior to the sentencing. I hadn't yet mailed my letter to the judge. As a member (inactive) of the bar, I record this impropriety with discomfort. Nobody need know. Zimmerman's liquor truck brought me a dozen delicious bottles too conscience-contaminated to be drunk. I gave them to hostesses, as dinner gifts. At least Tanky knew good wine.

At the Italian Village I had ordered Nozzole, a decent Chianti which Tanky barely tasted. Too bad he didn't allow himself to become tipsy. I might have made him an amusing cousinly confidence (off the record for us both). I, too, am involved in the lending of big sums. Tanky dealt in millions. As one who prepares briefing documents, I am involved with the lending of billions to Mexico, Brazil, Poland, and other hopeless countries. That very day, the representative of a West African state had been sent into my office to discuss aspects of his country's hard-currency problems; in particular, restrictions on the importing of European luxury products, especially German and Italian automobiles used by the executive class (in which they made Sunday excursions with their ladies and all the kids to watch the public executions—the big entertainment of the week: he told this to me in his charming Sorbonnish English).

But Tanky would never have responded with confidences about the outfit. So I never did get a chance to open this potentially intriguing exchange between two Jewish cousins who dealt in megabucks.

Where this private, confidential wit might have been, there occurred instead a deep silence. Gulfs of silence are what give a basso profundo like mine its oceanic resonance when talk resumes.

It should be said that it's not my office work that

most absorbs me. I am consumed by different interests, passions. I am coming to that.

With time off for good behavior, Tanky would have only about eight full months to serve in a decent jail in the Sunbelt, where as a trained accountant he could reckon on being assigned light work, mostly fooling with computers. You would have thought that this would satisfy him. No, he was restless and pressing. He apparently thought that Eiler might have a soft spot for low-rumbling, off-the-wall Cousin Ijah. He may even have concluded that Ijah "had something" on the judge, if I know anything about the way minds work in Chicago.

In any case, Cousin Eunice telephoned again, to say, "I *must* see you." In her own behalf, she would have said, "I'd *like* to see you." So I knew it was Tanky. What now?

I recognized that I couldn't refuse. I was trapped. For when Coolidge was President the Brodskys had slept on Cousin Shana's floor. We were hungry and she fed us. The words of Jesus and the prophets can never be extracted from the blood of certain people.

Mind, I absolutely agree with Hegel (lectures at Jena, 1806) that the whole mass of ideas that have been current until now, "the very bonds of the world," are dissolving and collapsing like a vision in a dream. A new emergence of Spirit is—or had better be—at hand. Or as another thinker and visionary has put it, mankind was long supported by an unheard music which buoyed it, gave it flow, continuity, coherence. But this humanistic music has ceased, and now there is a different, barbarous music welling up, and a different elemental force has begun to manifest itself, without form as yet.

That, too, is a good way to put the matter: a cosmic

orchestra sending out music has suddenly canceled its performance. And where, with regard to the cousins, does that leave us? I confine myself to cousins. I do have brothers, but one of them is a foreign service officer whom I never see, while the other operates a fleet of taxicabs in Tegucigalpa and has written off Chicago altogether. I am blockaded in a small historical port, as it were. I can't sail forth; I can't even extricate myself from the ties of Jewish cousinhood. It may be that the dissolution of the bonds of the world affects Jews in different ways. The whole mass of ideas that have been current until now, the very bonds of the world . . .

What has Tanky to do with bonds or ties? Years in the underworld. Despises his sister. Thinks his cousin Ijah a creep. Here before us is a life to which all have consented. But not Cousin Ijah. Why is he a holdout? What sphere does he think *he* is from? If he doesn't get into the action so gratifying for the most significant and potent people around, where does he satisfy his instincts?

Well, we met in the Italian Village to drink Nozzole. The Village has three stories and three dining rooms, which I call Inferno, Purgatorio, and Paradiso. We ate our veal limone in Paradiso. In his need, Tanky turned to Ijah. Jewish consanguinity—a special phenomenon, an archaism of which the Jews, until the present century stopped them, were in the course of divesting themselves. The world as it was dissolving apparently collapsed on top of them, and the divestiture could not continue.

Okay, now I take Eunice to lunch atop the First National skyscraper, one of the monuments of the most curious present (how weird can these presents get?). I show her the view, and far, far below us is the Italian Village, a thin slice of old-world architecture from Hansl-and-Gretl time. The Village is squeezed on one side by the green opulent swellings of the new Xerox headquarters and on the other by the Bell Savings Corporation.

I am painfully aware that Eunice has had cancer surgery. I know that there is a tormenting rose of scar tissue under her blouse, and she told me when we last met about the pains in her armpit and her terror of recurrence. Her command of medical terminology, by the way, is terrific. And you never get a chance to forget how much behavioral science she has studied. To counteract old affections and pity, I round up in self-defense any number of negative facts about the Metzger family. First, brutal Tanky. Then the fact that old Metzger used to frequent burlesque prick-tease shows when he could spare an hour from his duties at the Boston Store, and I would see him in those horny dark joints on South State Street when I was cutting school. But that was not so negative. It was more touching than sinful. It was his way of coming to life; it was artificial resuscitation. A man of any sexual delicacy may feel himself hit in the genitals by a two-by-four after doing his conjugal duty in the bungalow belt. Cousin Shana was a dear soul but there was nothing of the painted erotic woman about her. Anyway, South State Street was nothing but meat-and-potatoes lewdness in meat-and-potatoes Chicago. In the refined Orient, even in holy cities, infinitely more corrupt exhibitions were offered to the public.

Then I tried to see what I might convict Cousin Shana of, and how I might disown even her. Towards the end of her life, owner of a large apartment building, she hitchhiked on Sheridan Road to save bus fare. So as to leave more money to Eunice she starved herself, some of the cousins said. They added that she, Eunice, would need every penny of it because her husband, Earl, a Park District employee, deposited his weekly check as soon as he was paid, locked it in his personal savings account. Rejected all financial responsibility. Eunice put the children through school on her own entirely. She was a psychologist with the Board of Education. Mental testing was her profession. (Her *racket,* Tanky might have called it.)

Eunice and I sit down at our reserved table atop the First National Bank and she transmits Tanky's new request. Eagerness to serve her brother consumes her. She is a mother like her own mother, all-sacrificing, and a sister to match. Tanky, who would get to see Eunice once in five years, is now in frequent communication with her. She brings his messages to me. I am like the great fish in the Grimm fairy tale. The fisherman freed him from his net and has been granted three wishes. We are now at wish number two. The fish is listening in the executive dining room. What does Tanky ask? Another letter to the judge, requesting more frequent medical examinations, a visit to a specialist, a special diet. "The stuff he has to eat makes him sick."

The great fish should now say, "Beware!"

Instead he says, "I can try."

He speaks in his deeper tones, a beautiful depth, three notes bowed out on the double bass, or the strange baryton—an ancient stringed instrument, part guitar, part bass viol; Haydn, who loved the baryton, wrote moving trios for it.

Eunice said, "My special assignment is to get him out of there alive."

To resume his existence deeper within the sphere of illicit money, operating out of hotels of the Las Vegas type, looking well (in sickness) amid glittering fixtures designed to make everybody the picture of perfect health.

Eunice was crowded with masses of feeling for which there was no language. She transferred her articulate powers to accessible themes. What made communication difficult was that she was very proud of the special vocabulary she had mastered. She was vain of her degree in educational psychology. "I am a professional person," she said. She got this in as often as possible. She was the fulfillment of her mother's obscure, powerful drive, her ambition for her child. Eunice was not pretty, but to Shana she was infinitely dear. She had been as daintily dressed as other small girls, in print party dresses with underpants (visible) of the same print material, in the fashion of the twenties. Among other kids her age she was, however, a giantess. Besides, the strain of stammering would congest her face. But then she learned to speak bold declarative sentences and these absorbed and contained the terrible energy of her stammer. With formidable discipline, she had harnessed the forces of her curse.

She said, "You've always been willing to advise me. I always felt I could turn to you. I'm grateful, Ijah, that you have so much compassion. It's no secret that my husband is not a supportive individual. He says no to everything I suggest. All money has to be totally separate. 'I keep mine, you hang on to yours," he tells me. He wouldn't educate the girls beyond high school —as much education as he got. I had to sell Mother's building—I took the mortgage myself. It's a shame that the rates were so low then. They're sky high now. Financially, I took a bath on that deal."

"Didn't Raphael advise you?"

"He said I was crazy to spend my whole inheritance

on the girls. What would I do in old age? Earl made the same argument. Nobody should be dependent. He says we must all stand on our own two feet."

"You're unusually devoted to your daughters. . . ."

I knew only the younger one—Carlotta—who had the dark bangs and the arctic figure of an Eskimo. With me this is not a pejorative. I am fascinated by polar regions and their peoples. Carlotta had long, sharp, painted nails, her look was febrile, her conversation passionate and inconsequent. At a family dinner I attended, she played the piano so crashingly that conversation was out of the question, and when Cousin Pearl asked her to play more softly she burst into tears and locked herself in the toilet. Eunice told me that Carlotta was going to resign from the Peace Corps and join an armed settlement on the West Bank.

Annalou, the older daughter, had steadier ambitions. Her grades hadn't been good enough for the better medical schools. Cousin Eunice now gave me an astonishing account of her professional education. "I had to pay extra," she said. "Yes, I had to commit myself to make a big donation to the school."

"Did you say the Talbot Medical School?"

"That's what I said. Even to get to talk to the director, a payoff was necessary. You need a clearance from a trustworthy person. I had to promise Scharfer—"

"Which Scharfer?"

"Our cousin Scharfer the fundraiser. You have to have a go-between. Scharfer said he would arrange the interview if I would make a gift first to *his* organization."

"Under the table, at a medical school?" I said.

"Otherwise I couldn't get into the director's office. Well, I made a contribution to Scharfer of twelve-five.

His price. And then I had to pledge myself to Talbot for fifty thousand dollars.''

"Over and above tuition?"

"Over and above. You can guess what a medical degree is worth, the income it guarantees. A small school like Talbot, no endowment, has no funding. You can't hire decent faculty unless you're competitive in salaries, and you can't get accreditation without an adequate faculty.''

"So you had to pay?"

"I made a down payment of half, with the balance promised before graduation. No degree until you deliver. It's one of those concealed interfaces the general public never gets to see.''

"Were you able to manage all this?"

"Even though Annalou was president of her class, word came that they were expecting the final installment. It made me pretty desperate. Bear in mind that I held a five-percent mortgage, and the rate is now about fourteen. Earl wouldn't even talk to me about it. I took the problem to my psychiatrist. His advice was to write to the school director. We formulated a statement—a promise to make good on the twenty-five. I said that I was a person of 'the highest integrity.' When I went to my lawyer to check out the language, he advised against 'highest.' Just 'integrity' was enough. So I wrote, 'On my word as a person of known integrity.' Then Annalou was allowed to graduate, on the strength of this.''

"And . . . ?" I said.

My question puzzled her. "A twenty-cent stamp saved me a fortune.''

"You're not going to pay?"

"I wrote the *letter . . .*" she said.

A difference of emphasis separated us. She sat straighter, rejecting the back of the chair, stiffening herself upwards from the base of the spine. Little Eunice had become severely bony, just an old broad, except for the attraction of nobility, the high, prominent profile, the face charged with her mother's color, part blood, part irrationality. Put together, if you can, the contemporary 'smarts' she took pride in with these glimpses of patrician antiquity.

But if one of us was an anachronism, it was myself. Again, Cousin Ijah, holding out. With what motive? For unspecified reasons, I didn't congratulate Eunice on her exploit. She longed for me to tell her what a clever thing she had done, how dandy it was, and I seemed determined to disappoint her. What could my puzzling balkiness mean?

"Those words, 'high integrity,' saved you twenty-five thou . . . ?"

"Just 'integrity.' I told you, Ijah, I cut out the 'high.' "

Well, why shouldn't Eunice, too, make advantageous use of a fine word? All the words were up for grabs. Her grasp of politics was better than mine. I didn't like to see the word 'integrity' fucked up. I suppose the best reason I could advance was the defense of poetry. That was a stupid reason, given that she was defending her one-breasted body. A metastasis would bankrupt her.

The subject was changed. We talked a little about her husband. He had been busy in Grant Park, on the lakefront. Because of the alarming jump in the crime rate, the park board had decided to cut down concealing shrubbery and demolish the old-style comfort stations. Rapists used the bushes for cover, and women had been stabbed to death in the toilets, so now there were cans of the sentry-box type, admitting only one person at a time. Karger was administering the new installations. So Eunice said with pride, although the account she gave of her husband, when all references were assembled, did not make a favorable impression. Weirdly close-mouthed, he dismissed all attempts at conversation. Conversation not worthwhile. Maybe he was right. I saw his point. On the plus side, he didn't give a damn what people thought of him. He was a stand-up eccentric. His independence appealed to me. He had no act going, anyway.

"I have to pay half the rent," said Eunice. "And also the utilities."

I didn't buy her hard-luck story. "Why do you stay together?"

She explained, "I'm covered by his Blue Cross-Blue Shield . . ." Most people would have been convinced by this explanation. My response was neutral; I was taking it all under consideration.

When lunch ended, she asked to see what my office was like. "My cousin the genius," she said, very pleased by the size of the room. I must be important to rate so much space on the fifty-first floor of a great building. "I won't ask what you do with all these gadgets, documents, and books. For instance, these huge green books. I'm sure it bores you to have to explain."

The huge faded green books, dating from the beginning of the century, had nothing at all to do with my salaried functions. When I read them I was playing hooky. They were two volumes in the series of reports of the Jesup Expedition, published by the American Museum of Natural History. Siberian ethnography. Fascinating. I was beguiled of my griefs (considerable griefs) by these monographs. Two tribes, the Koryak and the Chukchee, as described by Jochelson and Bogoras, absorbed me totally. Just as old Metzger had been drawn magnetically from the Boston Store (charmed from his clerk's duties) by bump-and-grinders, so I neglected office work for these books. Political radicals Waldemar Jochelson and Waldemar Bogoras (curious Christian names for a pair of Russian Jews) were exiled to Siberia in the 1890s and, in the region where the Soviets later established the worst of their labor camps, Magadan and Kolyma, the two Waldemars devoted years to the study of the native tribes.

About this arctic desert, purified by frosts as severe as fire, I read for my relief as if I were reading the Bible. In winter darkness, even within a Siberian settlement you might be lost if the wind blew you down, for the speed of the snow was such as to bury you before you could recover your feet. If you tied up your dogs you would find them sometimes smothered when you dug them out in the morning. In this dark land you entered the house by a ladder inside the chimney. As the snows rose, the dogs climbed up to smell what was cooking. They fought for places at the chimney tops and sometimes fell into the caldron. There were photographs of dogs crucified, a common form of sacrifice. The powers of darkness surrounded you. A Chukchee informant told Bogoras that there were invisible enemies who beset human beings from all sides, demanding spirits whose mouths were always gaping. The people cringed and gave ransom, buying protection from these raving ghosts.

The geography of mental travel can't be the same from century to century; the realms of gold move away. They float into the past. Anyway, a wonderful silence formed around me in my office as I read about these tribes and their spirits and shamans—it doubled, quadrupled. It became a tenfold silence, right in the middle of the Loop. My windows look towards Grant Park. Now and then I rested my eyes on the lakefront, where Cousin Karger had sheared away the flowering shrubs to deprive sex maniacs of their cover, and set up narrow single-occupancy toilets. The monumental park, and the yacht basin, with sleek boats owned by lawyers and corporate executives. Sexual brutalities weekdays, at anchor; on Sundays the same frenzied erotomaniacs sail peacefully with the wife and kids. And whether we are preparing a new birth of spirit or the agonies of final dissolution (and this is the *suspense* referred to some pages back) depends on what you think, feel, and will about such manifestations or apparitions, on the kabbalistic skill you develop in the interpretation of these contemporary formations. My intuition is that the Koryak and the Chukchee lead me in the right direction.

So I go into trances over Bogoras and Jochelson at the office. Nobody bothers me much. At conference time I wake up. I become seerlike and the associates like to listen to my analyses. I was right about Brazil, right about Iran. I foresaw the revolution of the mullahs, which the President's advisers did not. But my views had to be rejected. Returns so huge for the lending institutions, and protected by government guarantees—I couldn't expect my recommendations to be accepted. My reward is to be praised as 'deep' and 'brilliant.' Where the kids in Logan Square used to see the eyes of an orangutan, my colleagues see the gaze of a clairvoyant. Nobody comes right out with it, but everybody reads my reports and the main thing is that I am left alone to pursue my spiritual investigation. I pore over an old photograph of Yukaghir women on the bank of the Nalemna River. The far shore barren—snow, rocks, spindling trees. The women are squatting, stringing a catch of big whitefish piled in the foreground, working with needle and thread at thirty degrees below zero, Fahrenheit. Their labor makes them sweat so that they take off their fur bodices and are half naked. They even 'thrust large cakes of snow into their bosoms.' Primitive women overheating at thirty below and cooling their breasts with snow lumps. As I read I ask myself who in this building, this up-up-upward skyscraper containing thousands, has the strangest imaginations. Who knows what secret ideas others are having, the dreams of these bankers, lawyers, career women—their fancies and mantic visions? They themselves couldn't bring them out, frightened by their crazy intensity. Human beings, by definition, half the time mad.

So who will mind if I eat up these books? Actually, I am rereading them. My first acquaintance with them goes back many years. I was piano player in a bar near the capitol in Madison, Wisconsin. I even sang some specialty numbers, one of which was "The Princess Papooli Has Plenty Papaya." I was rooming with my cousin Ezekiel on the wrong side of the tracks. Zeke, called Seckel in the family, was then lecturing in primitive languages at the state university, but his main enterprise took him to the north woods every week. He drove off each Wednesday in his dusty Plymouth to record Mohican folk tales. He had found some Mohican survivors and, in the upper peninsula, he did just as Jochelson had done, with the assistance of his wife, Dr. Dina Brodsky, in eastern Siberia. Seckel assured me that this Dr. Brodsky was a cousin. At the turn of the century, the two Jochelsons had come to New York City to work at the American Museum of Natural History with Franz Boas. Seckel insisted that at that time Dr. Brodsky had looked up the family.

Why were the Jews such avid anthropologists? Among the founders of the science were Durkheim and Lévy-Bruhl, Marcel Mauss, Boas, Sapir, Lowie.

They may have believed that they were demystifiers, that science was their motive and that their ultimate aim was to increase universalism. I don't see it that way myself. A truer explanation is the nearness of ghettos to the sphere of Revelation, an easy move for the mind from rotting streets and rancid dishes, a direct ascent into transcendence. This of course was the situation of Eastern Jews. The Western ones were prancing and preening like learned Germans. And were Polish and Russian Jews (in disgrace with civilized judgment, afflicted with tuberculosis and diseased eyes) so far from the imagination of savage practices? They didn't have to make a Symbolist decision to derange their senses; they were born that way. Exotics going out to do science upon exotics. And then it all came out in Rabbinic-Germanic or Cartesian-Talmudic forms.

Cousin Seckel, by the way, had no theorizing bent. His talent was for picking up strange languages. He went down to the Louisiana bayou country to learn an Indian dialect from its last speaker, who was moribund. In a matter of months he spoke the language perfectly. So on his deathbed, the old Indian at last had somebody to talk to, and when he was gone there was only Seckel in possession of the words. The tribe lived on in him alone. I learned one of the Indian love songs from him: *"Hai y'hee, y'hee y'ho*—Kiss me before you go."* He urged me to play it in the cocktail lounge. He passed on to me also a recipe for Creole jambalaya (ham, rice, crawfish, peppers, chicken, and tomatoes), which as a single man I have no occasion to cook. He had great skill also as a maker of primitive cat's cradles, and had a learned paper on Indian string-figures to his credit. Some of these cat's cradles I can still manage myself, when there are kids to entertain.

A stout young man, round-backed, Seckel had a Hasidic pallor. His plump face wore earnest lines, and the creases of his forehead resembled the frets of a musical instrument. Dark hair covered his head in virile curls, somewhat dusty from his five-hundred-mile weekly trips to Indian country. Seckel didn't bathe much, didn't often change his underclothes. It didn't matter to the woman who loved him. She was Dutch, Jennie Bouwsma, and carried her books in a rucksack. She appears in my memory wearing a tam and knee socks, legs half bare and looking inflamed in the Wisconsin winter. While in the sack with Seckel, she shouted out loudly. There were no doors, only curtains in our little rooms. Seckel hurried back and forth. His calves and buttocks were strongly developed, white, muscular. I wonder how this classic musculature got into the family.

We rented from the widow of a locomotive engineer. We had the ground floor of an old frame house.

The only book that Seckel picked up that year was *The Last of the Mohicans,* of which he would read the first chapter to put himself to sleep. On the theoretical side, he said he was a pluralist. Marxism was *out.* He also denied the possibility of a science of history—he took a strong position on this. He described himself as a Diffusionist. All culture was invented *once,* and spread from a single source. He had actually read G. Elliot Smith and was committed to a theory of the Egyptian origins of everything.

His sleepy eyes were deceiving. Their dazed look was a screen for labors of linguistics that never stopped. His dimples did double duty, for they were sometimes critical (I refer here to the modern crisis, the source of the *suspense).* I ran into Seckel in Mexico City in 1947, not too long before he died. He was leading a delegation of Indians who knew no

Spanish, and since no one in the Mexican civil service could speak their lingo, Seckel was their interpreter and no doubt the instigator of their complaints as well. These silent Indians, men in sombreros and white droopy drawers, the black hair growing at the corners of their lips, came out of the sun, which was their element, into the colonnades of the government building.

All this I remember. The one thing I forget is what I myself was doing in Mexico.

It was through Seckel, via Dr. Dina Brodsky, that I learned of the work of Waldemar Jochelson (presumably a cousin by marriage) on the Koryak. At a ladies' auxiliary sale I bought a charming book called *To the Ends of the Earth* (by John Perkins and the American Museum of Natural History), and found in it a chapter on the tribes of eastern Siberia. Then I recalled the monographs I had first seen years ago in Madison, Wisconsin, and borrowed the two Jesup volumes from the Regenstein Library. The women of Koryak myth, I read, were able to detach their genitalia when necessary and hang them up on the trees; and Raven, an unearthly comedian, the mythic father of the tribe, when he explored his wife's innards, entering her from behind, found himself first of all standing in a vast chamber. In contemplating such inventions or fantasies, one should bear in mind how hard a life the Koryak led, how they struggled to survive. In winter the fishermen had to hack holes in solid ice to a depth of six feet to drop their lines in the river. Overnight these holes were filled and frozen again. Koryak huts were cramped. A woman, however, was roomy. The tribe's mythic mother was palatial.

Very sympathetic to me (I'm sure she isn't being merely nosy), my assistant, Miss Rodinson, comes into the office to ask why I have been bent over at the window for an hour, apparently staring down into Monroe Street. It's only that these giant mat-green monographs borrowed from the Regenstein are hard to hold, and I rest them on the windowsill. In the eagerness of her sympathy Miss Rodinson perhaps wishes she might enter my thoughts, make herself useful. But what help can she be? Better not enter this lusterless pelagic green, the gateway to a savage Siberia that no longer exists.

Two weeks from now, I am being sent to a conference in Europe, on the rescheduling of debts, and she wants approval for travel arrangements. Will I be landing first in Paris? I say, vaguely, yes. And putting up for two nights at the Montalembert? Then Geneva, and returning via London. All this is routine. She is aware that she isn't getting to me. Then, because I have spoken to her about Tokyo Joe Eto (my interest in such items having increased since Tanky's patron, Dorfman, was murdered), she hands me a clipping from the *Tribune*. The two men who botched the execution of Tokyo Joe have themselves been executed. Their bodies were found in the trunk of a Buick parked in residential Naperville. A terrible stink had been rising from the car and there were flies parading over the lid of the trunk, denser than May Day in Red Square.

Eunice called me again, not about her brother this time but about her Uncle Mordecai, my father's first cousin—the head of the family, insofar as there is a family, and insofar as it has a head. Mordecai—Cousin Motty, as we called him—had been hurt in an automobile accident, and as he was nearly ninety it was a serious matter—and so I was on the telephone with Eunice, speaking from a dark corner of my dark

apartment. I can't really say why I should have had it
so dark. I have a clear preference for serene light and
simple outlines. Evidently I am not yet ready for this,
requiring instead a Holy Sepulchre atmosphere, far
too many Oriental rugs bought from Mr. Hering at
Marshall Field's (he recently retired and devotes
himself to his horse farm), and books with old bind-
ings, which I long ago stopped reading. Apart from
economics and international banking, my only reading matter for months has been the reports of the
Jesup Expedition, and I am attracted to certain books
by Heidegger. But you can't browse through Heidegger; Heidegger is hard work. Sometimes I read the
poems of Auden as well, or biographies of Auden.
That's neither here nor there. I suspect I created these
dark and antipathetic surroundings in order to force
myself to revise or rearrange myself at the core. (To
resolve the *suspense*.) The essentials are all present.
What they need is proper arrangement.

Now, why anybody should pursue such a project in
one of the great capitals of the American superpower
is also a subject of interest. I have never discussed this
with anyone, but I have had colleagues say to me
(sensing that I was up to something out-of-the-way)
that there was so much spectacular action in a city like
Chicago, there were so many things going on in the
outer world, the city itself was so rich in opportunities
for *real* development, a center of such wealth, power,
drama, rich even in crimes and vices, in diseases, and
intrinsic—not accidental—monstrosities, that it was
foolish, querulous, to concentrate on oneself. The
common daily life was more absorbing than anybody's
inmost anything. Well, yes, and I think I have fewer
romantic illusions about this inmost stuff than most.
Conscious inmosts when you come to look at them are
mercifully vague, considering the abominations that

lurk under their formlessness. Besides, I avoid anything resembling a *grandiose initiative*. Also I am not isolated by choice. I can't seem to find the contemporaries I require.

I'd like to get back to this presently. Cousin Mordecai has quite a lot to do with it.

Eunice, on the telephone, was telling me about the accident. Cousin Riva, Motty's wife, was at the wheel, Motty's license having been lifted years ago. Too bad. He had just discovered, after fifty years of driving, what a rearview mirror was for. Riva's license should have been taken away, too, said Eunice, who had never liked Riva (there had been a long war between Shana and Riva; it continued through Eunice). Riva overruled everybody and would not give up her Chrysler. She had become too small to drive that huge machine. Well, she had wrecked it, finally.

"Are they hurt?"

"She wasn't at all. *He* was—his nose and his right hand, pretty bad. In the hospital he developed pneumonia."

I felt a pang at this. Poor Motty, he was already in such a state of damage before the accident.

Eunice went on. News from the frontiers of science: "They can handle pneumonia now. It used to carry them off so fast that the doctors called it 'the old man's friend.' Now they've sent him home. . . ."

"Ah." We had gotten another stay. It couldn't be put off for long, but every reprieve was a relief. Mordecai was the eldest survivor of his generation, and extinction was close, and feelings had to be prepared.

Cousin Eunice had more to tell: "He doesn't like to leave his bed. Even before the accident they had that problem with him. After breakfast he'd get under the covers again. This was hard on Riva, because she likes

to be active. She went to business with him every day
of her life. She said it was spooky to have Motty
covering himself up in bed. It was abnormal behavior,
and she forced him to go to a family counselor in
Skokie. The woman was very good. She said that all
his life he had got up at five A.M. to go to the shop, and
it was no wonder after all the sleep he had missed if he
wanted to catch up."

I didn't go with this interpretation. I let it pass,
however.

"Now let me tell you the very latest," said Eunice.
"He still has fluid in the lungs and they have to make
him sit up. They force him."

"How do they do it?"

"He has to be strapped into a chair."

"I think I'd rather skip this visit."

"You can't do that. You always were a pet of his."

This was true, and I saw now what I had done:
claimed Motty's affection, given him my own, treated
him with respect, observed his birthdays, extended to
him the love I had felt for my own parents. By such
actions, I had rejected certain revolutionary developments of the past centuries, the advanced views of the
enlightened, the contempt for parents illustrated with
such charm and sharpness by Samuel Butler, who had
said that the way to be born was alone, with a
twenty-thousand-pound note pinned to your diaper; I
had missed the classic lessons of a Mirabeau and his
father, of Frederick the Great, of Old Goriot and his
daughters, of Dostoyevsky's parricides—shunning
what Heidegger holds up before us as "the frightful,"
using the old Greek words *deinon* and *deinotaton* and
telling us that the frightful is the gate to the sublime.
The very masses are turning their backs on the family.
Cousin Motty in his innocence was unaware of these
changes. For these and other reasons—mixed reasons

—I was reluctant to visit Cousin Motty, and Eunice was quite right to remind me that this put my affection in doubt. I was in a box. Once under way, these relationships have to be played to the end. I couldn't fink out on him. Now, Tanky, who was Motty's nephew, hadn't set eyes on the old man in twenty years. This was fully rational and consistent. When I last saw him the old man couldn't speak, or wouldn't. He was shrunken. He turned away from me.

"He always loved you, Ijah."

"And I love him."

Eunice said, "He's aware of everything."

"That's what I'm afraid of."

Self-examination, all theoretical considerations set aside, told me that I loved the old man. Imperfect love, I admit. Still, there it was. It had always been there.

Eunice, having discovered to what extent I was subject to cousinly feelings, was increasing her influence over me. So here I was picking her up in my car and driving her out to Lincolnwood, where Motty and Riva lived in a ranch-style house.

When we entered the door, Cousin Riva threw up her now crooked arms in a 'hurrah' gesture and said, "Motty will be so happy. . . ."

Quite separate from this greeting was the look her shrewd blue eyes gave us. She didn't at all care for Eunice, and for fifty years she had taken a skeptical view of me, not lacking in sympathy but waiting for me to manifest trustworthy signs of normalcy. To me she had become a dear old lady who was also very tough-minded. I remembered Riva as a full-figured, dark-haired, plump, straight-legged woman. Now all the geometry of her figure had changed. She had come down in the knees like the jack of a car, to a diamond posture. She still made an effort to move with speed, as if she were dancing after the Riva she had once been. But that she was no longer. The round face had lengthened, and a Voltairean look had come into it. Her blue stare put it to you directly: Read me the riddle of this absurd transformation, the white hair, the cracked voice. My transformation, and for that matter yours. Where is your hair, and why are you stooped? And perhaps there were certain common premises. All these physical alterations seem to release the mind. For me there are further suggestions: that as the social order goes haywire and the constraints of centuries are removed, and the seams of history open, as it were, walls come apart at the corners, bonds dissolve, and we are freed to think for ourselves—provided we can find the strength to make use of the opportunity—to escape through the gaps, not succumbing in lamentations but getting on top of the collapsed pile.

There were children and grandchildren, and they satisfied Riva, undoubtedly, but she was not one of your grannies. She had been a business woman. She and Motty had built a large business out of a shop with two delivery wagons. Sixty years ago Cousin Motty and his brother Shimon, together with my father, their first cousin, and a small work-force of Polish bakers, had supplied a few hundred immigrant grocery stores with bread and kaiser rolls, and with cakes—fry cakes, layer cakes, coffee cakes, cream puffs, bismarcks, and eclairs. They had done it all in three ovens fired with scrap wood—mill edgings with the bark still on them, piled along the walls—and with sacks of flour and sugar, barrels of jelly, tubs of shortening, crates of eggs, long hod-shaped kneading vats, and fourteen-foot slender peels that slipped in and out of the heat to bring out loaves. Everybody was coated in flour except Cousin Riva, in an office

under the staircase, where she kept the books and did
the billing and the payroll. My father's title at the
shop was Manager, as if the blasting ovens and the
fragrance filling the whole block had anything to do
with "Management." He could never Manage anything. Nerve Center of Anxieties would have been a
better title, with the chief point of concentration in
the middle of his forehead, like a third eye for all that
might go wrong in the night, when he was in charge.
They built a large business (not my father, who went
out on his own and was never connected with any
sizable success), and the business expanded until it
reached the limits of its era, when it could not adapt
itself to the conditions set by supermarkets—
refrigerated long-distance shipping, uniformity of
product, volume (demands for millions of dozens of
kaiser rolls). So the company was liquidated. Nobody
was to blame for that.

Life entered a new phase, a wonderful or supposedly wonderful period of retirement—Florida and all
that, places where the warm climate favors dreaming,
and people, if they haven't become too restless and
distorted, may recover the exaltation of a prior state
of being. Out of the question, as we all know. Well,
Motty made an earnest effort to be a good American.
A good American makes propaganda for whatever
existence has forced him to become. In Chicago,
Motty went to his downtown club for a daily swim. He
was a "character" down there. For a decade he
entertained the membership with jokes. These were
excellent jokes. I had heard most of them from my
father. Many of them required some knowledge of the
old country—Hebrew texts, parables, proverbs. Much
of it was fossil material, so that if you were unaware
that in the shtetl the Orthodox, as they went about
their tasks, recited the Psalms to themselves in an un-

dertone, you had to ask for footnotes. Motty wished, and deserved, to be identified as a fine, cheerful old man who had had a distinguished career, perhaps the city's best baker, rich, magnanimous, a person of known integrity. But when the older members of the club died off, there was nobody to exchange such weighty values with. Motty, approaching ninety, still latched on to people to tell them funny things. These were his gift offerings. He repeated himself. The commodity brokers, politicians, personal-injury lawyers, bagmen and fixers, salesmen and promoters who worked out at the club lost patience with him. He was offensive in the locker room, wrapped in his sheet. Nobody knew what he was talking about. Too much Chinese in his cantos, too much Provençal. The club asked the family to keep him at home.

"Forty years a member," said Riva.

"Yes, but his contemporaries are dead. The new people don't appreciate him."

I had always thought that Motty with his endless jokes was petitioning for acceptance, pleading his case, and that by entertaining in the locker room he suffered a disfigurement of his nature. He had spoken much less when he was younger. As a young boy at the Russian bath among grown men, I had admired Motty's size and strength when we squatted in the steam. Naked, he resembled an Indian brave. Crinkly hair grew down the center of his head. His dignity was a given of his nature. Now there was no band of hair down the middle. He had shrunk. His face was reduced. During his decade of cheer when he swam and beamed, pure affection, he was always delighted to see me. He said, "I have reached the *shmonim*"—eighties—"and I do twenty lengths a day in the pool." Then, "Have you heard this one?"

"I'm sure I haven't."

"Listen. A Jew enters a restaurant. Supposed to be good, but it's filthy."

"Yes."

"And there isn't any menu. You order your meal from the tablecloth, which is stained. You point to a spot and say, "What's this? *Tzimmes?* Bring me some.'"

"Yes."

"And the waiter writes no check. The customer goes straight to the cashier. She picks up his necktie and says, 'You ate *tzimmes.*' But then the customer belches and she says, 'Ah, you had radishes, too.'"

This is no longer a joke but a staple of your mental life. When you've heard it a hundred times it becomes mythic, like Raven crawling into his wife's interior and finding himself in a vast chamber. All jokes, however, have now stopped.

Before we go upstairs, Cousin Riva says, "I see where the FBI has done a Greylord Sting operation on your entire profession and there will be hundreds of indictments."

No harm intended. Riva is being playful, without real wickedness, simply exercising her faculties. She likes to tease me, well aware that I don't practice law, don't play the piano, don't do any of the things I was famous for (with intramural fame). Then she says, her measured way of speaking unchanged, "We mustn't allow Motty to lie down, we have to force him to sit up, otherwise the fluid will accumulate in his lungs. The doctor has ordered us to strap him in."

"He can't take that well."

"Poor Motty, he hates it. He's escaped a couple of times. I feel bad about it. We all do. . . ."

Motty is belted into an armchair. The buckles are behind him. My first impulse is to release him, despite doctor's orders. Doctors prolong life, but how Motty feels about the rules they impose cannot be known. He acknowledges our visit with a curt sign, slighter than a nod, then turns his head away. It is humiliating to be seen like this. It occurs to me that in the letter to Judge Eiler it had crossed my mind that Tanky in his high chair had struggled in silence, determined to tear free from his straps.

Motty is not ready to talk—not able. So nothing at all is said. It is a visit and we stand visiting. What do I want with Motty anyway, and why have I made a trip from the Loop to molest him? His face is even smaller than when I saw him last—*genio* and *figura* making their last appearance, the components about to get lost. He is down to nature now, and reckons directly with death. It's no great kindness to come to witness this.

In my first recollections, Eunice stood low, sucking her thumb. Now Eunice is standing high, and it's Riva who is low. Cousin Riva's look is contracted. No way of guessing what she thinks. The TV is switched off. Its bulging glass is like the forehead of an intrusive somebody who has withdrawn into his evil secret, inside the cokey (brittle gray) cells of the polished screen. Behind the drawn drapes is North Richmond Street, static and empty like all other nice residential streets, all the human interest in them siphoned off by bigger forces, by the main action. Whatever is not plugged into the main action withers and is devoured by death. Motty became the patriarch-comedian when his business was liquidated. Now there are no forms left for life to assume.

Something has to be said at last, and Eunice calls upon her strengths, which are scientific and advisory. She seems, moreover, to be prompted by a kind of comic instinct. She says, "You ought to have physiotherapy for Uncle Motty's hand, otherwise he'll lose the use of it. I'm *very* surprised that this has been neglected."

Cousin Riva is furious at this. She already blames herself for the accident, she had been warned not to drive, and also for the strapped chair, but she will not allow Cousin Eunice to take such a critical tone. "I think I can be relied upon to look after my husband," she says, and leaves the room. Eunice follows her, and I can hear her making a fuller explanation to the "layman," persisting. The cure of her stutter fifty years ago sold her forever on professional help. "Send for the best" is her slogan.

To sit on the bed, I move aside Riva's books and magazines. It comes back to me that she used to like Edna Ferber, Fannie Hurst, and Mary Roberts Rinehart. Once at Lake Zurich, Ill., she let me read her copy of *The Circular Staircase*. With this came all of the minute particulars, unnecessarily circumstantial. The family drove out one summer day in three cars and on the way out of town Cousin Motty stopped at a hardware store on Milwaukee Avenue and bought a clothesline to secure the picnic baskets on the roof of the Dodge. He stood on the bumpers and on the running board and lashed the baskets everywhich way, crisscross.

Like the dish in which you clean watercolor brushes, Lake Zurich is yellow-green, the ooze is deep, the reeds are thick, the air is close, and the grove smells not of nature but of sandwiches and summer bananas. At the picnic table there is a poker game presided over by Riva's mother, who has drawn down the veil of her big hat to keep off the mosquitoes and perhaps also to conceal her looks from the other players. Tanky, about two years old, escapes naked from his mother and the mashed potatoes she cries after him to eat. Shana's brothers, Motty and Shimon, walk in the picnic grounds, discussing bakery matters. Mountainous Shimon has a hump, but it is a hump of strength, not a disfigurement. Huge hands hang from his sleeves. He cares nothing for the seersucker jacket that covers his bulging back. He bought it, he owns it, but by the way he wears it he turns it against itself. It becomes some sort of anti-American joke. His powerful step destroys small vegetation. He is deadly shrewd and your adolescent secrets burn up in the blue fire of his negating gaze. Shimon didn't like me. My neck was too long, my eyes were too alien. I was studious. I held up a false standard, untrue to real life. Cousin Motty defended me. I can't say that he was entirely in the right. Cousin Shana used to say of me, "The boy has an open head." What she meant was that book learning was easy for me. As far as they went, Cousin Shimon's intuitions were more accurate. On the shore of Lake Zurich I should have been screaming in the ooze with the other kids, not reading a stupid book (it had an embossed monochrome brown binding) by Mary Roberts Rinehart. I was refusing to hand over my soul to "actual conditions," which are the conditions uncovered now by the FBI's sting. (The disclosures of corruption won't go very far; the worst of the bad guys have little to fear.)

Cousin Shana was on the wrong track. What she said is best interpreted as metaphysics. It wasn't the *head* that was open. It was something else. We enter the world without prior notice, we are manifested before we can be aware of manifestation. An original self exists or, if you prefer, an original soul. It may be as Goethe suggested, that the soul is a theater in which Nature can show itself, the only such theater that it has. And this makes sense when you attempt to account for some kinds of passionate observation— the observation of cousins, for example. If it were just

313

observation in the usual sense of the term, what would it be worth? But if it is expressed "As a man is, so he sees. As the Eye is formed, such are its powers," that is a different matter. When I ran into Tanky and his hoodlum colleague at O'Hare and thought what a disembodied William Blake Eye above us might see, I was invoking my own fundamental perspective, that of a person who takes for granted distortion in the ordinary way of seeing but has never given up the habit of referring all truly important observations to that original self or soul.

I believed that Motty in his silence was consulting the "original person." The distorted one could die without regrets, perhaps was already dead.

The seams open, the bonds dissolve, and the untenability of existence releases you back again to the original self. Then you are free to look for real being under the debris of modern ideas, and in a magical trance, if you like, or with a lucidity altogether different from the lucidity of *approved* types of knowledge.

It was at about this moment that Cousin Motty beckoned me with his head. He had something to say. It was very little. Almost nothing. Certainly he said nothing that I was prepared to hear. I didn't expect him to ask to be unbuckled. As I bent towards him I put one hand on his shoulder, sensing that he would want me to. I'm sure he did. And perhaps it would have been appropriate to speak to him in his native language, as Seckel in the bayous had spoken to his Indian, the last of his people. The word Motty now spoke couldn't have been *"Shalom."* Why should he give such a conventional greeting? Seeing how he had puzzled me, he turned his eyes earnestly on me—they were very large. He tried again.

So I asked Riva why he was saying this, and she

explained, "Oh, he's saying 'Scholem.' Over and over he reminds me that we've been receiving mail for you from Scholem Stavis. . . ."

"From Cousin Scholem? . . . Not *Shalom*."

"He must not have an address for you."

"I'm unlisted. And we haven't seen each other in thirty years. You could have told him where to reach me."

"My dear, I had my hands full. I wish you would take all this stuff away. It fills a whole drawer in my pantry, and it's been on Motty's mind as unfinished business. He'll feel much better. When you take it."

As she said "take all this stuff away" she glanced towards Eunice. It was a heavy glance. "Take this cross from me" was her message. Sighing, she led me to the kitchen.

Scholem Stavis, a Brodsky on his mother's side, was one of the blue-eyed breed of cousins, like Shimon and Seckel. When Tanky in that memorable moment at O'Hare Airport had spoken of geniuses in the family—"We had a couple or three"—he was referring also to Scholem, holding the pair of us up to ridicule. "If you're so smart, how come you ain't rich?" was the category his remark fell into, together with "How many divisions does the Pope have?" Old-style immigrant families had looked eagerly for prodigies. Certain of the children had tried to gratify their hopes. You couldn't blame Tanky for grinning at the failure of such expectations.

Scholem and I, growing up on neighboring streets, attending the same schools, had traded books, and since Scholem had no trivial interests, it was Kant and Schelling all the way, it was Darwin and Nietzsche, Dostoyevsky and Tolstoy, and in our senior year in high school it was Oswald Spengler. A whole year was invested in *The Decline of the West*. In his letters (Riva gave me a Treasure Island shopping bag to carry them in) Scholem reminded me of these shared interests. He wrote with a dated dignity that I rather appreciated. He sounded just a little like the Constance Garnett translations of Dostoyevsky. He addressed me as "Brodsky." I still prefer the Garnett translations to all later ones. It isn't real Dostoyevsky if it doesn't say, "Just so, Porfiry Petrovitch," or "I worshipped Tanya, as it were." I take a more slam-bang approach to things myself. I have a weakness for modern speed and even a touch of blasphemy. I offer as an example Auden's remark about Rilke, "The greatest lesbian poet since Sappho." Just to emphasize that we can't afford to forget the dissolution of the bonds (announced at Jena, 1806). But of course I didn't dispute the superiority of Dostoyevsky or Beethoven, whom Scholem always mentioned as the Titans. Scholem had been and remained a Titanist. The documents I brought home from Riva's pantry kept me up until four in the morning. I didn't sleep at all.

It was Scholem's belief that he had made a discovery in biology that did with Darwin what Newton had done with Copernicus, and what Einstein had done with Newton, and the development and application of Scholem's discovery made possible a breakthrough in philosophy, the first major breakthrough since the *Critique of Pure Reason*. I might have predicted from my early recollections of him that Scholem wouldn't do anything by halves. He was made of durable stuff. Wear out? Well, in the course of nature we all wore out, but life would never crack him. In the old days we would walk all over Ravenswood. He could pack more words into a single breath than any talker I ever knew, and in fact he resisted breathing altogether, as an interruption. White-faced, thin, queerly elastic in his gait, thumbs hooked into the pockets of his pants, he was always ahead of me, in a pale fever. His breath had an odor like boiled milk. As he lectured, a white paste formed in the corners of his mouth. In his visionary state he hardly heard what you were saying, but ran galactic rings around you in a voice stifled with urgency. I thought of him later when I came to read Rimbaud, especially the "Bateau Ivre"—a similar intoxication and storming of the cosmos, only Scholem's way was abstruse, not sensuous. On our walks he would pursue some subject like Kant's death categories, and the walk-pursuit would take us west on Foster Avenue, then south to the great Bohemian Cemetery, then around and around North Park College and back and forth over the bridges of the Drainage Canal. Continuing our discussion in front of automobile showrooms on Lawrence Avenue, we were not likely to notice our gestures distorted in the plateglass windows.

He looked altogether different in the color photo that accompanied the many documents he had mailed. His eyebrows were now thick and heavy, color dark, aspect grim, eyes narrowed, mouth compressed and set in deep folds. Scholem hadn't cracked, but you could see how much pressure he had had to withstand. It had driven hard into his face, flattened the hair to his skull. In one of the Holy Sepulchre corners of my apartment, I studied the picture closely. Here was a man really worth examining, an admirable cousin, a fighter made of stern stuff.

By contrast, I seemed to myself a slighter man. I could understand why I had tried my hand at the entertainment business instead, a seriocomic MC on Channel Seven—Second City cabaret stuff, dinner among the hoods and near-hoods at Fritzel's, even cutting a caper on Kupcinet's inane talk show before self-respect counseled me to knock it off. I now took a more balanced view of myself. Still, I recognized that in matters of the intellect I had yielded first honors to Cousin Scholem Stavis. Even now the unwavering intensity of his face, the dilation of his nose breathing fire earthwards, tell you what sort of man this is. Since the snapshot was taken near his apartment house, you can see the scope of his challenge, for behind him is residential Chicago, a street of Chicago six-flats, a good address sixty years ago, with all the middle-class graces available to builders in the twenties—a terrifying setting for a man like Scholem. Was this a street to write philosophy in? It's because of places like this that I hate the evolutionism that tells us we must die in stages of boredom for the eventual perfection of our species.

But in these streets Cousin Scholem actually did write philosophy. Before he was twenty-five years old he had already broken new ground. He told me that he had made the first real advance since the eighteenth century. But before he could finish his masterpiece the Japanese attacked Pearl Harbor, and the logic of his revolutionary discoveries in biology, philosophy, and world history made it necessary for him to enter the armed forces—as a volunteer, of course. I worked hard over the pages he had sent, trying to understand the biological and world-historical grounds of all this. The evolution of gametes and zygotes; the splitting of plants in monocotyledons and dicotyledons, of the animals into annelids and vertebrates—these were familiar to me. When he moved from these into a discussion of the biological foundations of modern politics, it was only my good will that he took with him, not my understanding. The great land masses were held by passive, receptive nations. Smaller states were the aggressive impregnating forces. No résumé would help; I'd have to read the full text, he wrote. But Right and Left, he wished to tell me now, were epiphenomena. The main current would turn finally into a broad, centrist, free evolutionary continuum which was just beginning to reveal its promise in the Western democracies. From this it is easy to see why Scholem enlisted. He came to the defense not only of democracy but also of his theories.

He was an infantry rifleman and fought in France and Belgium. When American and Russian forces met on the Elbe and cut the German armies in two, Cousin Scholem was in one of the patrols that crossed the river. Russian and American fighting men cheered, drank, danced, wept, and embraced. Not hard to imagine the special state of a Northwest Side Chicago kid whose parents emigrated from Russia and who finds himself a fighter in Torgau, in the homeland of Kant and Beethoven, a nation that had organized and carried out the mass murder of Jews. I noted just a while ago that an Ijah Brodsky, his rapt soul given over to the Chukchee and the Koryak, could not be certain that his thoughts were the *most* curious in the mental mass gathered within the First National Building, at the forefront of American capitalism in its subtlest contemporary phase. Well, neither can one be certain that among the embracing, weeping, boozing soldiers whooping it up in Torgau (nor do I omit the girls who were with the Russian troops, nor the old women who sat cooling their feet in the river—very swift at that point) there wasn't someone else equally preoccupied with biological and historical theories. But Cousin Scholem in the land of . . . well, Spengler—why should we leave out

Spengler, whose parallels between antiquity and modernity had worked us up intolerably when we were boys in Ravenswood?—Cousin Scholem had not only read world history, not merely thought it and untied some of its most stupefying, paralyzing knots and tangles just before enlisting, he was also personally, effectively experiencing it as a rifleman. Soldiers of both armies, Scholem in the midst of them, took an oath to be friends forever, never to forget each other, and to build a peaceful world.

For years after this my cousin was busy with organizational work, appeals to governments, activities at the UN, and international conferences. He went to Russia with an American delegation and in the Kremlin handed to Khrushchev the map used by his patrol as it approached the Elbe—a gift from the American people to the Russian people, and an earnest of amity.

The completion and publication of his work, which he considered to be the only genuine contribution to pure philosophy in the twentieth century, had to be postponed.

For some twenty years Cousin Scholem was a taxicab driver in Chicago. He was now retired, a pensioner of the cab company, living on the North Side. He was not, however, living quietly. Recently he had undergone cancer surgery at the VA Hospital. The doctors told him that he would soon be dead. This was why I had received so much mail from him, a pile of documents containing reproductions from *Stars and Stripes,* pictures of the embracing troops at Torgau, photostats of official letters, and final statements, both political and personal. I had a second and then a third look at the recent picture of Scholem— the inward squint of his narrow eyes, the emotional power of his face. He had meant to have a significant life. He believed that his death, too, would be significant. I myself sometimes think what humankind will be like when I am gone, and I can't say that I foresee any special effects from my final disappearance, whereas Cousin Scholem has an emotional conviction of achievement, and believes that his influence will continue for the honor and dignity of our species. I came presently to his valedictory statement. He makes many special requests, some of them ceremonial. He wants to be buried at Torgau on the Elbe, close to the monument commemorating the defeat of the Nazi forces. He asks that his burial service begin with a reading from the conclusion of *The Brothers Karamazov* in the Garnett translation. He asks that the burial service conclude with the playing of the second movement of Beethoven's Seventh Symphony, the Solti recording with the Vienna Philharmonic. He writes out the inscription for his headstone. It identifies him by the enduring intellectual gift he leaves to mankind, and by his participation in the historic oath. He concludes with John 12:24: "Verily, verily, I say unto you, Except a corn of wheat fall into the ground and die, it abideth alone; but if it die, it bringeth forth much fruit."

Appended to the valedictory is a letter from the Department of the Army, Office of the Adjutant General, advising Mr. Stavis that he will have to find out what rules the German Democratic Republic (East Germany) has governing the bringing into their country of human remains for the purpose of burial. Inquiries may be made at the GDR chancery in Washington, D.C. As for expenses, the liability of the U.S. Government is unfortunately restricted, and it cannot pay for the transportation of Scholem's body, much less for the passage of his mourning family. Allowances for cemeteries and burial plots may be available through the Veterans Administration. The letter is decent and sympathetic. Of course, the colonel who signs it can't be expected to know how remarkable a person Scholem Stavis is.

There is a final communication, concerning a gathering next year in Paris (September 1984) to commemorate the seventieth anniversary of the Battle of the Marne. This will honor the taxi drivers who took part in the defense of the city by carrying fighting men to the front. Cabbies from all countries have been invited to this event, even pedal-cab drivers from Southeast Asia. The grand procession will form near Napoleon's tomb and then follow the route taken in 1914. Scholem means to salute the last of the venerable taxicabs on display in the Invalides. As a member of the planning committee, he will soon go to Paris to take part in the preparations for this event. On the way home he will stop in New York City, where he will call upon the five permanent members of the Security Council to ask them to respect the spirit of the great day at Torgau, and to take a warm farewell of everybody. He will visit the French UN delegation at nine-thirty A.M., the Soviet Union at eleven, China at twelve-thirty, Great Britain at two P.M., the U.S.A. at half past three. At five P.M. he will pay his respects to the Secretary-General. Then return to Chicago and a "new life"—the life promised in John 12:24.

He appeals for financial assistance in the name of mankind itself, referring again to the dignity of humanity in this century.

Lesser documents contain statements on nuclear disarmament and on the hopeful prospects for an eventual reconciliation between the superpowers, in the spirit of Torgau. At three A.M. my head is not clear enough to study them.

Sleep is out of the question, so instead of going to bed I make myself some strong coffee. No use sacking out; I'd only go on thinking.

Insomnia is not a word I apply to the sharp thrills of deep-night clarity that come to me. During the day the fusspot habits of a lifetime prevent real discovery. I have learned to be grateful for the night hours that harrow the nerves and tear up the veins—"lying in restless ecstasy." To want this, and to bear it, you need a strong soul.

I lie down with the coffee in one of my Syrian corners (I didn't intend to create this Oriental environment; how did it come into existence?), lie down in proximity to the smooth, lighted, empty moon surface of the Outer Drive to consider what I might do for Cousin Scholem. Why do anything? Why not just refer him to the good-intentions department? After he had been in the good-intentions chamber five or six times, I could almost feel that I had done something for him. The usual techniques of evasion would not, however, work in Cousin Scholem's case. The son of Jewish immigrants (his father was in the egg business in Fulton Market), Cousin Scholem was determined to find support in Nature and History for freedom and to mitigate, check, or banish the fear of death that governs the species—convulses it. He was, moreover, a patriotic American (a terribly antiquated affect) and a world citizen. Above all he wanted to affirm that all would be well, to make a distinguished gift, to bless mankind. In all this Scholem fitted the classical norm for Jews of the diaspora. Against the Chicago background of boardrooms and backrooms, of fraud, arson, assassination, hit men, bag men, the ideology of decency disseminated from unseen sources of power—the moral law, never thicker, in Chicago, than onionskin or tissue paper—was now a gas as rare as argon. Anyway, think of him, perhaps the most powerful mind ever to be placed behind the wheel of a cab, his passengers descendants of Belial who made II Corinthians look sick, and Scholem amid unparalleled decadence being ever more pure in thought. The effort gave him a malignant tumor. I have also been convinced always that the strain of driving ten hours a day in city traffic is enough to give you cancer. It's the enforced immobility that does it; and there's also the aggravated ill will, the reflux of fury released by organisms, and perhaps by mechanisms, too.

But what could I do for Scholem? I couldn't go running to his house and ring the bell after thirty years of estrangement. I couldn't bring financial assistance—I don't have the money to print so many thousands of pages. He would need a hundred thousand at least, and he might expect Ijah to conjure it out of the barren air of the Loop. Didn't Ijah belong to a crack team of elite financial analysts? But Cousin Ijah was not one of the operators who had grabbed off any of the big money available for "intellectual" projects or enlightened reforms, the political grant-getters who have millions to play with.

Also I shrank from sitting down with him in his six-flat parlor to discuss his life's work. I didn't have the language it required. My college biology would be of no use. My Spengler was deader than the Bohemian Cemetery where we discussed the great questions (dignified surroundings, massy tombs, decaying flowers).

I didn't have a language to share with Cousin Motty, either, to open my full mind to him; and from his side Cousin Scholem couldn't enlist my support for his philosophical system until I had qualified myself by years of study. So little time was left that it was out of the question. In the circumstances, all I could do was to try to raise funds to have him buried in East Germany. The Communists, needing hard currency so badly, would not turn down a reasonable proposition. And towards morning, as I washed and shaved, I remembered that there was a cousin in Elgin, Illinois —not a close cousin, but one with whom I had always had friendly and even affectionate relations. He might be able to help. The affections have to manage as they can at a time so abnormal. They are kept alive in storage, as it were, for one doesn't often see their objects. These mental hydroponic growths can, however, be curiously durable and tenacious. People seem able to keep one another on "hold" for decades or scores of years. Separations like these have a flavor of eternity. One interpretation of "having no contemporaries" is that all valuable associations are kept in a time-arrested state. Those who are absent seem to sense that they have not lost their value for you. The relationship is played *ritardando* on a trance instrument of which the rest of the orchestra is only subliminally aware.

The person I refer to was still there, in Elgin. Mendy Eckstine, once a free-lance journalist and advertising man, was now semiretired. He and Scholem Stavis were from altogether different spheres. Eckstine had been my pool-hall, boxing, jazz-club cousin. Mendy had had a peculiar relish for being an American of his time. Born in Muskingum, Ohio, where his father ran a gents' furnishings shop, he attended a Chicago high school and grew up a lively, slangy man who specialized in baseball players, vaudeville performers, trumpeters and boogie-woogie musicians, gamblers, con artists, city hall small-rackets types. The rube shrewdie was a type he dearly loved—"Aaron Slick from Punkin Crick." Mendy's densely curled hair was combed straight up, his cheeks were high, damaged by acne, healed to a patchy whiteness. He had a wonderful start of the head, to declare that he was about to set the record straight. He used to make this movement when he laid down his cigarette on the edge of the pool table of the University of Wisconsin Rathskeller and picked up his cue to study his next shot. From Mendy as from Seckel I had learned songs. He loved hick jazz numbers like "Sounds a Little Goofus to Me," and in particular,

Oh, the cows went dry and the hens wouldn't lay
When he played on his ole cornet.

Altogether an admirable person, and a complete American, as formal, as total in his fashion as a work of art. The model on which he formed himself has been wiped out. In the late thirties he and I went to the fights together, or the Club de Lisa for jazz.

Cousin Mendy was the man to approach on Scholem's behalf because there was a fund, somewhere, set up by a relative dead these many years, the last of his branch. As I understood its provisions, this fund was set up to make essential family loans and also to pay for the education of poor relations, if they were gifted, perhaps even for their higher cultural activities. Vague about it myself, I was sure that Mendy would know, and I quickly got hold of him on the telephone. He said he would come downtown next day, delighted, he told me, to have a talk. "Been far too long, old buddy."

The fund was the legacy of an older Eckstine,

Arcadius, called Artie. Artie, of whom nothing was expected and who had never in his life tied his shoelaces, not because he was too stout (he was only plump) but because he announced to the world that he was *dégagé*, had come into some money towards the end of his life. Before the Revolution, he had brought to America a Russian schoolboy's version of Pushkin's life, and he gave Pushkin recitations incomprehensible to us. Modern experience had never touched him. Viewed from above, Artie's round, brownish-fair head was the head of a boy, combed with boyish innocence. He grew somewhat puffy in the cheeks and eyelids. His eyes were kiwi green. He lost one of his fingers in a barbed-wire factory in 1917. Perhaps he sacrificed it to avoid the draft. There is a "cabinet portrait" of Artie and his widowed mother, taken about seventy years ago. He poses with his thumb under his lapel. His mother, Tanya, is stout, short, and Oriental. Although she looks composed, her face is in reality inflated with laughter. Why? Well, if her legs are so plump and short that they don't reach the floor, the cause is a comical deficiency in the physical world, ludicrously incapable of adapting itself to Aunt Tanya. Tanya's second marriage was to a millionaire junkman, prominent in his synagogue, a plain man and strictly Orthodox. Tanya, a movie fan, loved Clark Gable and never missed a performance of *Gone with the Wind*. "Oy, Clark Gebble, I love him so!"

Her old husband was the first to die. She followed in her mid-eighties, five years later. At the time of her death, Artie was a traveler in dehydrated applesauce and was demonstrating his product in a small downstate department store when the news came. He and his wife, a childless couple, retired at once. He said he would resume his study of philosophy, in which he

327

had majored at Ann Arbor God knows how many years ago, but the management of his property and money kept him from the books. He used to say to me, "Ijah, wot is your opinion of Chon Dewey—ha?"

When these Eckstine cousins died, it was learned that a fund for higher studies had been set up under the will—a sort of foundation, said Mendy.

"And has it been used?"

"Very little."

"Could we get money out of it for Scholem Stavis?"

He said, "That depends," implying that he might be able to swing it.

I had prepared an exhibit for him. He quickly grasped the essentials of Scholem's case. "There wouldn't be money enough to publish his life's work. And how do we find out whether he really is to Darwin what Newton was to Copernicus?"

"It would be hard for us to decide."

"Who would you ask?" said Mendy.

"We'd have to retain a few specialists. My confidence in academics is not too great."

"You think they'd steal from a defenseless genius-amateur?"

"Contact with inspiration often disturbs your steady worker. . . ."

"Assuming that Scholem is inspired. Artie and his missis didn't live long enough to enjoy their inheritance. I wouldn't like to blow too much of their dough on a brainstorm," said Mendy. "I'd have more confidence in Scholem if he weren't so statuesque."

People nowadays don't trust you if you don't show them your trivial humanity—Leopold Bloom in the outhouse, his rising stink, his wife's goat udders, or whatever. The chosen standards for common humanity have moved towards this lower range of facts.

"Besides," said Mendy, "what's all this Christianity? Why does he have to quote from the most anti-Semitic of the Gospels? After what we've been through, that's not the direction to take."

"For all I know, he may be the heir of Immanuel Kant and can't accept an all-Jewish outlook. He's also an American claiming his natural right to an important position in the history of knowledge."

"Even so," said Mendy, "what's this asking to be buried behind the iron curtain? Doesn't he know what Jew-haters those Russians are—right up there with the Germans? Does he think by lying there that he'll soak up all that hate like blotting paper? Cure them? Maybe he thinks he can—he and nobody else."

He was working himself up to accuse Scholem of megalomania. These psychological terms lying around, tempting us to use them, are a menace. They should all be shoveled into trucks and taken to the dump.

It was interesting to consider Mendy's own development. He was very intelligent, though you might not think so if you had observed how he had dramatized himself as a middle American of the Hoover or early Roosevelt period. He pursued the idiocies and even the pains of his Protestant models, misfortunes like the estrangement of husbands and wives, sexual self-punishment. He would get drunk in the Loop and arrive swacked on the commuter train, like other Americans. He bought an English bulldog that irritated his wife to madness. He and his mother-in-law elaborated all the comical American eccentricities of mutual dislike. She went down to the cellar when he was at home and after he had gone to bed she came up to make herself a cup of cocoa in the kitchen. He would say to me, "I sent her to a nutritionist because I couldn't understand how she could look so well and rosy on a diet of sweet rolls and cocoa." (Histrionics, I guess, had kept her in splendid condition.) Mendy made an ally of his young son; they went on fishing trips and visited Civil War battlegrounds. He was a man-and-boy Midwesterner, living out of a W. C. Fields script. And yet in the eyes under that snap-brim fedora there had always been a mixture of Jewish lights, and in his sixties he was visibly more Jewish. And, as I have said, the American model he had adopted was not utterly obsolete. The patriarchs of the Old Testament were infinitely more modern than the Punkin Crick smart alecks. Mendy was not returning to the religion of his fathers, far from it, but in semiretirement, stuck out there in Elgin, he must have been as hard up for comprehension as Cousin Motty had been in the locker room of his club. Accordingly, it didn't surprise him that I should take so much interest in cousins. His own interest was stirred. Unless I misinterpreted the expression of his now malformed, lumpy, warm face, he was appealing to me to extend this interest to him. He wished to draw nearer.

"You aren't being sentimental, are you, Ijah, because you and Scholem went on such wonderful walks together? You'd probably be able to judge if you read his blockbusting book. They didn't hire dummies at the Rand Corporation—someday I'll ask you to tell me about that super think tank."

"I'd rather call it sympathy, not soft sentiment."

In the moral sphere, a wild ignorance, utter anarchy.

Mendy said, "If you tried talking to him, he'd lecture you from on high, wouldn't he? Since you don't understand about these zygotes and gametes, you'd be forced to sit and listen. . . ."

What Mendy intended to say was that he and I—*we* could understand each other, owing to our common ilk. Jews who had grown up on the sidewalks of America, we were in no sense foreigners, and we had brought so much enthusiasm, verve, love to this American life that we had become *it*. Odd that *it* should begin to roll towards oblivion just as we were perfecting ourselves in this admirable democracy. However, our democracy was passé. The *new* democracy with its *new* abstractions was cruelly disheartening. Being an American always had been something of an abstract project. You came as an immigrant. You were offered a most reasonable proposition and you said yes to it. You were *found*. With the new abstractions you were *lost*. They demanded a shocking abandonment of personal judgment. Take Eunice's letter to the medical school as an example. By using the word "integrity" you could cheat with a good conscience. Schooled in the new abstractions, you no longer had to worry about truth and falsehood, good and evil. What excused you from good and evil was the effort you put into schooling. You worked hard at your limited lesson, you learned it, and you were forever in the clear. You could say, for instance, "Guilt has to die. Human beings are entitled to guiltless pleasure." Having learned this valuable lesson, you could now accept the fucking of your daughters, which in the past would have choked you. You were compensated by the gratification of a lesson well learned. Well, there's the new thoughtfulness for you. And it's possibly on our capacity for thoughtfulness that our survival depends—all the rational decisions that have to be made. And listen here, I am not digressing at all. Cousin Scholem was a noble creature who lived in the forests of *old* thoughtfulness. An excellent kind of creature, if indeed he was the real thing. Cousin Mendy suggested that he was not. Cousin Mendy wished to remind me that he and I were representatives of a peculiar Jewish and American development (wiped out by history) and had infinitely more in common than any superannuated prodigy could ever understand.

"I want to do something for Scholem, Mendy."

"I'm not sure we can spend Cousin Artie's money to bury him in East Germany."

"Fair enough. Now, suppose you raise the money to have his great work read . . . find a biologist to vet it. And a philosopher and a historian."

"Maybe so. I'll take it up with the executors. I'll get back to you," said Mendy.

I divined from this that he himself was all of the executors.

"I have to go abroad," I said. "I may even see Scholem in Paris. His valedictory letter mentions a trip to plan the taxis-of-the-Marne business."

I gave Mendy Miss Rodinson's number.

"Flying the Concorde, I suppose," said Mendy. Devoid of envy. I would have been glad of his company.

I stopped in Washington to confer with International Monetary Fund people about the intended resumption of loans from commercial banks to the Brazilians. I found time to spend a few hours at the Library of Congress, looking for Bogoras and Jochelson material, and to get inquiries under way at the East German chancery. Then I telephoned my former wife at National Public Radio. Isabel has become one of its most familiar voices. After three marriages, she has resumed her maiden name. I sometimes hear it after the prancing music of the program's signature: "We will now hear from our correspondent Isabel Greenspan in Washington." I invited her to have dinner with me. She said no, offended perhaps that I hadn't called earlier from Chicago. She said she would come to the Hay-Adams Hotel to have a drink with me.

The thought persistently suggested by Isabel when we meet is that man is the not-yet-stabilized animal. By this I mean not only that defective, diseased, abortive types are common (Isabel is neither defective nor sick, by the way) but that the majority of human beings will never attain equilibrium and that they are by nature captious, fretful, irritable, uncomfortable, looking for relief from their travail and angry that it does not come. A woman like Isabel, determined to make an impression of perfect balance, reflects this unhappy instability. She identifies me with errors she has freed herself from; she measures her progress by our ever-more-apparent divergence. Clever enough to be a member of the Mensa (high-IQ) society, and, on the air, a charming person, she is always somewhat somber with me, as if she weren't altogether satisfied with her "insights." As a national figure in a program offering enlightened interpretation to millions of listeners, Sable is "committed," "engaged"; but as an intelligent woman, she is secretly rueful about this enlightenment.

She talked to me about Chicago, with which, in certain respects, she identified me. "White machine aldermen tying the black mayor in knots while they strip the city of its last buck. While you, of course, see it all. You always see it all. But you'd rather go on mooning." There was a noteworthy difference in Sable this afternoon. At cocktail time, she was made up like the dawn of day. Her dark color was the departing night. She was more perfumed than the dawn. It was otherwise a very good resemblance. No denying that she is an attractive woman. She was dressed in dark, tea-colored silk with a formal design in scarlet. She didn't always make herself so attractive for our meetings.

Vain to pretend that I "see it all," but what she meant when she said "mooning" was quite clear. It had two distinct and associated meanings: (1) my special preoccupations, and (2) my lifelong dream-connection with Virgie Dunton née Miletas, the eight-fingered concert harpist. Despite her congenital defect, Virgie had mastered the entire harp repertoire, omitting a few impossible works, and had a successful career. It's perfectly true that I had never been cured of my feeling for Virgie—her black eyes, her round face, its whiteness, its frontal tendency, its feminine emanations, the assurances of humanity or pledges of kindness which came from it. Even the slight mutilation of her short nose—it was the result of a car accident; she refused plastic surgery—was an attraction. It's perfectly true that for me the word "female" had its most significant representation in her. Whenever possible, I attended her concerts; I walked in her neighborhood in hopes of running into her, imagined that I saw her in department stores. Chance meetings—five in thirty years—were remembered in minute actuality. When her husband, a heavy drinker, lent me Galbraith's book on his accomplishments in India, I read every word of it, and this can only be explained by the swollen affect or cathexis that had developed. Virgie Miletas, the Venus of rudimentary thumbs, with her electric binding power, was the real object of Sable's "you'd rather go on mooning." The perfect happiness I might have known with Mrs. Miletas-Dunton, like the longed-for union of sundered beings in the love myth of Aristophanes—I refrain from invoking the higher Eros described by Socrates during the long runs of the blatting El trains that used to carry me, the inspired philosophy student, from Van Buren Street and its hockshops to Sixty-third Street and its throng of junkies—was an artificial love dream and Sable was quite right to despise it.

At the Hay-Adams, where we were drinking gin and tonic, Sable now made a comment which was surprising, nothing like her usual insights, which were not. She said, "I don't think mooning is such a satisfactory word. To be more exact, you have an exuberance that you keep to yourself. You have a crazy high energy absolutely peculiar to you. Because of this high charge you can defy the plain dirty facts that other people have to suffer through, whether they like it or not. What you are is an exuberance-hoarder, Ijah. You live on your exuberant hoard. It would kill you to be depressed, as others are."

This was a curious attack. There was something to it. I gave her full credit for this. I preferred, however, to think it over at leisure instead of answering at once. So I started to talk to her about Cousin Scholem. I described his case to her. If he were to be interviewed on National Public Radio and received the attention he deserved (the war hero-philosopher-cabby), he might succeed in stimulating the interest and, more important, the queer generosity of the public. Sable rejected this immediately. She said he'd be too heavy. If he announced that in him Kant and Darwin had a successor at last, listeners would say, Who is this nut! She admitted that the taxis of the Marne would be rich in human interest, but the celebration would not take place until 1984; it was still a year away. She also observed that her program didn't encourage fund-raising initiatives. She said, "Are you sure the man is really dying? You have only his word for it."

"That's a heartless question," I said.

"Maybe it is. You've always been soft about cousins, though. The immediate family threw a chill on your exuberance, and you simply turned to the cousins. I used to think you'd open every drawer in the morgue if somebody told you that there was a cousin to be found. Ask yourself how many of them would come looking for you."

This made me smile. Sable always had had a strong sense of humor.

She said also, "At a time when the nuclear family is breaking up, what's this excitement about collateral relatives?"

The only answer I could make came from left field. I said, "Before the First World War, Europe was governed by a royalty of cousins."

"Yes? That came out real good, didn't it?"

"There are people who think of that time as a golden age—the last of the old *douceur de vivre*, and so on."

But I didn't really mean it. The millennial history of nihilism culminated in 1914, and the brutality of Verdun and Tannenberg was a prelude to the even greater destruction that began in 1939. So here again is the all-pervading *suspense*—the seams of history opening, the bonds in dissolution (Hegel), the constraints of centuries removed. Unless your head is hard, this will give you nothing but dizzy fits, but if you don't yield to fits you may be carried into a kind of freedom. Disorder, if it doesn't murder you, brings certain opportunities. You wouldn't guess that when I sit in my Holy Sepulchre apartment at night (the surroundings that puzzled Eunice's mind when she came to visit: "All these Oriental rugs and lamps, and so many books," she said), wouldn't guess that I am concentrating on strategies for pouncing passionately on the freedom made possible by dissolution. Hundreds of books, but only half a shelf of those that matter. You don't get more goodness from more knowledge. One of the writers I often turn to concentrates on passion. He invites you to consider love and hate. He denies that hate is blind. On the contrary, hate is perspicuous. If you let hate germinate, it will eat its way inward and consume your very being, it will intensify reflection. It doesn't blind, it increases lucidity, it opens a man up; it makes him reach out and concentrates his being so that he is able to grasp himself. Love, too, is clear-eyed and not blind. True love is not delusive. Like hate, it is a primal source. But love is hard to come by. Hate is in tremendous supply. And evidently you endanger your being by waiting for the rarer passion. So you must have confidence in hate, which is so abundant, and embrace it with your whole soul, if you hope to achieve any clarity at all.

I wasn't about to take this up with Sable, although she would be capable of discussing it. She was still talking about my weakness for cousins. She said, "If you had cared about me as you do about all those goofy, half-assed cousins, and such, we never would have divorced."

"Such" was a dig at Virgie.

Was Sable hinting that we try again? Was this why she had come painted like the dawn and so beautifully dressed? I felt quite flattered.

In the morning I went to Dulles and flew out on the Concorde. The International Monetary Fund was waiting for the Brazilian parliament to make up its mind. I jotted some notes towards my report and then I was free to think of other matters. I considered whether Sable was priming me to make her a proposal. I liked what she had said about hoarded exuberance. Her opinion was that, through the cousins, through Virgie, I indulged my taste for the easier affects. I lacked true modern severity. Maybe she believed that I satisfied an artist's needs by visits to old galleries, walking through museums of beauty, happy with the charms of kinship, quite contented with painted relics, not tough enough for rapture in its strongest forms, not purified by nihilistic fire.

And about marriage . . . single life was tiresome. There were, however, unpleasant considerations in marriage that must not be avoided. What would I do in Washington? What would Sable do if she came to live in Chicago? No, she wouldn't be willing to move. We'd be flying back and forth, commuting. To spell the matter out, item by item, Sable had become a public-opinion molder. Public opinion is power. She belonged to a group that held great power. It was not the kind of power I cared about. While her people were not worse jerks than their conservative opposites, they were nevertheless jerks, more numerous in her profession than in other fields, and disagreeably influential.

I was now in Paris, pulling up in front of the Montalembert. I had given up a hotel I liked better when I found cockroaches in my luggage, black ones that had recrossed the Atlantic with me and came out all set to conquer Chicago.

I inspected the room at the Montalembert and then walked down the Rue du Bac to the Seine. Marvelous how much good these monumental capitals can do an American, still. I almost felt that here the sun itself should take a monumental form, something like the Mexican calendar stone, to shine on the Sainte-Chapelle, the Conciergerie, the Pont Neuf, and other medieval relics.

Returning to the hotel after dinner, I found a message from Miss Rodinson in Chicago. "Eckstine fund will grant ten thousand dollars to Mr. Stavis."

Good for Cousin Mendy! I now had news for Scholem, and since he would be at the Invalides tomorrow if he was alive and had made it to Paris for the planning session, I would have more than mere sympathy to offer when we met after so many decades. Mendy meant the grant to be used to determine whether Scholem's pure philosophy, grounded in science, was all that he claimed it to be, an advance on the *Critique of Pure Reason.* Immediately I began to devise ways to get around Mendy. I could choose Scholem's readers myself. I would offer them small sums—they didn't deserve fat fees anyway, those academic nitwits. (Angry with them, you see, because they had done so little to prevent the U.S. from sinking into decadence; I blamed them, in fact, for hastening our degradation.) Five experts at two hundred bucks apiece, whom I would pay myself, would allow me to give the entire ten grand to Scholem. By using my clout in Washington, I might get a burial permit out of the East Germans for two or three thousand, bribes included. That would leave money enough for transportation and last rites. For if Scholem had a clairvoyant conviction that his burial at Torgau would shrink the world's swollen madness to a small pellet, it might be worth a try. Interred at Waldheim in Chicago, beside the pounding truck traffic of Harlem Avenue, one could not hope to have any effect.

To catch up with European time, I stayed up late playing solitaire with a pack of outsized cards that made eyeglasses unnecessary and this put me in a frame of mind to get into bed without a fit of exuberance. Given calm and poise, I *can* understand my situation. Musing back and forth over the cards, I understood Sable's complaint that I had ruined our marriage by denying it a transfusion of exuberance. Speaking of my sentiments for the cousins, she referred indirectly to the mystery of being a Jew. Sable had a handsome Jewish nose, perhaps a little too much of one. Also, she had conspicuously offered her legs to my gaze, knowing my weakness for them. She had a well-turned bosom, a smooth throat, good hips, and legs still capable of kicking in the bedroom—I used to refer to "your skip-rope legs." Now, then, had Sable continued through three marriages to think of me as her only true husband, or was she trying her strength one last time against her rival from (Egyptian) Alexandria? Guiltless Virgie was the hate of her life, and hate made you perspicuous, failing love. Heidegger would have approved. His idea had, as it were, infected me. I was beginning to be obsessed with the two passions that made you perspicuous. Love there isn't too much of; hate is as ubiquitous as nitrogen or carbon. Maybe hate is inherent in matter itself and is therefore a component of our bones; our very blood is perhaps swollen with it. For moral coldness in the arctic range I had found a physical image in the Siberian environment of the Koryak and the Chukchee—the subpolar desert whose frosts are as severe as fire, a fit location for slave-labor camps. Put all this together, and my idyll of Virgie Miletas might be construed as a fainthearted evasion of the reigning coldness.

Well, I could have told Sable that she couldn't win against an unconsummated *amour* of so many years. It's after all the woman you *didn't* have whose effect is mortal.

I concede, however, that the real challenge is to capture and tame wickedness. Without this you remain suspended. At the mercy of the suspense over the new emergence of spirit . . .

But on this I sacked out.

In the morning on my breakfast tray was an express envelope from Miss Rodinson. I was in no mood to open it now; it might contain information about a professional engagement, and I didn't want that. I was on my way to the Invalides to meet with Scholem, if he had made it there. The world cabbies' organizing session, attended, as I noted in *Le Monde,* by some two hundred delegates from fifty countries, would begin at eleven o'clock. I put Miss Rodinson's mail in my pocket with my wallet and my passport.

I was rushed to the great dome in a cab, and went in. A wonderful work of religious architecture— Bruant in the seventeenth century, Mansart in the eighteenth. I took note of its grandeur intermittently. There were gaps in which the dome was no more to me than an egg cup, owing to my hectic excitement— derangement. The stains were growing under my arms. Loss of moisture dried my throat. I went to get information about the taxis of the Marne and had the corner pointed out to me. The drivers had not yet begun to arrive. I had to wander about for half an hour or so, and I climbed up to the first *étage* to look down in the crypt of the Chapelle Saint-Jérôme. Hoo! what grandeur, what beauties! Such arches and columns and statuary, and floating and galloping frescoes. And the floor so sweetly tessellated. I wanted to kiss it. And also the mournful words of Napoleon from Saint Helena. "Je désire que mes cendres reposent sur les bords de la Seine in the middle of that nation, ce peuple Français, that I loved so much."

Now Napoleon was crammed under thirty-five tons of polished porphyry or alizarin in a shape suggestive of Roman pomp.

As I was descending the stairs I took out Miss Rodinson's envelope, and I felt distinctly topsy-turvy, somewhat intoxicated, as I read the letter from Eunice—that was all it contained. Here came Tanky's third wish: that I write once again to Judge Eiler to request that the final months of his prison term be served in a halfway house in Las Vegas. In a halfway house, Eunice explained, you had minimal supervision. You signed out in the morning, and signed in again at night. The day was your own, to attend to private business. Eunice wrote, "I think that prison has been a tremendous learning experience for my brother. As he is very intelligent, under it all, he has already absorbed everything there was to absorb from jail. You might try that on the judge, phrasing it in your own way."

Well, to phrase it in my own way, the great fish tottered on the grandiose staircase, filled with drunken darkness and hearing the turbulent seas. An inner voice told him, "This is it!" and he felt like opening a great crimson mouth and tearing the paper with his teeth.

I wanted to send back a message, too: "I am not Cousin Schmuck, I am a great fish who can grant wishes and in whom there are colossal powers!"

Instead I calmed myself by tearing Eunice's notepaper six, eight, ten times, and then seeking discipline in a wastepaper basket. By the time I reached the gathering place, my emotions were more settled, although not entirely normal. There was a certain amount of looping and veering still.

Upwards of a hundred delegates had gathered in the taxi corner, if gathered is the word to apply to such a crowd of restless exotics. There were people from all the corners of the earth. They wore caps, uniforms, military insignia, batik pants, Peruvian hats, pantaloons, wrinkled Indian breeches, crimson gowns from Africa, kilts from Scotland, skirts from Greece, Sikh turbans. The whole gathering reminded me of the great UN meeting that Khrushchev and Castro had attended, and where I had seen Nehru in his lovely white garments with a red rose in his lapel and a sort of baker's cap on his head—I had been present when Khrushchev pulled off his shoe to bang his desk in anger.

Then it came to me how geography had been taught in the Chicago schools when I was a kid. We were issued a series of booklets: "Our Little Japanese Cousins," "Our Little Moroccan Cousins," "Our Little Russian Cousins," "Our Little Spanish Cousins." I read all these gentle descriptions about little Ivan and tiny Conchita, and my eager heart opened to them. Why, we were close, we were one under it all (as Tanky was very intelligent "under it all"). We were not guineas, dagos, krauts; we were cousins. It was a splendid conception, and those of us who opened our excited hearts to the world union of cousins were happy, as I was, to give our candy pennies to a fund for the rebuilding of Tokyo after the earthquake of the twenties. After Pearl Harbor, we were obliged to bomb hell out of the place. It's unlikely that Japanese children had been provided with books about their little American cousins. The Chicago Board of Education had never thought to look into this.

Two French nonagenarians were present, survivors of 1914. They were the center of much eager attention. A most agreeable occasion, I thought, or would have thought if I had been less agitated.

I didn't see Scholem anywhere. I suppose I should have told Miss Rodinson to phone his Chicago number for information, but they would have asked who was calling, and for what purpose. I wasn't sorry to have come to this mighty hall. In fact I wouldn't have missed it. But I was emotionally primed for a meeting with Scholem. I had even prepared some words to say to him. I couldn't bear to miss him. I came out of the crowd and circled it. The delegates were already being conducted to their meeting place, and I stationed myself strategically near a door. The gorgeous costumes increased the confusion.

In any case, it wasn't I who found Scholem. I couldn't have. He was too greatly changed—emaciated. It was he who spotted me. A man being helped by a young woman—his daughter, as it turned out—glanced up into my face. He stopped and said, "I don't dream much because I don't sleep much, but if I'm not having hallucinations, this is my cousin Ijah."

Yes yes! It was Ijah! And here was Scholem. He no longer resembled the older man of the Instamatic color photo, the person who squinted inward under heavy brows. Because he had lost much weight his face was wasted, and the tightening of the skin brought back his youthful look. Much less doomed and fanatical than the man in the picture, who breathed prophetic fire. There seemed a kind of clear innocence about him. The size of his eyes was exceptional—like the eyes of a newborn infant in the first presentation of *genio* and *figura*. And suddenly I thought: What have I done? How do you tell a man like this that you have money for him? Am I supposed to say that I bring him the money he can bury himself with?

Scholem was speaking, saying to his daughter, "My

cousin!" And to me he said, "You lived abroad, Ijah? You got my mailings? Now I understand—you didn't answer because you wanted to surprise me. I have to make a speech, to greet the delegates. You'll sit with my daughter. We'll talk later."

"Of course. . . ."

I'd get the girl's help; I'd inform her of the Eckstine grant. She'd prepare her father for the news.

Then I felt robbed of strength, all at once. Doesn't existence lay too much on us? I had remembered, observed, studied the cousins, and these studies seemed to fix my own essence and to keep me as I had been. I had failed to include myself among them, and suddenly I was billed for this oversight. At the presentation of this bill, I became bizarrely weak in the legs. And when the girl, noticing that I seemed unable to walk, offered me her arm, I wanted to say, "What d'you mean? I need no help. I still play a full set of tennis every day." Instead I passed my arm through hers and she led us both down the corridor.

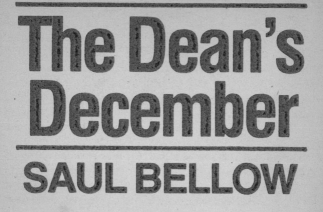